Leslie Stephen

Life of Henry Fawcett

Leslie Stephen

Life of Henry Fawcett

ISBN/EAN: 9783337332341

Printed in Europe, USA, Canada, Australia, Japan

Cover: Foto ©Andreas Hilbeck / pixelio.de

More available books at **www.hansebooks.com**

LIFE

OF

HENRY FAWCETT

BY

LESLIE STEPHEN

𝔚𝔦𝔱𝔥 𝔗𝔴𝔬 𝔓𝔬𝔯𝔱𝔯𝔞𝔦𝔱𝔰

FIFTH EDITION

LONDON
SMITH, ELDER, & CO., 15 WATERLOO PLACE
1886

PREFACE.

Not long after Fawcett's death, Mrs. Fawcett requested me to write a memoir of her husband. She added that the other members of his family concurred in the request. I, of course, could not hesitate to accept the task, though fully sensible of the responsibility as well as of the honour. I was qualified for the duty in this respect, that Fawcett had been for thirty years one of my most intimate and valued friends. It would be strange if, during that period, I had not learnt to understand one of the simplest and most transparent of men. Our mutual regard never cooled; it rather grew warmer; but after the first ten years our intercourse had ceased to be so frequent as before. I had not followed with any minute attention the details of his political career, and I could therefore not have hoped to put together a satisfactory narrative, had I not counted upon the help of better informed persons. Any shortcomings in the following pages must, however, be due to faults of my own; for I have had most generous assistance, which it is now a pleasure and a duty to acknowledge in detail.

Mrs. Fawcett has done everything in her power. She has placed at my disposal all the letters and other documents in her possession which can throw any light upon the facts. She has also been kind enough to read each portion of the work as it was written; and she has made numerous suggestions of the greatest value. I will add that, although she has helped me at every point, and has often modified my opinions and cleared up difficulties, she has not in any way placed me under restraint. I have said nothing which does not appear to me to be strictly true, and I have concealed nothing which, in my judgment, can be revealed without breach of confidence.

I must, in the next place, offer my grateful thanks to my friend's sister, Miss Fawcett. Miss Fawcett has communicated to me many recollections of her own and of her parents. She had made a practice, from the beginning of her brother's career, of preserving reports of his speeches, and newspaper articles referring to him. She kindly entrusted these collections to me, and I have found them exceedingly serviceable.

I have also to thank Mr. Dryhurst, who was Fawcett's private secretary from 1871, and soon became a confidential friend. Mr. Dryhurst has been most zealous in helping me, both by communicating his own recollections and by collecting and arranging statements of fact. My readers have also to thank him for the index, which he has been good enough to prepare.

Another old friend of Fawcett's, Mr. R. Hunter, now Solicitor to the Post-Office, has placed me under an obligation, the full extent of which I find a difficulty to acknowledge adequately. I cannot quite say that the chapter upon Commons Preservation is his instead of mine, or the actual words are my own, and I am entirely

and solely responsible for every opinion expressed. But
he provided, if I may say so, the whole stamina of the
chapter, and he in conjunction with Mr. Dryhurst helped
me equally in my account of the Post-Office. But for
his assistance I should not only have had much additional labour, but should have been forced to be content
with a far more incomplete account of the facts.

Two old college friends of Fawcett's have been especially helpful. Mr. C. B. Clarke, now of the Education
Department in India, was the most intimate of all
Fawcett's friends in college days; and his recollections
of Fawcett down to the end of 1865, when they were
separated by Clarke's departure for India, have been
very useful. Mr. W. A. Porter, formerly a fellow of
Peterhouse and since of the Indian Education Department, has given me some recollections and made some
valuable suggestions in regard to the chapter upon
India.

I must also thank the following, who have helped me
in regard to various details : Mr. Willmore, now President
of Queenwood College, and Messrs. J. Mansergh, William
Milne, and H. P. Blackmore, schoolfellows of Fawcett at
the same college ; Sir John Lambert, Mr. A. T. Squarey
of Liverpool, Mrs. Hodding and Dr. Roberts of Salisbury,
old family friends ; Mr. Wright of Salisbury and Mr.
Wheaton, now of St. Thomas's Hospital ; Mr. W. H.
Hall, of Six Mile Bottom ; Sir John Pope Hennessy ;
Mr. Hawke, of Liskeard ; the Rev. F. L. Hopkins and
Mr. Dale, Fellows of Trinity Hall ; Mr. Sedley Taylor,
Fellow of Trinity College ; Dr. Besant, formerly Fellow
of St. John's ; Prof. Wolstenholme, of Cooper's Hill

College; Mr. Alexander Macmillan, the publisher; Mr.
Halpin, of the Hospital Saturday Fund, formerly resident
in Southwark; Messrs. Willett, Merrifield, and Botting,
of Brighton; Mr. Fitch, of the Education Department,
who has helped me very kindly in regard to Fawcett's
part in school legislation; Sir Charles W. Dilke, Mr.
Mundella, Mr. Leonard Courtney, Mr. Shaw Lefevre, and
Mr. John Morley; Mr. G. A. Critchett and Dr. Latham,
of Cambridge. Finally, I must thank the Rev. J. C.
Egerton, vicar of Burwash, Sussex; Mrs. Hodding, of
Salisbury; Mrs. Hertz, Mr. F. Darwin, and Mrs. Cairnes,
widow of the late Professor Cairnes, for communicating
or allowing me to use various letters. No approval could
be so welcome as the opinion of these and others of
Fawcett's friends that I have not been an inadequate
representative of the sentiments common to us all.

The portraits in this volume are from photographs,
one taken a year or so before his accident, the other, by
Messrs. Bassano, in the last year of his life. I may
mention that M. Richeton has prepared, and is, I
understand, about to publish an etching which represents with remarkable fidelity Fawcett's expression in
later years. The only portraits taken during life were
one by Mr. Ford Madox Browne, now in possession of
Sir Charles Dilke (this picture includes a portrait of
Mrs. Fawcett); and a chalk-drawing and two oil-paint-
ings by Mr. Harold Rathbone, executed in 1884. A bust
was taken during life by Mr. Pinker, who exhibited a later
bust at the Grosvenor Gallery in 1885.

LESLIE STEPHEN.

LONDON: *November* 1885.

CONTENTS.

CHAPTER   PAGE

I. EARLY LIFE 1

II. BLINDNESS 43

III. CAMBRIDGE 73

IV. POLITICAL ECONOMY 134

V. EARLY POLITICAL LIFE 182

VI. MEMBER FOR BRIGHTON 218

VII. COMMONS PRESERVATION 291

VIII. INDIA 341

IX. THE POST-OFFICE 402

X. CONCLUSION 449

APPENDIZ 469

INDEZ 473

LIFE

OF

HENRY FAWCETT.

HENRY FAWCETT was born at Salisbury on August 26,
1833. His father, William Fawcett, born at Kirkby
Lonsdale, Westmoreland, on March 31, 1793, had left
his native place for London about 1812. He was in one
of the crowds which welcomed the allied sovereigns in
1814, and there achieved the honour of shaking hands
with Blücher. In April 1815 he moved to Salisbury,
and soon afterwards turned to account the remarkable
clearness and power of his voice by springing upon a
coach to read out the news of the battle of Waterloo.
At Salisbury, which he has never quitted, he was first
employed in the shop of Mr. Pinckney, a leading draper,
who treated him with great kindness. Upon Mr.
Pinckney's retirement in 1825, Mr. Fawcett set up
in business for himself, opening a draper's shop in the
market-place. On April 25, 1827, he married Mary

Cooper (born 1804), daughter of a solicitor who was agent for the Liberal party in the town. His other children, William, Sarah Maria, and Thomas Cooper, were born in 1828, 1830, and 1839. Mr. Fawcett prospered in business, and in the year of the Reform Bill (1832) was Mayor of Salisbury. His election by a close corporation, the majority of which belonged to the opposite political party, was a remarkable proof of a popularity acquired by various qualities.

Mr. Fawcett was a man of great athletic vigour, though throughout a long life he has never enjoyed very robust health. In the North he had practised jumping, then a popular amusement in the schools, and had in particular a surprising power of leaping from great heights. The place is still shown where he astonished his southern companions by leaping from the second ring at Old Sarum—a height of thirty feet. He was a keen sportsman, a good shot, and a first-rate fisherman in a district where the clearness of the chalk streams raises the sport to the level of a fine art. He was thoroughly sociable: he laid in a good cellar of wine and played a good rubber of whist. These tastes were transmitted to his son, who inherited other and higher qualities. The son strikingly resembled the father (as Sir John Lambert, an old friend of both, has remarked to me) in perseverance, manly straightforwardness, and in a warmth of friendship specially shown to those who, from sickness or distress, were most in need of it. Henry was strongly influenced by the political views of both his parents. For Mrs. Fawcett, like her husband, was an ardent reformer. She took a keen interest in

politics, and her son not only inherited her strong
common sense but, doubtless, received an early intellectual bent from the combination of paternal and
maternal influence. Mr. W. Fawcett was active in all
electioneering matters. He was a remarkably good
speaker—a better orator, as I have been told, than his
son; more skilful in modulating his voice, and more
felicitous in finding apt expressions on the spur of the
moment. He was generally put forward as proposer or
seconder of the Liberal candidate. Until quite recently
he attended political meetings, especially some held in
support of his son, and showed that age had not destroyed oratorical powers manifested long before. He
presided at a great dinner held in the market-place at
Salisbury on June 27, 1832, to celebrate the passing of
the Reform Bill. Processions with banners, decorations
of houses, illuminations representing Minerva, Mercury,
Victory, and Britannia trampling on the hydra of cor-
ruption, whilst Sir Robert Peel and the Duke of Wellington
uttered appropriate maledictions in the background, had
testified on the previous day to the exultation of Salisbury;
sheep were roasted whole in the streets, and meat and
beer distributed to the poor. An old inhabitant (Mr.
T. H. Hayward) wrote to Henry Fawcett fifty years later
to give his recollections of the day, which was wound up
by a ball, in which the mayor 'led off the merry dance
with an elderly lady in the Green Croft cricket-ground.'

Liberalism, when not quenched by the shadow of a
cathedral, burns there perhaps with an intenser flame.
In spite of the burst of enthusiasm evoked by the advent
of the millennium in 1832, years were to come in which

Mr. Fawcett's zeal was to encounter plenty of opposition. The upper ranks of society in and round Salisbury, the clergy and country gentlemen, were nearly to a man staunch Tories and Protectionists. An almost solitary exception was the Earl of Radnor, of Longford Castle, close to Salisbury. Lord Radnor's political activity brought him into connection with Mr. Fawcett, to whom, in 1841, he gave a lease of the home farm of Longford. The comfortable farmhouse lies about three miles to the south of Salisbury, where the valley of the Avon is entered by the smaller valley of the Chalke, coming down from the west. Mr. Fawcett was on the pleasantest terms with his landlord. His eldest son, William, and a bailiff generally occupied the farmhouse, until 1851, when Mr. Fawcett settled there himself for some years. Mr. Fawcett thus became that rare pheno-menon—an anti-Protectionist farmer. In the year 1843, Messrs. Cobden, Bright, and Moore visited Salisbury to carry the agitation for free trade into the heart of the enemy's country. After their meetings, they used to sup alternately with Mr. Fawcett and with Mr. Squarey, another leading Liberal, and some knowledge of what was going on doubtless reached the little Harry (the name by which he always went in his family), whose ears were already open to the talk of his elders.

The influences which surrounded Fawcett's infancy have been thus sufficiently indicated. A boy brought up at Salisbury might well have been impressed by some of the many historical traditions of the district. An antiquarian, a High-Churchman, or a Tory might derive ample nourishment for his characteristic prepossessions in the neighbourhood. Fawcett's family associations impressed upon him from the first a different set of convictions. To trace the influences of his 'environment' we must not turn to the mysterious antiquity of Stonehenge, or the aristocratic splendour of Wilton, or the almost unrivalled symmetry of the most perfect of English cathedrals. It will be more to the purpose to open Cobbett's 'Rural Rides,' a book in which Fawcett took great pleasure in later days. In August 1826 that sturdy demagogue, who was not only a master of vernacular English, but, in spite of all errors, had a keen eye for rustic beauty and a genuine interest in the rustic population, came riding down the valley of the Avon from Milston (Addison's birthplace) to Salisbury, moralising after his fashion.

He was in ecstasies at the beauty of the scenery— the steep chalk downs standing out into the valley like piers into the sea; the sheltered bottoms below; each farm with its portion of down, arable, and water meadow; its orchards and clumps of noble elms; and the rich harvests which had been gathered into the great farmyards. 'This is certainly,' he exclaims, 'the most delightful farming on earth.' But then he asks, what of the people who produce the food? Each family, he calculates, raises enough to support five families, and yet those who do the work are half-starved. They get at the outside about 9s. a week. Whence is help to come? He rages as he goes; he curses 'the monster Malthus;' he declares, after computing the number of churches and manor-houses, that the inhabitants are fewer than of old—spite of the twaddle of 'beastly

Scotch *feelosophers*,' and the fellows that call themselves country gentlemen, who prate of over-population. It is 'the worst-used labouring people upon the face of the earth;' and somehow or other the mischief is caused, he thinks, by the taxes and paper-money, which drain the population away to the 'Wen' (London, to wit). A cure, however, may be hoped. As he rides he comes to the 'accursed Hill' of Old Sarum. He meets a man going home from work, who says that the times are bad. '"What *times*?" said I; "was there ever a finer summer, a finer harvest; and is there not an *old* wheat-rick in every farmyard?" "Ah," said he, "they make it bad for poor people for all that." "*They*?" said I, "who is *they*?" He was silent. "Oh, no, no! my friend," said I, "it is not *they*: it is that accursed Hill that has robbed you of the supper that you ought to find smoking on the table when you get home." I gave him the price of a pot of beer and on I went, leaving the poor dejected assemblage of skin and bones to wonder at my word.'

The 'accursed Hill' was stormed in 1832; but Cobbett's question, 'Who is *they*?' might still be asked; and Fawcett, who in his childhood saw the same scenes as Cobbett, and may have talked to the same dejected peasant, learnt very early to take a keen interest in a problem still unsolved. For the present it hardly weighed upon his mind. As a child he was not precocious, at any rate at his lessons. His first teacher, Mrs. Harris, mistress of a dame-school in Salisbury, said that she had never had so troublesome a pupil. His head was like a cullender. 'Mrs. Harris says that if we go on we shall kill her,' was Master Harry's version of the

case to his mother; 'and we do go on,' he added wist-
fully, 'and yet she does not die!' The boy, it seems,
preferred the streets to the schoolroom for a study.
His house opened upon the market-place and was just
opposite the hustings. There he found matters more
attractive than the A B C. His father's patience was
often tried by the ceaseless string of questions prompted
by his early curiosity. What is the price of cheese or of
bacon? What was it yesterday and what will it be to-
morrow, and why? This eager curiosity was doubtless
a proof, though at the moment not the most acceptable
proof, of intellectual ˙activity, and took a form oddly
characteristic of the future economist. About 1841
Fawcett was sent to his next schoolmaster, Mr. Sopp (at
Alderbury, five miles from Salisbury, on the line to
Romsey). Family traditions seem to imply that he
had been petted at home, and resented a little his first
entrance into a larger circle. He used to tell how he
once demanded at dinner 'more meat, well done, no fat,
and plenty of gravy.' The schoolmaster seems to have
responded more generously than might have been expected, and made his pupil comfortable enough. Fragments of letters of somewhat doubtful authenticity
(they depend upon oral and not quite consistent tradition) are recalled to show a certain recalcitrance. 'I
have begun Ovid: I hate it,' is one such passage; and
another, 'This is a beastly school—milk and water, no
milk; bread and butter, no butter. Please give a
quarter's notice.' But this apparently represents the
first plunge into school life; his family agree that he
was really well treated, and evidence to the same effect

appears a short time later in a quaint contemporary
document.   .

Before he left Mr. Sopp's school, Fawcett had been
seized by the normal attack of diary-writing. A little
pocket-book contains the records of his childish expe-
riences during September and October 1846, and from
March to October 1847. The handwriting is excellent,
the contents fragmentary. Frequently the young author
is forced to condescend to bare meteorology: 'It was a
very fine day,' is often the sole entry. We gather, however, that he often goes home for a half-holiday, and
has a full share of the true delights of a country-bred
lad. Fishing, his life-long recreation, comes in for
frequent mention: on June 21, 1847, he has the pleasure
of recording the capture of the first fish he ever took with
a fly, 'an Humber' (*i.e.* grayling) 'of about ¾ lb.' He
receives a present of a hedgehog with four young ones;
he sees a party rabbit-shooting; he pays a visit to the
Isle of Wight and goes on board H.M.S. Howe of 120
guns. He goes once to the theatre and once or twice gets
into court at sessions and hears 'Mr. New's girl tried.'
He begins Greek on September 16, 1846; which day had
also its compensations, for 'Trollope had a cake come.'
On July 3, 1847, he notes the state of the poll at the Salisbury election, but refrains from any comment indicative
of his own views. On October 3 following we read with a
sympathetic twinge that he had a new tooth extracted with
'the corkscrew instrument—it hurt very much indeed !'
The later part of the journal records an important change
in his life. On August 3, 1847, he enters Queenwood
College. The house at Queenwood had been built in

1841 by the famous Robert Owen for his last socialistic experiment, and was then called 'Harmony Hall.' In 1847 it had been opened as a school and agricultural college by Mr. Edmonson, Fawcett being the first pupil to arrive on the opening day. Mr. Edmonson was an enthusiastic educationalist. He had previously kept a school in Lancashire, and upon starting at Queenwood he engaged several of the assistants of Fellenberg, whose establishment at Hofwyl had just been broken up. Mr. Edmonson tried to carry into practice some ideas not familiar in England. The course included a good scientific training, and much attention was paid to English literature. At Mr. Sopp's, as we have seen, Fawcett had begun Greek; he had also practised writing letters to his sister in French; and he had acquired some knowledge of shorthand (on Pitman's system). He had not gone far in the usual line of an English classical education, for which he never showed any aptitude. But his intellectual powers were rapidly developing. On Saturday, August 14, the diarist tells us, ' we fixed the election for various officers on the following Wednesday.' On the 18th he says, ' We elected the various college officers: J. Mansergh and I were elected without opposition editors of the " Queenwood Chronicle." ' This choice, within a fortnight of his arrival, seems to prove that he must have speedily impressed his fellows with his literary propensities. His father promises (August 29) to take him to Stonehenge upon hearing that he had been elected to this office, and also that he had been ' studying most determinedly.' One of Mr. Edmonson's educational schemes was the issue of a juvenile paper. I have seen

some copies of the 'Queenwood Reporter' (apparently
a continuation of the 'Chronicle,' but edited by the school
authorities). It contains some articles signed 'H. F.'
One or two are solutions of elementary mathematical
problems. Another, upon 'The End of the Half-Year,'
at Christmas 1848, contains a reference to the death of
a schoolfellow creditable to the writer's feelings. Another
(without signature) is a description of a visit to London,
and is continued through two numbers—August and
October 1848. The original manuscript is still preserved.

The diary gives us sufficient proofs of Fawcett's
interest in his lessons. On August 21, we are told, 'Mr.
Tindal, the surveyor, came.' Afterwards we find that
Mr. Tyndall (whose name is now spelt in the fashion known
to all the world as that adopted by the person indicated,
now Professor Tyndall) takes the boys out surveying and
lectures them 'on the skin.' Fawcett renewed his acquaintance with Professor Tyndall in after years. One
of his colleagues was Dr. Frankland, now professor at the
School of Mines, who lectured upon botany and chemistry.
Fawcett was interested in the scientific lectures. Mr.
Edmonson, he tells us, lectured on fire, and the learner
notes that 'there is fire in almost everything, even in ice.'
He works in the laboratory, and on October 5 'finishes
his first substance in the laboratory; it was some bi-
chromate of lead or chrome yellow.' His English composi-
tions are also noticed. On September 8 he notes, 'I began
writing my lecture on phonography, on the uses of steam'
(some slip of the pen seems to have run two lectures
into one), 'without copying any of it.' A fragment

of the lecture on phonography is still extant, which, after stating that out of 50,000 words in the language only fifty are written as they are pronounced, goes off into a eulogy of Mr. Pitman's system of shorthand, and is followed by several pages written apparently in that character. The lecture on the uses of steam had more important results. On September 16 he acknowledges the receipt from his sister of some mining journals, a paragraph of which is required for his lecture. The lecture fully written out is described as 'delivered by H. Fawcett at Queenwood College, September 27, 1847.' On October 2 he goes home and reads the lecture to the family party. They were 'all much pleased with it,' and 'papa promised to give me a sovereign for it.' It was, as Miss Fawcett tells me, the first thing which convinced the father that there was really 'something in the boy.' The lecture is, in fact, a very promising performance for a boy of fourteen. There are abundant traces of the future economist. The lecturer gives a great many statistics as to the cost of construction of railways, the number of passengers and so forth ; for some part of which he was doubtless indebted to the mining journals. He explains with perfect clearness the advantages to the Wiltshire farmer and the London consumer of a cheap transport of cheese. It is evident that his mind was already running upon the same topics which interested him in later life, and had the same tendency to reason upon the facts of daily observation. In another direction the essay shows a tendency which afterwards diminished. It is highly rhetorical. He begins with an edifying passage upon final causes and

the great Power which amongst other things has provided steam for human use; he becomes florid in
dwelling upon the wonders of modern civilisation and
the glories of the nation which has produced Watt and
Shakespeare; and he winds up with some 'striking
verses,' called the 'Song of Steam,' extracted from an
American paper.

An exuberance of high-flown language, if not a
merit, is at least a very venial fault at fourteen.
Fawcett's flow of language at this time indicates very
considerable intellectual energy. Other more or less
fragmentary essays survive. There is a long one upon
'Reflection,' dated May 19, 1848, enlarging upon the
difference between man and brute; another (title and
beginning lost) which points out that statesmen depend
upon their brains, and then passes into a long eulogy
upon phrenology; there is a short paper called 'A Visit
to Netley Abbey;' and another described as 'Reflections
upon a First Visit to London,' published, as we have seen,
in the 'Reporter'; and some fragments upon 'Satire,'
'Angling and Izaak Walton,' and one upon Ireland.

A sufficient specimen of this boyish rhetoric may be
taken from the essay called 'Reflection.' Inventions
of all kinds, as the essayist remarks, are the fruit of
reflection; and he illustrates their value by an imaginary
traveller. This person, after experiencing the benefits
of bells, newspapers, and a 'buss' (which knocks down
two or three people, but has wheels so formed that
'they get up again quite uninjured'—an invention of
the future, apparently), gets into a railway, where the
heating of a few gallons of water takes him at a rate of

sixty miles an hour, now elevated at a fearful height, 'and now in a dungeon far below the earth.' ' Unfortunately, as he is getting from the carriage he slips and his leg is very seriously injured, in two minutes after the accident is heard of in the town some hundreds of miles distant from where he had just come, it gets no better, soon he has to have it amputated, it is done, and under the most pleasant feelings possible he lays in an hotel, more like a palace, in fact, than anything else ; ' he goes in a steamship past Spain, where Fawcett moralises on the phenomena often noticed in his later studies of a people 'made poor by gold ; ' and so to Egypt, the ancient glories of which are enumerated, whilst we are told parenthetically to depend upon it that Mahomet was 'in many respects a worthy man ' (had Professor Tyndall been lecturing on Carlyle's 'Hero-worship ' ?) ; and finally reaches India, where a small body of men, ' occupying a house of no very considerable size in London, have, entirely from their enterprise and powers of mind, got possession of many thousand acres of land.' He winds up by quotations from Shakespeare (his ' Ode to Mercy '—*i.e.* the passage in Portia's speech) and Cicero's Oration on Verres, both of which, as he justly observes, show powers of reflection.

The quaint boyish declamation is already directed to subjects which occupied much of his later thought ; the general line of remark being of course a version of many contemporary eulogies on progress, familar enough to the Radicals of that day. Fawcett used to tell us how he had once ventured into poetry, the subject being a 'Prairie on Fire,' and the sole surviving fragment

describing the 'bisons in despair,' and stating that they
'tore their grizzly hair.' A letter to his father dated
November 17, 1848, throws some light upon the influences which presided over his early eloquence. He
has been taking lessons in elocution; he has 'pronounced a very impassioned speech in presence of the
whole school' as composedly as if he had been repeating
it to himself. Such composure, as he observes, is a
desirable acquirement for one who wishes to speak well.
He has learnt various famous passages from Shakespeare
and Addison's 'Cato.' The elocution master certainly
seems to have been consulted in the composition of
the letter, which is full of moral reflections after the
manner of Mr. Barlow. 'What talents will not do,' says
the lad, after professing his own resolutions to be indus-
trious, 'industry will. This was a maxim ever in the
mind of Napoleon.' He observes in the same letter
that Cambridge students are henceforth to know something of political economy, history, and science, as well
as classics and mathematics, and states that in a recent
examination he has been first both in history and
geography.

Fawcett, as his schoolfellows remember, was at this
time tall for his age, loosely made, and rather ungainly.
He preferred study to boyish sports, and, in spite of
prohibitions, would desert the playground to steal into
a copse with his books. He was best at mathematics,
caring little for Latin and French. He learnt long
passages by heart, and would wander in the fields
repeating them aloud. In an old chalk-pit, which was a
favourite greenroom, he would gesticulate as he recited,

till passing labourers had doubts as to his sanity. Even
at this time, when the boys talked of their future lives,
he always declared that he meant to be a member of
Parliament—an avowal then received by 'roars of
laughter.' The rather peculiar course of study certainly seems to have been favourable to his development.
On December 15, 1880, he presided at a dinner of old
Queenwood scholars, and spoke cordially of the value of
the training. He insisted especially upon the absence
of injudicious forcing, and upon the charms of the free
country life in a retired situation.

His Queenwood experience only lasted some eighteen
months. He was sent to King's College School after the
Christmas holidays, 1848-9. He was now shooting up
rapidly to his great height, and had for the time outgrown
his strength. It was thought desirable that he should
live as near as might be to the school; and after a short
residence with Dr. Major, the head-master, he was
therefore transferred to the house of a Mr. Fearon. Mr.
Fearon, who was in some way connected with Fawcett's
family, was for many years a chief office keeper in the
Stamps and Taxes Department in Somerset House, and
consequently had apartments there, in convenient proxi-
mity to King's College. Fawcett's delicacy at this time
was probably some hindrance to his studies. Mr. C. B.
Clarke, who had been at school in Salisbury and knew
his parents by sight, was also at King's College School
at this time. He remembers Fawcett as 'a very tall
boy, with pale whitey-brown hair, who always stood at
the bottom of the lower sixth class.' The master of
this class was Thomas Markby, a good scholar, who was

afterwards lecturer at Trinity Hall, Cambridge. A boy's position in the school was determined exclusively by his classical attainments. Fawcett's knowledge in that direction was scanty enough. Fawcett (as Mr. Clarke believes) distinctly refused to have anything to do with Beatson's 'Iambics,' and was serenely indifferent to the petty distinctions between aorists, perfects, and so forth, which are not beneath the notice of Greek grammarians. Markby had the good sense to excuse him from the hated verses, being satisfied that he was at work in other directions. Mr. Cunningham, secretary to King's College, kindly informs me that Fawcett gained the arithmetic prize in the Easter Term 1849; the 'class work' prize in the Michaelmas Term 1849; the first prize for German and the second for French in the same term (a fact which implies, I fear, that the contemporary standard of foreign languages was not exalted); a prize for mathematics in the Lent Term, 1850; and the first prize for mathematics in the Michaelmas Term 1850. The mathematical master at that time (as Mr. Clarke tells me) was Mr. James Hann, a self-taught man who had begun life in a coal-mine, and retained the appearance of a miner. When once detected in a perusal of Horace, he apologised on the ground that, although Horace could not teach you to make a steam-engine, there was pretty reading in him when you were not in working humour. Hann was a shrewd observer. He recognised Fawcett's mathematical power and took him on from Euclid to the Integral Calculus—a range of reading then very unusual before entering the University. I may add that in July 1849 his master, the Rev. J. Edwards, reports that Fawcett showed 'great power in writing English prose.' At Easter 1851 Fawcett left the school and attended the mathematical and classical classes at the college until the summer of 1852. Here, for the first time, he became intimate with Mr. C. B. Clarke, who was attending the same mathematical lectures under Professors Hall and Goodeve. The friendship was destined to be lifelong. At this time Fawcett was the best mathematician of the two. It does not seem, however, that he made any special mark at the college. He always attributed much influence to his conversations with Mr. Fearon. I am told that he played cribbage unweariedly with Mrs. Fearon in order to have greater opportunities of hearing her husband talk. Mr. Fearon, as I learn from Sir John Lambert, was a keen politician, though not a highly educated man. He was a Unitarian in religion, a staunch Liberal in politics and creed, and especially a strong free-trader. Fawcett preserved a high respect for Fearon's common sense, and in later days often recalled his 'quaint and forcible' phrases in conversation with Sir J. Lambert. I have a faint recollection that Fawcett told me that he had even at this time found his way to the gallery of the House of Commons. He occasionally played cricket, though King's College had not the athletic advantages of some other schools, and he acquired some skill at billiards.

The then Dean of Salisbury, Dr. Hamilton, was consulted by Mr. Fawcett senior, who showed him some of the boy's mathematical papers. The dean said emphatically that the lad ought to go to Cambridge. This opinion fortunately decided the question. The expense was a matter of some importance, as Mr. Fawcett was not a rich man, and University education was not usual for a man of Fawcett's social position. The choice of a college was characteristic. Parents generally seem to consider that the choice of the place at which a young man is to be under the most decisive influences of his whole life is of so little importance that it may be decided by the most trivial circumstance. Boys themselves are more likely to think of the position of the college boat than of more serious merits. Fawcett, however, was already thoughtful enough to choose his college for more weighty reasons. He chose Peterhouse[1] deliberately, on the ground that its Fellowships were supposed to be of more than the average value and were tenable by laymen. He had already to some extent chalked out his future career; though I am unable to say precisely at what period his mind had been made up.

I saw Fawcett for the first time a few months after his entrance (in October 1852). The circumstances imply that his appearance was then sufficiently striking. My memory is very irretentive of such matters in general; but I could point to the precise spot on the bank of the Cam where I noticed a very tall, gaunt figure swinging along with huge strides upon the towing-path. He was over 6 feet 3 inches in height. His chest, I should say, was not very broad in proportion to his height, but he was remarkably large of bone and massive of limb. The face was impressive, though not hand-

---

[1] I cannot bring myself to the barbarism of ' St Peter's College,' under which the oldest college in the University has apparently tried to conceal its identity.

some. The skull was very large; my own head vanished as into a cavern if I accidentally put on his hat. The forehead was lofty, though rather retreating, and the brow finely arched. The complexion was rather dull, but more than one of his early acquaintance speaks of the brightness of his eye and the keenness of his glance. The eyes were full and capable of vivid expression, though not, I think, brilliant in colour.[1] The features were strong, and, though not delicately carved, were far from heavy, and gave a general impression of remarkable energy. The mouth, long, thin-lipped, and very flexible, had a characteristic nervous tremor as of one eager to speak and voluble of discourse. In after years, the expression rather suggested that his inability to see stimulated the desire to gain information through his other senses. A certain wistfulness was a frequent shade of expression. But a singularly hearty and cordial laugh constantly lighted up the whole face with an expression of most genial and infectious good-humour.

On my first glimpse of Fawcett, however, I was troubled by a question of classification. I vaguely speculated as to whether he was an undergraduate, or a young farmer, or possibly somebody connected with horses at Newmarket come over to see the sights. He had a certain rustic air, in strong contrast to that of the young Pendennises who might stroll along the bank to make a book upon the next boat-race. He rather resembled some of the athletic figures who may be seen at the side

[1] In the portrait from an early photograph engraved in this volume, the rather peculiar expression of the eyes results, I think, from the weakness of sight presently to be noticed, which made him shrink from any strong light.

of a North-country wrestling ring. Indeed, I fancy that Fawcett may have inherited from his father some of the characteristics of the true long-legged, long-limbed, Dandie-Dinmont type of North-countryman. The impression was, no doubt, fixed in my mental camera because I was soon afterwards surprised by seeing my supposed rustic dining in our college hall.

I insist upon this because it may indicate Fawcett's superficial characteristics on his first appearance at Cambridge. Many qualities, which all his friends came to recognise sooner or later, were for the present either latent or, it may be, undeveloped. The first glance revealed the stalwart, bucolic figure, with features stamped by intelligence, but that kind of intelligence which we should rather call shrewdness than by any higher name. The earliest anecdote of his college days is significant of the impressions which he made. There was at Peterhouse a youth nicknamed the 'Captain'— apparently by way of tribute to his sporting tendencies. The Captain saw first in Fawcett only the country bumpkin, and challenged him to a game at quoits. Fawcett could beat most Salisbury lads at this, which was a Salisbury game, and made short work of his antagonist. The Captain then proposed the more refined game of billiards. They played a single game of 100. After a time the Captain had scored ninety-six to Fawcett's seventy-five. Fawcett was to play, and the spectators taunted him with offers of ten to one on his opponent. Fawcett accepted all bets offered at this, and then at lower rates. He then played, and made the necessary twenty-five in a single break. 'The bets,' he said to

Clarke, 'were forced on me; but the odds were really
more than ten to one against my making twenty-five in
any position of the balls, though I saw a stroke which I
knew that I could make and which would leave me with
a fine game.' Clarke thinks that Fawcett was in his first
week of residence. He won what seemed a large sum
to undergraduates and obtained a reputation for shrewdness which earned for him for a short time the nickname
of the 'Old Serpent.' One of Fawcett's intimates tried
to repeat his success, and challenged the Captain to a
game of chess. The Captain, however, was no fool, and
won his game triumphantly.

Fawcett's remarkable nerve and powers of rapid cal-
culation would have made him a formidable antagonist
in such games of skill. But he never condescended to
gambling. He was a good whist-player, but he gave up
billiards, and when some of his college acquaintance fell
into a foolish practice of playing for more than they
could afford, he did what he could to discourage them,
and spoke of their folly with hearty contempt. He had,
in truth, too much sense and self-command—to say
nothing of higher motives—to fall into errors of this
kind. I may add here—and the testimony of a college
contemporary before whom no reserve was necessary
may be taken as sufficient—that as a young man he was
free from errors too common in the undergraduate world
of those days. The moral standard of Cambridge was,
in certain respects, far from elevated; but Fawcett,
though no ascetic or strait-laced Puritan, was in all
senses perfectly blameless in his life.

Fawcett's friends soon came to value him for

intellectual qualities displayed in a higher sphere than that of games. The strong, shrewd common sense of the man was the first quality to be recognised; and upon that head there could be no mistake. The circle of friends to which he belonged was propitious to its early development and recognition. The years spent at the University, when the buoyancy of the schoolboy blends with the exulting sense of manly independence and the growing consciousness of power, are amongst the most delightful in the lives of most men, especially when they have the good fortune to find congenial spirits. We can still form friendships with boyish facility, which are yet more than the mere comrade-ship of boyish days. Of all men whom I have ever known, Fawcett most fully retained the power of forming new friendships till later years. Yet even he probably made more friendships at this than at a later period, and, what is more remarkable, he never lost a friend once attracted. An undergraduate's 'set' generally represents the most important influences of his academical career. Half-a-dozen promising lads can do more to educate each other than all the tutors and professors can do for them. Fawcett's set included several men of distinguished ability. Peterhouse was a small college, in which everyone could soon become known to everyone else. There he became acquainted with his seniors, Tait, Steele, Routh, and W. D. Gardiner. His King's College connection brought him into friendly relations, through his special intimate C. B. Clarke, with Messrs. E. Wilson, Rigby (now Q.C.), Daniel Jones, and M. M. U. Wilkinson now vicar of Reepham, Norfolk).

These last formed a kind of inner circle. Clarke and Rigby were at Trinity and in Fawcett's own year. All the set were mathematicians and reading men. Some of them were musical, though Fawcett at this time took the unappreciative view of the difference between tweedle-dum and tweedle-dee. He was also pre-eminent for classical ignorance, and was often rallied by his friends for his literary deficiencies. Literature, indeed, was not the strong point of the set. They were typical Cambridge men : believers in hard facts and figures, admirers of strenuous common sense, and hearty despisers of sentimentalism. They seem to have carried on the tradition of the earlier set, described in Mill's 'Autobiography,' of which Charles Austin was the leader, who swore by Bentham and used the dyslogistic words, 'sentimentalism,' 'declamation,' and 'vague generalities,' as a kind of Shibboleth. The phrase current in Fawcett's set, by which a man was placed beyond the pale of serious notice, was 'gush.' 'Is he not a gusher?' meant 'Is he not a consummate imbecile?' The whole set, it must be remembered, were still in the semi-schoolboy stage, looking upon their studies as a clever schoolboy regards his lessons—chiefly as a providential machinery for prize-winning. They played whist and billiards and had constant social meetings, 'wines,' and 'tea-fights,' and did not condescend ('muscular Christianity' was hardly on foot) to take much part in athletic games. They had, however, genuine intellectual interests. At that period the more 'sentimental' youth learnt Tennyson by heart, wept over 'Jane Eyre,' and was beginning to appreciate Browning. If more seriously disposed, he

read 'Sartor Resartus' and the 'French Revolution';
he followed the teachings of Maurice and had some
leaning to 'Christian Socialism.' But the sterner utilitarians looked to Mill as their great prophet. They
repudiated Carlyle as reactionary, and set down Maurice
as muddle-headed. The chief of Fawcett's set in these
matters was Edward Wilson, three years his senior, who
was eighth Wrangler in 1853, and whose place in the
Tripos very inadequately represented his real abilities.
Wilson specially delighted in discussing political economy,
and vindicating Mill. When an outsider joined the
parties of the set, he was liable to be entrapped into an
argument upon the theory of population or the wage-
fund; and Wilson, after tearing to pieces the fallacies
of some ignoramus, would always add sententiously,
'Read Mill! read Mill!' Fawcett took the advice to
heart.

Meanwhile he applied himself resolutely to mathematics. In his first year he read with Steele, and afterwards with W. Hopkins.[1] Peterhouse had then a remarkable mathematical reputation. Mr. Fuller, now
Professor of Mathematics at King's College, Aberdeen,
had been fourth Wrangler in 1842; (the present Sir
William) Thomson was second in 1844; W. A. Porter,
one of Fawcett's closest friends, was third in 1849;
James Porter, another close friend, now Master of Peter-

---

[1] A conflict of testimony of which I spoke in previous editions has
been kindly cleared up for me. Fawcett was not a private pupil of Mr.
Routh's, but after leaving Peterhouse he continued to attend a weekly
problem paper in the college, which during part of the time was set by
Mr. Routh.

house, was eighth Wrangler in 1851. In 1852 Tait,
now the eminent professor at Edinburgh, was senior
Wrangler, and Steele, Fawcett's first tutor, who died
young, was second. In 1854 Mr. Routh, the most
eminent mathematical tutor at Cambridge for a great
number of years, was again senior, and J. Clerk Maxwell, the great physicist, who was second, had also been
entered originally at Peterhouse. All these except the
two first, who had left Cambridge, became friends of
Fawcett. One of Fawcett's qualifications for making
friendships was his utter incapacity for being awed by
differences of position. He was as sensitive as anyone
to the claims of intellectual excellence, but his freedom
from affectation or false pretensions saved him from
any awkward shyness. He was equally at his ease with
an agricultural labourer, or a prime minister, or (what
to me seemed more surprising) a senior Wrangler. To
this day I do not realise—though on purely intellectual
grounds I accept—the fact that even a senior Wrangler
is made of flesh and blood. I cannot forget the surprise
with which I once found Fawcett chatting on terms of
perfect equality with the great Tait and Steele, then
in all the glory of recent pre-eminence in the Tripos.
Fawcett always took other people for what they were,
and expected to be taken in the same way himself. He
was capable, I think—and he was, I may say, the only
man I have ever known capable—of joining cordially in
a laugh at a false quantity made by himself; not that he
often ventured into the regions environed by such perils.
He was no more ashamed of his deficiencies as a scholar
than of the shape of his nose.

He thus became intimate with men apparelled in all the terrors of seniority and academic reputation. With none did he become more friendly than with Hopkins, an old Peterhouse man (B.A. 1827) then Esquire-Bedell, and for many years the leading mathematical ' coach ' at Cambridge. He always spoke of Hopkins with enthusiasm. In 1880 Fawcett had some correspondence with the family about an intention of writing some account of his old tutor's work in the University (Hopkins had died in 1867). The intention fell through, probably on account of the pressure of official work, which fully occupied Fawcett's energies. I can, however, say with certainty that he would have rejoiced to do justice to his teacher. Hopkins used to form a class of select pupils, admitting only those who in their first year had shown themselves to be qualified for a good place amongst the Wranglers. A weak point of the Cambridge system was the tendency of students to think too exclusively of winning marks in the Senate-house. Hopkins was conspicuous for inculcating a more liberal view of the studies of the place. He endeavoured to stimulate a philosophical interest in the mathematical sciences instead of simply rousing an ardour for competition. Fawcett had no desire nor the necessary aptitude to be a mathematical specialist. He meant to win a Fellowship by examination ; and his success was to be a stepping-stone to his future career. He used to say that he would rather be senior Wrangler in the worst year than second to a Sir Isaac Newton. No man was more fully awake to the tangible commercial utility of a good degree. But it was very characteristic that his robust common sense led him to aims which lay beyond the range of mere temporary expediency. He did not despise the pecuniary rewards of intellectual prowess, but he saw distinctly that it would be the reverse of sensible to win such rewards at the expense of his intellectual development. He read for honours and with a view to a Fellowship, but he worked in the spirit of the official Cambridge theory, expounded in its best sense by Hopkins—that the true value of the mathematical training was its excellence as a branch of intellectual gymnastics. He formed what was (in my own opinion) an even excessive estimate of its merit, in this respect; and in later life took more than one opportunity of saying that, although he had been forced by circumstances to drop his mathematics entirely, he did not regret a single hour spent in the study. Fawcett's keen appreciation of this advantage was doubtless due in part to Hopkins's mode of treatment and the direct personal influence of his singularly lofty character. In any case, he always regarded Hopkins as one of the best representatives of all that he most admired in his well-loved University. Another occupation was characteristic in the same sense. One day at the beginning of his third year (October 1854) Fawcett looked in at the Union, and was prompted to speak in the debate which was proceeding. He became from that time a regular debater. Many young men of ability have first tried their powers in that arena. Charles Austin, Macaulay, Monckton Milnes, and others had been famous orators in the early years of the century. Just before Fawcett's time Sir William Harcourt and Mr. Justice Stephen had been protagonists in many keenly contested debates.

Since Fawcett's time many conspicuous orators from the Union have distinguished themselves in various public careers ; yet there was a kind of tacit agreement amongst the undergraduates, who specially affect a stern contempt for all kinds of ostentatious display, to treat debates at the Union as legitimate matter for ridicule. The shame-facedness of British youth is unfavourable to oratory. Perhaps success at the Union is a promising symptom just because it indicates superiority to this prevalent weakness. Fawcett, at any rate, the least shamefaced of men, perceived that common sense might recommend a practice ridiculed by sensible men. His friends mocked at his efforts and held aloof from the Union. He went steadily to work, and after some comparative failures became one of the most prominent orators. He not only spoke but sometimes carefully prepared his speeches. I find amongst his papers two rough drafts of speeches upon National Education and University Reform, upon both of which subjects he opened debates. He thus at any rate acquired the power which, as we have seen, he desiderated at Queenwood, of addressing an audience with perfect composure. Between November 1854 and the summer of 1856 (when he was a young B.A.) he made many speeches recorded in the Annals of the Union. The most conspicuous of his rivals were H. M. Butler (subsequently Head-master of Harrow, and now Dean of Gloucester), to whose remarkable powers as a youthful orator I can still bear witness, Mr. Vernon Lushington, Mr. W. C. Gully, Mr. A. G. Marten (all of them now Queen's Counsel), Mr. (now Sir) J. E. Gorst (now Solicitor-General), Mr. E. E. Bowen (now Master at Harrow), and Mr. W. T. Marriott (now Judge Advocate-General).

The main topic of the debates was provided by the Crimean War. Had the sovereigns of Austria and Prussia listened to Fawcett, Butler, and a great majority of the Union, they would have formed an alliance with England in November 1854. Fawcett, again in a majority, held that the character of the late Emperor Nicholas was not worthy of respect. In May 1855 he held with a small minority that the independence of Poland must be secured as a condition of a satisfactory peace. In October 1855 he objects to a Prussian alliance. In November he argues with Mr. Marriott and against Mr. Bowen that the time has not yet come for negotiating a peace. In the same month he defends the 'Times' against Mr. Gorst, who maintains that its conduct has been unpatriotic. In February 1856 he objects to the Russian proposals, which are approved by Messrs. Marriott, Bowen, and Butler. In March he holds that Lord John Russell deserves the gratitude of his country, and in May 1856 that the annexation of Oude was justifiable.

Fawcett was clearly not at this time in sympathy with the party opposed to the war. His other speeches, however, show that he was already avowing the principles to which he adhered throughout his life. On December 1, 1854, he brings forward a resolution in favour of an unsectarian system of National Education. In March 1855 he supports a motion for the abolition of purchase in the army; in May 1855 he holds (in a minority of four to twenty-two) that the 'party called the Cobdenites have done the country good service; '

and in December 1855 he approves of a 'considerable
extension of the franchise.' One motion brought forward
by him on February 5, 1856, is worth giving, as it expresses an opinion upon which he was soon to take
decided action. He moves, 'That it is highly desirable
that the term of tenure of Fellowships should be limited;
that the restriction of celibacy should be abolished; that
all who have ever been Fellows should have equal claim
with present Fellows to college livings, and should have
a voice in the presentation to Church patronage.' His
notes show that he elaborately argued for this resolution,
of which he was the only supporter in the debate, and
which was rejected by thirty-seven to sixteen. His chief
ground of argument was the evil effect of celibacy and
clerical restriction in lowering the character of Fellows.
He said that many men of high power waited for
college livings until they were fit for nothing better
than making brilliant puns in combination rooms. His
practice at the Union seems to have led Fawcett to
overcome that boyish tendency to stilted rhetoric which
appears so quaintly in his early essay. Perhaps the
last trace of it was in a college essay (in 1854 or 1855)
upon the merits of Pope's poetry, of which he has left
a fair and a rough copy. It is not more and perhaps not
less likely than more pretentious essays upon English
men of letters to throw new light upon that venerable
topic.

Fawcett when he joined the Union had been for more
than a year a member of Trinity Hall. He was admitted
as a pensioner at that college October 18, 1853, and won
a Scholarship in the college examination of the following

May. He had found that his chances of a Fellowship at Peterhouse were diminished by the presence of several strong competitors. He therefore 'migrated' (in the college phrase) to Trinity Hall, which had recently been at its very nadir. The story ran that Mr. Latham (who was appointed tutor from Trinity College at Christmas 1847) asked his colleague a short time afterwards when the freshmen were coming up? The reply was, that they had all come up; the numbers were too small to be visible to the naked eye. Trinity Hall has steadily risen under Mr. Latham's judicious government to a leading place amongst the small colleges. Its depression had been partly due to the fact that its Fellowships had been regularly confined to law students, and very little interest was then taken in law studies at Cambridge. It had now been decided that Fellowships should be given to men distinguished in the ordinary Triposes. Several migrations took place of men who, like Fawcett, desired lay Fellowships and anticipated vacancies at Trinity Hall. The change of college made little immediate difference to Fawcett except by the addition of some new friends to his circle. I may boast that I was of the number, and so gained one of the greatest privileges of my life.

Fawcett's set had read to the last term of their undergraduate course with a vague belief that the honours of the Tripos would fall to St. John's College. It then began to dawn upon them that they, too, were mathematicians. Fawcett was thought to show most promise; and though it was generally held that Hadley of St. John's was the best man of his year, it began to

be whispered that Fawcett had some chance of even the
senior Wranglership. The contest for that honour is
always most exciting. In the Tripos, for, as I imagine,
the first and last time of his life, Fawcett's nerve failed
him. He could not sleep, though he got out of bed and
ran round the college quadrangle to exhaust himself.
He failed to gain the success upon which he had counted
in the concluding papers.[1] Not only was Hadley senior
Wrangler and far ahead of the second, but Fawcett
sank to be seventh. His intimates, Rigby and Clarke,
were second and third. In spite of his comparative
failure he had shown marked ability. Dr. Besant, one
of the Moderators for 1856, tells me that he was much
impressed by Fawcett's work. Fawcett was wanting in
technical skill and the manipulation of mathematical
analysis. He overcame his deficiency by sheer mental
force and his power of directly applying mechanical
principles. He used plain English where most candidates would apply mathematical machinery. Fawcett
had in any case done more than enough to win a Fellowship at his college, where he was far ahead of all rivals.
He was elected to a Fellowship at Christmas 1856.

Fawcett had clearly decided upon his plan of life.

---

[1] Dr. Wolstenholme, junior examiner for the Tripos in 1856, has
kindly shown me the marks. Fawcett was seventh at the end of the
first three days (which then formed a separate section of the examination). He rose to be sixth, passing C. B. Clarke, on the first of the
five days, and at the end of each succeeding day was seventh on the
total marks, neither passing nor being passed. On the separate days'
marks he was sixth on the first day, second on the fourth, and only
thirteenth, twelfth, and tenth on the second, third, and fifth day
respectively. He was distanced by Rigby and Clarke on the last day
especially, when he had probably hoped to gain places.

I cannot fix the precise date at which his mind was
made up: even at Queenwood his mind, as we have
seen, had been fixed upon political success, and his desire
of acquiring the art of public speaking was probably
significant of the same boyish ambition.   It was known
to all his friends whilst he was yet an undergraduate.
He was, however, a poor man.   He had no income
beyond his Fellowship (worth about 250*l.* a year),
and such allowance as could be made by his father, who
was not a rich man, and had three other children.   He
resolved therefore to approach Parliament through a
successful career at the bar.   He was justified in counting upon such success as almost a certainty.   His indomitable energy, his strong practical intellect and aptitude
for business, combined with his remarkable power of falling into friendly relations with men in all classes, were
admirable qualifications for a young barrister.   He had
also reason to be certain that an opening would not be
wanting to him.   Mr. A. T. Squarey, whose family was
long connected with Salisbury, had known him from
childhood and had formed a high opinion of his abilities.
Mr. Squarey was now at the head of one of the principal
firms of solicitors in Liverpool, with a very large mer-
cantile practice.   He encouraged Fawcett to go to the
bar, and promised that he should have opportunities
of showing his powers in the conduct of important
business.

Fawcett had entered Lincoln's Inn on October 26,
1854.   After his degree, he considered that he had a
right to a short holiday.   He was at Cambridge in the
summer of 1856, and for a time he took lodgings on

D

Putney Heath, to be near an old family friend, Mrs.
Hodding.   In November he settled in London to begin
his legal studies.   He attended some of the reader's lectures, upon which he made careful notes, still preserved
amongst his papers.   I remember the warm admiration
which he expressed for the lectures of Mr. (now Sir
Henry) Maine; and, indeed, he never came in contact
with a man of marked ability without being moved to
enthusiasm.   He continued to practise himself in public
speaking.   He was a member, as Sir John Pope Hennessy (now Governor of Mauritius) kindly informs me, of
the Westminster Debating Society, which met in an old-
fashioned room in the Westminster Tavern, near Westminster Bridge.   Several young barristers and journal-
ists belonged to this society, which imitated the forms of
the House of Commons.   The tradition ran that Sir E.
B. Lytton had once paid it a visit, and said afterwards
that he had entered in a fit of abstraction, mistaking
it for the House of Commons.   He only discovered his
error upon finding that there were no dull speeches and
no one asleep—which seems to prove that it must have
been a very remarkable society indeed.   Fawcett became
leader of the Radical party in this mimic Legislature,
and Sir J. Hennessy remembers his 'resonant voice,'
'wild hair,' and 'expressive eyes.'   No contemporary of
Fawcett's, I should imagine, can have entered the struggle of life better qualified to take his own part, or with
greater confidence of success.   None of his friends had
the slightest doubt that in some way or other he would
force his way to the front.   We recognised as fully as
at a later period his energy and his keen intelligence.

If we were still a little blind to some of his nobler qualities, we at least recognised in him the thoroughly 'good
fellow,' whose success would be as gratifying to his
friends as it was confidently anticipated. But soon
after he had taken his degree the shadow of a great
calamity fell across his path. In the winter of 1856–7
he wrote to his friend Clarke to say that something was
wrong with his eyesight. In the early part of 1857 he
consulted Critchett, one of the first oculists of the day.
Critchett (as his son, Mr. G. Anderson Critchett, kindly
informs me) found that Fawcett was suffering 'from a
sprained condition of the ciliary or adjusting muscles,
consequent upon over-use of the eyes. The retina had
also become very sensitive to light, but no organic change
had taken place to threaten any serious or permanent
loss of sight.' Critchett ordered perfect rest, forbidding
him to try his eyes by reading or by exposure to strong
light. This warning certainly caused some anxiety.
I do not myself, nor do the surviving members of his
family, remember that his spirits were visibly depressed.
Clarke, however, to whom he paid a visit shortly after
this time, says that at no point of his career was Fawcett so unhappy. I think that on this, as upon other
occasions, he was careful to conceal his anxieties unless
circumstances prompted some special confidence, and
especially to conceal them from the parents and the
sister who would have been so deeply pained by a full
knowledge of his misgivings.

His temporary incapacitation and the possibility of
permanent disqualification for his chosen career must
in any case have been a severe trial for the young man.

then in the first flush of his ambition. In 1857 he found
some employment by taking a pupil, Charles Cooke,
nephew of the Master of Trinity Hall, who was reading for
a military examination. With Cooke and Miss Fawcett,
Fawcett went to Paris towards the end of 1857, where
the pupil might learn French whilst he read mathematics with his tutor. Fawcett hoped for some advantage
from change of scene, and consulted some of the French
oculists. In a letter dated November 9, he wrote to an
old friend, Mr. Egerton, then curate of Nunton, close to
Longford, and now rector of Burwash, Sussex. He has
spent six weeks in Paris and his sister is about to leave
him. He has been under the care of Sichel, who says
' that it is one of the most extraordinary cases he has
ever had,' but hopes to be of some service. Should
his eyes not improve by Christmas, Fawcett says that he
shall go to Düsseldorf. Miss Fawcett tells me that her
brother consulted two oculists at Paris, one of whom
ordered high and the other low living. Fawcett followed
the latter prescription, but derived from it no distinct
advantage.

Fawcett's letter to Egerton, as I may remark in
passing, contains some remarks upon French characteristics which are I fear of the conventional British
type. No man, to say the truth, could well be more out
of his element. The weakness of his eyes now made him
specially dependent upon his favourite resource of conversation ; but in spite of his linguistic successes at
school, Fawcett was through life even oddly incapable of
acquiring new languages. His tongue, fluent enough
in the vernacular, was a stubborn member, and adhered

rigidly to the tricks of early days. Some Wiltshire forms of speech hung about him, I think, to the last. I doubt whether he ever perceived the difference between 'February' and 'Febuwerry'; and I remember how hard we found it to convince him that although Professor Tyndall might be right in saying that glacier ice was a 'viscous fluid,' he had never asserted it to be 'vicious.'

Fawcett came back from Paris by Christmas as true a Briton as he had set out. The state of his eyes had not improved. Idleness was still enforced upon him; and for a few months he spent his time chiefly, I believe, at his father's house, occasionally writing a few letters to the papers upon topics of the day. The accident was soon to happen which brought this period of suspense to a strange and unexpected close. For reasons which I have tried to explain, Fawcett's character had not hitherto been fully revealed to his friends, even so far as it had hitherto been fully developed. The kind of stoical severity which was our pet virtue at Cambridge, the intense dislike to any needless revelations of feeling, had certainly its good side. It was at worst an exaggeration of a creditable and masculine instinct. We preferred to mask our impulses under a guise of cynicism rather than to affect more sensibility than we really possessed. I for one should be sorry to see the opposite practice come into fashion. But it must be admitted that the habit of systematically acting the cynic may generate a real cynicism. Fawcett was a man of cordial and generous nature, and of exceedingly strong domestic affections. But he rarely trusted himself at this time to utter his emotions, especially to the friends who were inclined to an excessive severity. Staunch utilitarians and political economists, we were always on our guard against sentimentalism and keenly alive to the absurdity of excesses in that direction. Fawcett sympathised fully with our prejudices; and it was only as he grew older and his character became mellowed that the juvenile affectation finally passed away, and that he came not only to appreciate but to act openly, without false shame, upon the great truth that warmth of heart is not incompatible with, but essential to, a thoroughly masculine nature. Though no one could think him brutal or cynical, early acquaintance might still think him hard. It is fortunate, however, that his friend Mrs. Hodding has preserved some letters of this period which prove that he had higher motives than he cared to lay bare to the ordinary circle, and could relax his severity under the influence of feminine sympathy. I will quote some passages from them (by her kind permission). Perhaps they show some touches of his youthful magniloquence; but the genuineness of the sentiment is proved by his later fulfilment of the early aspirations. Fawcett, as I have said, had been lodging near her on Putney Heath, in the summer of 1856. She left England for Australia shortly afterwards. He writes to her on September 21, 1856: 'I regard you with such true affection that I have long wished to impart my mind on many subjects. . . . You know somewhat of my character; you shall now hear my views as to my future. I started life as a boy with the ambition some day to enter the House of Commons. Every effort, every endeavour, which I have ever put forth has had this object in view. I have continually tried and shall, I trust, still try not only honourably to gratify my desire, but to fit myself for such an important trust. And now the realisation of these hopes has become something even more than the gratification of ambition. I feel that I ought to make any sacrifice, to endure any amount of labour, to obtain this position, because every day I become more deeply impressed with the powerful conviction that this is the position in which I could be of the greatest use to my fellow-men, and that I could in the House of Commons exert an influence in removing the social evils of our country, and especially the paramount one—the mental degradation of millions.

'I have tried myself severely, but in vain, to discover whether this desire has not some worldly source. I could therefore never be happy unless I was to do everything to secure and fit myself for this position. For I should be racked with remorse through life if any selfishness checked such efforts. For I must regard it as a high privilege from God if I have such aspirations, and if He has endowed me with powers which will enable me to assist in such a work of philanthropy.

'This is the career which perhaps the too bright hopes of youth have induced me to hope for. Speaking of myself, I trust that I bear little malice to anyone. Still I know and am well aware that I am impetuous.'

On November 3 he says that he has an invitation to the 'great manufacturing centres,' where he is 'particularly anxious to observe certain things with respect to the social condition of the people in those parts.'

On November 20 he reports that his trip has been delightful. He has met many friends and seen many interesting objects. Especially he met the 'great philanthropist,' Mr. Wright, of Manchester—a 'second Howard,' who showed him gaols and ragged schools, and received him hospitably in his family. 'I have never met,' says Fawcett, 'so fine and perfect an example of a venerable Christian.'

On February 22, 1857, he has heard the Budget debate. He had gone at one o'clock and spent twelve hours in the House. 'No one,' he says, 'need fear obtaining a position in the House of Commons now; for I should say never was good speaking more required. There is not a man in the Ministry can speak but Lord Palmerston; Disraeli is the support of the Opposition; but although he was considered to have achieved a success that night, it was done by uttering a multitude of words and indulging in a great deal of claptrap. Gladstone made the speech of the evening, and he *is* a fine speaker. He never hesitates, and his elocution and manner are admirable; in fact, in this he resembles Bright, but is, in my opinion, inferior to Bright in not condensing his matter. Wilson's speech showed by far the most sound sense, but he is no orator and therefore was hardly listened to. You who know so well my deep ambition to be one day in Parliament will believe that I shall use every endeavour to fit myself for the duties of such a life, and I now see no reason to despair of having my desire gratified and of obtaining what to me would be by far the greatest of worldly triumphs— namely, the assurance of my own conscience that my days had been usefully passed in behalf of my country.

'Long before you went to Australia, I had eagerly desired to visit that country, for to my mind it must within a few years exercise a most important influence on the future of England. India, too, is the land I much desire to see and know; and it ought to be by anyone who takes part in public life.'

On March 9, 1857, we have an account of his eye troubles, which shows him, perhaps for reasons similar to those already suggested, in a more cheerful mood than Clarke's recollections would imply.

'I must tell you that my eyes have not been well lately. I therefore went with my father to one of the first oculists of the day, as I was naturally becoming somewhat alarmed. However, his opinion was very consoling; he tells me that for a twelvemonth I must relinquish all reading; but, as there is no disease whatever, he feels no doubt at all that I shall then find them as strong as ever they were, and I myself have every confidence in their becoming so. I cannot be sufficiently thankful that it has occurred just now, when perhaps I can spare the time with so little inconvenience. I go home to-morrow. Maria will resign her needle with great composure to devote herself to reading to me. I shall thus get quite as much reading as I desire, and I can well foresee that, far from being a misfortune, it may become an advantage, since it will perhaps for the next year induce me to *think* more than young men are apt to do; it will give me an opportunity to solidify and arrange my knowledge, and *you* will know how happy Maria and I shall be together.

'Not being able to read, in the evening I have been a constant visitor to the House of Commons. I heard the whole debate on China, which certainly elicited the best of our parliamentary talent and which resulted (most sadly to the people of India) in the defeat of the Ministry.' He goes on to criticise the chief speakers. Lord Derby's intellect 'is by no means of a high order,' but he has every qualification for oratory except a good voice. Gladstone's 'mind is too subtle,' but he has made the most effective speech to which the hearer ever listened. 'It caused a great excitement, . . . and I could not help feeling it was a triumph which you may well devote a lifetime to obtain. He discussed the question on high moral grounds; his speech was said to have obtained many votes, for Lord Palmerston lost his temper and seemed entirely to fail in replying to it.'

I will only call attention to the interest already manifest in the great social questions of the day and in the condition of India. I may add that the events of 1857 were calculated to strengthen any impressions already formed upon Indian matters. His thoughts upon these subjects were to have a predominant influence upon his future career. At this time, however, the accident happened which appeared to everyone but himself to put a conclusive end to any political ambition. The hopes so deeply rooted in his nature were to be apparently blasted at once and for ever.

CHAPTER II.

On September 17, 1858, Fawcett went out shooting with his father upon Harnham Hill. Harnham Hill commands a view of the rich valley where the Avon glides between the great bluffs of the chalk downs and beneath the unrivalled spire of Salisbury. It is one of the loveliest views, as Fawcett used to say, in the south of England. He now saw it for the last time. The party was crossing a turnip field and put up some partridges, which flew across a fence into land where Mr. Fawcett had not the right of shooting. In order to prevent this from happening again, Fawcett advanced some thirty yards in front of his party. Shortly afterwards another covey rose and flew towards him. His father was suffering from incipient cataract of one eye. He therefore could not see his son distinctly, and had for the moment forgotten their relative change of position. He thus fired at a bird when it was nearly in a line with his son. The bird was hit by the greatest part of the charge, for it was 'completely shattered.' A few pellets, however, diverged and struck Henry Fawcett. Most of these entered his chest, but, passing through a thick coat, only inflicted a trivial wound. Two of them went higher.

He was wearing tinted spectacles to protect his eyes from the glare of the sun. One shot passed through each glass of the spectacles, making in each a clean round hole.[1] Their force was partly spent, and was further diminished by the resistance of the spectacles. They might otherwise have reached the brain and inflicted a fatal injury. As it was, they passed right through the eyes, remaining permanently embedded behind them. Fawcett was instantaneously blinded for life.

Fawcett's first thought, as he told his sister, was that he should never again see the view which he had just been admiring in the light of a lovely autumn afternoon. He was put into a cart and taken to the Longford farmhouse—about two miles and a half distant —whilst doctors were summoned from Salisbury. His sister received him as he got down at his home, and his first words were, 'Maria, will you read the newspaper to me?' They were prompted by the wish to encourage his family by showing his own calmness. He was, however, persuaded to go to bed and keep himself as quiet as possible. There was very little hope from the first. The doctors, indeed, declined to pronounce an absolute sentence. At the outside, they could scarcely have expected more than some faint perception of the difference between light and darkness. The general condition of the patient was happily as favourable as possible. He was in thorough health, and he suffered no actual pain. About six weeks after the accident he regained for a short time some power of perceiving light; but after

---

[1] The spectacles thus injured are still in possession of the family.

about three days this last glimmer vanished, and he passed the rest of his life in complete darkness. In the following June his left eye began to waste : and he then (and only then) suffered a good deal. About the end of the following October, Critchett performed an operation for making an artificial pupil in the remaining eye, in the faint hope that he might yet regain some useful perception of the difference, at least, between light and darkness. The retina, as it turned out, had been too extensively injured. Fawcett took lodgings with his sister and his attendant near Critchett's house, and the operation was performed under chloroform. For two or three days his eyes were bandaged. His friend W. Porter was with him constantly, and remembers the 'terrible anxiety' with which he tried the first experiments upon his power of vision, and asked whether the sun was shining. Yet he bore himself calmly and cheerfully, and submitted without apparent emotion to the final discovery that there was no longer room for any hope whatever.

The calamity was crushing. The father deserved pity almost as much as the son, for the son had been the very pride of his heart. A year or two before I had been to Longford, where I had been struck by the eager delight with which the father had spoken of the son's University honours, and the superabundant cordiality of the welcome which he had bestowed upon me as one of his son's friends. Clearly, nothing could be too good for anyone whom Harry honoured by his friendship. The relations between the two men were suggestive rather of affectionate comrade-ship than of the more ordinary relation, where affection is coloured by deference

and partial reserve. The father shared the son's honourable ambition, or rather made it his own ; and the son's
hopes of success included the liveliest anticipation of the
delight which it would cause at home. The close union
was the more remarkable because neither father nor son
could be accused of sentimentalism, and both of them
were rather apt to condemn the excessive sacrifices
sometimes made by parents to children as implying a
kind of vicarious selfishness, injurious to both parties
in the long run. Fawcett's family affections (for his love
of his mother and sister was as marked as his love of
his father) were through life unusually strong. Perhaps
the severest letter which he ever wrote to a real friend
was prompted by the belief that the friend had spoken to
his father in a way calculated to produce uneasiness.
And now it seemed that the father's hand had ruined the
son's brilliant prospects. When I visited Longford a few
weeks after the accident, I found Fawcett calm and even
cheerful, though still an invalid. But the father told me
that his own heart was broken, and his appearance confirmed his words. He could not foresee that the son's
indomitable spirit would extract advantages even from
this cruel catastrophe. One of Fawcett's favourite
quotations ever afterwards (he had not a large stock of
such phrases, for his verbal memory was as weak as his
memory for facts and figures was retentive) was the
phrase from Henry V. :—

> There is some soul of goodness in things evil,
> Would men observingly distil it out.

The danger in which Henry V. stood before Agincourt

was not a more efficient stimulus to his heroism than the shot through his eyes to Fawcett's resolute temper.

Meanwhile, though Fawcett was surrounded by the tenderest cares of his family, he had a sore trial to go through. He said a few years later [1] that he had made up his mind 'in ten minutes' after the accident to stick to his pursuits as much as possible. But that last clause admitted a wide margin of uncertainty. How far was it possible for a blind man, a man without fortune and without any great family connection, even to approach a parliamentary career? Success at the bar, by which alone he had hoped to achieve an independent position, was apparently out of the question. As he lay in his darkened room he meditated upon this problem. Letters of condolence poured in upon him. He found, as he told a friend soon afterwards, that they gave him 'more pain than comfort.' The impression seems to have been deep. 'Nothing,' he said in the speech just quoted, 'pained him so much as the letters he received after the accident.' The reason, as I gather, was that the letters fell into the ordinary form, and consisted of well-meant exhortations to resignation, assuming that his life was ruined, though, somehow or other, the ruin was to be a blessing. Only be resigned! But though resignation to the inevitable is a clear dictate of prudence, the question remains, What is inevitable? How distinguish between cheerful acceptance of the dictates of fate or Providence and the cowardly abnegation of duty under apparent difficulty? Fawcett insisted upon

---

[1] Speech in St. James's Hall, May 17, 1866.

having the letters read to him by his sister; and he put
them aside with a sigh.   They depressed him, and he
appeared for a time to be at best in a fixed state of stoical
calm.   The blow had apparently stunned him.

At last, however, a letter came pitched in a different key.   It was from his old and revered friend
Hopkins.   He said to his sister, 'Keep that letter for
me;' and from that time his mood changed and he took
a more cheerful and resolute tone.   I am happy to be
able to give the timely word of good cheer, spoken so
much in season:—

Cambridge: Oct. 10, 1858.

'I have rarely been more grieved, my dear Fawcett,
than I was by your father's letter, which informed me
of the very sad accident you have met with.   Your
father writes almost broken-hearted and requires comfort,
I doubt not, almost as much as yourself.

'That you will receive from him every comfort which
the thoughtful affection of a parent can suggest, I well
know; and I feel equally certain that you will give to
him the best consolation he can receive by cultivating
as cheerful a tone of mind as your sad deprivation will
admit of.   It would indeed be not only useless, but false,
to endeavour to console you by pretending that loss of
sight, the having wisdom at one entrance quite shut
out, is not one of the greatest afflictions that can happen
to us.   It is so; and though especially so to those who
delight in all the varied aspects and beauties of external
nature, it cannot but be deemed, alike to all, one of the
severest bodily calamities that can befall us.   But

depend upon it, my dear fellow, it must be our own fault if such things are without their alleviation. It has always seemed to me a beautiful and touching form of the expression of this sentiment, that "God tempers the wind to the shorn lamb;" and so, I doubt not, you will find it, even should the injury you have received realise your worst fears.

'Yesterday I saw the letter you have sent to the college porter for the perusal of your friends. Mr. Critchett's statements afford evidently some ground of hope, but of the expectations which they justify I am, of course, unable to judge. I have no hesitation, however, in recommending you not to build your hopes upon them. Give up your mind at once to meet the evil in the worst form it can hereafter assume.

'The course of life and objects of study which you may heretofore have proposed to yourself must of necessity be much modified, and you will be obliged by circumstances to depend on intellectual pursuits almost entirely for your future happiness, so far as it may depend on efforts of your own. Now it seems to me that your mind is eminently adapted to many of those studies which may be followed with least disadvantage without loss (the help?) of sight.

'You must almost necessarily exclude, more or less, those subjects which involve practical details and facts; and I would suggest your directing your attention to subjects of a philosophical and speculative character, such as any branch of mental science and the history of its progress; the Philosophy of Physical Science, as Herschel's work in "Lardner's Encyclopædia," Whewell's

R

"Inductive Philosophy," &c., or any work treating on
the general principles, views, and results of physical
science. Political economy, statistics, and social science
in general are assuming interesting forms in the present
day.

'What a wide range of speculative study, full of
interest, do these subjects present to us! for any part of
which, if I mistake not, your mind is well qualified. How
often have I wished I had more time to devote to them
myself! I know that I should find in them a great
compensation (as I trust you will yourself) for any
circumstances which might restrict me to the pursuit
of them. But still I can throw out all this as affording
suggestions to you, and possibly an inducement and
encouragement to look forward with determination and
courage to the future, and to the formation of some
systematic plan for your intellectual pursuits.

'The evil that has fallen upon you, like all other
evils, will lose half its terrors if regarded steadfastly in
the face with the determination to subdue it as far as it
may be possible to do so.

'But I seem, my dear fellow, to be writing you a
hard-hearted letter, something like a hard-hearted doctor
prescribing for a suffering patient; and yet I could weep
while I write, to think of the bright hopes and aspirations, so naturally entertained on the threshold of
life, which must be crushed under this sad calamity.
But again I say, "Courage." Cultivate your intellectual
resources (how thankful you may be for them!), and
cultivate them systematically; they will avail you much
in your many hours of trial. Under any circumstances

I hope you will visit Cambridge from time to time ! I'll lend my aid to amuse you by talking philosophy or reading an act of Shakespeare, or a canto from Byron.

'I shall certainly avail myself of the first opportunity I have of paying you a visit at Longford, and shall engage you for my guide across the chalk hills. I may then perhaps find the means of indoctrinating you with a few healthy geological principles. Mrs. Hopkins desires to unite with me in kindest regards to your father and sister, whom we do know, and also to your mother, to whom, though we do not know her personally, we equally extend our sympathy. I have not yet seen your brother, but I suppose we shall hear of you soon through him. A great many men will not be up before the end of next week.

'Believe me, dear Fawcett,

'Yours very truly,

'W. HOPKINS.

This affectionate and judicious letter showed how clearly Hopkins had divined the mental condition of his old pupil. The right key was struck, and Fawcett, roused from his temporary prostration, responded gallantly to the inspiring summons. Though crippled, he would not fall out of the ranks; rather he would keep step with the stoutest. I do not doubt that in any case the reaction would have come, and that Hopkins's letter was rather the occasion than the cause of his speedy and victorious reaction. In truth, it would be unworthy of Fawcett were I to exaggerate the force of the blow ; and he would have been the last to sanction any phrases which might exalt his own courage at the price of appearing to justify discouragement in men of less stalwart mould. The calamity was severe enough. But it was not so severe as to mean permanent disablement for a man in the full flush of youth, health, and mental energy. Blind men have done much and are often said to lead happier, at least more placid, lives than others. And I do not think that it would have been more than might have been expected if Fawcett had gradually roused himself and worked out some tolerable solution of the great problem before him. What was wonderful, however, and beyond the powers of any but the bravest, was the indomitable resolution with which he immediately encountered his misfortune. He determined not that he would in some way evade, but that he would conquer his fate; not that he would find a new path by which the new difficulty might be turned, but that he would persevere in the old; not only this, indeed, but that he would go all the straighter to his mark and take by storm the position which he was to have assailed by the usual approaches.

For a time, he had even some thoughts of being called to the bar. The benchers of Lincoln's Inn consented in 1859 to his dispensing with the usual certificate from the Council of Legal Education. In June 1860, however, he finally abandoned this plan, from which he probably anticipated little at any time, and took his name off the books. Very soon, though I cannot fix the precise date, his friends knew that he had resolved to stick to his old ambition. Blind, poor, unknown, he would force his way into the House of Commons. And within a year or so from the accident he was taking the first steps in his difficult career. It will be my task to describe his success in the following chapters. Here I propose to bring together some of the facts which illustrate the spirit with which he bore himself in the daily conduct of life. I must ask my readers hereafter to bear in mind what his courageous cheerfulness often tended to make us forget—the fact that everything I have to say of him is said of a blind man. Fawcett had resolved within ten minutes to do as far as possible whatever he had done before. This from first to last was the principle upon which he acted through life. He determined for one thing that he would still be as happy as he could, and I will not quote moral philosophers to prove that this resolution was not only wise but virtuous. Fawcett was no ascetic. He heartily enjoyed all the good things of life—a good glass of wine, a good cigar, or a bit of downright gossip, not less than more intellectual recreations. 'One of the first things I remember about him,' says his wife, 'was his saying how keenly he enjoyed life.' He expressed, she adds, some impatience with people who avowed or affected weariness of life. 'There is only one thing that I ever regret,' he would say, 'and that is to have missed a chance of enjoyment.' He would, for instance, seriously ponder at the end of a frost whether he could not have contrived another hour's skating. He intended, he would tell me, to live to be ninety and to relish every day of his life. Should anyone be offended at a doctrine which seems to me more sound than easy to put in practice, he must remember that all Fawcett's enjoyments

were wholesome and innocent, that they emphatically
included a strenuous exertion of all his faculties, and
excluded with equal emphasis every tinge of ill-nature.
No man was more persistently cheery and genial. He
never enjoyed anything which could give pain to others.
He never fully enjoyed anything unless his pleasure
were shared by others. Nothing, for instance, would
have induced him to keep a horse for his own riding
unless he could have his wife or daughter to ride
with him. When towards the end of his life—to mention
a trivial but characteristic incident—he was ordered
to drink champagne, he resolutely refused to touch it
until he was promised that his family should have a share
of it.

At first cheerfulness required some effort. We who
watched him as friends immediately after his accident detected occasional fits of depression. They vanished even
then under the influence of society, and disappeared altogether with the trying period of suspense. Eyes guided by
stronger affection than ours detected no permanent depression. A phrase or two in his letters suggests that
he had occasional trials in the way of low spirits, and at
times a slight shade of weariness would seem to come
over his features in repose. He was careful to conceal
any such feeling, if he was ever conscious of it, and
especially to conceal it from those dearest to him. But
it may, I think, be safely said that to very few men is
granted so large a share of happiness or an enjoyment of
life qualified by so few drawbacks. There was only one
thing, he told his sister, which he dreaded—namely, a

loss of energy. Life might become a burden if life no longer meant action. He was spared that trial.

With his usual good sense Fawcett set to work to provide himself with means of enjoyment. He deliberately learnt to smoke, for example. He never worshipped tobacco with the zeal of some devotees; but he thought that it would help to smooth some weary hours. He resolutely set himself to improve his taste for music, the recreation most open to a blind man. It is also one of the few recreations, as he used to observe, which a blind man may enjoy without immediate dependence upon others. Fawcett was unable to exemplify this in his own case, as he could not learn to perform upon any instrument. He did, however, acquire so much musical taste as to enjoy an evening at a concert or the opera, and his enjoyment increased observably in the last two years of his life, when, after his illness, he had more enforced leisure. At the same period he also tried successfully to play cribbage and écarté with packs marked for the purpose. He, with his secretary, Mr. Dryhurst, devised a system of pricking them, and learnt to play correctly with remarkable quickness. Three days after he had begun the experiment he could play and win a game, without making mistakes and without hesitating over the cards longer than his antagonist. He had tried the same experiment immediately after his accident, but had then given it up.

He tried for some time to continue writing with his own hand, and I have seen an autograph letter of his dated in 1860. He found the practice irksome, however, as is, I believe, the general experience of men who lose their sight, and soon confined himself to dictation. He thought that the habit was useful to him as a speaker, because it accustomed him to produce a regular flow of grammatical sentences. In some little things Fawcett never acquired the dexterity of the blind from birth. He had lost his sight too late.

He kept up more successfully the various athletic sports to which he was already devoted. I have, indeed, noticed that during his undergraduate days he could scarcely be called an athlete, as judged by a more modern standard. He would have thought it foolish to sacrifice his reading to mere sport. He never went into regular training or belonged to a racing crew, except of humble pretensions. The Peterhouse boat of those days was low on the river, and he did not belong to the first crew at Trinity Hall. That he occasionally performed in the second boat I remember by this circumstance, that I can still hear him proclaiming in stentorian tones and in good vernacular from an attic window to a captain of the boat on the opposite side of the quadrangle, and consequently to all bystanders below, that he had a pain in his inside and must decline to row. I have some reason to think that he had felt bad effects from some previous exertions, and had been warned by a doctor against straining himself. I have an impression that there was some weakness in the heart's action. Fawcett, like many men who enjoy unbroken health, was a little nervous about any trifling symptoms. One day we found him lying in bed, complaining lustily of his sufferings, and stating that he had despatched a messenger to bring him at once the first doctor attainable. A doctor arrived, and his first question as to the nature of Fawcett's last dinner resolved the consultation into a general explosion of laughter, in which the patient joined most heartily. A steady pull down the Cam was one of his favourite amusements in later years. He used to row stroke to a club of graduates founded by Augustus Vanssittart, and christened the 'Ancient Mariners' by the well-known scholar, Dr. Donaldson. Fawcett took pains to get up a crew three times a week during his later residences at Cambridge. It was a good healthy exercise, and the age of his comrades was a security that they would not over-exert themselves. He had played cricket fairly, and I once saw him felled to the earth by an over-excited fieldsman, who had forgotten to allow for his last six inches of height. I remember, too, his racket-playing, because my own temper broke down under the irrepressible amusement with which he witnessed some of my vagaries as a learner.

These games, of course, became impossible. He adhered to other exercises resolutely. He had always been a regular and vigorous walker, and I am much inclined to measure a man's moral excellence by his love of this pursuit. All Cambridge men believed (I hope they still believe) in a daily 'constitutional' as one of the necessities of life. Very soon after his accident, he went out for a walk with his elder brother and a friend. He went between them and chose a path through the water-meadows, where some guidance was necessary. Yet, even on the first experiment, he was rather the guide than the guided. In later years he was constantly to be encountered upon the roads round Cambridge. He rather despised the familiar round by Granchester and Trumpington as 'an old gentleman's walk.' He preferred to all other walks the ascent of what, by an abuse of speech pardonable at Cambridge, are called the 'hills,' or, more familiarly, the 'Gogmagogs,' or, by an affectionate diminutive, the 'Gogs.' The air, he used to declare, was fresher there, because there was nothing higher than a molehill between him and the Ural Mountains. He would pause on what passes for the summit to point out to his friends the distant view over King's College Chapel to the towers of Ely. He often strode down the towing-path to 'see' (in his own phrase) a boat race or the practice of the crews. He was as keenly interested as anyone in the success of the college eight, and as ready to give a shrewd opinion as to its right constitution. He was a regular attendant at the Oxford and Cambridge contests at Putney till almost the end of his life. He walked with a friend through the streets, but dropped a guiding arm as soon as he was fairly on the road, and it was no slight effort for the short of wind or limb to keep up with his vigorous strides. The best plan was to equalise the strain on the lungs by engaging him in a steady flow of talk—no difficult task —when, especially if a steady gale were blowing in his teeth, his pace might be kept within reasonable limits.

Fawcett retained a very accurate recollection of all the places he had known before his accident. When, after his marriage, he went to Alderbury, where he had been at school as a child, he could direct his wife through all the intricacies of the surrounding lanes. Within the college, of course, he could ramble about

alone, and the sound of his stick tapping on the walls
for guidance was a familiar sound, sometimes a little
disturbing the light sleepers when he would indulge in a
meditative stroll at dead of night. When walking in
London, he could tell by the difference in the echo and
by the current of air when he was opposite to the
opening of a cross street. In all these walks he took a
special pleasure in listening to his companion's descrip-
tions of the scenery—whether to retain his hold on the
vanishing pictures of old days or to endeavour to construct some image of the now invisible world. He still
loved the works of Nature, he said, and had associations
with the light of sun and moon unknown to him before
he was blind. I do not imagine that Fawcett would at
any time have cared to indulge in the rhapsodies about
the beauties of scenery which have become fashionable
of late. But he certainly loved most heartily the country
sounds, as the rustle of leaves, the song of birds, and the
leap of a fish, which he had learned to appreciate in
early days. The picture of a glorious moonlight night
with a long trail of silvery cloud on the hills above
Longford, in a stroll which we took together before his
accident, remains with me; and though I believe that
our talk was of supply and demand, and though we
certainly made a burglarious assault on the larder when
we returned, I am equally sure that Fawcett was fully
sensitive to its beauties. In after days he delighted in
driving about the country with his sister and friends,
and would always stop the carriage at certain favourite
points and go with them to places where he could enjoy
the view through their eyes. His friend, Mr. Botting, of

Brighton, tells me that Fawcett often telegraphed to him beforehand to take him for a walk along the cliffs to Rottingdean.   The delightful air, the smooth turf of the chalk-down, and the murmur of the waves below never failed to throw him into a reverie, and he would say that it was for him the most charming walk in England. Another friend, Mrs. Roberts, saw him in the last autumn of his life waiting in Salisbury Close, and on being asked where he was going, he said that he wanted to see the Clarendon Woods, as he understood that the autumn tints were especially fine this year.   One summer (1872) he went to Switzerland, and there made the ascent of the Cima di Jazzi, a well-known point of easy access for the enjoyment of the keen mountain air and a vast panorama of snowy peaks.   The blind, I believe, usually employ the language of sight, but it was certainly startling at times to hear Fawcett's remarks. ' How old so-and-so is looking! ' he said to me once; ' but when men with hair of that colour turn grey, they do look prematurely old.'   Such language was, one may say, part of his system of behaving in his blindness as much as possible as he behaved when he could see. Once, as a friend tells me, Fawcett was speaking to him of another friend, known to him only after his blindness, who had an odd trick of moving his limbs.   Fawcett re- marked upon this, and, to explain his meaning, gave a lively mimicry of the gesture in question.

Though not specially dexterous, his nerve was sur- prising.   He walked from the first with absolutely un- faltering steps, and he kept up his skating with equal courage.   Before his accident, his weight and length of

limb made him a very powerful skater, though he had not
acquired more than the rudiments of the art of figure-
skating. He told me that he once accompanied a race in
the Fens, keeping up on the rough ice outside with the
competitors, who had the advantage of the smooth swept
course within the bounds. I accompanied him on his first
attempt after the accident. After a few strokes the only
difficulty was to keep his pace down to mine. We each
held one end of a stick, and, as we were on the crowded
Serpentine, we came into a good many collisions. As,
however, we were a couple, and one of us a heavy man,
we had decidedly the best of these encounters, especially
as the conscience of our antagonists was on our side
when they saw that they had tripped up a blind man.
Some severe winters followed, and I shall not forget the
delights of an occasional run beyond Ely on the frozen
Cam. I remember how we flew back one evening, at
some fifteen miles an hour, leaning on a steady north-
easter, with the glow of a characteristic Fen sunset
crimsoning the west and reflected on the snowy banks;
whilst between us and the light a row of Fenmen, following each other like a flight of wild fowl, sent back the
ringing music of their skates. As we got under shelter
of the willows above Clayhithe, the ice became trea-
cherous and we began to remonstrate after a threatened
immersion. 'Go on!' said Fawcett; 'I only got my legs
through.' That, however, seemed a sufficient quantity
of the human body for sub-glacial immersion, and the
rest of us insisted upon putting the final edge upon
our appetites by a tramp homewards to a Christmas
dinner along the towing-path. He kept up the practice,

and declared in 1880 that no one had enjoyed more than he a skate of fifty or sixty miles in the previous frost.

In later years, Fawcett used to insist that everyone in the house, except an old cook, should partake of his amusement. His wife and daughter, his secretary, and two maids would all turn out for an expedition to the frozen Fens. On the wide open spaces he would skate quite alone, guided only by the sound of his companions' voices and skates. When his daughter was about nine, she guided him in this fashion, whistling to give him notice of her whereabouts.

A pursuit in some ways more difficult was riding. In the early days, Fawcett rode rarely, partly because it was an expensive amusement, and also, I think, because one or two narrow escapes (he was nearly crushed against a cart at Salisbury) made the prudence doubtful. Later, however, and especially after his illness of 1882, when his walking powers rather declined, he rode regularly and with great enjoyment. He speaks of the delights of a gallop over the turf which borders the roads round Cambridge. He generally had with him a riding-master whom he could trust. He constantly went out with large parties of friends. Miss McLeod Smith, of Cambridge, was a very frequent and always most welcome companion. One of his especial friends in later life, Mr. W. H. Hall, of Six Mile Bottom, near Newmarket, tells me that Fawcett often rode over to see him, sometimes staying over the Sunday, when he would walk his friends off their legs, as he would try his horse's legs on the other days. He had a 'perfect passion' for a gallop over Newmarket Heath, where there was abundant space and the best of air. He would ride over from Cambridge at Christmas time with a box of sandwiches, to provide luncheon on the sunny side of the ' Devil's Ditch.' He loved the chalk-down, and often stopped at a cottage to ask for a draught of the sparkling water from the deep wells. He always enjoyed, too, a gossip with the shepherds about the flocks; for his early interest in agricultural matters was through life a marked characteristic. Occasionally he came across the harriers, which often meet in the neighbourhood, and would then, as Mr. Hall says, ' join in our gallops, trusting implicitly to the sagacity of his horse to select the most favourable gaps in our stunted hedgerows.'

Of all his recreations there was none which he enjoyed so heartily as his fishing. He had, as we have seen from his early diary, been educated as a fisherman from his childhood. His father was a keen fisherman, and caught a trout so late as his ninetieth year. Fawcett's great height and strength of arm enabled him to throw a fly with remarkable power and precision. Clarke tells me how, in early days, Fawcett would combine two favourite amusements. He would wade in the river, fishing slowly up stream, whilst Clarke was instructed to walk along the bank at such a distance from the river as not to throw his shadow upon the water, and then to talk to his heart's content. Trout, as Fawcett said, hear very badly (and, it may be added, care nothing for the soundest political economy), but see remarkably well. A letter from his first secretary, Edward Brown, tells how he used to go with Fawcett to the river, where, in the intervals of sport, they could retire to an outhouse, drink tea, and read Mill's 'Political Economy.' Fawcett had resumed the sport very soon after his accident. In April 1868 I find him saying that he and a friend had caught twelve pike; the friend had caught the largest, weighing 15 lb., but Fawcett had caught ten of the twelve, one of them an eleven-pounder. He remembered his native stream with minute accuracy. The letters written to his father during the last four or five years of his life are full of references to past and future expeditions. Whenever he can spare a few hours, he delights to run down to Salisbury. He gives directions about his fishing-boots; makes appointments with Wright, a famous performer, who generally accompanied him; asks to have the weeds cut at a particular point, or suggests the most promising scheme for inveigling some wily monster, whose fame has spread in the neighbourhood, and who lies ensconced under some hardly approachable bank.

Many friends in the neighbourhood of Salisbury and elsewhere were glad to give him opportunities of fishing, and Fawcett was always delighted to accept their kindness. Lord Normanton was especially kind in offering salmon fishing at Ibbesley on the Avon, between Ringwood and Christchurch. Lord Nelson, with equal kindness, gave him trout and jack fishing in the Avon below, and Lord Pembroke at Wilton above, Salisbury. Lord Mount-Temple made him welcome to the Itchen at Broadlands. In the summer he often visited Scotland, where his old friend Mr. Bass received him at Glen Tulchan on the Spey. The late Duke of Roxburgh often gave him fishing on the Tweed, where he used to stay in the house of an old fisherman at Kelso. Fawcett enjoyed the surroundings of the sport as well as the sport itself. He often combined an excursion to the New Forest with his salmon fishing at Ibbesley. At Ibbesley he often stayed at the house of the fisherman, Samuel Tizard, and his wife, where he liked to enjoy a friendly supper and a good chat with his hosts. Their place is full of birds, whose singing gave him particular pleasure.[1] Here he caught a large salmon, part of which he contributed to the feast upon the golden wedding of his father and mother.

On his expeditions round Salisbury he was generally accompanied by Mr. Wright, already mentioned, and by Mr. Wheaton, of Salisbury, now student of medicine, both of whom have been kind enough to give me their recollections. They agree that Fawcett was a remarkably good fisherman. He performed, if anything, better than the seeing, whether because he waited more patiently to strike until he felt his fish, or because he was more docile in following the directions of his skilled companions. He had great success in catching salmon and trout, and in trolling for pike in the winter. He showed his usual nerve in crossing narrow planks across streams, though he once had an immersion with Mr. Wright, whose comparative shortness of stature made it total in his case. He would wade in the streams where necessary,

---

[1] I remember, however, that Fawcett told me how he had once been tried beyond bearing by the song of a nightingale close to his bedroom window, and how he had at last risen and endeavoured to drive away the intruder by pelting at it with the only available missile—a piece of soap.

F

and Mr. Wheaton remembers his hearty enjoyment of a rough drive in a donkey-cart full of fish, along a road in Wales, where they made a month's expedition in October 1879. As memorials of his sport, I have found among his papers an envelope containing the hook 'that caught the 20 lb. salmon,' and another huge envelope turns out to be the canvas on which is drawn (by Mr. Wheaton) the pencil outline of 'a trout caught by me at Mr. Hoare's (in Hertfordshire) with an Alexandra fly.' The date is July 9, 1881. The trout was 21¾ in. in length and weighed 10 lb. Fawcett, as Mr. Wheaton tells me, was a remarkably good judge of the weight and condition of a fish. A local journal, which makes the same remark, adds that at Ringwood 'he was seen smoking a pipe in our streets;' it is a more characteristic statement that he made there the acquaintance of a local postman, and obtained for him an annual holiday, and an appointment entitling him to a superannuation allowance. It was, in fact, one of the collateral charms of fishing to Fawcett, that it brought him to easy and friendly intercourse with men in a humble position of life.

A friend once made some remark to Fawcett upon the cruelty to animals involved in fishing. Without discussing that point (though upon other occasions he would adduce some of the familiar arguments against the existence of any keen sensibility in fish), Fawcett apologised for his own delight by a very important consideration. He could not, he said, relieve himself by some of the distractions which help others to unbend. Every strenuous worker knows the worrying persistency with which the swarm of thoughts which occupy his business hours returns to tease and distract his hours of relaxation. No small part of the art of living consists in learning to command the spells which lay these vexatious spectres and conjure them into temporary quiescence. But Fawcett's blindness made many modes of relief impossible or difficult. He could not, for example, glance through the pages of a magazine or a novel, or join in the games of the young, or could only do so with difficulty, and in constant dependence upon others. Blindness increased concentration by shutting out distractions. We close our eyes to think, and his were always closed. His mental strength and weakness, the power with which he grasped certain principles, and the comparative want of versatility and consequent indifference to many of the literary amusements which relieve the strain of some men's minds, made every available relaxation more important, and fishing served admirably to give enough exercise to muscle and mind to keep his faculties from walking the regular treadmill of thought from which it is often so hard to escape. His delight in conversation was unfailing; and if possible —for it is hardly possible—he became more sociable as life went on. Yet our conversation is apt to return to the well-worn grooves of thought; and nothing served so well to vary his life as throwing a fly on the Scotch rivers or his beloved Salisbury Avon.

What I have said will show how Fawcett adhered to his great maxim, to let blindness interfere as little as possible with his course of life, whether in his serious pursuits or his amusements; and he was never tired of enforcing this maxim for the benefit of his fellow-sufferers.

In conversation he very rarely referred expressly to his blindness. In reading his speeches, I noticed one occasion upon which another debater spoke of Fawcett's having something read to him. Fawcett took up the phrase and said in his reply, not that he had read the passage in question, but that it had been read to him. This recognition of his disqualification struck me as something quite exceptional, and implied, I think, a shade of annoyance at any notice being taken of his blindness as an excuse for a supposed inaccuracy. He claimed tacitly to have no allowance made for him; and the feeling, as we shall see, comes out on one or two occasions of his political life. He naturally felt it to be a duty to speak of himself when he delivered addresses on behalf of various institutions for the benefit of his fellow-sufferers. But he shrank from such efforts. He observes in one of the first I have seen (May 16, 1866) that he had never felt so nervous in speaking; and I believe that this feeling was always present to him. Of course it did not prevent him from speaking, and from speaking very effectively. But he no doubt felt the difficulty of citing his own case without appearing in the attitude, most painful to him, of one putting forward a plea for compassion; or in the attitude, only less disagreeable, of one who is making a boast of his own courage. In fact, however, no one can read the speeches without being stirred to sympathy by the unobtrusive gallantry of his spirit. Briefly, his advice to his fellows was always, 'Do what you can to act as though you were not blind; be of good courage and help yourselves;' and his advice to the seeing was, 'Do not patronise; treat us without reference to our misfortune; and, above all, help us to be independent.' The principle applied in this case blended, as I may briefly observe, with his general political sentiments.

He spoke on behalf of various benevolent institutions, and always very much to the same purpose. In one meeting, an eminent philanthropist who was to precede Fawcett accidentally came late and had to follow. Fawcett insisted upon his usual topics, and wound up by saying that on previous occasions he had heard remarks which unintentionally gave the utmost pain to some of the hearers. Nothing was so hard to bear as to hear people assume a 'patronising tone towards the blind, as if they were suffering from something for which in some mysterious way they should be thankful. The kindest thing that could be done or said to a blind person was, not to use patronising language, but to tell him as far as possible to be of good cheer, to give him confidence that help would be afforded him whenever it was required; that there was still good work for him to do, and the more active his career, the more useful his life to others, the more happy his days to himself.'

The unlucky philanthropist came just in time to hear these observations, primed with a speech in the exact spirit condemned—recalling the usual 'pity the poor blind' of the professional beggar. He could not strike out a new path, and was forced to go through his regular appeal, after an apology to the eminent professor, 'but still,' and so forth. No one, I am told by a hearer, more heartily enjoyed the awkward performance than the eminent professor himself. I may add here that when Fawcett in his walks met one of the blind beggars in question, he always spoke to him kindly, without administering needless didactic remarks, and gave him a trifle in spite of political economy.[1]

Amongst the various institutions which he helped to support, he was specially interested in the Royal Normal College founded at Norwood, in March 1872, by the efforts of the energetic Dr. Campbell. Its great merit, in his opinion, was that it enabled a large proportion of the blind to earn their own living. In an appeal made for it in 1875, he observes that the greatest of all services to the blind was to give them this power, and that it was the special object of the institution to render that service. Five years later, June 30, 1880, he insists upon the same point. He found that eighty per cent. of the pupils were earning their own living. He urged that the Gardner bequest (of 300,000*l*.) would be applied most efficiently if a considerable portion of it were devoted to the development of existing institutions such as the Normal College; and he ended by a characteristic remark. He protested against 'walling up' the aged blind in institutions. For training the young they are of course necessary; to the old they are actually prisons. 'Home associations,' he said, 'are to us as precious as to you. I know from my own experience that the happiest moments that I spend in my life are when I am in companionship with some friend who will forget that I have lost my eyesight, who will talk to me as if I could see, who will describe to me the persons I meet,

[1] I mention this on unquestionable authority, that of his constant companion, Mr. Dryhurst, because an anecdote implying a contrary practice appears in one of the obituary notices. It must have been in some way mistaken.

a beautiful sunset, or scenes of great beauty through which we may be passing. For so wonderful is the adaptability of the human mind that when, for instance, some scene of great beauty has been described to me, I recall that scene in after years and I speak about it in such a manner that sometimes I have to check myself and consider for a moment whether the impression was produced when I had my sight or was conveyed by the description of another. Depend upon it, you have the power of rendering invaluable services to the blind. Read to them, talk to them, walk with them, and treat them in your conversation just in the same way as if you were in the companionship of one who was seeing.' He made some remarks to the same effect in the last year of his life (March 18, 1884), enlarged upon the services rendered by Dr. Campbell, who possessed, he said, a genius for organising the best methods of educating the blind, and begged his hearers to help to 'replace the depressing misery of dependence by the buoyant activity which comes from self-reliance and from the consciousness of the power to earn one's own living.' In the same speech he approvingly notices a plan which was soon afterwards decided upon, but which, though let drop for a time in consequence of his death, has been recently revived, for the appointment of a Royal Commission to examine into the best means of educating the blind.

Another remark may be made, and not the least characteristic. Speaking on February 18, 1880, he says: 'The chief compensation, the silver lining to the dark cloud, is the wonderful and inexhaustible fund of human kindness to be found in this world, and the appreciation which blind people must have at every moment of their life of the cordial and ready willingness with which the services which they needed were generously offered to them.' I am glad to think that these simple and pathetic words represented Fawcett's own experience, and prove that his trouble was alleviated, not only by his own energy, but by the sympathy of his innumerable friends. They, indeed, could claim little credit for showing kindness to one so ready to help himself and so grateful for all the help given by others. But in this eager recognition of the kindness upon which he had so paramount a claim, we may notice, as in many other ways, how misfortune affected Fawcett as it only affects a large-hearted man. It not merely brought out his buoyant vigour of character, but mellowed and sweetened his nature, and strengthened the tenderness which at all times underlay his masculine courage, by making every little service, given or received, a new bond in the great web of kindly attachments which connected him with his family and the wider circle of his friends. Fawcett's friendship always seemed to be tacitly blended with gratitude; and he rendered any little service, not as one who is conferring a favour, or even as one who is simply fulfilling the duty of a friend, but as one who is unobtrusively recognising an obligation for previous kindness. No one ever took more obvious pleasure in helping those whose claims were only that they had not been neglectful of a friend's duty. Sometimes his eagerness on such occasions was felt by them (though certainly not by him) as almost a tacit reproach for not having been more zealous in their own duty to him.

CHAPTER III.

CAMBRIDGE.

Soon after his accident Fawcett returned to Cambridge,
which continued to be his headquarters for some years,
and was his home for part of every subsequent year.
He took rooms in Trinity Hall. Although the Universities should be natural homes of tradition, the generations of students succeed each other so rapidly that
minor details are soon forgotten. I will therefore specify
that Fawcett's rooms were on the first floor between the
two staircases on the north side of the main quadrangle.
They were entered from the eastern staircase, whilst he
could reach the other through a lecture-room into which
his sitting-room or, in the Cambridge phrase, 'keeping-
room' opened. His bedroom also opened out of the
keeping-room, and above were some garrets occupied by
the lad whom he now engaged to act as guide and
amanuensis. This was Edward Brown, son of a college
servant at Corpus Christi College, an intelligent boy whom
Fawcett treated with great kindness and familiarity, and
who was warmly attached to his employer.[1] From my

[1] Soon after Fawcett's marriage in 1867 Brown entered Trinity
College with a view to taking orders, but in 1869 or 1870 emigrated to
Natal. Bishop Colenso was very kind to him, and had agreed to ordain

own rooms I could pass through the lecture-room into
Fawcett's; and until the end of 1864, when I ceased
to reside in Cambridge, I considered his rooms to be
almost part of my own. C. B. Clarke, who had become a
Fellow of Queens' College, was on the old terms of friendly
intimacy. Fawcett's other undergraduate friends (with
the sole exception of Mr. M. M. U. Wilkinson) had left
the University ; but he speedily acquired a large circle of
new acquaintance, and within a very short time became one of the most familiar figures in the society of
Cambridge.

That society had some characteristics which are
already modified and which, under the influence of
recent changes, are likely to undergo still greater modifications. I do not doubt that the changes have been in
the main for the better. The old state of things had,
however, its merits, and merits which were singularly
congenial to Fawcett's temper. He loved Cambridge so
well as to pardon or even to approve what others held to
be its faults. A quaint phrase often occurs in biographies,
according to which schools and colleges receive credit
for having 'produced' all the remarkable men whom they
have not suppressed. Cambridge might claim with more
than the usual plausibility to have 'produced' Fawcett,
were it not that the affinity between his University and
himself may be better explained as a case of pre-estab-
lished harmony. He was a typical Cambridge man,

him after a year's probationary work. Before the year was completed
Brown died of dysentery, in 1870 or 1871. Brown was succeeded by
Mr. Albert Haynes, and Haynes in 1871 by Mr. F. J. Dryhurst, who
remained with Fawcett till the end, and is now in the Post Office.

whether as moulded by Cambridge or as one of the class by which Cambridge has been itself moulded.

Fawcett's residence coincided with the culminating period of the old college system. An undergraduate belonged to his college exclusively. He knew of 'out college' men only through school friendships or meetings in the rooms of his private tutor. The University was for him a mere abstraction, except when it revealed itself as the board of examination for 'little go' and degree. His chief ambition, if of a studious turn, was to win first a Scholarship and then the more permanent dignity of a Fellowship in his own college. To the Fellow the college became a substitute, sometimes a permanent substitute, for a family. To a certain number, indeed, a Fellowship represented merely a stepping-stone towards professional success. The resident Fellows were more closely bound to the colleges. Had their celibacy been permanent they might, like monks, have lost their identity in the corporate body. But celibacy during the tenure of a Fellowship implied the possibility and generally the desirability of a divorce. As the normal desire of a young man is to acquire a wife, the college bond soon became irksome to most of us. The clerical Fellows, a large majority amongst the residents, began to long for a retiring pension in the shape of a college living. University society thus consisted mainly of young men who at about the age of thirty departed, or were eager to depart. A few belated seniors remained behind as bachelors by predilection or compulsion. Some were waiting for a good college living whose incumbent survived with inconsiderate vitality ; some had found a life amongst libraries

and in a circle of scholarlike tastes too congenial to be
hastily quitted; and some had come to think that the
vicinity of the college cellar and kitchen would be ill
exchanged for the comparatively crude arrangements by
which a country parsonage endeavours to supply the
needs of a large circle of hungry mouths. A drawback
to the society of the place was the extraordinary rapidity
with which the more permanent residents became super-
annuated in the eyes of their colleagues. A don of thirty
was ten years older than a rising young barrister of
forty.

The youthfulness of the majority, however, had its
charms for the youthful. We were young men, sanguine,
buoyant, and sociable. We might boast of such superiority to the average intellectual standard as was indicated by the fact that we had won our places in an open
contest; and we were naturally not inclined to under-
estimate the value of that test of excellence. A youth
just fresh from his first classmanship often impresses
his seniors as a little too condescending. We gave too
frequent ground for the famous admonition of the present Master of Trinity: 'We are none of us infallible, not
even the youngest of us.' Yet a certain innocence tempered our youthful arrogance. The young don's socia-
bility among his fellows was unbounded. His appetite
for many intellectual pursuits was keen and genuine.
Though he was not rich, his income more than supplied
the wants of a bachelor at college, and he found it easy
to be hospitable and to freshen his wits during the
bountiful vacations by a run across the Continent or
an indulgence in London society. Amongst a number of

bright, sociable young men, full of many interests, Fawcett, the most heartily sociable of all, soon gained a wide popularity, and was welcome in most of the college halls. If grave seniors, dwelling in the empyrean atmosphere of Master's lodges, thought the young Radical ' dangerous,' they were speedily disarmed by his unmistakable good humour in personal converse.

Our own college, Trinity Hall, was founded in 1350 by Bishop Bateman. That farsighted prelate had been alarmed by the terrible Black Death. He founded the college to guard against the sad possibility of a scarcity of lawyers. His statutes were still nominally in force; though, in process of time, the Fellows, instead of devoting themselves, as he intended, to the canon and civil law, had become for the most part barristers of the ordinary type. Three clerical Fellows resided to act as tutors; the remaining ten were practising or courting practice in London, and visited Cambridge with a view to auditing accounts and granting leases at Christmas. A later benefactor had provided that we should relieve ourselves during that dry employment by a modest conviviality; first raising our minds to a due elevation by a service in chapel, where a Latin oration was delivered in praise of the Civil Law. The Christmas ' exceedings,' as they were called in our official language, had a certain reputation. A dinner is, of course, strictly speaking, a dinner; but the college feast, though resembling from the materialist point of view the ordinary meal, might also be regarded poetically as possessed of a certain historic dignity. It was almost a religious ceremony. If we could not rival the luxury of a civic banquet, there

was an impressive solemnity about the series of festivities which lasted some ten days at Christmas time. The
college butler swelled with patriotic pride as he arranged
the pyramid of plate—the quaint little enamelled cup
bequeathed by our founder, which had, I think, a shadowy
reputation for detecting poison ; the statelier goblet given
by Archbishop Parker, which made its rounds with due
ceremonial that we might drink 'in piam memoriam
fundatoris ; ' and the huge silver punchbowl, which represented Lord Chesterfield's view of the kind of conviviality likely to be appreciated by the Fellows of his
own period.

The Master, Dr. Geldart, a most kindly, old-fashioned
gentleman, beamed hospitality from every feature as he
presided at the table, prolonging the after-dinner sitting
till the port and madeira had accomplished the orthodox
number of rounds. At an earlier period dinner had
begun about the middle of the day, and the fine old race
which was laying in our supplies of gout had felt itself
in need of supper as a crown to the proceedings. Civilisation, postponing the hour of dinner, had not yet
dared to abolish so solemn an institution on the prosaic
ground of its superfluity. From the hall, therefore, we
adjourned in due time to the combination room, lighted
from silver sconces on the dark oak panels whence Lord
Chesterfield, with other more rosy-faced dignitaries of
the last century, gazed approvingly on boar's head, and
game pie, and oysters, and certain tins of baked apples
ripening before a generous fire, and credited with a
medicinal virtue for preventing any evil consequences of
the accompanying milk-punch. Legends told how many

glasses of that seductive fluid, the great boast of our
butler, Miller, had thus been rendered innocuous to
Judge Talfourd and other distinguished guests of a previous generation. The younger withdrew for a time to
enjoy an interlude of tobacco; whilst the steady old
dons settled comfortably to their orthodox rubbers of
whist.

No one entered more cordially into the spirit of such
convivialities than Fawcett. In later days the strain
upon the digestive faculties of the guests has, I understand, been lightened. But Fawcett was a steady conservative as to the essentials. He kept up the hospitality,
and delighted in bringing down old friends to revisit the
scenes of youthful pleasure and chat over the old days
and knit closer the bonds of college friendship. The
talk was always most animated and the laughter loudest
in the neighbourhood of his chair. Amidst the clatter
of forty pairs of knives and forks and the talk of forty
guests, his ringing volleys of laughter would assert their
supremacy. We used to argue whether Fawcett or one
of his friends, whose lungs could emit a crow of superlative vigour, was capable of the most effective laughter;
but if the single explosion of his rival was most startling,
no one could deny that Fawcett was superior in point of
continuous and infectious hilarity.

These Christmas performances showed the convivial
Fawcett in all his glory. But there was also a continuous current of pleasant sociable gatherings. Other
colleges held their grand days in term-time. There were
dining-clubs of one or two of which Fawcett was a member. One of these brought together periodically the dons

of Oxford and Cambridge; and in it Professor Henry
Smith and Fawcett might be taken as typical representatives of the two Universities. Curiously contrasted as
they were in many ways, they were rivals in diffusing a
thoroughly social spirit, and each heartily appreciated the
other's good qualities. There was no lack of less formal
meetings—down to the simple *tête-à-tête* with an old
friend, when the talk, if less noisy, was more intimate and
serious. Visions come before me of quiet talks in quaint
old college rooms, to which we retired as the curfew was
sounding to hold a tobacco-parliament till St. Mary's had
long given notice of midnight. And summer brought
pleasant hours in the charming college gardens and
bowling greens; above all in the Fellows' garden at
Trinity Hall, which Mr. Henry James—a most capable
judge—pronounces to be unsurpassed in Europe. There
we would take our wine in the shade of the noble chest-
nut trees, whose boughs make a cascade of flowers and
foliage down to the dry smooth-shaven green, or enjoy a
meditative stroll when the nightingales at the 'backs'
were singing their loudest in the pleasant May Term. I
remember a friend who came to see Cambridge for the
first time, and, strolling into the garden after breakfast,
found it so strongly impregnated with the *genius loci*
that he decided to cut short his round of sight-seeing at
its first stage. Sitting there all day, he felt that he had
imbibed the very essence of Cambridge life. In logical
phrase, the intensity of his experience more than
atoned for its want of extension.

Fawcett was never tired of praising Cambridge
society. He exalted it far above the frigid formality of

what passes for society in London. In Cambridge there could still be real talk such as Johnson enjoyed at the Mitre or the Turk's Head. London has become a chaos; society means intercourse for a couple of hours with a fortuitous concurrence of human atoms; little circles are swept away in the great current; you make a small journey to a friend's house; you are set down by a stranger and have to beat the bush for an hour before you discover what little segment of the vast circle of human interests is common to both; you must be on your guard in view of possible collisions, and keep to the superficial topics which hurt no sensibilities because they excite no real interest. Fawcett specially detested the early break-up of the guests at a London dinner-party enforced by the dismal ceremonial of 'at homes,' gatherings which he absolutely declined to attend. In Cambridge it was otherwise; friends could meet daily by crossing a court or a couple of streets. There was no formality where all were equal, and no tentative dallying with topics where each man's tastes and prejudices were known to all his fellows; the parts in the dialogue were assigned beforehand and could be taken up at once; and we were young and eager enough really to discuss important questions and to fancy that our discussions were enlightening. In our gatherings, we could realise Johnson's familiar requirements: there a man could 'fold his legs and have his talk out;' there he could find plenty of men ready fairly 'to put their minds to his;' and there, too, though the circle was small, there was enough come and go from the outside world to

G

prevent any danger of stagnation or of the painful discovery that we had exhausted each other's topics.

Some distinguished men came to us at Christmas or at other times; and Fawcett's constantly widening circle of friends offered abundant variety. Once, in the early time, we walked over to Babraham, and, with some audacity, called on Mr. Jonas Webb, the famous breeder of Southdown sheep, whose statue now stands in the Cambridge Corn Exchange. Though we interrupted his Christmas dinner, he politely sent a shepherd to exhibit his flocks; and he returned our visit to talk agriculture with Fawcett and his father in our college hall. A nearly contemporary guest was an Oxford don who proclaimed his favourite study to be 'dogmatic theology,' but who had struck up a friendship with Fawcett, certainly not from any common interest in the study. Fawcett was not the less hospitable or less hearty in his laughter, when our theologian had a sharp encounter with a friend from the opposite pole of the circle who boasted that he was a 'hard-headed Scotchman,' and scoffed at all the wiles of Jesuits in disguise. Other and more famous friends were glad of a day or two at Cambridge. Fellow disciples of Mill's, Professor Cairnes, Mr. Hare, and W. T. Thornton were amongst the most welcome. Fawcett, as I find by an early letter, had the courage to invite Mill himself at Christmas 1859 to meet Hare, who was already a guest. The philosophic recluse did not come to try our milk-punch. Thackeray had promised to come to stay with Fawcett at the Christmas of 1863; and only put us off at the last moment, just before we heard of his death. Cobden came to see Fawcett in the summer of 1864; and I do not know whether the dons were more impressed by the charming urbanity of the great agitator, or Cobden himself by the discovery that dons could be as free from political and sectarian prejudices as any class of the community. Lawyers, politicians, and men of science (I especially remember Professor Huxley) were glad occasionally to breathe the academic atmosphere, and Fawcett was always anxious to welcome them. Our home resources, however, were not despicable. It may be that I am under an illusion; but it certainly seems to me that I have never heard such excellent talk as I heard in Cambridge in those days. My appetite for talk was doubtless keener and my faculty for admiration less blunted; and yet I think that the conditions already described were really favourable, whilst we were free from that uneasy desire to justify a reputation which is so injurious to the talk of more famous conversationalists. There were several men of real talent in the art. There was W. G. Clark, the graceful scholar and wit, who brought more than usual knowledge of the outside world to our academic retirement; and J. L. Hammond, who in those days was the brightest of companions. With a singularly penetrative voice, a very retentive memory stocked with many anecdotes, a keen interest in politics as well as in more academic topics, and a wit always tempered by good-nature, he often became the centre of conversational attraction to all guests in the Trinity combination room. Once, indeed, as he was declaiming with more than usual freedom, Fawcett's secretary came hastily into the room and announced the fact that a group of Hammond's

pupils were seated outside the open window drinking
in the overflow of their tutor's remarks. Fawcett was
rather more delighted than Hammond. Then, too,
there was Gunson, of Christ's, a big North-countryman
with a Cumbrian burr, whose figure was not unlike
Fawcett's, but who, unlike Fawcett, prided himself especially on his Greek, and had done more than any
college tutor of his time to raise his pupils in the Tripos.
It was Fawcett's special delight to indulge in some
outrageous confession of classical ignorance by way of
oblique flattery to Gunson ; and he would chuckle with
intense appreciation of the simple-minded utterances
of harmless vanity which he succeeded in provoking. I
have not mentioned those who are still with us. This,
alas ! does not now prevent me from mentioning H. A. J.
Munro, the pride of all Cambridge scholars, whose
extraordinary classical attainments were combined with
a charming simplicity, unaffected kindliness, and a
refreshing bluntness of speech, and who used to delight
Fawcett by his talk, especially by his enthusiastic cele-
brations of Miss Byron and Clarissa Harlowe. Three of
the Fellows of Trinity—Blore, Hotham, and Munro, whose
names are most associated with the Trinity of those days
—have died since Fawcett ; and only a dwindling minority
is left of those who some twenty years ago joined in our
friendly meetings.

These names remind me of one very marked feature
of Fawcett's character. I first discovered it one day,
when I heard to my shame that a common friend had
been for some time in bad health, and that Fawcett had
been visiting him regularly. Nothing gave him greater

pleasure than to render such services. Hammond suffered cruelly under a protracted and painful disorder, of which he ultimately died. It was depressing to the spirits, and he fell into a rather morbid state of feeling, creating the imaginary grievances natural to the sick. Fawcett was the friend who adhered most closely to him. When refusing other invitations, Hammond would always go to Fawcett's house; and I remember the good-natured triumph which Fawcett expressed to me upon inducing his old friend to pay him a visit at Cambridge and cheering him into forgetfulness of his sufferings. Once, when an old gentleman who shared some of Fawcett's tastes was on his deathbed, Fawcett was admitted to a talk, and with such cheering results that the old man became his former self, sent for his fishing tackle, and even proposed, I think, a bottle of. his famous port. The family were so scandalised by the introduction of such topics at a period when meditation on death seemed to them to be the only proper occupation, that they objected to any fresh administration of a similar cordial. He was equally ready to visit humbler friends who had fallen into any variety of distress. I may safely say that Fawcett never forgot a friend and never missed an opportunity of this kind of service, which is too frequently omitted even by the good-natured. Whenever I met him in later years, I was sure to hear from him the last news of friends, some of whom had drifted away from the rest of their circle, but who never lost their hold, whether depressed in mind or body or fortune, upon his cordial goodwill.

There was another maxim upon which he would

sometimes insist, which coincides with a remark of
Johnson's.   The doctor spoke of the importance of
keeping friendships in repair and of filling up gaps by
new acquisitions.   Fawcett would often tell me that he
made it a principle to make friendships with younger
men; and this, he said, was the great secret of his
continued enjoyment of Cambridge society.   He did
not, like some of us, age prematurely.   He never drifted
away from the sympathies of the young or became a
'don' in the offensive sense of the word.   Many of the
most distinguished of the younger men found him a warm
friend.   Amongst them, I may especially mention Mr. J.
F. Moulton, and the late Professor Clifford, in whose
exuberant and almost boyish spirits and good-humour
there was something especially congenial to Fawcett's
taste.   After Clifford's premature death, Fawcett was
foremost in pressing upon Mr. Gladstone the claims of
his widow to a proper recognition of her husband's intellectual achievements.   He had been, he said, 'one of
Clifford's most intimate friends,' and it was ' only possible for those who enjoyed his intimate friendship fully
to understand the beauty and worth of his character.'
Good judges, he said, agreed that if Clifford had lived
he might have ranked with Laplace or Lagrange.   The
metaphysical writings to which Clifford had latterly devoted his attention had drawn public attention from his
merits as a mathematician.   Fawcett's judicious advocacy
was rewarded with success; though, of course, he was one
of many influential applicants.

What, I have sometimes asked myself with a certain
wonder, did we talk about in those pleasant days, when

sleep seemed an impertinent interruption to a perpetual
flow of conversation ? I have gone to breakfast with
Fawcett at Christmas time, read and discussed the
newspapers till lunch, taken a good constitutional, returning just in time to dress for dinner, and then dined,
talked, and smoked till past midnight, having enjoyed,
and most heartily enjoyed, some fifteen hours of uninter-
rupted talk. What supplied the matter of this abundant
flow ? I must reply, in the first place, that Fawcett
was not above the trivial. Of course we talked of the
events of our little circle : who was to be the next senior
Wrangler, or stroke to the University boat, or to succeed
to the vacant Fellowship or Mastership? On all such
matters his interest was unfailing, and I have heard him
discuss the last boating news from the Thames with a
member of the London Rowing Club as eagerly as he
would discuss proportional representation with Mr. Hare.
Nor did he despise downright personal gossip. Once his
friends observed him deeply engaged in what was supposed
to be a profound political discussion with a member of
Parliament ; when Fawcett was suddenly heard to inquire
eagerly, ' Was it *his* fault or *hers* ?' He would often tell
a story, showing how he had been one link in a chain by
which an outrageous and entirely fictitious bit of scandal
had been circulated all round Cambridge between breakfast
and dinner time, so as to reach the person affected and give
—if custom had sanctioned the practice—occasion for a
duel. He was not puritanical in such matters ; he used to
say that other people loved gossip as well as he did, and
only differed from him in dissembling their love. I fancy
that he also differed by retaining in full measure the eager

curiosity of his childhood. But it must be at once added
that I never heard Fawcett say an ill-natured thing or
intentionally spread a possibly mischievous rumour. He
despised certain classes of mankind heartily enough ; but
his social influence was invariably on the side of kindly
feeling and judicious reticence. Still he delighted im-
measurably in any little anecdote bringing out the
harmless foibles of his acquaintance. I shall not forget
his intense enjoyment of an anecdote which used to be
spun out through several courses at dinner by the simple
narrator— a well-known Cambridge don. It told of the
series of ingenious manœuvres by which a turtle had
been transported from Bristol to a remote part of
the Highlands in time for conversion into soup, and
of the anxiety which supervened when it was discovered
that there was not a lemon within thirty miles ; and
there was a final tableau picturing the assembled guests
looking out, like sister Anne, for the approach of the
horseman who had been despatched on the chance of
bringing back the necessary condiment. Another narrative of equal length told of the sad consequences of the
inconsiderate death of an elderly connection in the same
gentleman's house. But for an almost providential coincidence, which brought the son of the deceased to remove
the body to a distant burial-place, the unhappy man
would have lost a day's fishing. Fawcett, instead of
being bored, enjoyed the repetition of these famous nar-
ratives as if he had been assisting at a comedy. Few
people, indeed, were less easily bored. He would beg
with a kind of childlike eagerness for the repetition of
some story familiar to him for a quarter of a century.

One of his friends had a marvellous power of reviving both the voice and the characteristic language of old Cambridge dons of the port-wine period, now for the most part vanished from an uncongenial world. Fawcett never to the last day of his life lost his power of relishing these admirable anecdotes—which I would fain hope may be embalmed in some future volume of reminiscences. He would begin to listen with anticipatory delight, and as the well-known anecdote proceeded, every muscle of his body would quiver with enjoyment, and he would end by laughter-choked petitions for more.

If our conversation did not exclude such topics, its main staple was serious enough. It included constant and eager discussions of political and economical problems. In those days the most exciting topic was the Civil War in America. Fawcett, as a staunch advocate of the Federal cause, was, as he was so often destined to be in later life, the champion of a small minority. We had long arguments as to the merits of Mr. Hare's scheme; the prospects of an extension of the franchise; or the principles represented by Cobden and Palmerston, Gladstone and Disraeli. In Clarke's rooms the conversation often ran upon points of political economy; for Clarke was not only a keen economist and a most ingenious disputant, but had a singular faculty for producing (from memory or imagination) the most crushing statistical statements, with which Fawcett especially delighted to wrestle. We used to say that no event in history could be mentioned which Clarke could not instantaneously match by a parallel from his native town of Andover — such is the power of acute observation.

Perhaps a listener would have been more inclined to complain of the dryness than of the frivolity of our talk. The dominant influences of Cambridge in those days were indeed favourable to a masculine but limited type of understanding. The intellectual atmosphere, bracing as it might be to congenial minds, was not so propitious to the development of the less robust varieties. The average student scarcely contemplated the existence of any kind of culture except that represented by the two old-fashioned Triposes. Classical or mathematical training was the only alternative suggested, and in either case the study was confined within the limits of a rather narrow definition. The attempt made under the influence of Whewell to introduce the study of moral and physical sciences, was still in its infancy. The new Triposes flagged and showed no signs of really taking root. The University, as was often pointed out, was little but a continuation of the public school. Cambridge men could, of course, defend this characteristic narrowness by a good à priori theory; although, in truth, it was less the product of any conscious theory than the natural outcome of the indigenous system of competitive examination. When challenged for a defence, they would lay down the very sound principle that education should be directed rather to train the faculties than to store the memory. The best education was that which afforded the best course of mental gymnastics; not that which imparted the greatest quantity of practically useful knowledge. They would add, and with equal truth, that the Cambridge course provided in fact a most strenuous and masculine training; success was impossible for the most skilfully crammed ; it was open to hard-headed, thoroughly practised intellectual athletes, and to them alone. Fawcett was heartily convinced of the truth of these assertions. He felt, I have no doubt rightly, that his own mental fibre had been invigorated by the mathematical course, though he had derived from it no knowledge useful in the ordinary sense. His gratitude to the University for this service was unfailing. He held that it had turned him out, and, of course, had turned out others, thoroughly well equipped for the battle of life. He triumphantly confuted the narrow utilitarianism of the cram theory. A senior Wrangler, as he would urge, might be absolutely ignorant of law; but three years after his degree he would be a far better lawyer than the man who had been crammed with legal knowledge in place of being trained in the use of his logical faculties.

Having confuted the vulgar objection, Fawcett took for granted too easily that he had won his case. Granting that the true function of a University is to supply a good course of mental gymnastics, and granting that Cambridge supplied such a course, there was still a gap in his logic. Studies which found no favour at Cambridge have also this pre-eminent virtue. The mind may be trained as well as stored by philosophical, and scientific, and historical, and literary studies. For some minds such studies may even be more stimulating than the regular classical and mathematical round. Gymnastics are good for the body, though they do not train a man for the specific trade by which he is to gain his living. But it does not follow that they should be limited to lifting weights and pulling an oar. The Cambridge system might be criticised as resembling a physical system which should thus train only one set of muscles or one mode of applying them. This peculiarity was connected with the excessive value attached to the competitive system. Having got a test, excellent in its way for fairness and severity, Cambridge did not care to look further. In all competitions there is a tendency to regard the test too much as an ultimate end. Cambridge looked askance at all studies which did not lend themselves to examination. It disliked studies in which cramming was possible or probable: historical studies, for example, because in them it is easier to test the quantity of knowledge than the power of investigation; and studies which by their nature are not so susceptible of a definite numerical test of excellence, such as philosophical studies, where it is impossible to say, as in arithmetic, that a result is clearly right or clearly wrong, and where, in consequence, it is harder to distinguish the pretence from the reality of originality. For such reasons Cambridge was content with the sound masculine training which it actually provided, and which had merits now, perhaps, in some danger of being overlooked. Any new-fangled scheme had great difficulty in establishing itself alongside of the old course, in which there was an accepted and thoroughly well-understood test of relative merit. Fawcett's high estimate of the value of a fair and open competition increased his respect for a system vigorous, if narrow, which at least gave plain, tangible, definable results.

His complete satisfaction with the Cambridge system limited any inclination which he may have had to extend

the area of his studies. He worked hard after his
degree; but he did not make many excursions into new
fields. His own education had been limited; his tendency fell in with the general disposition of the society
to which he belonged. Cambridge men were rather
proud of their limitations. The limitations represented
contempt for mere intellectual frippery and empty pretence. It was exceptional for a don of that day to
extend his inquiries into new fields of speculation. He
was content to make his knowledge more thorough within
the accepted sphere, without annexing new regions of
thought. Whether from this or from other causes, Cambridge was curiously indifferent to certain controversies.
It is strange to turn from the Cambridge of this period
to the Oxford so vividly described by the historians of
the Newman generation. It is like passing to the history
of a remote century or a different civilisation. Theological discussion had doubtless (as Pattison's memoir
has lately told us) ceased to excite the old interest at
Oxford itself. At Cambridge it was difficult to realise
that such controversies could ever have occupied any
reasonable mind. Arguments upon the merits of alchemy
would hardly have been a greater anachronism at Cambridge than argument about the *Via Media,* or the rival
claims of Reason and Authority. We had, of course,
our High-Churchmen and our Evangelicals, and I have
no reason to doubt that the great majority did more than
simply acquiesce in the creed to which they were pledged.
But there was no active spirit of theological investigation.
The cardinal virtue in such matters, according to us, was
a common sense which might be taken to imply a liberal

and tolerant spirit or simple indifference. Indifference
was certainly the characteristic of Fawcett's inner circle
and of Fawcett himself. There were, in fact, wide
spheres of thought which he scarcely cared to enter.
Once, when directly asked for his opinion upon a question which to most philosophers seems to be of primary
importance, he replied with his usual simplicity, ' I never
could bring my mind to take any interest in the
subject.'

Within a certain limit Fawcett's mind was surprisingly
active and powerful. I have never known a man to
whose judgment I should have more readily deferred in
all matters in which he was really at home. But his
mental activity was strictly confined within certain
limits. His want of interest in the questions generally
called philosophical was no doubt due in part to his
perception of the familiar fact that such questions are
never finally answered and have no immediate bearing
on the questions which must be answered. That consideration, however, would have failed to deter any man
who had the natural aptitude from an inquiry which to
men so qualified is delightful in itself, even where they are
convinced beforehand that the inquiry must be fruitless
of any definite result. Fawcett's intellect was not of the
type which would prefer the search after truth to the
truth itself. On the literary side, Fawcett's tastes were
at this period equally undeveloped. His classical training had been of the scantiest, and his Cambridge friends
had few purely literary interests. Nor did Fawcett ever
make the slightest pretension to be a literary connois-
seur. His enjoyment of good literature when it came in

his way was probably not the less keen, and certainly
was all the freer from affectation. At leisure hours he
took pleasure in listening to some of the masterpieces of
our literature. He heartily enjoyed a sonorous passage
from Milton or Burke. He was fond of Shelley and
Wordsworth and of Lamb's and De Quincey's essays; he
read all George Eliot's novels; he read and re-read
'Esmond' and 'Vanity Fair,' and he was very fond of Miss
Austen and the Brontës. He enjoyed, too, a conversation
with men of more literary pretensions upon their special
subjects, as with Mr. Aldis Wright upon Shakespeare or
Bacon. Whenever, indeed, he was convinced that any
man was a genuine worker in any department he respected him accordingly. Even if his friends ventured
into the barren fields of metaphysics he was generous to
excess in crediting them with real accomplishments.

Believers in 'Culture' naturally set him down as
a Philistine, a name which—as I have elsewhere ventured to suggest—is best definable as that which a
prig bestows on the rest of the species. Between
Fawcett and a prig there was a natural antipathy.
The only human beings more objectionable to him
were those whom Cambridge men used to describe as
'impostors'—a phrase equivalent to Carlyle's 'quacks.'
Thoroughness was our pet virtue. An impostor is one
who substitutes fine phrases for thoughts. He flourishes
pre-eminently in the region of metaphysics. If we too
summarily identified metaphysicians with impostors we
perhaps went a little too far. But the opinion is tenable.

I have dwelt upon these considerations because they
help to explain Fawcett's characteristic qualities and his

enthusiastic love of the Cambridge system. He delighted above all things in its absolute fairness. He would say that Cambridge was almost the only place where a man won his position exclusively on his merits. There was no real taint nor even suspicion of unfairness in the distribution of the prizes. When a man had won a position the respect paid to him was proportioned to his intrinsic merits. No one inquired into his social position or the length of his purse. There was no sordid interest in money making. If success in University competitions might be valued too highly, it was at least a genuine test of real ability. No point about the University more endeared it to Fawcett than the homage thus paid to moral or intellectual excellence. The little world of Cambridge had the republican spirit in the best sense of the word. It despised all adventitious claims to respect. Fawcett's chief desire as a University reformer was to bring all classes and sects within the influence of its generous encouragement. The intellectual vigour fostered by the open competitions, and the masculine common sense encouraged by the positive nature of the studies, were thoroughly congenial to him. What he learnt he learnt well. Political economy, to which he had already paid attention in undergraduate days, became his main pursuit. He always studied it in connection with actual experience. In his infancy he had preferred the market-place to the dame-school. He tested the theories of Mill and Ricardo by applying them to the facts, so familiar to him, of agricultural life in Wiltshire. He widened his knowledge by following with the keenest interest the course of contemporary politics. He read the parliamentary debates from end to end. He would complain pathetically of one friend who used to shorten his own labour and Fawcett's enjoyment by skipping the peroration or, as he contemptuously called it, the ' blow off.' Through life his appetite for newspapers was omnivorous. One of his favourite enjoyments was to collect all accessible newspapers and spend a quiet Sunday in reading them steadily through. He enriched his mind less by indulgence in abstract theory than by persistently immersing it in the discussion of affairs in actual course of transaction.

Fawcett was sufficiently familiar with the English literature of his favourite study. I used to maintain that he had read no book except Mill's ' Political Economy.' This was, of course, untrue; but it was true that he had then read no book so thoroughly and elaborately. In some of his later addresses he recommended his hearers to study some good book until they were prepared to give the substance and fully to analyse the argument of every chapter. He would suggest Mill's ' Political Economy ' as desirable for the purpose, and his advice was founded upon his own experience. Besides Mill, he had read such authors as Adam Smith, Malthus, and, above all, Ricardo, in whose terse logic he especially delighted. I remember, too, the frequency with which he would clench an argument by a reference to that entertaining work, Tooke's ' History of Prices.' His admiration for Mill led him to study the ' Logic ' and the later works in which his favourite teacher deals with questions of political philosophy, and to read them with almost unconditional accept-ance. The affliction of his eyesight and his subsequent blindness had naturally limited his studies in the years following his degree. He was, however, greatly impressed by two books which stirred the minds of all young men of his generation.

The first volume of Buckle's 'History of Civilisation' appeared in 1857. Some letters from his friend Mr. Egerton show that he was eagerly discussing it soon afterwards. Buckle impressed many men (Mark Pattison amongst others) of intellectual temperament very different from Fawcett's by his daring and (in a literary sense at least) brilliant generalisation. Fawcett's enthusiasm was roused by this bold attempt to apply scientific methods to historical inquiry. He was not, indeed, blind to the weak side of Buckle. He thought that Buckle's language betrayed a superficial knowledge of political economy. He used, too, to tell with some amusement an anecdote of a (probably fictitious) feminine disciple of the new prophet who went about proclaiming that she was ' panting for a wider generalisation.' His admiration for Buckle, however, was not quenched by these suspicious symptoms of that writer's affinity with the great class 'Impostor.' In February 1860 he lectured at Bradford on ' The New School of History.' Adopting a view taken by Mill, he maintains that history which had previously belonged to mere partisans like Hume and Voltaire, and afterwards to the graphic or imaginative writers, like Macaulay and Carlyle, was in the hands of Buckle to become a genuine science. Fawcett was venturing with the courage of youth beyond his proper province, and the lecture is only valuable as indicating his sympathies.

A greater impression was made upon him by Darwin's

'Origin of Species.' Though Fawcett's scientific studies
had hardly gone beyond the mathematical theories included in the Tripos, he took a general interest in
scientific methods. In 1859 the publication of Darwin's
great book initiated the most fruitful controversy of the
day. Fawcett became an enthusiastic Darwinian. He
was disgusted at the bitterness of the theological on-
slaught upon the new teaching, and at the tone of ungenerous hostility exhibited by some of the old-fashioned
men of science. He had been present at the smart
passage of arms (in 1860) between Professor Huxley
and Bishop Wilberforce at the British Association meeting in Oxford; and in the December of the same year
published an article in 'Macmillan's Magazine' in which
he came to the rescue. He states with his usual firmness the true logical position of Darwin's theory; dis-
tinguishing carefully between a fruitful hypothesis and
a scientific demonstration; exhibiting the general nature
of the argument and the geological difficulty with great
clearness, and taking some pains to prove that religion is
in no danger from Darwinism. In any case, he says, life
must have been originally introduced by an 'act of
creative will.' His old friend Hopkins criticises him in
a very kind letter. Hopkins was of the old school in
this respect, and thinks that Darwinism 'utterly fails'
by confusing the difference between hypothesis and
proof. Fawcett did not bow to his teacher's authority;
and at the British Association meeting at Manchester
(September 1861) he read a paper which was substantially
a reassertion of the arguments in his article. This controversy, which went no further, led to a correspondence

with Darwin himself. I quote a passage or two from Darwin's letters, as anything that can throw additional light upon their writer is of interest.

'You could not possibly have told me anything,' writes Mr. Darwin, July 20, 1861, 'which would have given me more satisfaction than what you say about Mr. Mill's opinion. Until your review appeared I began to think that perhaps I did not understand at all how to reason scientifically.' Fawcett has told me that Mill had said to him that the ' Origin of Species ' was admirable as a piece of thorough logical argument (I forget the precise phrase), and I presume that Fawcett had repeated this to Mr. Darwin. The later letter, dated September 18 (1861), refers to Fawcett's paper at the British Association :—

'My dear Mr. Fawcett,—I wondered who had so kindly sent me the newspapers, which I was very glad to see ; and now I have to thank you sincerely for allowing me to see your MS. It seems to me very good and sound ; though I am certainly not an impartial judge. You will have done good service in calling the attention of scientific men to means and laws of philosophising. As far as I could judge by the papers, your opponents were unworthy of you. How miserably A. talked of my reputation, as if that had anything to do with it. . . . How profoundly ignorant B. [who had said that Darwin should have published facts alone] must be of the very soul of observation ! About thirty years ago there was much talk that geologists ought only to observe and not theorise ; and I well remember some one saying that at this rate a man might as well go into a gravel-pit and count the pebbles and describe the colours. How odd it is that anyone should not see that all observation must be for or against some view if it is to be of any service!

'I have returned only lately from a two months' visit to Torquay, which did my health at the time good; but I am one of those miserable creatures who are never comfortable for twenty-four hours; and it is clear to me that I ought to be exterminated. I have been rather idle of late, or, speaking more strictly, working at some miscellaneous papers, which, however, have some direct bearing on the subject of species; yet I feel guilty at having neglected my larger book. But, to me, observing is much better sport than writing. I fear that I shall have wearied you with this long note.

'Pray believe that I feel sincerely grateful that you have taken up the cudgels in defence of the line of argument in the "Origin;" you will have benefited the subject.

'Many are so fearful of speaking out. A German naturalist came here the other day, and he tells me that there are many in Germany on our side, but that all seem fearful of speaking out, and waiting for some one to speak, and then many will follow. The naturalists seem as timid as young ladies should be, about their scientific reputation. There is much discussion on the subject on the Continent, even in quiet Holland, and I had a pamphlet from Moscow the other day by a man who sticks up famously for the imperfection of the " Geological Record," but complains that I have sadly *understated*

the variability of the old fossilised animals! But I must
not run on.   With sincere thanks and respects,
    'Pray believe me,
        'Yours very sincerely,
           'CHARLES DARWIN.'

The influence of evolutionist doctrines has been
hardly less marked in philosophy than in the scientific
movement.   Fawcett, however, did not follow such discussions far; nor did he, I think, care for any applications
of the same ideas to questions of political theory.   He
was becoming more and more absorbed in the political
questions of the day.   And here he still preserved his
early zeal for Mill's teaching.   The influence upon his
opinions will be shown in my next chapter.   Here I may
note one or two proofs of his feeling towards Mill, before
the growth of a personal intimacy.   In the letter already
noticed (December 23, 1859) Fawcett calls himself 'personally a stranger to you,' but mentions 'the very kind
sympathy you have expressed to me.'   He tells Mill
that his books are producing a deep impression on many
young men in Cambridge.   'For the last three years,'
he says, 'your books have been the chief education of
my mind.   I consequently entertain towards you such a
sense of gratitude as I can only hope at all adequately to
repay by doing what lies in my power to propagate the invaluable truths contained in every page of your writings.'
    There is another undated fragment, clearly intended
for Mill, and possibly referring to the expression of
sympathy noticed in the last.   'My dear Sir,' he says,
'pray accept my most sincere thanks for your letter.   I

cannot tell you how much I value your words of kind encouragement. , Often, when I reflect on my affliction, I feel that it is rash on my part to attempt anything like a career of public usefulness; and again and again, I am sure, my heart would fail me if I was not stimulated by your thoughts and teaching. I can, therefore, assure you that your kind words will remove many an obstacle to my course.'

No teacher could ever boast of a more ardent and attached disciple. He never lost an opportunity of referring to Mill and the value of his teaching. In distributing prizes at Manchester on October 1, 1866, he remarks on the value of converse with great minds. 'As I was reading Mill's "Liberty,"' he says, 'perhaps the greatest work of our greatest living writer, as I read his noble, I might almost say his holy, ideas, I thought to myself, If everyone in my country could and would read this work, how infinitely happier would the nation be! How much less desirous should we be to wrangle about petty religious differences! How much less of the energy of the nation would be wasted in contemptible quarrels about creeds and formularies; and how much more powerful should we be as a nation to achieve works of good, when, as this work would teach us to be, we were firmly bound together by the bonds of a wise toleration!'

We used sometimes to rally Fawcett upon his enviable —and really honourable—absence of the modest awkwardness so common with over-sensitive youth. He would reply, 'If you could ever see me meeting Mill, you would see me awkward enough!' The introduction came about through Mr. Hare, I believe, who had himself made the acquaintance of Fawcett as an energetic advocate of his own scheme. Whether Fawcett was awkward at the first meeting I know not; he met our inquiries with a resolute refusal to confess; but, in any case, the two men soon became familiar, and Fawcett could talk to Mill as easily as to anyone. He soon perceived the peculiar charm of a feminine tenderness underlying a character which superficial readers of his books had taken to be stern and chilling. In a speech upon unveiling Mill's statue (January 26, 1878) Fawcett said that Mill possessed qualities supposed to be the peculiar privileges of women —a gentleness and tenderness such as no woman could exceed. His adherence as a disciple was blended with strong personal affection; something of the chivalrous desire to stand up for a friend blended with the spirit in which he defended their common beliefs, and, as some people thought, made him less impartial than usual in giving a hearing to their common opponents.

From the date of his return to residence in Cambridge, Fawcett had a double set of interests. His main energies were soon diverted into the political direction. But through life, in spite of all distractions, he clung fondly to Cambridge and his college. I shall here bring together the main incidents of his purely academical career, before taking up the thread of political affairs. Fawcett was elected to a Fellowship at Christmas 1856. He found the college on the eve of a revolution. Our five-hundredth anniversary had been celebrated in 1850, and during our whole previous existence we had jogged along quietly, without any nominal alteration in the

old statutes. It was, however, beginning to be understood that the University was to be overhauled. New
studies were beginning to be introduced; and it was
now perceived that the constitution of the colleges
would require a corresponding change. A commission
of inquiry had reported, and in the session of 1856
an Act had been passed, appointing an executive Commission to carry out suggested improvements. The
colleges were permitted to frame new statutes before
January 1, 1858. If no settlement had been effected
by that time, the Commission might itself propose new
statutes, which could only be rejected by a majority of
two-thirds of the governing body. It was further provided that no religious test should be imposed for the
ordinary degrees or for Scholarships; but no one was
to acquire a vote in the senate or to hold a Fellowship
until he had declared himself to be that rather indefinite
entity—' a *bonâ fide* member of the Church of England.'
This last provision marks the point in removal of
religious tests which had then been reached by reformers. It afterwards became the cause of a prolonged
agitation in which Fawcett took a very prominent part
as a politician. For the present, however, our hands
were tied, and we could do nothing to affect the connection between the Church and the Universities.

The main desire of the reformers, both at Oxford
and Cambridge, was simple. Their primary object was
to do away with all restrictions which hampered the full
efficiency of the prizes offered to intellectual excellence.
The function of the University was education; the
mainspring of the educational system was the rewards

obtainable by success in examination; the more attractive the prizes, and the more open the field, the greater
would be the success of the system. Another school of
reformers has since arisen, which holds that Universities
should be also institutes of learning, and which took
for its watchword the 'endowment of research.' This
view was partly represented under the Commission of
1856, in so far as it was proposed to do something
towards strengthening the professorial system. The
Commissioners proposed to levy a tax of five per cent.
upon the college incomes for University purposes.

At Cambridge generally there were few of the close
Fellowships which were a main grievance with the
Oxford reformers. At Trinity Hall there were none.
Cambridge Fellowships, however, unlike those at Oxford,
were by custom confined to members of the college.
The small colleges invariably accepted success in the
University examinations as the test of merit. The
Commissioners suggested the advantage of imitating
Oxford in this respect, and electing to Fellowships by
examinations open to the University. Cambridge men
generally clung to their own system; and a meeting
(held October 24, 1857) protested so unanimously against
the proposed change that the Commissioners withdrew
their proposal. Fawcett, I find, was almost alone in
advocating the Oxford system. He argued, in a letter to
the 'Times,' that under that system there would be less
uncertainty; the standard of merit would not vary from
one college to another, and the supply of vacancies would
be more regular; colleges would be compelled to attract
students by improving their educational staff, instead of

keeping up their numbers by confining the offer of prizes to members of their own body. His own case was in point; for he had 'migrated' to Trinity Hall to improve his chances of a Fellowship, not for any superiority in the college itself. His arguments, though certainly deserving attention, failed to affect the existing prejudice.

Another point gave us far more trouble at Trinity Hall. The Fellowships were tenable for life, subject only to the condition of celibacy. Of our thirteen Fellows ten were barristers. A barrister who does not marry is, as a rule, of the class called 'briefless.' The result was that the prize for youthful excellence became too often a pension for adult incompetence. The number of vacancies was diminished by a system which clogged the college revenues by creating small sinecures for men who had failed in the open field of professional enterprise.

This was clearly an abuse of the prize system. The obvious remedy was to limit the tenure to a term of years. The value of the reward would hardly be diminished, for no clever young man cares much for the prospect of securing his retreat when he is setting out on his adventures. What was lost by this change would be more than made up by allowing marriage, and by the increased number of vacancies resulting from the limitation. Fawcett's great object, therefore, was to limit the Fellowships, and remove the restriction of celibacy. A battle raged over this question for many months; and Fawcett's part in it was too characteristic to be passed over. The changes affected only one small college, and subsequent legislation has made our discussions obsolete.

Yet the struggle in our combination room resembled in
its conduct and in the principles at issue more important
battles waged in the House of Commons, and curiously
illustrates some of Fawcett's permanent principles.

Fawcett was the leader of the opposition. His
followers were R. Campbell, F. Fitzroy, and myself (his
seniors in the University by a year or two), and Lumley
Smith (now Q.C.), his junior by a year (elected Fellow,
June 1857). Our opponents, the Master and the older
Fellows, were in a majority of eight or nine to five. I
remember vividly Fawcett's first appearance in the field.
At the college meeting at which he was elected Fellow
(Christmas 1856) the statutes came up for discussion.
The new Fellow proceeded at once to expound his
theories in a speech of some length. A dignified senior
then began a few observations, destined to an abrupt
close. At an early pause, Fawcett interrupted and told
him in the plainest English that he had said quite
enough. Dumb surprise ensued, and the startled senior
collapsed on the spot. This was the only occasion I can
remember upon which Fawcett was not only brusque but
distinctly rude. Whether from the essential good-humour
beneath his occasionally rough manner, or from a similar
quality in his opponents, or from the harmonising influences of the evening's milk-punch, the sun never went
down upon any serious irritation. We wrangled up and
down; we wrangled long and sore; we got into tangled
skeins of logic, till we hardly knew what were the issues
before us; but the spirit of good fellowship was never
extinct, and before long Fawcett was on the best of
terms with everyone. At this first meeting we were out-

voted. The statutes, framed by the majority, adopted the essential points of the old system. Life Fellowships, subject to the restriction of celibacy, were still to be the rule. The Commissioners, however, for some reason did not act upon our proposals. It was not till February 1859 that they sent us a scheme of their own, making an essential alteration in our draft. The Fellowships were to be tenable for ten years from the M.A. degree, whilst the restriction of celibacy was to be preserved. This suited neither party. The war broke out afresh. We met and wrangled and broke up into several sections, each of which drew up its own platform for the consideration of the Commission. We printed and circulated professions of our various faiths. In one which (I do not remember why) Fawcett signed alone, the youthful Radical roundly informs the Commissioners that he can 'neither understand nor imagine the reasons' which have induced them to preserve the restriction of celibacy along with a limited tenure. Nor, to say the truth, can I. At last, however, this tangled controversy came to an end. The minority triumphed by a diplomacy of which Fawcett often spoke with complacency. The essential point was this. The statutes proposed by the Commission could only be rejected by a majority of two-thirds of the governing body. The majority objected both to the limitation of tenure and to the abolition of celibacy. The minority were in favour of both. Either party, being more than a third of the whole, could secure the adoption of a proposal of the Commission by abstaining from voting against it. If, therefore, the Commission adhered to their proposal, it was possible that it might be rejected by our united votes. But the majority might, if they pleased, retain celibacy, though only on the disagreeable terms of also accepting limitation of tenure; whilst the minority could obtain all they required if the Commission would withdraw the restriction of celibacy. The great point with the Commission was to secure a limited tenure; and we of the minority took care that they should understand that they could secure this by withdrawing the condition of celibacy, whilst, if they proposed both, it was possible that they might unite the whole college against them.

This consideration apparently was conclusive. The Commissioners were probably glad to have the thing settled; at any rate they accepted our view. They sent down statutes in the form desired, and, as the requisite two-thirds majority could not be obtained against them, we were one of the first colleges in the University to carry out the now accepted system of Fellowships of limited tenure without any restriction upon marriage. Great was our triumph!

On certain collateral issues we were less successful. A distinction was made in the statutes between the ten lay Fellowships to be held by lawyers, and the three clerical Fellowships intended for the educational staff of the college. The last were still to be celibate, though under certain conditions. A life Fellowship free from restriction might be·voted to them as a reward for services of a certain length. We protested—reasonably, I think—that celibacy was specially injurious in the case of the clerical Fellows, because it hindered the adoption of teaching as a permanent career. We held that no professional condition should be imposed, for every such condition depreciated the value of the Fellowship, and that the only difference should be a permission to retain Fellowships during service in a college office. Our seniors were greatly scandalised by our audacious proposal, which would, they held, destroy the connection of the college with the bar, besides rendering unnecessary its connection with the Church. We failed, at the time, in this, and in another protest (specially insisted on in Fawcett's letter) against a provision that ' open secession from the Church of England ' should vacate a Fellowship.

One other controversy bore upon a different point. The proposed levy of five per cent. on the colleges for University purposes broke down. Seniors and juniors agreed in rejecting it, and we juniors stated in explanation of our part in the protest that we were very willing to contribute to strengthen the professoriate; but that we preferred a different scheme. We objected to taxing Fellowships, but we were quite ready to sacrifice our Master. Let his office be annexed to a professorship, a contribution which would be more than the proposed five per cent. I remember Fawcett's delight in securing the adhesion of one of the senior Fellows to this (as it was thought) audacious proposal. The poor man weakly admitted that he could not answer Fawcett's arguments, and was then fairly terrorised by appeals to his conscience into the logical consequence of signing a proposal, which thus received the adhesion of half the Fellows. But the interference with so delightful a sinecure was too much even for reforming zeal at the time.

I owe gratitude to one of our opponents who collected

and deposited in our college library the documents bearing
upon this dispute.   He has prefixed to it a pious aspiration that the evils which he foresees may not fall upon
the college.   It may perhaps be now admitted that, in
some respects, our opponents saw farther than we did.
Undoubtedly we were striking a blow at the old autonomy
of the colleges.   The holder of a prize Fellowship is no
longer connected by such close ties as of old with his
college.   We were virtually acting upon the principle
that the college is not an end in itself, but merely a part
of a larger body, to whose needs its own interests must
be subordinated.   The changes made by the Commission appointed under the Act of 1877 brought out the
tendency of the reform.   Our statutes, instead of obtaining the venerable antiquity of their predecessors, barely
reached their majority.   Their provisions became obsolete
whilst the ink was fresh.   Under the new statutes (finally
approved on March 16, 1881) there is no longer any
question of a religious test; there is no restriction to
professions, legal or clerical; there is no mention of
celibacy in any case; and the tenure is restricted within
still narrower limits.   A Fellow holds for only six years
from the date of appointment, but Fellowships are tenable
during the tenure of college offices, and twenty years of
such tenure may be rewarded by a life Fellowship.

The effect of these changes is that part of the college
revenue is to be devoted to prize Fellowships, implying a
very transitory connection with the college; whilst the
remainder goes chiefly to the support of a permanent
educational staff.   Fawcett considered that the tenure
was too short, for he continued to attach great value to

the prize Fellowship system. For the same reason he looked with doubtful approval upon another change of great importance. It was now decided that a large contribution should be levied upon the colleges for University purposes. The old system of a lax federation of seventeen independent bodies, each teaching the same subjects, involved great waste of power and implied a most defective organisation. Professors' lectures were mainly of the ornamental kind; college lectures, given by men anxious to go off to a living, and confined to the students who entered a college for any other reason than its educational advantages, were almost equally ineffective. The real work was done by private tutors, and the college endowments, mainly devoted to rewarding competitors, increased instead of diminishing the expense of education. To remedy these evils, it has seemed desirable to most reformers to re-organise the whole University system; to make each college co-operate instead of competing with its neighbours; to subordinate it to the University; and to put fresh life into the central body, which should thus be not only capable of teaching more efficiently, but become an institute for 'original research' and a leading organ of national education.

Fawcett looked with a certain suspicion upon these proposals. His view was indicated very frankly in a speech in June 1876, when the new Commission was in prospect. It is true that as the speech was made after dinner, on the occasion of the presentation to the college of a portrait of Chief Justice Cockburn, it should not be taken too seriously. He spoke, as usual, of his gratitude to the old college. 'There was,' he added, 'a

I

certain school, not a great school, which, having gained
great advantages from the emoluments and rewards of
the Universities, turned round and said poor men were
not to be helped; examinations were not to be rewarded;
young men were not to be encouraged; but everything
was to be thrown into an undefined hodge-podge of what
they called "original research."' He claimed to have
as much sympathy with the ostensible end as its professed advocates; but he earnestly hoped that the
number of Fellowships might not be diminished. He
proposed an amendment to this effect (June 4, 1877),
during the passage of the University Bill of 1877.

Fawcett was in fact a Conservative, as viewed by the
younger school of reformers. What he really valued in
the University system, as he said again and again, was
that it provided, however imperfectly, a ladder by which a
young man might climb to success by the exercise of his
own talents, in a fair contest, however poor or socially
depressed. To reform the University meant with him
chiefly to remove all obstructions which limited the
beneficial influence of this open competition to any
particular class. He held, too, that the new system was
in danger, if not of encouraging jobbery, at least of
favouring 'impostors.' The 'endowment of research'
is a pretty phrase; but it may cover much that was
condemned by the old narrow but masculine school. It
might mean the foundation of comfortable posts for
gentlemen who prefer regions of inquiry which do not
always atone by loftier merits for their want of immediate
practical utility. Instead of the old strenuous competition, the students would be encouraged to listen to pro

fessors spinning fine phrases and creating sham sciences
to justify the existence of their chairs, rather than to
extend the borders of genuine science. He held that
the obligation to take part in the actual work of education would serve as a beneficial restraint upon such
waste of energy, and was really compatible with original
research. A prize openly offered and fairly won has
certain definite and intelligible merits. A post created
to enable a gentleman to air his last new philosophical
crotchets may contribute to the multiplication of empty
verbiage and sham illumination. And possibly a little
body of gentlemen connected by family ties may not
show that aversion to jobbery which Fawcett regarded
as the most honourable characteristic of the old order.

I will not argue the question. I only wish to show
the natural tendency of Fawcett's strong common sense
and love of the definite and tangible. I may add that
he did not object to the principle of raising some contribution to the University, though he was doubtful as
to the special method proposed. Change became the
natural state of the Universities when once the old
system was broken up, which had seemed to be almost a
part of the necessary order of nature. Fawcett confined
himself to criticising some of the proposed measures in
detail. He was anxious that the contribution should
not be so levied as to be a first charge upon the college
revenues. He feared that bodies dependent in great
part upon landed property, and therefore likely to suffer
from agricultural depression, were liable to be seriously
crippled by such a charge. And he held that whatever
materially lowered their power of rewarding success in

examinations would be a very heavy fine to pay for the endowment of readers and professors.

I have anticipated events in order to bring together Fawcett's views upon this group of questions. It will, I think, appear hereafter that his attitude in regard to them throws some light upon his later divergence from one school of Radicals. I now return to an earlier period.

During his first years of residence Fawcett was rapidly making himself known both within and without the University. He was becoming conspicuous as a speaker at the British and the Social Science Associations, and as a candidate for a seat in Parliament. He was becoming known as an expounder of economic principles. Amongst our friends of those days was Mr. Alexander Macmillan, already rising as a publisher, though his business was still limited to Cambridge. Fawcett contributed to the early numbers of the magazine. Macmillan was often in our rooms, trying rather fruitlessly to stimulate Fawcett's interest in the writings of Carlyle, Maurice, and Kingsley. At Macmillan's we occasionally met men of some literary eminence, whom we respected with juvenile simplicity. Macmillan, I believe, was the first to suggest an undertaking which was of great importance in Fawcett's career. He proposed that Fawcett should write a popular manual of political economy. The result was profitable to both parties; and I will add that Macmillan always continued to be both friend and publisher—a combination happily more common than the complaints of some querulous authors would suggest. Fawcett was at work upon his book in the autumn of 1861, and it appeared in the beginning of 1863. It was favourably received from the first; and the reputation gained was of great service. Professor Pryme had received the title of Professor of Political Economy in May 1828. He was now breaking in health and announced his intended resignation. It was generally understood that a more substantial professorship would be created when a vacancy should occur. Fawcett naturally desired such an appointment, and Macmillan had pointed out to him the advantage of having some public proof of his capacities as one reason for writing the book. Pryme resigned in the summer of 1863 (he died in December 1868), and the professorship, with a salary of 300*l.* a year, was founded by grace of the senate, October 29, 1863. The choice lay with the electoral roll—a body consisting chiefly of resident M.A.'s, with a few examiners and others as *ex-officio* members. Ultimately, four candidates declared themselves. Besides Fawcett, they were Mr. Joseph Bickersteth Mayor, of St. John's; Mr. Leonard H. Courtney, also of St. John's, who has now made a wider reputation; and Mr. Henry Dunning Macleod, of Trinity. The electoral poll was tolerably certain to prefer a resident, personal friendship counting for a good deal in a body too large to have a keen sense of responsibility. Mr. Macleod, though a learned writer upon the subject, was not only a non-resident, but generally regarded as an economical heretic. Courtney's abilities were already generally recognised; but he, too, was non-resident, and the contest came to be between Fawcett and Mayor. Mayor had lectured on political economy

in his college, but had given no public proofs of his
capacity. Fawcett's book stood him in good stead, and
he produced a strong body of testimonials from Sir
Stafford Northcote, Robert Lowe, Thorold Rogers, professor at Oxford; R. H. Mills, professor at Cork; J.
Waley, professor at University College, London; Cliffe
Leslie, professor at Belfast; R. H. Hutton, G. W. Norman, W. Newmarch, W. T. Thornton, J. S. Mill, and
Herman Merivale, formerly professor at Oxford. Most
of them refer to his book, and some to his discussions at
the London Political Economy Club, of which he had
become a member in 1861. I will not quote from a kind
of literature proverbially untrustworthy and abounding
in platitude, even in the hands of eminent men beyond all
suspicion of insincerity. The names, however, show that
Fawcett was already widely known amongst the official
representatives of the science. He could certainly produce far stronger evidence of fitness for the post than his
most dangerous rival. But much was to be set against
him. There were some real doubts as to the power of a
blind man to preserve order in his classes. One at least
of his most intimate friends withheld his support upon
this ground. Yet I think that no one who knows the
average undergraduate will doubt that he has too much
good feeling to take advantage of an infirmity in a man
at least who knows how to make himself respected.
Other considerations told against him. Fawcett's Radicalism had scandalised the older members of the University. He had contested Southwark, and in the preceding summer Cambridge itself under the very eyes
of the dignitaries. He was an active and pugnacious

antagonist of Conservatism in and out of college. He
had encountered the great Whewell, too, on an economic
question: he read a paper at the British Association
meeting at Oxford in 1860, in which he assaulted
Whewell's preface to the works of Richard Jones. A
large meeting had gathered to witness the encounter.
Fawcett had learnt by heart a sentence from Whewell's
preface. Whewell replied and repudiated the phrases
quoted. Fawcett slowly and accurately repeated the
words, which Whewell again disavowed. Then Fawcett
called to his secretary, E. Brown, to produce the volume
in which the unlucky sentence had been marked. The
chairman, Nassau Senior, read it out, when Fawcett's
quotation appeared to be perfectly correct. He thus
gained an apparently conclusive triumph. 'There were
not half a dozen people in the room,' he observed, 'who
would have understood if I had got the best of the argument as to the inductive method; but they all heard the
passage repeated distinctly three times.' The common
impression was that Whewell had been defeated by his
junior. Whewell has left a traditional reputation for
roughness; and yet, though his manner was at times
overbearing, he was thoroughly magnanimous. I can
testify from personal experience to his real courtesy to
young men who had to take a part with him in University work and were almost grotesquely his inferiors in
knowledge and reputation; and on this occasion, instead
of owing Fawcett a grudge, he was from that time on
thoroughly good terms with his antagonist. Still it was
not to be expected that he, a good Conservative, should
support a young Radical with unsound views of true

methods. Whewell, and the dons of highest dignity, were in favour of Mayor.

Against Mayor, indeed, there was only one word to be said. His character and abilities were all that could be desired. But if it were right to bestow the chair upon the man who had given the most unequivocal public proofs of his capacity, Fawcett's claim was undeniably superior. The election really turned upon other questions than this, which would surely be the main question in a satisfactory contest. One consideration turned out to be decisive. Members of St. John's College, unless they were belied, had a private decalogue, including the commandment, Thou shalt not vote against a Johnian. Fawcett had some very warm friends in St. John's, who sincerely thought him the best man, but who would not allow that opinion to divert them from the plain path of duty. Courtney, however, was a Johnian as well as Mayor; and, though his chances were known to be infinitesimal, they could vote for him without inconsistency. Such votes would be taken from Mayor, though not transferred to Fawcett. Fawcett's chance thus came to depend upon Courtney's continuing to stand, and thus to divide the solid Johnian phalanx. The fact that the election, in this and other ways, turned upon considerations quite irrelevant to the merit of the candidates may be some excuse for one manœuvre of Fawcett's, to which, I think, he would not have condescended at a later time. Fawcett managed to secure the nomination to an examinership, and therefore to a place on the electoral roll, of one gentleman at least upon whose vote he had reasons—not generally obvious—for counting.

He was, I must add, a thoroughly competent examiner. The result was that all the examiners in one department voted for Fawcett, and Fawcett was rather wickedly amused, when a friend remarked upon this coincidence without suspecting it to be other than purely accidental. The anecdote, perhaps, shows more of his characteristic shrewdness than of the scrupulous fairness to antagonists for which his later conduct was always conspicuous. He had, however, a sufficient majority without such a device, which, at the outside, only secured one or two votes. Courtney fortunately held that he was pledged to his supporters to go to the poll, and they held him to the pledge. His action, though serviceable to Fawcett, was therefore not decided by a personal friendship, which afterwards became very intimate.

The great day came on, and Clarke, who delighted in such affairs, acted as Fawcett's amateur agent, calculated the votes, and directed Fawcett's supporters when to poll. The result is given in a letter from Fawcett, dated Trinity Hall, November 28, 1863 :—

'My dear Mother,—1 hope you duly received the telegram. The victory yesterday was a wonderful triumph. I don't think an election has produced so much excitement at Cambridge for years. At last excitement was greatly increased by its being made quite a Church and political question. All the masters opposed me, with two exceptions, but I was strongly supported by a great majority of the most distinguished resident Fellows. My victory was a great surprise to the University. I thought on the whole that I should win, but

I expected a much smaller majority. Clarke, however, was very confident. He managed the election splendidly for me, and curiously enough predicted that I should poll exactly ninety votes, and made a bet with Stephen that I should beat Mayor by ten or twelve. We are going to publish a list of the votes, which I shall send to you. My great strength after all was in Trinity. This says much for the independence of the college, as the Master was one of my strongest opponents. At the end of the first hour I was five behind. I might then have easily had a majority, but we kept many of our safe voters in reserve, as we thought if we got ahead of Mayor it would make his party more active. Directly the polling commenced in the second hour, we put on a majority of ten, and kept steadily ahead until the close.

'All my friends in the town regard it as a great political triumph. The Fosters [who had supported him in the election for Cambridge] were in a wonderful state of delight, and I have been quite overwhelmed with congratulations. I must now conclude, as I have many more letters to write. Give my kindest love to Maria, and believe me to be, dear Mother, ever yours affectionately,   'HENRY FAWCETT.'

The actual numbers were—Fawcett, 90; Mayor, 80; Courtney, 19; Macleod, 14.

The election was of great value to Fawcett. It was a proof that he not only was respected by the University, but trusted to discharge duties rendered difficult by his blindness. It also secured him a certain income. With the Fellowship—at that time worth about 250*l.* or 300*l.*

a year—and his professorship, he had an income sufficient for a bachelor. He continued to deliver his annual course of lectures for the rest of his life. His professorship bound him to a residence of eighteen weeks annually, an obligation which to him was a pleasure.

Since Fawcett's election the view taken of a professor's duties has materially changed. At an earlier period, professors' lectures were considered to be mainly ornamental. Few students attended, and they scarcely formed a part of the real educational system. When it was thought desirable to introduce more vigour into this part of the University, the lecture-rooms were filled by compelling the ' poll ' men to attend a certain number of lectures, though it was felt that it would be cruel to waste the time of candidates for honours by such exactions. Whilst this regulation remained in force, Fawcett had a large share of the compulsory attendance. In 1876 the regulation was repealed. After that time his lectures were, for a short period, nearly deserted ; but in his later years he had again a respectable audience.

Fawcett was, I believe, the only professor who objected to the withdrawal of compulsion. In a letter to the Vice-Chancellor, dated January 1876, he gives his reasons. He had been convinced by experience that his hearers profited more than he had anticipated. Examinations showed that they had really acquired useful knowledge. He did not feel the objection, upon which his colleagues chiefly insisted, that they had to lecture above the capacities of their compulsory audiences, or to lower the standard of their lectures. He should not, he said, alter in any case the character of his own lectures. This opinion is characteristic of the view taken by Fawcett of his subject, upon which I shall have more to say. It illustrates, also, the merits and the shortcomings of his lectures.

According to him, in fact, the leading principles of political economy, and those which were really valuable, were few, simple, and therefore capable of an exposition on the level of average intelligence. Refined and subtle reasonings were not required to set forth the great truths which had really been established, and which alone possessed much importance or bore directly upon the really interesting questions. His exposition of these was always forcible and lucid, and did, in fact, stimulate many of his hearers. Nor, it may be added, did Fawcett confine himself to setting forth the A B C of the science, or, like many of his predecessors, confine himself to a repetition of his previous courses. The substance of several courses has been published, and shows the keenness with which he followed the illustration of his principles by the great events of contemporary history. His lectures upon pauperism and free trade are those of a man who values his science, not as a field for logical subtlety, but for the light which it throws upon great political topics of pressing interest. The freshness of this method was well calculated to stimulate the interest of his hearers, and is enough to show that he never fell into the academical indolence which is content with the mere dry bones of established formulæ.

Fawcett's main energies were of course directed to politics. He could not therefore fulfil the ideal of those who think that a professor should have no duties beyond those of his chair, and devote all his energy either to teaching or to extending his science. Fawcett did, however, as much as was required, and more than had been customary. Few professors' lectures at Cambridge had been of equal value as real contributions to the study of their respective topics. And it may be asked whether it is not a greater advantage on the whole to secure a part of the energy of an eminent man who always keeps his studies fresh by application to outside interests, than to secure the whole energy of a purely academical student.

I am also bound to say that exception was taken by some of the younger men to one aspect of Fawcett's teaching. They held, rightly or wrongly, that political economy needed to be re-written, that Ricardo and Mill were obsolete, and that a professor should have had his eyes more open to recent speculations in Germany and elsewhere. I am certainly not prepared to say that this criticism was groundless. My own opinion is that it represents the failing natural to an intellect wanting in versatility and less open to new ideas than powerful in its grasp of the old. But this is a question of theory upon which I cannot now enter. It is enough to say that, accepting Fawcett's own point of view, he discharged his duties vigorously and did his best to keep his hearers alive to the vast importance of the principles in which he believed by applying them to the great problems of the day.

Fawcett's professorship attached him permanently to Cambridge. In the autumn of 1866 an event occurred which was of the greatest importance to his future life. He was engaged to Miss Millicent Garrett.

The prospect of marriage made a considerable difference in his academical status. He had remained under the old college statutes; for, at the time, to have placed himself under the new regulations would have been to sentence himself to lose in 1869 his only independent means of support. His Fellowship, however, would be vacated by marriage. But his professorship, which on the old system made no difference in the tenure of his Fellowship, would, under the new regulations, enable him to hold it even after marriage, so long as he continued to be professor. At Christmas 1866 he therefore re-signed his Fellowship and offered himself for re-election under the new statutes. The re-election made to him the difference of retaining half his independent income. I cannot resist the pleasure of quoting from a letter in which he announces his success. It was, he says, 'most fortunate that I decided to resign at the present time, for if Stephen had given up his Fellowship [as I was about to do soon afterwards] I should have had no chance of being re-elected. There were only two or three votes to spare, and two or three would probably not have voted for me if they had not been influenced by Stephen's strong will and earnest determination.' I would gladly take all the credit I can for this, which was my last action as a Fellow of the college. But I am bound to add, first, that whatever I did was only returning a very similar service which Fawcett had rendered to me a couple of years before; and, secondly, that my difficulty, so far as I can remember, was not to prove that the re-election was desirable, for we were nearly unanimous upon that point, but that it was legally within our powers. In fact, our beautiful new statutes were a constant source of difficulty. They declared that the lay Fellowships were designed for persons intending to pursue the legal profession. Fawcett certainly had no such intention, and some of us had prejudices, which I will hope that I helped to soften, against making a breach in our bran-new constitution.

Fawcett was married on April 23, 1867. I write under conditions which compel a certain reserve. I must confine myself therefore to saying that Mrs. Fawcett was the daughter of Mr. Newson Garrett, of Aldeburgh, Suffolk, and that she was fully qualified to take an interest in all Fawcett's intellectual pursuits, and shared his main political principles. They published together a volume of lectures and essays, which is sufficient to show that in political and social questions their alliance implied the agreement of independent minds, not the relation of teacher and disciple. In the prefaces to his books, Fawcett invariably acknowledges with due gratitude the assistance which he had received from his wife's revision and suggestions. He took an equally keen interest in her independent writings. When Mrs. Fawcett was invited to address a meeting at Brighton upon women's suffrage, some of his constituents protested that it would cause a prejudice against himself. Fawcett emphatically refused to listen; and he was always ready to support her efforts in a cause in which she naturally took the leading part. Those who have the best means of judging are convinced that his marriage was a main source of the happiness and success of his later career. I will only add that on one occasion Fawcett gave a public expression to his feelings during the election contest at

Brighton in February 1874. Mrs. Fawcett was starting
for a ride with her husband, when her horse fell with
her, and she was thrown with great force and rendered
unconscious.   Eye-witnesses have told me of his terrible
agony, and of the pathetic weeping of the strong man.
It was hard to persuade him that he was not being
deceived, and that the unconsciousness was not a name
for death.   Fawcett was unable to attend political meetings that night, but on the next day, February 4, he
met a large gathering in the Dome, and there made
one touching reference to his anxiety.   He thanked the
constituency which was about to reject him for its
previous generosity, and added that if he had overcome
obstacles, it was because of the assistance given by others,
and because he had had 'a helpmate whose political
judgment was much less frequently at fault than his
own.'   Many later circumstances prove that this was no
mere phrase, but an expression of his genuine feeling.

Upon his marriage, Fawcett took a house at 42
Bessborough Gardens, and in 1874 one at 51 The
Lawn, Lambeth, which he occupied during the parliamentary sessions until his death.   The last house, with
which his friends especially associate his memory, is
in a region not very attractive at first sight.   It is
within hearing of the ceaseless roar of trains at Vauxhall
Station, in the smoky and grimy neighbourhood which
welcomes the astonished stranger on entering London
by the South-Western Railway.   But it had the great
recommendation that it was within an easy walk, chiefly
along the Embankment, of Westminster Bridge and the
Houses of Parliament.   The inferiority of the district

in a social sense implied cheapness, and therefore enabled him to have a strip of garden, about three-quarters of an acre in extent, in which he could at any moment enjoy a stroll. It included a couple of small greenhouses, in which he could raise flowers, and it was his special pride to send presents of asparagus and sea-kale to his parents to show the superiority of the London climate for the growth of vegetables. The house itself was small, but a very pretty old-fashioned residence, suitably adorned by the taste of his wife. In this he always took a lively pleasure. He preserved a letter from his friend, Munro, apparently on account of a reference to their house at Cambridge. 'Again and again,' says this gentleman, 'I have been on the way to call on you and Mrs. Fawcett and see your new house, the beauty and taste of the decorations of which throw, I am told, my own poor rooms entirely in the shade.' The said 'poor rooms,' it should be added, were amongst the sights of the most distinguished college at Cambridge.

During his periods of residence he lived in furnished houses in various parts of Cambridge, until in 1874 he took a lease of 18 Brookside. He was always glad to run down during intervals of his parliamentary work, and occasionally occupied rooms in his old college. At Cambridge he made a special point of keeping up sociable relations with old friends and cultivating the younger men who were graduating and taking their place as Fellows. Fawcett was not only sociable but a really serviceable friend. No one was a better adviser on all matters within his scope. He was at once cordially sympathetic and scrupulously careful not to encourage false hopes

K

or give way to personal partialities. In the old college meetings I can remember more than one occasion on which his strong sense of justice came into effective play. No one was more righteously indignant than he when he fancied (erroneously or otherwise) that some attempt was being made to dispose of just claims by a side-wind. He hated all injustice, and injustice complicated by a want of straightforwardness was the fault most opposed to his whole nature. I do not say that there was any risk of such errors being committed even in Fawcett's absence; but, so long as he was present, there was small chance indeed of their escaping notice or succeeding in spite of it.

He thus acquired a very strong popularity amongst the younger men of his old college, as well as in the University generally. A strong proof of this was given on the death of the Master, T. C. Geldart, on September 17, 1877. The Mastership is not one of great value. The salary is that of two Fellowships, and it gives also a right to occupy the lodge. It would, however, have this advantage—that, as the duties are scarcely more than nominal, Fawcett would be able to hold it permanently even if he should abandon his professorship. Residence is not obligatory, though half the salary depends upon residence for a certain period. Fawcett's popularity amongst the junior Fellows seemed to give him a good prospect of success. Whatever the fairness of elections to Fellowships, the same character hardly attaches to elections for Masterships. They have generally been considered as sinecures, in the appointment to which personal friendships and private interests may have their share; and many legends are current in Cambridge combination rooms of the peculiar practices which have sometimes been brought to bear. On the present occasion no vote was determined by private interest; but a very warm dispute arose and some temporary bitterness of feeling. The first meeting for election was held on October 6, when the votes of the twelve electors present were equally divided between Fawcett and Mr. Latham. Fawcett's wide reputation beyond the University might be alleged in his favour. On the other hand, Mr. Latham completed at Christmas, 1877, his thirtieth year of service as a college tutor. During his tenure of office, and mainly owing to his management, the college had risen from almost the lowest place to the very front rank amongst the smaller colleges. In the college, and still more in the University, there was a strong feeling that such services deserved the reward of the Mastership. On the other hand, there was a college tradition in favour of electing a layman. Trinity Hall had been, until recent changes, almost the only college at which a layman could be a Master. It had come to be a kind of principle to elect a lawyer who should maintain the legal character of the college, and at any rate not to bestow the office upon one of the class which had a monopoly elsewhere. Against this, it was again said that the election of Fawcett—a known Radical and a strong opponent of all ecclesiastical restrictions—would tend to throw the college into a Nonconformist connection; and to some prejudices this was a formidable consideration.

I need not go into the details of a contest carried on so recently. The election was adjourned to the 22nd of

December, then again to the 24th, and afterwards to
the 27th. The deadlock had so far continued. If no
election could be made the appointment would lapse
to the Chancellor. Meanwhile many and complicated
diplomatic processes had been going on to secure a solution by combining the votes on a third candidate. It
was announced at the Christmas meetings that either Sir
Alexander Cockburn or Sir Henry Sumner Maine would
be willing to accept the post. Cockburn was a contemporary of Lord Lytton at Trinity Hall; he had been Fellow
and afterwards Honorary Fellow, and was a candidate
for the Mastership on the last election in 1852. Sir
Henry Maine, though a Pembroke man, had been for
a short time tutor of Trinity Hall and held college
rooms as Professor of Civil Law. A small college has
rarely had before it such a list of distinguished candidates. At the meeting of. December 24, Fawcett proposed certain resolutions, savouring a little of the
complexity attributed to Hare's scheme, for gathering
the opinions of the Fellows on various hypotheses as to
the withdrawal of Mr. Latham and himself. No agreement could be reached, and some of the Fellows preferred
a lapse of the appointment to the Chancellor. At last,
however, the deadlock was broken up by Mr. Latham,
who proposed the retirement of Fawcett and himself and
the unanimous election of Sir Henry Maine.

The college undoubtedly secured a most distinguished
Master, eminently fitted to carry on the legal tradition;
and I believe that both the rival candidates came to be
satisfied with the result. This, like every other contest
in which Fawcett engaged, left no personal bitterness.

The principal combatants, so far from being alienated, were afterwards upon more cordial terms than before. I have, however, to say that Fawcett came to regret his own part in the contest. He had become eager, and did his best to win; but on cooler reflection he thought that a purely academical honour of this kind would mean more to Mr. Latham than to himself, and be a fitting close to a singularly successful career in a college office.

The discussion of the new statutes which followed in the next year has been already noticed. I may, therefore, here close my account of Fawcett's academical career. Radical as he was called, and as in many ways he rightly claimed to be, no staunch old Conservative or High-Churchman, from the days of Bishop Bateman downwards, was ever a more loyal member of the old foundation. His action may have tended materially to alter and, as Conservatives may hold, to lower its position. But Fawcett's intention was to develop and strengthen both the college and the University, and only to widen their influence upon every class of his countrymen. In Cambridge, his reluctance to make rash changes in the system which he valued so highly caused him to be reckoned as so Conservative that, as I have been told, it was even contemplated to nominate him as a Conservative candidate for the council. At any rate, no man could be a stauncher admirer of the high qualities, the fair play, and the manly industry which he specially loved in his favourite place. And Cambridge men soon came to return his affection, and consider him not only as one of the familiar figures of the place, but as one who had an almost unique hold upon their regard and esteem.

CHAPTER IV.

POLITICAL ECONOMY.

BEFORE following Fawcett into active life, it will be convenient to speak of his contributions to economic literature. It may be said at once that he did not claim a place beside the founders of the science. He confined himself chiefly to expounding or applying principles already enunciated by his predecessors. No new theory is specially identified with his name. In his first book, the 'Manual of Political Economy,' he frankly avows his dependence upon Mill. Mill's great treatise, he thinks, ' will be remembered amongst the most enduring literary productions of the nineteenth century.' He would not have published the 'Manual' had he thought that readers could regard it as a substitute for his teacher's work, rather than as an introduction. Some parts of the 'Manual,' indeed, especially in the first edition, are almost a summary of the corresponding passages in Mill. Fawcett was never a passive recipient of Mill's teaching, for he always tested and frequently departed from its conclusions; but he was so much a follower of Mill and of the ' orthodox ' economists, that to criticise him would be to criticise the whole school. It is only in considering the first teachers of a doctrine that such a discussion would be desirable or permissible.

Nor can it be said that Fawcett's work has any special claims to consideration on the ground of literary elegance. He never attempts rhetoric or epigram, or adduces such felicitous illustrations from remote departments of speculation as enliven the pages of some economists. His style is a good plain homespun, thoroughly congenial to the substantial merits of his work. For the 'Manual' has striking merits as an exposition of the orthodox creed. It shows in every page the downright masculine thinker, thoroughly convinced of the truth and importance of the doctrines set forth. He is less anxious to be elegant than to be clear and solid, and he wins the respect of his readers even where he does not produce full conviction. He has the merit—much rarer in such a case—of remarkable freshness. He writes as from personal experience. The true secret of his success is given in the incidental remark, that we can only become familiar with economical principles by applying them to the problems ' suggested by the facts of everyday life.' It is to his constant observance of this precept in his own case that the book owes its highest merit. The doctrines are no mere playthings for the schools. They will stand the test of real work, for they are selected by a real worker, and expressed in the forms which he has found helpful in his own labours. Fawcett prepared himself in the first instance, not only by studying Mill, but by obtaining information from official sources and from men of practical experience, such as the founders of the 'Rochdale pioneers,' with whom he had much correspondence in the years 1859-60. He carefully revised every later edition of the book, re-writing many chapters with a view to the latest discussion on the subject. His books on ' The Economic Position of the British Labourer,' on ' Pauperism,' and on ' Free Trade and Protection ' may be put in the same class. Some of Fawcett's writings (a list of which will be found in the Appendix) will be more properly noticed in the story of his active life. Those of which I now speak are of less special application; but they lay down so clearly the principles by which his public conduct was invariably guided, that some account of them will form the best introduction to an account of his political career.

Fawcett was an economist almost from his infancy. His shrewd mathematical understanding and remarkable command of figures made him a born statistician. He took positive pleasure in dealing with a budget or a balance-sheet. He was therefore attracted rather than repelled even by the driest parts of his subject. The Preface to the ' Manual ' expresses his confidence that an acquaintance with the first principles of political economy will produce such a perception of its ' attractiveness and importance ' that the study once begun will not be relinquished. He once asked me, purely in the tone of a man applying for information, why Carlyle called political economy the ' dismal science ' ? Few of Carlyle's oracular sayings require less interpretation for the average reader.

The antagonism between the disciples of Mill and the disciples of Carlyle upon this topic is indeed significant. Mr. Ruskin once challenged Fawcett to a discussion upon the first principles of political economy. Fawcett sensibly declined a discussion which would at most have been an amusing illustration of argument at cross purposes, with an utter absence of any common ground. I should conjecture that, in any case, part of Mr. Ruskin's assault would have been represented by the statement that political economy is radically opposed to Christianity. Political economists, as Mr. Froude puts it in his 'Life of Carlyle,' hold that the proper end of man is money-making, whereas Christians profess to hold that the love of money is the root of all evil. The antithesis is therefore complete.

Fawcett's answer to assaults of this kind was simple. Political economy, in the first place, is a science, not a code of morality. It deals with 'laws' in the scientific, not in the moral sense. It tell us what actually happens, not what ought to happen. It does not pronounce the 'proper end of man' to be money-making, or to be anything else. It confines itself to showing what are, in point of fact, the conditions and the consequences of money-making and money-spending. The economist, as such, no more assumes that the *summum bonum* of man is to make money than the physiologist assumes that the *summum bonum* is to digest. A newspaper article which Fawcett was fond of quoting described Malthus as a morose and coldhearted old man, whose principles were now happily exploded. Both statements are curiously wide of the mark; but, in any case, the warmth or coldness of Malthus's heart has no more to do with the validity of his principles than the moral qualities of Newton with the validity of the law of gravitation. Malthus's 'law' is a statement of general fact: it is true or false, but is no more right or wrong in the ethical sense than the statement that the planets describe their orbits under the influence of gravitation.

Our scientific theory and our ethical system are, indeed, closely connected. A strong conviction as to the facts implies almost necessarily certain moral prepossessions. St. Simeon Stylites, one may conjecture, would have cared little for theories of supply and demand. The more ascetic the religious principle the greater will be the indifference to all theories of money-making; and, conversely, interest in such theories generally implies a belief in the innocence of the pursuit. If we are convinced that the love of money is the root of all evil, we shall be the less disposed to investigate calmly the workings of the evil principle. Before admitting, however, that Christians are bound to condemn professors of economic science, we must venture to ask, What is really the Christian view? Is all love of money bad? So far as love of money means greed and selfishness it means qualities condemned by all moralists. But love of money or desire for wealth includes, in the language of economists, the hatred of starvation. Nine men out of ten desire wealth chiefly in the sense of wishing to supply the most pressing material wants of themselves and their wives and children. It is with this desire that economists are mainly concerned. Does Christianity condemn such a desire as radically evil? If so, Christians will doubtless condemn most teachers of political economy. If, however, Christianity admits that such a desire is innocent or even praiseworthy, Christians may sanction the morality generally taught by economists. Whether consistently or inconsistently, most Christians of the present day disavow the extreme asceticism of some earlier teachers. The rhetoricians who denounce political economists take advantage of the equivocation. Political economists, they declare, are un-Christian. That is true, but not damnatory, if all who object to the grinding poverty of the masses are un-Christian. It is damnatory, but not true, if those alone are un-Christian who refuse to condemn selfishness, luxury, and avarice. Political economists are proved to be 'un-Christian' in the first sense, and reviled for being 'un-Christian' in the second sense.

I think, indeed, that Carlyle was justified in some applications of his scorn. Some of the older economists may be plausibly, and I think truly, accused of having looked too exclusively and complacently upon the growth of national wealth without considering its diffusion. They took for granted too easily that when some grew rich all would be made happier. They were inclined to the practical fatalism which regarded the helpless poverty of the millions as the normal and inevitable condition of things. They were often blind to many vital conditions of national welfare which lay outside their own special sphere. But, however true this might be of some reasoners (and it would be necessary to make great deductions from this admission if I were writing a history of the study), it was more nearly the reverse of the truth when applied to men like Mill and Fawcett. They will not receive the barest justice unless we fully recognise the fact that their interest in political economy was

rooted in an ardent desire for the elevation of the masses.
That is no mere phrase, but an expression of their
strongest convictions. Fawcett's great principle (which,
of course, he shared with Mill) was one which would
only be disputed in general terms by an Egyptian an-
chorite or an Indian faquir. Live in camel's-hair raiment,
and you may fairly denounce the rich and regard poverty
as a blessing. Fawcett, who preferred broadcloth, held
that the master evil of the day was the crushing poverty
of great masses of the population. To make men better,
you must make them richer—that is, less abjectly poor,
less stunted and shackled by the ceaseless pressure of
hard, material necessities. Religious, moral, and intellectual reforms are urgently needed, but they cannot
become fruitful unless the soil be prepared. Apply all
your elevating influences, but also drive the wolf from
the door or they will never have fair play. Men ought
to desire more, or rather ought to have further-reaching
desires. They should be more prudent and thoughtful—
oftener at the savings' bank and less often at the public-
house. That was the pith of Fawcett's teaching as an
economist, and few who call themselves Christians will
admit that it is condemned by Christianity. Fawcett
often referred to a little anecdote which gives the key to
his real sentiment. A common friend remembers how
strongly Mill was affected when Fawcett related the incident in conversation. Fawcett went to see a Wiltshire
labourer—a man of more than average ability—and found
him going to bed at the dusk of a winter day. The man
gave as his reason that he could not afford to buy candles,
and that, even if he could, he had not learnt to read.

Why should he spend money uselessly or sit up in the dark? And how, asked Fawcett, could such a man's spirit be raised or his interests widened, whilst he had to keep a wife and family on 9s. a week? That was Cobbett's old question, not answered, as it now turned out, by the disfranchisement of Old Sarum. Mr. George has recently excited the public mind by asking it in order to suggest a very different remedy. Fawcett had put the same question with equal lucidity. After giving the familiar statistics about the growth of national wealth, he asks[1] again and again, Why has this increase of wealth done so little for the poorest? 'Let us endeavour,' he says, 'to understand the true causes of poverty.' That is the vital problem. His answer differs from that of his opponents, for he applies a different method. It is the method of a man of science, not that of an inspired reformer. He wishes, like Spinoza, 'neither to mock, to bewail, nor to denounce men's actions, but to understand them.' Most people prefer the denouncing and bewailing, and consistently object to those who think it essential to begin by constructing as coolly and completely as they can a tenable theory of the true causes of poverty, or (which is the same thing) of the true causes of wealth. Shrieking is easier and more popular. Fawcett preferred, with such helps as lay at hand, to study the question first and propose remedies afterwards; but he was as anxious as any philanthropist that sound remedies should be discovered and applied.

The different, and far more difficult, question remains: how far the method adopted by Mill and Fawcett was

[1] *E.g., Manual* (1st ed.), p. 154.

sound, or the conclusions to which it led them valid?
Mill, and his most original disciple, Cairnes, held that
a science of political economy had been definitely constituted. The foundations were securely laid, and we
might proceed to erect a superstructure. They were
apt to regard opponents as illustrating Hobbes's famous
aphorism: 'If reason be against a man, a man will be
against reason.' Some people would argue against
Euclid as readily as against Malthus, if they had an
interest in maintaining that two sides of a triangle were
less than the third. On the other hand, recent doubts
as to the finality and completeness of the science have
led to depreciation of its value, even within its own
sphere. If political economy be not a science, is it
not a mere bundle of prejudices? Our guides are not
infallible. Should we follow them, even upon their own
ground? Such doubts, rightly or wrongly, have clearly
tended to discredit the old doctrines in public opinion,
and even its professors have abated something of the old
authoritative tone. The great cause of misunderstanding
lies in the very nature of the method adopted. Political
economy, as all its teachers admit in one sense or
other, begins by making an abstraction. It deals in
the facts, only so far as they come within a certain
category. Every social phenomenon, even if it has an
economic aspect, has other aspects which must be remembered when we pass to concrete applications. The
abstraction, as a logical artifice, is not merely convenient,
but necessary, in the discussion of all complex industrial
phenomena. It may, however, lead, if its true nature
be not recognised, to important errors in practice—to a

one-sided dealing with the most vital problems, and an attempt to settle great social questions upon grounds which leave out of sight the most essential considerations. Ample illustrations of such fallacious processes might be drawn from the writings of distinguished economists. On the other hand, the weakness of the more impulsive and imaginative minds is that they instinctively resent all analysis. They think that to take one question at a time is to ignore all other questions. Not content with pointing out the danger of a misunderstanding, they denounce the method itself. They decline to reason upon the only terms on which any approach to scientific reasoning is possible. Instead of saying, as may be truly said, that the most vital laws of social growth cannot be deduced from economical formulæ about supply and demand, they refuse to pay any attention to arguments in which the application of such formulæ is essential, within a certain sphere, to all sound reasoning.

Political economy, as the word is generally understood, includes many inquiries corresponding to the various elements of the problem which come successively into view. The narrowest and driest part of the subject corresponds to the old theory, according to which, political economy was simply a kind of national book-keeping. From this point of view the economist was mainly occupied with the old problems about the balance of trade, the ebb and flow of the currency, and the effects upon prices of variations of supply and demand in different branches of trade. Such problems are analogous to questions about the equilibrium of the forces in a piece of mechanism, and may be discussed without taking into

account principles other than such as may be called
mechanical. It may freely be granted that these discussions form a tolerably 'dismal science.' Arguments
as to the Bank Charter Act or the advantages of 'Bi-
metallism' are amongst the dreariest to which the human
intellect can apply itself. They are the chosen ground
upon which the most consummate bore delights to dis-
port himself. It would, however, be silly to deny the advantage of forming sound opinion upon questions of this
class. If dry, they are not barren. It is not amusing to
inquire into the principles involved in a sound currency;
but the possession of a sound currency system is of vast
importance to the welfare of a nation.

For questions of this order, Fawcett had a genuine aptitude. He possessed the logical faculties which enabled
him to argue them forcibly, and the exercise of the
faculties was a source of genuine pleasure. Some of his
earliest essays deal with the effects of the great discoveries
of gold. He lectured at Warminster on March 7, 1858,
on the rather ambitious topic of 'Spain and England.'
The lecture is mainly an attempt to compare the effects
of the gold discoveries of the Spaniards in America with
the effects of the later gold discoveries in California and
Australia. The drain of precious metals to the East is
noticed in this lecture, and occupied him at intervals
during many years. An early paper upon this subject
at the British Association meeting at Aberdeen in 1859
attracted the notice of Cairnes, Jevons, and other economists; and, in later years, his interest in the subject
qualified him for speaking weightily upon one of the
most perplexing difficulties of Indian finance. In the

first edition of the 'Manual' he shows his command of similar questions in an independent criticism of Mill's opinions upon the currency. His thorough command of intricate considerations involved, puts the remarkable independence and soundness of his judgment in the clearest light.

If a mastery of currency questions takes us but a short step towards the solution of deeper social problems, it is not the less true that it is a step of importance. Till we have made it, our footing is unsafe. For the social quack finds one of his favourite lurking places amidst the intricacies and perplexities of these regions. There he can find plausible cover for the various nostrums which are to remedy all social evils by some ingenious sophistication. Sound book-keeping will not, by itself, make a prosperous merchant, nor supply the place of industry and honesty. But it is not less important that a merchant should keep his books accurately, if he would avoid the most ruinous illusions. Political economy, considered merely as national book-keeping, has a similar value. Figures, we know, can be made to prove anything. Although dexterous book-keeping cannot alter facts, it may mystify the ignorant. Mystification on a large scale is the great weapon of economical sophists. They have been able to disguise bankruptcy and the plunder of creditors under plausible names, and to prove that a nation can be made rich or poor by processes which amount to skilful manipulation of balance-sheets. To unravel their labyrinthine sophistries is an excellent application of a clear intellect.

Thus, for example, many of the arguments still

current in regard to the question of free trade and protection are simply a rehabilitation of old sophistries of
this class. The ancient fallacy of the balance of trade
constantly reappears, and may be exposed without going
beyond a sound theory of supply and demand. To these
questions Fawcett had paid special attention. He gave
a course of lectures in the October Term, 1877, which
were published as ' Free Trade and Protection ' in 1878,
and have just (1885) reached a sixth edition. It is
perhaps his ablest book. It is singularly terse, tempe-
rate, and exhaustive. He had spent much time and
labour in studying the arguments of the heretics, and
had got up the most recent statistics with his usual
command of figures. The result is, I think, an unanswerable refutation within a moderate space of the
leading arguments of his opponents. He can, of course,
advance no arguments of substantial novelty upon so
well-worn a topic. But as a thorough-going application of established principles to recent facts, his book is
masterly and conclusive.

One conspicuous merit of Fawcett's book is his clear
perception of the true logical limitations of his inquiry.
He carefully limits himself, in the first place, to the
purely commercial argument. The function of the
economist is simply to show what is the actual profit or
loss due to a certain policy. When he has shown the
economical advantage or disadvantage of a given tax or
duty, he has fulfilled his proper function. It is still open
to the statesman to argue, if he pleases, that political considerations make it worth while to incur the loss, or,
possibly, that some ulterior social benefit may arise from

the temporary sacrifice of commercial profits. What Fawcett attempts to prove, and, as I think, proves triumphantly, is simply that protection implies a sacrifice, and not, as his opponents maintain, an immediate advantage. His argument is limited in another sense, which deserves special attention. Opponents of free trade often take advantage of the vulgar prejudice against theorists. They call upon us to prefer practical men to abstract reasoners and the spinners of pretended sciences. In point of fact, the protectionist is at least as open to this line of attack as his opponent. He has quite as definite a theory. The misfortune is that his theory is self-contradictory. He asks for a tax in order to encourage trade. The assumed connection between the suggested cause and the anticipated effect is a theory just as much as the contrary assertion. Fawcett points out that it is a theory made out by an arbitrary selection of one set of consequences. It assumes that we may fix our minds exclusively upon the advantages gained by one class of producers, without attending to the consumers or the nation generally. Explicitly and fairly stated, the arguments generally advanced by protectionists may, as he urges, be shown to involve a variety of familiar fallacies. They take for granted that wealth consists exclusively of money; or that we can buy without selling; or that a people as a whole can be enriched by transferring wealth from one set of pockets to another; or that arguments, admittedly true in respect of provinces, cease to be true when the provinces are called states. Their reasoning would imply that you can increase the volume of a stream by pumping water from below to pour it into the source ; or that it would be wise to darken the sun to encourage the gas companies; or, as Mandeville urged, that the fire of London was an advantage, because it gave employment to the masons and carpenters. To press home these fallacies, to show that they were essentially involved in the protectionist theory, was Fawcett's aim. He does not, so far, set up a rival theory, nor is he under any obligation to do so. A proposed tax is justified by a theory. The theory cannot be right, for it contradicts itself, or leads to admitted absurdities. Therefore the policy which embodies the theory cannot be wise. To admit this is to give up the whole case; for it is all that Fawcett urges. His theory is simply that his opponents' theory is inconsistent with itself; and unless they can meet this contention, they are so far confuted. A direct appeal to facts is of course still open. It may be urged that, theory or no theory, protectionist countries prosper, and free-trading countries decline. On this ground, Fawcett was fully prepared to meet his adversaries ; but with this I am not at present concerned.

Political economy, which to the popular mind meant chiefly the theory of free trade, has so far what may be called a negative value. It is, in substance, a negation of vital errors. It does not set up in their place a positive theory as to the conditions of prosperous trade. Certain restrictions are bad, because they imply inconsistent aims. It does not follow that the mere absence of bad restrictions will make trade prosperous. The conditions of prosperity include such things as honesty, energy, industry, and social welfare generally, which lie to a great extent beyond the sphere of the economist.

Moreover, a belief in free trade is not even, as Fawcett was careful to say, necessarily connected with an acceptance of the general principle of *laissez-faire*. The clearest proof that this mode of State interference is foolish does not prove (though it may suggest some presumption) that all modes of State interference with trade are absurd. Some of them are clearly not obnoxious to the same objections. It would be as wrong to lay down the general principle at once as to say that because the old method of bleeding was mischievous, therefore all surgical operations must be mischievous. It is conceivable, so far at any rate, that the State may foster commerce by judicious methods, though the kind of interference most generally adopted has been injudicious because hopelessly illogical.

The importance of these considerations appears, as I think, equally in regard to those deeper social questions in which Fawcett found his main impulse to the study. Political economy, as I venture to think, has been especially valuable in what I have called its negative aspect. It has been more efficient in dispersing sophistries than in constructing permanent theories. Economic writers have exploded many absurd systems, though, unfortunately, a system too often survives when its absurdity has been demonstrated. They have so far cleared the way for an application of sounder methods. But the complexity of the problem is so great, and the working of industrial forces so essentially bound up with other more inscrutable forces, that I confess to a certain scepticism as to the truly scientific character of their more positive conclusions. The importance, however, of the service rendered by clearing the air of sophistry is not diminished. An important illustration of the principle may be found in one of the most fundamental economic principles. The great book of Malthus was first suggested by the facile optimism of Godwin and his followers. He was accused of brutality and heartlessness because he brought out with unanswerable force a fatal obstacle to the schemes by which mankind was to be regenerated out of hand. The Malthusian doctrine is for that reason still a stumbling-block with all believers in some speedily attainable Utopia. Its importance in the history of political economy is comparable to the importance of Darwin's generalisation of the same principle in the history of recent speculation. Fawcett, in particular, was profoundly impressed by the teaching of Malthus. He always speaks of Malthus with especial respect, and retorts the scorn of the popular assailants of his vital principle. Malthus was not the first to call attention to the evils which he specially denounced. Nobody is ever first in such discoveries. Nor was he aware—no one is ever aware—of the full import of his own theories. But his theory was of the highest importance because it involved the implicit recognition of a cardinal truth. A great principle which lay beneath his arguments is now more generally recognised. Society is not a mere aggregate of independent atoms, but a complex living organism. However faulty may be its operations, it represents a system worked out by the experience of generations. Its structure has been developed by the wants of mankind ; the principles on which it rests have been felt out, not reasoned out ; and though it is undoubtedly in need

of constant improvement and, perhaps, of thorough reconstruction, genuine reform is only possible by a careful
examination of the functions discharged by its various
constituent parts and a provision for the wants by which
their constitution has been actually, if unconsciously,
determined. The rash reformers, who undertake to cut
and carve and re-mould in obedience to some à priori
guesses, or in wrath provoked by real grievances, are
mangling it at the risk of vital injury. Malthus confined
himself to a particular application of this truth. The
revolutionists, as he showed, had mistaken the nature
of the evil which they proposed to cure. Lazarus, they
said, is starving whilst Dives is revelling; yet Lazarus
is as good a man as Dives. The remedy is obvious.
Cut up Dives and distribute his wealth amongst the
multitudinous representatives of Lazarus. Malthus
pointed out that, unluckily, Lazarus was capable of indefinite multiplication. To relieve a pauper may be a
blessing for the individual pauper; but, if the pauper
class multiplies in proportion to the relief bestowed, the
end of charity is the boundless increase of the class of
paupers. The remedy is therefore founded on a neglect
of the most important fact. You are not simply redis-
tributing wealth amongst a set of independent and invariable units, but trying to tamper with the processes
of growth and nutrition of a living organism. Granting
that the unequal distribution of wealth involves gross
injustice, it has yet been a condition of all progress
above barbarism, and must be a condition of further
progress until at least some radical remedy can be
worked out. When, therefore, Godwin and the believers

in 'perfectibility' anticipated, as the result of absolute equality, a vast population governed only by pure laws of reason, Malthus pointed out the inevitable obstacles. Population has an indefinite elasticity. It is already pressing everywhere upon its means of support. War, famine, and disease are the 'positive checks' which keep it within bound. They are the symptoms of the universal 'struggle for existence.' The only real remedy is to encourage the 'preventive check'—in other words, to raise the standard of prudence, which will make the struggle less severe and diminish the operation of the causes of the worst evils which afflict mankind.

I need not inquire how far Malthus himself was led into a misstatement of his argument, and gave a pretext for the common accusation of his opponents that he looked upon the 'positive checks' as a providential, and therefore inevitable, arrangement. Fawcett, at any rate, took him in the sounder sense. Poverty and its attendant evils may be diminished, but diminished only by judicious measures, by looking beyond the momentary need, and especially by raising the moral standard of the poor themselves. Whoever professes to raise the position of a class without elevating its character is a charlatan. The principle was especially relevant to the great question of pauperism, upon which he had thought much and felt strongly from his earliest years. The crying evils which led to the new poor-law system of 1834 had made the subject sufficiently familiar to the economists of Fawcett's school. He differed from many contemporaries, not in his theory, but in the strength of his convictions and of his aversion to the method of the mere sentimentalists. He held that the poor-law system was responsible for a great deal of the misery which it professed to remedy. The principle is, of course, simple, and had been more or less recognised by many observers in pre-Malthusian periods. By the generation of economists which followed Malthus it had been both expounded and partly applied in legislation. Fawcett was strongly impressed by the necessity of maintaining and extending their views. The relief of beggars, as we all know, may come to mean the support of beggary as a permanent institution. 'You may have as many paupers as you choose to pay for,' was a phrase of his friend Clarke, often on his lips. His book upon 'Pauperism' gave a forcible application of this principle. It helped in particular to call attention to the abuses springing from a lax administration of outdoor relief. A poor-law inspector, in one of whose reports Fawcett had been greatly interested, says some years later that his first clear ideas upon the subject had been derived from Fawcett's book. Fawcett brought home, in this as in many cases, the 'theoretical' objection to men of practical experience. One special application may be cited in illustration of his method. The 'boarding-out' system had at this time (1871), as he says, received the unanimous approval of the press. Kindly philanthropists had been content to contrast the comfort of the rescued children with their previous misery. Fawcett points out the set-off to the benefit. The system, in the form advocated by enthusiasts, meant, as their figures proved, that a labourer might receive as much for the support of two pauper children as he would gain by his whole labour for him-

self and his family. A man, therefore, would do better
for his children by deserting them than by maintaining
them. It would be an act of folly to provide for his
family by insuring his life. He would do better for his
children as well as for himself by raising an illegitimate,
than by raising a legitimate, family. The prudent, who
supported their own children, would be taxed for the
support of the immoral and the imprudent. So soon,
therefore, as the system began to work there would be a
direct discouragement to prudence and a premium upon
demoralisation. Even if we suppose that some safeguard
may be found against these abuses, no safeguard was
contemplated in the scheme actually proposed. In any
case, therefore, Fawcett was calling attention to a
danger overlooked by philanthropists, which threatened
the moral standard of the class which they desired to
benefit. No one, I think, can doubt the extreme importance of these warnings, or the danger of shutting our eyes
to such consequences in the name of a spurious charity.

Fawcett, it must be observed, admitted fully that the
poor-law was a practical necessity. He saw and regretted the socialistic tendency involved in it. But he
held, not merely that it could not in fact be abolished,
but that it might be worked in accordance with his
fundamental principle. If the mischievous system of
outdoor relief were duly restricted, and the principle of
local responsibility maintained, it might serve to correct
the worse evil of promiscuous charity, and prevent the
bitterness which prevails where the State simply washes
its hands of all responsibility. His real principle,
moreover, was not that of absolute non-interference.

The 'crucial test,' he says, 'of the value of all agencies which are brought into operation to improve the condition of the labouring poor is this: Do they exert a direct tendency to make the labourer rely upon self-help?' This in fact was the fundamental consideration. It does not condemn all attempts at meeting the evil, but those alone which really stimulate the true cause of the evil. Wise Malthusians do not proclaim an absolute *non-possumus*: they only assign one necessary condition of all permanent improvement. The 'preventive check' must be brought into play. In other words, men must be made more prudent and self-reliant, or all the schemes of reformers will be a mere weaving of ropes of sand. This principle runs through all Fawcett's criticisms of schemes for the amelioration of the poorer classes.

Other great principles, generally associated with the name of Ricardo, are connected with that of Malthus. Malthus had pointed out how the struggle for existence imposes certain conditions upon the growth of society as a whole. Its internal structure is equally determined by that struggle. Society becomes organised into classes in attempting to meet the pressure upon the means of subsistence. Those who are able to secure certain natural advantages become possessors of a monopoly, the nature of which is explained by the theory of rent. The class, again, which lives from hand to mouth must depend upon the wealth accumulated by others, and by trying to work out the conditions on which they will secure a share of the products, we reach the theory of the 'wage-fund.' Rent constitutes a separate fund, rigidly defined by natural conditions, which may belong to a special class, or be

appropriated by Government, or distributed amongst the
actual labourers, but which in any case grows according to certain laws as the social pressure on a given area
increases.   The labourer's wage depends equally on fixed
conditions.   To increase it is to diminish the share of
the capitalist and therefore to retard the accumulation of
capital.   To diminish it would conversely increase profits
and   therefore   the   wage-fund.   There   is   therefore   a
fixed rate about which the actual rate may oscillate, but
from which it can never permanently or widely diverge.
By the help of various assumptions which I need not
pause to specify, the whole economist theory is thus
rounded   off   and   assumes   a   kind   of   mathematical
symmetry.   If the labouring class chooses always to
multiply up to the verge of its means of subsistence, the
rule is greatly simplified and gives rise to what has been
called the 'iron law' of Ricardo.   His critics, as the
phrase implies, sometimes speak as if he had intended
to demonstrate the absolute impossibility of a permanent
rise of wages.   That is only true on the assumption of
the improvidence of the labouring class.   His argument
is substantially that they can only raise the price of their
services by limiting the supply—that is, by keeping down
their own numbers.   Assuming that they have sufficient
self-command to raise the standard of comfort, the action
of supply and demand will be in their favour, as, in the
contrary case, it will be against them.

The doctrine thus elaborated was used to crush all
manner of socialist schemes, and used with the air of conclusive demonstration.   Socialists denounced it, without
perhaps taking the trouble to understand it ; and political

economists were supposed to accept a fatalistic theory, announcing the utter impossibility of all schemes for social regeneration. Fawcett, of course, did not accept this reading of their doctrines. Economists, he held, pointed out the crucial difficulty, and a clear recognition of its nature must be the first step towards surmounting it. Fawcett was himself satisfied of the substantial truth of the wage-fund theory. He, like Cairnes, adhered to it when Mill abandoned it in consequence of Thornton's attack. In the first edition of his 'Manual' Fawcett used some unguarded phrases which have been quoted against him. He pronounces it to be 'physically impossible that any permanent rise in wages should take place without a corresponding diminution of profit.'[1] In later editions, the chapter was rewritten, and this statement disappeared. Even in the first edition there are explanations which considerably modify the sweeping character of the phrase just quoted. He was, however, fully satisfied of the general validity of the main principle. He held that it really contained the fatal objection to the crude schemes of socialism. Hasty thinkers assume, whether consciously or otherwise, that the rate of wages is something arbitrary, which can be fixed by the will of legislators or indefinitely altered by an agreement between the parties concerned. They attribute therefore the inadequate remuneration to the tyranny or avarice of the employers. Fawcett insisted upon the necessity of looking beyond this to the permanent conditions imposed by the structure of society. The rate of wages is fixed by such conditions,

[1] *Manual* (1st ed.), p. 264.

even though the economic theory may be in various ways
an imperfect expression of their precise nature. A
summary interference will defeat its own ends. The
necessity of attracting capital; the impossibility of arbi-
trarily raising wages without interfering with the profits
of others, and diminishing the immediate demand for
labour is undoubtedly one of the main conditions of the
problem. It may be stated too absolutely, but cannot be
neglected without fatal consequences.

Fawcett did not speak as a mere closet theorist. On
several occasions he discussed these questions with large
bodies of artisans. He had visited Manchester, as we
have seen, so early as 1857, to examine social questions.
He had made the personal acquaintance of the leaders
in the remarkable co-operative movement at Rochdale.
In 1859 he discussed the question of strikes at the meeting
of the Social Science Association at Bradford. Sir James
Kay Shuttleworth, who presided, was much struck by his
speech; and at Shuttleworth's request he held a meeting
at St. Martin's Hall in the following spring, and dis-
coursed very successfully to the workmen, then excited
by a great strike in the building trade, upon the true
principles of political economy. A Tory statesman and
friend came to him on this occasion to say that he
thought him the most dangerous man in England.
Fawcett had, again, a remarkable conference at Sheffield
on October 11, 1865, with the Filesmiths' Union. The
men defended themselves against the charge of encouraging outrages, whilst they expressed their strong dislike to a proposed introduction of machinery. Fawcett
argued with them frankly and forcibly. He denounced

intimidation, and pointed out the risk of their cutting their own throats by driving business elsewhere. His theories were thus strengthened by a familiarity with the immediate practical arguments which could be brought home to sensible men on both sides. Even if his doctrine was too rigid, it was thoroughly to the point, and brought out the merits of the actual discussions in workshops and counting-houses.

So far Fawcett's teaching fell in with that *laissez-faire* doctrine which was generally ascribed to economists of his school, and which is now, it appears, rather out of fashion. It is represented by enthusiasts as a barren fatalism, and an excuse for evading the most important problems of the day. If it be true, they say, the struggle for existence must be allowed to work itself out; all that rulers can do is to stand by, keep the peace, and let the poor starve, to teach them that poverty is an evil. I have tried to show that Fawcett was as far as possible from holding that because difficulties must not be blinked they must be regarded as insuperable. He was also far from holding that Government could safely or justly limit itself to a mere policy of inaction. The point is one of great importance in regard to his whole career, and deserves a brief consideration.

Fawcett's intellect, as I have said, was eminently shrewd and practical. He cared comparatively little for abstract discussions of the primary grounds of political or ethical principles. He was content, so far as he cared at all, to take his doctrine pretty directly from Mill. I do not think that he was specially interested in the more abstract arguments against State interference advanced by some theorists. He refers indeed to Mr. Spencer [1] as giving 'the most powerful and exhaustive statement' of the argument on that side. But he regards the association of political economy with the *laissez-faire* school as in some sense 'accidental.' To my mind this is of doubtful accuracy; but it is true that, upon Mill's principles, the *à priori* objections to State interference are scarcely available. Fawcett only followed his teacher in declaring, emphatically and frequently, that every proposed measure must be considered on its own merits. He observes that opponents of socialism are accused of being slaves to the *laissez-faire* theory. He is, on the contrary, 'quite prepared to admit that nothing is more hazardous than to pay a too implicit obedience to any such principle.' He frequently repeats the same view with even greater emphasis in regard, for example, to such questions as State education. He is, in brief, a consistent empiricist. The one general principle is that Government should do what experience proves it can do efficiently.

It is, however, undeniable that on most of the important questions of the day Fawcett's judgment was on the side of non-interference. His strong objection to increased action of the State separated him emphatically from a large and growing section of his own party. He adhered to the doctrines of the earlier Radicals, and saw a serious danger in the leaning of their successors to the socialistic movement. This was not simply the result of what was certainly a characteristic of his powerful mind —an indisposition to accept new theories which occasionally savoured too much of unreasoning prejudice.

[1] *Essays and Lectures*, p. 32.

He was, in fact, governed by a principle already stated. He held, as I have said, that each case must be tested by itself. He therefore did not consider himself entitled to reject any proposal without further hearing on the ground of its incompatibility with some general formula. He asked whether it could or could not be supported by specific reasoning, and in his own arguments he always relies upon definite practical objections. But his real conviction appears from the test which he invariably applies. It is that which, as we have already seen, he calls the ' crucial test ' in all proposed remedies for poverty : Does the remedy tend to raise or to lower the spirit of self-help ? If you make the poor more dependent, no immediate benefit will compensate for the moral injury. Help them to be prudent and self-reliant, and you do more than can be done by any machinery whatever. A society in which every class does not take its own part is one in which the surviving energy will be oppressed by an ever-growing and ultimately insuperable burden. To call out therefore the energy of all classes, to open the widest field for the application of all their faculties, is the aim which should preside over every genuine effort for social improvement. How strongly Fawcett was penetrated by this conviction will appear as we proceed.

For the present I shall only observe that the *laissez-faire* doctrine, so far as it falls in with this view, is entirely free from the blame insinuated in the popular travesty of its teaching. It implies the very reverse of any want of sympathy with suffering. The advocates of toleration are sometimes charged with indifference to truth, because they object to drive their own conceptions

M

of truth into reluctant minds by main force. They reply, triumphantly as I think, that it is precisely because they believe the power of truth that they refuse to attempt its propagation by force. A method which begins by imposing insincerity will not end by favouring truth. The case is the same in regard to other modes of State interference now less out of fashion. Fawcett's sympathy with the poor and the helpless was not only deep and genuine; it was the mainspring of his most energetic political action. For that very reason he was heartily opposed to all the quack remedies which, whilst professing the same aim, injured the only force which can permanently raise the poor—namely, their own self-respect. To him the principle of *laissez-faire* commended itself by its nobler aspect. It did not mean, Leave the blind struggle to work itself out, and apply no remedy to the most cruel grievances. It meant, on the contrary, Give free play to all men's intellects and faculties; be exceedingly jealous of all restrictions upon the energies of any class, especially of the poorest class. There is no social restriction which cannot find some appropriate plea. Slavery of the worst kind ever known was justified by the supposed interests of the slave. Privileges of all kinds, political and social, have been defended on the ground that the excluded were the better without them. Even laws which were undoubtedly the product of benevolent motive have failed wherever they have tried to force people to be better off without enabling them to be better in themselves. All new proposals therefore should be subject to a jealous scrutiny, and we should not approve till we are satisfied that the motives alleged are genuine and that the means are calculated to stimulate the energies of the persons affected instead of to force them into the mould of some mechanical system. Interference, briefly, may be tyranny in disguise, even when it makes the most virtuous professions and is really based on amiable motives. A chivalrous sympathy with the helpless is not the exclusive property of either side, but it may certainly render a man jealous of State nterference as well as eager to apply it. Whether Fawcett's view was the product of mere indifference or of a desire that sympathy should be guided by forethought and sound principle will best appear from other applications of his doctrine.

Many of the schemes of modern reformers undoubtedly sinned against his fundamental criterion. A weighty article in ' Macmillan's Magazine' for July 1883 (which has been reprinted separately, and is added to the last edition of the ' Manual ') sets forth his objections to State socialism and the nationalisation of the land. Such schemes, as he urged, regarded the State as a kind of supernatural milch cow—a body capable of making something out of nothing, of directly commanding supplies of manna from the heavens and water from the rock; whereas, in point of fact, they were simply schemes for taking money from the prudent and handing it over to the idle. On the other hand, he was from the first profoundly interested in schemes of co-operation. That system, instead of discouraging self-help, implies a voluntary process of self-education in thrift. It strikes at the evil system of credit, which directly encourages imprudence, and it enables the poor man to find invest-

ments for saving. He had been greatly impressed by
the Rochdale experiment at a time when co-operation
was comparatively in its infancy. An article upon
strikes, published in the 'Westminster Review,' which
had the honour of attracting the notice of George Eliot,
led to a more important practical result. It was read
by Mr. Briggs, of the Whitwood Colliery, at Methley,
near Leeds, and led to an adoption by the proprietors
of the system suggested by Fawcett. Throughout his
career, Fawcett was a warm advocate of the co-operative
system, and outspoken in its defence when speaking out
was by no means the way to conciliate constituents. His
zeal rather strengthened than otherwise, and towards the
end of his life he said that, if he should resign office, he
would join his friend, Mr. Sedley Taylor (author of 'Profit-
sharing between Labour and Capital'), in a systematic
attempt to promote the spread of the co-operative system.

In his first edition, Fawcett says that he has just
heard of the co-operative farms at Assington, and gives
some information supplied by their founder, Mr. Gurdon.
His permanent interest in this experiment was characteristic. Through life he kept up his interest in agriculture and his personal relations with agricultural
labourers. He speaks of his 'intimate friendship' with
some of them; his knowledge of their wants and feelings
was at first hand, and his sympathies correspondingly
keen. Mr. Wright, the Salisbury fisherman, gives me
a significant anecdote. Fawcett, after a day's fishing,
had some beer with a farmer, who told him that the
labourers' wages were to be lowered after the harvest.
Fawcett, after vainly protesting, refused more beer and

walked home. On his way he met one of his labouring friends, who accounted for his best clothes by saying that he was going to a harvest-home celebration at the church. Fawcett fell into a long reverie, and at last asked Mr. Wright how he would like to give thanks for a bountiful harvest when his wages were to be docked of a shilling a week. Such little incidents often gave him food for reflection, and this apparently prompted a letter upon the subject which appeared in the ' Times.' Many of the proposed remedies seemed to him impolitic. He accepted, to a great extent, the views of Mill and Thornton as to the advantages of peasant-proprietorship; but I think that in earlier times he thought that the English conditions were scarcely suitable to its introduction here, and he was decidedly opposed to a direct legislative attempt in that direction. The great changes in later years rather modified his opinion upon this point. His writing, however, was chiefly in support of the opinions prevalent with his school. He argued against the obstacles imposed upon the easy sale of land by settlements and entails. A better system, he thought, would make room for the desirable state of things in which the cultivators should also be the owners of the land. He had a smart controversy in 1868 with the lawyers upon the general question. Some of the experts, indeed, came to his help anonymously; though the general professional view was of course in favour of the perfection of the existing system. He would not follow Mill's theory about the ' unearned increment,' which has been turned to account by socialists. He held that proposals founded on this doctrine tended to hinder the most essential improvement, 'the free flow of capital to agriculture.'[1] He saw also that the ownership of land was in this respect in precisely the same position as other kinds of property, and that it was therefore grossly unjust to subject it to special burdens.

Co-operation was, in fact, Fawcett's great panacea. In spite of the small success which has hitherto attended its application to agriculture, he clung to this belief. He thought that co-operation would reconcile the advantages of large and small farming, and that in all industries it represented the only solution of the perpetual conflict between labour and capital. It would lead workmen to recognise the necessity of leaving sufficient profits to the capitalist, give them interest in their work, and ultimately replace some of the advantages of the old domestic system which had been broken up under the growth of gigantic factories.

Co-operation, though attacked by some rigid economists of the older generation, has won its way to general favour. Fawcett did something, along, of course, with many others, in promoting the change of opinion. The sternest advocate of *laissez-faire* might so far go with him. Co-operation was valuable in his eyes just as it was a mode of elevating the poor by the application of their own resources. But other consequences followed, where the *laissez-faire* theorist begins to have his qualms. Admitting that many modes of State interference are suicidal, admitting that the moving power must come from the energy of the labourers themselves, it may still be asked whether the State cannot do more than simply

[1] *Manual* (6th ed.), pp. 286, 7.

look on or remove the impediments which now hamper private energy. Can it not so act as to stimulate instead of simply permitting private energy ? In certain respects Fawcett held that it could, and upon these questions he separated himself from the school of absolute *laissez-faire*, or, as Professor Huxley calls it, of State nihilism. In the first place came one great question. The main obstacle to the spread of co-operation was the want of intelligence of the classes which most needed it. The labourer who had to go to bed with the sun was cut off from the intellectual influences of the superior artisan. His mental darkness isolated him ; he could not take advantage of a rise in wages elsewhere, for he heard nothing of what was going on in regions as strange to him as the remotest part of Australia. The periodical press now acts like a nervous system of the nation, spreading every central impulse to the most distant ramifications of the social body. The man who cannot read or write is out of touch with all the impulses of his day. To raise the educational standard of the labourer, especially in agricultural districts, was therefore a first condition for bringing direct impulses to bear. This, as Fawcett held, could only be done effectually by a national and unsectarian system of education. Even in his Cambridge days he had brought this question forward at the Union. It became one of his strongest political interests. As we shall see hereafter, there was no subject to which he devoted more time and attention. He spoke constantly and laboured strenuously in Parliament and elsewhere on behalf of the introduction of a compulsory system of education into the agricultural

districts.   He defended the proposal even upon the
strictest grounds of political economy.   To the argument,
for example, that such a system would impose additional
burdens upon the poor, he replied that the wages of
agricultural labourers were in fact determined, not by
open competition, but by a consideration of what was
absolutely necessary to keep soul and body together.   The
payment for schools would therefore not come out of
their pockets, but be made up in their wages.   The
employer would be repaid either by a reduction of his
rent or, it might be confidently hoped, by the increased
efficiency of new labour.   A man is repaid by keeping
his horses in good condition whilst he leaves his labourers
in a state of semi-starvation.   To use the machinery of
legislation to break up the isolation and intellectual
darkness of the agricultural labourer was an end which
thus appeared to him to be recommended by all the
principles most deeply rooted in his mind.

There were many other methods in which he held
that the State could interfere, and was therefore bound to
interfere, without infringing his fundamental principles.
Thus, for example, it may do much to encourage thrift.
The support of savings-banks, the provision of a
system of deferred annuities, and plans for facilitating
the investment of small sums in national securities,
are instances of a kind of interference which may stimulate instead of depressing the tendency to self-help.   All
such schemes had therefore his heartiest approval and,
in time, his effectual help.   His jealousy, indeed, was
not to be laid asleep.   The recent outcry about the
dwellings of the most abject classes did not lead him to

favour spasmodic remedies. At a much earlier period he had maintained that the State might legitimately do something towards improving the dwellings of the poor. But in the last edition of his ' Manual ' he points out the dangers of ineffectual administration, of burdening those who are just above pauperism by taxing them to help those who are just below, and, above all, of discouraging the efforts to self-help exemplified by the growth of building societies. In 1875 he explained with great clearness the obstacles which, as he thought, and I believe rightly, as shown by subsequent experience, would neutralise the working of Sir Richard Cross's Building Act in that year.

I have tried to show briefly how far Fawcett might be properly called an adherent of the *laissez-faire* school. He leaned generally, and I think more decidedly, as he grew older, against many applications of the opposite principle. In theory, he denied that either principle could be regarded as true without qualification. In practice he became more jealous of a tendency which was growing more pronounced. Those who approve of the tendency will of course regard him as so far antiquated or even reactionary. Others will consider him as a faithful Abdiel upholding the true Radical theory, from which modern Radicals are too apt to depart. Without arguing so wide a question, I shall only venture to suggest certain considerations, sufficient, I think, to justify Fawcett's good feeling and good sense.

Fawcett was sometimes condemned for a supposed inconsistency. It was observed that this great opponent of State action became the head of the department which,

more than any other, infringes his favourite principle.
He was active in setting up a State education which is
crushing the voluntary system, and he had a main share
in extending the action of the State in regions previously
left to private enterprise.. I have shown indeed, or tried
to show, that Fawcett was thoroughly convinced of the
propriety of State interference in these cases. That, it
may be urged, is not a sufficient apology. By encouraging State interference in cases where he approved, he
actually encouraged it in cases where he strongly disapproved. The 'logic of facts' was too strong for him.
He helped to set in motion forces which he was unable
to control.

I do not think that Fawcett would himself have
denied the partial truth of this criticism. Fawcett, like
Mill, was a democrat, and yet, like Mill, strongly convinced that democracy had a very evil side. His strong
conviction of this was shown by his persistent advocacy
of Mr. Hare's doctrine of proportional representation.
He held that in the adoption of that principle in some
form lay the only remedy against the great danger of an
oppression of minorities. Upon that question he entirely
sympathised with the views of his teacher, and his
feeling is only one more illustration of his intense hatred
of all oppression in whatever shape it may be masked.
One very important form is that of State interference.
The tendency of recent times to an extended action of
the State is only a fresh illustration of the old truth.
Power has been conceded to the ignorant and helpless.
It is only too likely that they will often use it ignorantly
and oppressively. They will fancy, as of old, that as

soon as they have votes they can order that the three-hooped pots shall have ten hoops. As the old governing classes tried to keep down the rate of wages, the new governing classes will try to raise wages by a summary process. They are the new emperor, and above the laws of political economy.

This, it may be said, is simply the old Tory doctrine. Such views may be permissible to a reactionary, but not to an advocate of democracy. Fawcett would substantially answer that adherence to democratic principles did not involve blindness to the evil side of democracy. He was a democrat, in the first place, because he thought the advance of democracy inevitable. The attempt to keep up the old system, which was incompatible with the whole tendency of social development, was hopeless and absurd. Democracy will come ; all we can do is to try to introduce it in the best shape. But he was also a democrat because he believed in the justice of the democratic principle. The old privileges were unjust, because they imposed arbitrary disqualifications upon men's employment of their own faculties. This, he argued, sinned against an indefeasible principle, and, moreover, was injurious as well as unjust. The fact that new grievances might arise does not justify us in retaining the old. But, finally, he was also a democrat because he held that democracy would be in the long run beneficial. There is a common kind of political fatalism which assumes that the fashionable principles of the day are justified by their existence, and irrevocable when once asserted. Because the new rulers of the State have fancied themselves omnipotent and adopted all kinds of quack remedies for the grievances which once seemed irremediable, it is assumed that anyone who opposes their blunders may be set aside as a mere theorist and ridiculed as an antiquated doctrinaire. Fawcett had more faith in the power of reason and the ultimate common sense of his countrymen. He saw that a new current of erroneous opinion had acquired power and carried many politicians off their legs; but he did not doubt that it might be successfully opposed and, like other prejudices, gradually dispersed by manly and outspoken criticism. And, finally, I may repeat what I have already said in regard to special cases. Fawcett followed the orthodox economists in pointing out certain grave obstacles to easy-going schemes for off-hand social regeneration. He asked for a definite and specific answer to his allegations. He never held that the obstacles were incapable of being in some way surmounted. On the contrary, it was his great aim to surmount them. But he would not ignore a difficulty because it was easier and more popular to deny its existence. Now, whatever may be thought of his views, I certainly think that he was so far amply justified. The evils may be cured; they may be cured by means not contemplated by Fawcett; but, at the very lowest, he did good service by resolutely calling attention to the difficulties in question, and by unmasking the common sophistries used by those who would ignore their existence. We must all hope that social evils may admit of some remedy; but our progress in finding a remedy will depend upon our willingness to adopt Fawcett's method of looking facts in the face and carefully considering every proposal on its merits, without giving way to the shrieks of charlatans, ready to drown all opposition to their favourite nostrums, and without flattering our new masters by assigning miraculous powers to the laws they would impose.

The application of these principles to matters political as well as economical may be briefly illustrated. If Fawcett often agreed with the *laissez-faire* theory where it condemned schemes prompted by short-sighted benevolence, he was its enthusiastic supporter in its nobler aspect. He was prejudiced against restrictions in general. He hated restrictions which held the hands of the weak for the benefit of the strong. He approved a competition which gave the prize to the most vigorous, but was righteously indignant when it was so contrived as to impose additional burdens on the feeblest. He was upon such grounds a chivalrous supporter of women's rights. He cared comparatively little for the abstract reasonings which have sometimes been used upon that question and have thrown some discredit upon its allies. He does not urge that women are 'naturally' equal to men, but maintains that they should in any case have equal opportunities for developing whatever faculties they possess. He supported the first proposal for admitting women to the Cambridge local examinations in a speech for which he was warmly thanked by the Conservative head of a house. This gentleman had female relations who had been compelled to earn their living as governesses. Fawcett had dwelt upon the vast importance to women in that position of obtaining a weighty testimonial to their qualifications. He dwelt with keen sympathy upon the number of women condemned under

our present system to profitless and inactive lives. He
was greatly touched by facts which showed how difficult
it was for them to earn an independent living. He
would refer, for example, to a fact which came under his
notice at the Post Office, where there were 900 candidates
for forty places of 65*l.* a year, though the vacancies had
been scarcely advertised. Serious evils of this kind
touched the noblest part of his nature, roused his
interest in the political question, and made him specially
indignant at the flippant dismissal of such evils too
common with his opponents in controversy. His characteristic mode of feeling appears in one case which may be
taken separately as it lies outside the main line of his
political career.

In 1873 a report was made by Dr. Bridges and Mr.
Holmes as to the sanitary condition of persons employed
in the textile manufactures. A bill was brought in during the session of that year by Mr. Mundella imposing
restrictions upon the hours of labour of women and
children. Ultimately the matter was taken up by the
Government, and in 1874 a bill was introduced by
Mr. (now Sir Richard) Cross, then Home Secretary, which
adopted Mr. Mundella's main proposals and was passed
with general approval. Fawcett stood almost alone as a
determined opponent of that part of the measure which
imposed restrictions upon the labour of adult women. He
investigated the question with great pains. He corre-
sponded with many of the persons interested and best
able to give information. He carefully studied the
attainable documents, and he made himself conspicuous
by speeches of which the general criticism seems to have

been that they were too logical—an epithet which, somehow or other, is considered by many people to be a conclusive refutation. The advocates of the bill relied upon the evidence which proved, as they thought, that the existing hours of labour were injurious to health, and upon the precedent of the Factory Acts, which are generally supposed to justify all proposed interference with labour. Many issues were raised, as to the exact effect of the evidence, and so forth, which need not be considered. Fawcett's position was simple. He distinguished, in the first place, between the cases of women and of children. Compulsory education, as he frequently urged, is not only justifiable, but eminently desirable, because children are necessarily dependent. The non-interference of the State means the irresponsible power of the parents. A parent may be forced to teach his children by the same right as that by which he may be forced to feed or clothe them. But this does not apply to the case of adult women, unless, indeed, as his opponents were sometimes driven to argue, they too must be considered as virtually slaves. Fawcett repudiated this doctrine as a mere pretext put forward to justify the proposed interference. Against all such interference he urged the familiar arguments—the risk of foreign competition, the rigidity of any Government action, which is necessarily incapable of adapting itself to various trades, and the great superiority of the action of the persons concerned, which had already shown itself capable of limiting the hours of labour. But his special point was the covert injustice to women. He considered the movement to be, in part at least, the result of the jealousy so often exhibited by trades-unions. The effect of limiting women's labour was necessarily to make it less available to employers. He produced evidence to show that manufacturers would be driven to employ men where, but for this restriction, female labour would have been more advantageous. Fawcett was, of course, opposed to a strong popular prejudice. He was accused of inconsistency because in his first Parliament (in 1867) he had supported an extension of the Factory Acts. He frankly admitted that he had changed his mind upon further reflection; and I need only mention the charge because it illustrates the fact that he had changed in a direction opposed to that of his party generally. He was accused of pedantic adherence to the precepts of a cold-blooded political economy, though his motives were generally appreciated even by his opponents. His warm friend, though on this occasion his determined antagonist, Mr. Mundella, certainly did full justice to the generosity of his motives, though disapproving his conclusions. Secure himself of his own purity of motive, Fawcett stuck resolutely to his views, though he was in 1873 representative of a popular constituency just slipping away from him, and in 1874 newly elected for Hackney, where many voters were likely to be alienated by his action.

The bearing of this controversy upon the question of women's votes is obvious. Fawcett considered it to be one illustration of the fact that women's interests were neglected because they could bring no pressure to bear upon the Legislature. His strong conviction that such injustice constantly resulted from their exclusion from the franchise, much more than any theory about

abstract rights, stimulated his zeal for their admission.
He argued that the evils of pauperism were clearly connected with this question. A large proportion of able-
bodied paupers are women. This mischief, he said, was
intensified by all legislation which interfered with their
power of taking up any employment of which they were
capable. Every such restriction forces more women to be
crowded into the employments still left open, and more,
of course, to toil for wages insufficient to maintain them
in the barest decency. Their would-be benefactors
forgot that any industry was better than dependent
pauperism,[1] or, as he said in the debate, that there was
one thing worse than work – namely, want. Social
customs and legal enactments, he says,[2] combine to
discourage women of every class from earning their
livelihood. This, he argues, is one fruitful cause of
pauperism. He looked upon the franchise as a powerful
lever for breaking up this system of enforced idleness,
and invariably based his arguments upon this solid
practical ground. He did not, I think, anticipate any
great change in the ordinary career of women—he
admitted that, for the most part, it would continue to
lie chiefly in the domestic circle ; but his sense of justice
revolted against the virtual condemnation of a large
number of women in every class to inability to use
their faculties freely, and he held that their political
disabilities were one more obstacle to freer and more
varied activity.

I have thus endeavoured to point out Fawcett's leading principles. When he first entered active political

[1] *Manual* (6th ed.), p. 593.   [2] *Essays and Lectures*, p. 104.

N

life, I was frequently asked whether he was not a fana-
tical and pedantic theorist: one who, like Robespierre,
would unflinchingly enforce doctrines—in his case the
doctrines of 'cold-hearted political economy'—in the
name of benevolence. I used then to make the (very
inadequate) reply that Fawcett was one of the shrewdest,
most hard-headed, and practical of men, and that his
common sense was the quality by which he would force
his way to the front. Though either statement taken
alone would be a misrepresentation so gross as to be a
caricature, both were founded upon observation of some
real characteristics. Fawcett was often called a doctrinaire in his earlier years, and the name was, up to a
certain point, merely the reverse aspect of a most
honourable quality. Every man must be in some sense
a theorist who is not a mere timeserver. Unless his
theory is that of simple self-interest, or unless his mind
is a mere kaleidoscope of shifting views, he must have
some fixed principles. It was one of Fawcett's finest
qualities that he had the strongest conviction of the
truth of certain principles. The policy which would in
his opinion do most to raise the condition of his countrymen was the policy to which he manfully adhered. He
would not sacrifice it either to his party or to his constituents. He would not flatter his leaders or truckle to
immediate popularity; and it is one of his special merits
that he thus achieved a well-founded reputation for absolute political honesty. I should not, however, be speaking openly if I did not admit that in my opinion he had
also some of the defects indicated by the criticism. I
cannot deny that he had some of the rigidity and

narrowness of a mind attached to the solid and practical, and immersed from infancy in a rather exclusive consideration of one set of topics. Culture may be pushed to mere dilettantism and flippancy. But no man's culture can be conspicuously narrow without some injury to his mind. I have explained the circumstances which narrowed Fawcett's intellectual sphere, and probably his mind was from the first indisposed to a wider sphere of thought. In reading his speeches and essays, one is struck by the recurrence of particular views expressed in the same phrases ; and it would be easy enough to give illustrations of the consequent limitation of his views of many great questions. I may safely leave the task to other critics. If Fawcett might be in some respects called a man of one idea, we must remember first that the real possession of a single idea indicates an unusual wealth of thought, and confers remarkable power upon the possessor. Firmly to grasp any belief, to hold to it unflinchingly in spite of good and evil report, is unfortunately to be an exception amongst politicians, and perhaps amongst any class. And, moreover, the phrase would be unjust, except so far as it indicates a dominant tendency to approach all questions from a particular direction.

I think, again, that I was justified in referring to Fawcett's strong common sense as a sufficient guard against any excessive impracticability. My account of his career should be a sufficient proof of his possession in an eminent degree of this quality. It showed itself in the soundness of judgment which he displayed in his political campaigns, and equally in the character of his more abstract doctrines. He never lost himself in mere

generalities, but was prepared to show in detail and to justify by specific arguments the application of his theories
to tangible facts, and was therefore eminently fitted on
all occasions to put the doctrines of his political teachers
into the dialect of the market-place. But I must add
here emphatically what will, I hope, become more obvious as we proceed. The shrewdness which all his early
friends recognised in Fawcett, and which in youth was
perhaps his most conspicuous quality, was combined with
another quality of more importance—I mean, of course,
the thorough kindliness and generosity of his nature.
I have spoken more than once of Fawcett's chivalrous
feeling. It is the epithet which recurs to me most
frequently in dwelling upon his career. It is the more
striking, because the phrase often calls up certain associations of external graces which seem scarcely in harmony with the robustness and the sturdiness and even, in
some sense, the apparent roughness of Fawcett's manner. The last phrase, indeed, was applicable only in his
youth, and was even then compatible with substantial
gentleness. But, essentially, I have never known a man
of more chivalrous nature. For chivalry of feeling, as I
understand the word, means a refinement of the sense of
justice—an instinctive capacity for sympathising with
everyone who is the victim of oppression in any of its
forms; and this was really the chief constituent of the
character which we all came to recognise. A spontaneous and intense hatred of everything unfair showed
itself in all his most active impulses; whether it took
the form of sympathy for the ignorant and depressed
agricultural labourer, for the children deprived of the

means of cultivating their intellectual faculties, for women ousted by men from the provinces of labour in which they could achieve independence, for the townspeople shut out from the only places in which they could enjoy healthy recreation, or for the millions of India governed by an alien race too apt to neglect the real interests of the subject or to allow their policy to turn upon totally different considerations. Fawcett was invariably upon the generous side. It seems to me that the interest of his character is mainly due to this rare combination. He was a man of superlative common sense, who could see that common sense dictated the noblest line of conduct, and whose sound judgment of facts always led him to judge justly, because he judged reasonably, and to find the best field for his intellectual vigour by employing it in obedience to the dictates of a large and generous heart. What was harshest in him became softened; and before we had lost him we had found out how imperfectly we had at first estimated the gentleness, which had been overlaid, though never suppressed, by the strength of his character.

CHAPTER V.

EARLY POLITICAL CAREER.

I MAY now take up the history of Fawcett's first attempts to realise the dreams of his boyhood. IIis success has made it difficult fully to realise the apparent extravagance of his enterprise at the time. He was not the man to win the favour of such patrons as could still dispose of family boroughs. Yet he was not in all respects a promising candidate for a popular constituency. A successful orator had occasionally been carried into Parliament by some great wave of public feeling. But this was the period of political calm, when Palmerston was the appropriate representative of the prevailing sentiment. Free trade had triumphed, and faint proposals for parliamentary reform had expired amidst general indifference. Nor was Fawcett likely to give complete satisfaction to the Radical leaders. He had identified himself with theories most obnoxious to the practical man. If the regular party managers had an instinctive suspicion of Mill as a theorist and a crotchet-monger, they were not likely to be favourable to Mill's ardent disciple. They would greatly prefer some rising barrister, or a successful merchant who was ready to pay his money and accept the regular platform without dispute. Fawcett's blind-

ness added a conclusive argument. A good-natured man
would regard it as a claim to some tenderness, but not
the less as a sufficient reason for suppressing, as gently
as might be, a too romantic aspiration. It was really a
kindness to intimate quietly, but firmly, that his ambition
was illusory, and coax him back to his study to amuse
himself with speculations on abstract politics. Even
Fawcett's friends, so far as I can remember, were inclined
to fear that he might be flying too boldly in the face of
common sense. They could not refuse admiration to his
audacity, but they were unable to feel confident in his
success. Fawcett, however, set to work undauntedly.
He had to make his name known, to show that his
blindness did not prevent him from dealing with matters
of business, and to convince practical men that he could
force them to take him seriously. During the years
which immediately succeeded his accident he was vigorously putting himself forward in every direction. Wherever he became known he made friendships, and was
recognised as a man of genuine force of mind. His first
public appearance, I think, was at the meeting of the
British Association at Aberdeen in September 1859.
He went there accompanied only by the lad, Edward
Brown, and his solitary journey was regarded as rather
adventurous. At this meeting he read a paper upon the
' Social and Economical Influence of the New Gold.'
He astonished an audience, to most of whom even his
name had hitherto been unknown, by the clearness with
which he expounded an economic theory and marshalled
the corresponding statistics as few men could have done
even with the advantage of eyesight. The discovery of

Fawcett was the most remarkable event of the meeting. He came south to attend the Social Science Association at Bradford. Here he read a paper upon the ' Protection of Labour from Immigration,' and the paper already mentioned upon the theory and tendency of strikes which so much impressed Sir James Kay Shuttleworth. He made several friends at Bradford, especially Mr. and Mrs. Hertz. Some of them were so much impressed by his abilities as to consider the possibility of procuring an invitation for him to stand for some Northern borough. Nothing, however, came of this. A discussion took place at the Bradford meeting upon proportional representation, papers having been read by Mr. Hare and A. T. Mayo. It was on this occasion, I think, that Fawcett first made Mr. Hare's acquaintance. He returned to town to undergo the operation which finally dissipated all hopes of eyesight. In the following year he served on a committee appointed by the Social Science Association to investigate the question of strikes, and in the September of that year took part in a discussion of the report presented by this committee at the Glasgow meeting. Fawcett decidedly preferred meetings of the British Association to those of its younger rival. The latter body was less unpropitious than might have been desired to the emptier kinds of rhetoric. It brought him into contact, however, with some men of real distinction, who, as a matter of course, became his friends. He saw a little of Lord Brougham, who had become the perpetual president of the association. Brougham, whose powers were now decaying, was put forward in a way which suggested more desire to exploit a great reputation than care to avoid an exhibition of his infirmities. Fawcett would have been the last to object to a respectful treatment of the veteran reformer, but he was disgusted by what he took to be downright servility. He would be content, he said, if they would permit Brougham to be contradicted. His annoyance became marked when in 1863 Brougham indulged in some remarks upon the American War which, as Fawcett says, ' drove me half wild.' He attended a meeting, however, at Sheffield in 1865, when it may be worth noting that he took part in a discussion on the management of railways by the State, and said that Government had a right to interfere with the monopoly, though he suspended his opinion until further inquiry. Until he became absorbed in political life, he was a pretty regular attendant at the British Association, where he enjoyed the society of eminent men of science, and occasionally read papers upon economical questions.

By this time he was coming forward more decisively as a politician. He put forward a kind of manifesto in two pamphlets published in 1860. They attracted, so far as I know, very little notice. The first of them, as C. B. Clarke tells me, was even suppressed, because it seemed to identify him too completely with the details of a scheme of which he never concealed his general approval, but which was not yet ripe for practical application. This was a popular exposition of Mr. Hare's scheme. The second was a plan for a new Reform Bill, suggested by the abortive measure introduced by Lord John Russell on March 1, 1860. These pamphlets, written under the influence of Mill and Mr. Hare, are

chiefly remarkable as illustrating a point noticed in the
last chapter. Fawcett called himself a Radical, and
even professed to hold extreme opinions. Yet, Radical
as he was, and writing with the specific intention of
calling attention to his political pretensions, he is chiefly
preoccupied with the dangerous tendencies of democracy.
He holds, and he thinks that even a wise Conservative
must admit, that progress in the direction of democracy
is inevitable. But a Radical should be equally ready to
admit that democracy may be favourable to the tyranny
of the majority. The first pamphlet argues that the
adoption of Mr. Hare's scheme would provide a sufficient
safeguard against this serious danger. Although he
labours to prove the practicability of this scheme, he
could scarcely expect to attract many converts from the
ranks of active politicians. In his second pamphlet he
admits that there is at present no chance of the adoption
of his proposal. He suggests, therefore, a partial application of the principle, by allowing each member of a
constituency to vote for only one candidate. In order
to secure a further advantage to intelligence, he would
give the franchise to all who had saved 60*l.* under
certain defined conditions. This proposal takes up a
plan suggested by Disraeli in 1859, with modifications
intended to obviate the objections which had been fatal
to the original proposal. The constituencies are to be
so redistributed as to give a voice to all interests. Candidates of more intelligence than wealth are to be encouraged by throwing the cost of elections upon the rates.

Fawcett in later years ceased to care for some of the
details of these plans ; but he invariably and inflexibly

adhered to the main principles in after life. They express with all possible clearness his dominant conviction that political justice demanded, above all things, that a career should be thrown open to all men of ability, and that a full and fair hearing should be assured to every member of the body politic. They show that, from the first, he was as anxious to guard against the abuses of power generally condoned by Radicals, as against those which they denounce. The doctrine of proportional representation, which seemed to him, as to Mill, to secure these objects, had through his life his heartiest support. Although, as I have said, he thought it impossible, for the present, to introduce a complete embodiment of the scheme into any political platform, he was anxious to bring its discussion forward as much as possible. In the course of 1860 he made the personal acquaintance of Mill, with whom he had already been in correspondence during the early part of that year, chiefly in reference to possible ways and means of bringing Mr. Hare's scheme into greater prominence. No practical result appears to have followed, though there was some talk of the formation of a committee and some discussion of the best recruits to be enlisted. In one letter Mill, after expressing his pride that his teaching had been regarded as useful to such a disciple, congratulates Fawcett on his selection of a political object. He speaks of the importance of meeting the political dangers of the future by securing the adoption of Hare's scheme. Time presses, for if the democracy once seize power, untrammelled by such conditions, it will be no more inclined than would a single ruler to abandon its despotic rule. The only chance, however, is to recommend the scheme from the Liberal point of view. Conservatives show their blindness by resisting and pouring scorn upon this truly Conservative principle ; and here, as in many other cases, Radicals will have to play the part which ought to be assumed by Conservatives. In another letter Mill cordially encourages Fawcett to persevere in his political ambition. His loss of sight could only be a disqualification so far as it had depressed his zeal. He has only to take all fair opportunities of showing his powers in public, and his misfortune will then turn out to be an advantage, because it will excite sympathy, neutralise jealousy, and help to spread his reputation.

Fawcett was no doubt encouraged by this judicious opinion. His zeal was stimulated by the cordial good will of the teacher, who was soon to become a warm personal friend. He was now looking out in every direction for an opening into political life. He had called upon men in high position. He had an interview with Lord Stanley (the present Lord Derby) about the Reform Bill, introduced by the Derby Cabinet in 1859. Lord Stanley, as Fawcett reported to Clarke, 'thought me, I fancy, rather young.' He had visited the Marquis of Exeter (then Lord High Steward of Cambridge) upon a scheme for opening Fellowships to Dissenters. He had also made inquiries at more than one borough supposed to be in want of a candidate. In October 1860 Mr. Bright, to whom he had spoken about some Scotch borough, gave him very good reasons against the particular place, and recommended him, kindly but decidedly, to wait until he had made himself better known.

Fawcett, however, was straining for a start. He soon afterwards took a step which showed in the most emphatic way his remarkable moral courage. The death of Sir Charles Napier, the admiral (November 6, 1860), made a vacancy in the representation of Southwark. Fawcett shrewdly perceived that the absence of local interest, fatal in a small borough, would be of less account in a shapeless slice from the wilderness of London. But another circumstance induced him to come forward. A report in the 'Morning Star' of November 8 stated that a meeting of Southwark electors had been held the day before; speeches had been made denouncing the bondage of electors to paid agents; it was said that Mr. John Locke, the sitting member, had been forced to spend 10,000l. on an election; and a committee was appointed to look out for some independent candidate who would stand upon principles of purity. Fawcett saw this report, which gave exactly the opening he wished. On the following day, as we learn from the 'Morning Star,' the committee was waited upon by 'a Mr. Fawcett, who announced himself as of Norfolk Street, Strand, and a Fellow of Trinity College, Cambridge.' He stated that he had read the report of the previous proceedings, and gave a satisfactory account of his principles. He brought as his credentials a letter from Lord Brougham, who had, as I have said, seen Fawcett at the Social Science Association, and had, no doubt, felt a genuine sympathy for a youthful audacity, in which, if in little else, there was some likeness between the two.

The Southwark committee was so far impressed that

its chairman, Mr. Love, consented to preside at a meeting
to be held next day (Saturday, November 10) at the St.
George's Tavern. It was, I fancy, to this meeting that
a story applies which Fawcett used to tell with considerable glee, and which probably received a little colour in
the telling. Mr. Love and Mr. Archer, who had made
the speeches denouncing money influence at the first
committee meeting, both attended ; but few people had
come to hear the unknown candidate. Fawcett therefore sent to the bar of the tavern for an increase to his
audience, and moreover undertook to supply the report of
his speech, presenting a guinea to the gentleman whose
function he discharged. His speech at any rate appeared in the 'Morning Star.' He spoke of Brougham,
and of Mill's encouraging letter, and pledged himself to
conduct the election on terms of absolute purity. He
expounded his principles, and made so good an impression that his future meetings were full and rapidly
became overflowing. He declared emphatically that
he would not spend a shilling to influence votes. The
meetings passed resolutions declaring rather guardedly
that his claims deserved attention. On the 15th he
issued an address. Five days ago, he says, he had been
an entire stranger. Three most influential meetings
had now passed unanimous resolutions declaring that
his claims deserved serious attention. He promises to
attend a series of meetings and allow the electors to
question him. Meanwhile he declares his main principles.
He would have supported their late member, Sir William
Molesworth, as a political leader. Molesworth, in fact,
was one of the philosophical Radicals, whose tradition

had been inherited by Fawcett. He is for a lodger franchise; abolition of church-rates; removal of religious restrictions (as he has shown at Cambridge); economy; the volunteer movement; the equalisation of poor-rates, and the reform of local government in London. He will go to the poll if he can obtain the support of 'any considerable section of the electors,' and he will devote himself to his duties, having no profession to distract him. His vigorous popular speaking, the interest attracted by his blindness, and the coolness, good humour, and frankness with which he replied to cross-questioners soon won ardent support. Hearers soon came from all parts of London, and the street outside the place of meeting was often crowded. Mr. Halpin, who was present, tells me, as a specimen of his answers, that he was asked whether he approved of the separation of married couples at workhouses—a question which then excited some feeling. He answered that they need not perhaps be separated after sixty, but that he could not wish the workhouses to be converted into breeding establishments. At a 'crowded meeting' on the 16th, a Mr. Dredge, who became a most ardent supporter, moved that the meeting should pledge itself to elect him, and the resolution was carried unanimously.

By this time the more regular forces were coming into play. Mr. Apsley Pellatt came forward, but retired on the 17th. Mr. Scovell, a gentleman of local influence, who had previously contested the borough, had meanwhile been induced to stand. His first meeting resolved itself into a mere bear-garden; furniture was smashed, and speaking became impossible. Fawcett, a few days later, held a most successful meeting at the same place (Taylor's South London Repository, opposite the Elephant and Castle). The smashed furniture had been removed, and perfect order prevailed in testimony to Fawcett's command of his audience. He won another remarkable triumph. A small meeting was held (on November 21) of some influential electors who were supposed to be in Mr. Scovell's interest. Mr. Dredge attended and carried a motion expressing preference for Fawcett by 36 to 7. A deputation, however, was appointed to wait upon another and more formidable candidate—Mr. (now Sir Austin Henry) Layard, whose name had for some time been mentioned.

Hitherto Fawcett had carried on the game with surprising success. He had. as he used to tell the story, a committee room, duly announced by external placards ; but the committee consisted solely of himself and his boy, and the porter's orders were simply to admit no one on any pretence. This may have been a humorous exaggeration. He certainly had a committee of a more substantial character before the election had gone on long ; but, at any rate, he had still to fight against the difficulty of an absence of influential support, and the doubts of his *bonâ fide* action were increased by his inability to pledge himself definitely to go to the poll. I believe that he never seriously expected that he would be able to do so, unless by some fortunate and very improbable combination of circumstances; though his surprising success seemed at times to make it possible. Mr. Layard's acceptance of the candidature made the prospect far less hopeful, for he was a man of wide reputation, and he was understood to be the Government candidate, and the influence of the great employers of labour was decidedly upon his side. Fawcett, however, fought on gallantly. He spoke every night. He proposed in vain that a mass meeting of electors should decide between his claims and Mr. Layard's. Should they reject him, he said, he would retire ; should they accept him, he would pledge himself to poll against Mr. Scovell ; but the proposal was not accepted. Fawcett's blindness now became almost the principal topic of the election. It roused the enthusiasm of his friends, and his antagonists pronounced it to be a fatal objection. He complained that the deputation to Mr. Layard had, without authority, declared him to be disqualified in the opinion of the electors by this defect. Mr. Layard himself stated that he regarded the objection as an insuperable one, whilst professing personal respect for his antagonist. The gallantry and perfect good temper with which Fawcett defended himself on this point roused the heartiest enthusiasm of his hearers. On November 30 he replies to a letter in the ' Times ' signed ' Common Sense,' which had put this difficulty in a way which, one must suppose, seemed sensible. ' Common Sense' wanted to know how Fawcett would find his way into the lobby ; how he would catch the Speaker's eye, and so forth. The last argument would have been more to the purpose if Fawcett had been a candidate for the Speakership. Fawcett had no difficulty in rebutting such attacks. He challenged Mr. Layard to argue with him any point supposed to require eyesight, when he would show his power of dealing with statistics and figures. One elector asked him how he

could understand local questions, in regard, for example,
to laying out new streets. Fawcett explained how he could
inform himself thoroughly by putting pins in a map.
Friends came forwards to bear witness to his powers. Mr.
Duncan McLaren, who had heard him at Glasgow, came
without notice to a meeting and spoke of him in the
warmest terms. Sir James Kay Shuttleworth sent an
enthusiastic letter, saying that the supposed obstacle had
only strengthened Fawcett's powers. Mr. Washington
Wilks—then, I think, the editor of the ' Morning Star '—
attended another meeting to deliver a vigorous popular
oration. The general sympathy became intense, and
Fawcett used to speak of the energy with which unpaid
supporters had circulated the necessary bills. He had
(as he announced on December 2) been able to fight a
large borough for a month for less than 250*l.* At last,
however, the struggle came to an end. Fawcett was compelled to decide that his prospects of success were not
sufficient to justify him in going to the poll, though he
had been able some time before to count upon 2,000 votes.
In an address dated December 8 he announces his
retirement. The poll took place on the 11th, and Mr.
Layard was returned by a majority of more than 1,000
over Scovell, the latter obtaining over 3,300 votes. The
defeat was a victory. Shortly afterwards I find Fawcett
telling a friend that he is certain that his contest will
enable him to succeed on another occasion. He had
conclusively proved, in spite of all odds, that he was
a dangerous antagonist in a popular constituency. But
there was still much to be done. He had to show that
he could convert vague enthusiasm into active support.

The prominence given to the ' physical infirmity ' argument, upon which his opponents were constantly dwelling, though with ostensible reluctance, showed plainly
enough that the objection was still insuperable in the
eyes of practical men.

The Mr. Dredge of the Southwark contest was for
some time an important figure in Fawcett's parliamentary campaigns. He was an intelligent citizen, earning
2l. or 3l. a week by ' wool sorting,' and possessed of a
shrewdness which would have qualified him to be an
admirable solicitor or election agent. His enthusiasm
for Fawcett was, I believe, perfectly genuine, though
some years afterwards he fell into difficulties and behaved badly to his old friend. For the present he was
an ally who could be very useful, but was not altogether
safe. Fawcett's position was a difficult one. He had
not merely to impress himself upon the public at large,
but to carry on negotiations with the under-world of
politics, the party managers, wirepullers, and so forth, who
had strong objections to any interference with their
established modes of procedure. Every candidate in
those days—perhaps the case is not altogether changed
—was tempted to make friends with the mammon of
unrighteousness. The temptation was of course especially strong for a man who was regarded as an intrusive
outsider. Fawcett's conduct in these matters, so far as
he was personally concerned, was strictly and invariably
honourable. He did his best to keep clear of personal
entanglements ; he never allowed himself to be inveigled
into giving pledges to which he could not fully adhere in
spirit as well as in letter ; he never acted ungenerously

to friend or foe ; and it may, I think, be safely said that no active politician has ever been freer from any suspicion of want of straightforwardness. But some of his allies and supporters were not conspicuous for delicacy. The ordinary code of political morality admits of manœuvres of which it may be said that their adroitness is more conspicuous than their lofty morality. Fawcett would never at any time have lent himself to any such manœuvre which was tainted by a want of generosity or by political dishonesty. But I may say frankly that at this period his own shrewdness and his hearty appreciation of shrewdness in others led him to take rather too lenient a view of some ingenious devices. His sense of humour was tickled, and he could not help enjoying a stratagem which was free from malevolence. He looked at it rather in the light of a good practical joke, and could not find it in his heart to be over-severe upon the contriver.

His friend Dredge acted as a kind of volunteer agent. Fawcett of course paid his expenses, which were very moderate compared with those of a regular professional, and believed implicitly in Dredge's disinterested zeal. Dredge went about to various constituencies. He made, as I find, inquiries at Finsbury, Canterbury, Bolton, Oldham, Leicester, and probably elsewhere ; and at such places was apt to surround himself with a mysterious halo of political importance not corresponding very accurately to his real position. Some anecdotes as to his respectful reception by local magnates, who would certainly have been less effusive had they known his true position, caused a good deal of amusement in Fawcett's inner circle.

For two years, however, nothing came of these diplomatic proceedings. Fawcett was active intellectually,
and was rapidly enlarging his circle of friends. He
was working at his 'Manual,' and writing articles in
'Macmillan's Magazine' and elsewhere. He was especially becoming intimate with some friends of Mill's.[1]
Mr. Hare, as we have seen, was at Trinity Hall at
Christmas 1859. Another friend of Mill's, Mr. W. T.
Thornton, then Secretary to the Public Works Department
in the India Office, became especially intimate with
Fawcett and with C. B. Clarke at this time. He was a
man of singular amiability, of calm, slow-working intellect, who would go on cross-examining any acquaintance
who had thrown out a remark not perfectly intelligible
with an amusing persistency. His favourite virtue was
candour, and it was not the less genuine because, like
other very candid people, he had a certain mild obstinacy
which secured him from the risk of conversion, however
benevolently he could listen to arguments. The self-
approbation fairly won by calmly listening to an opponent
rather strengthened the firmness of his adherence to his
own views. It was characteristic that he was practically
quite ignorant of agriculture, although he had written a
book of real value, for it was founded upon painstaking
research, upon peasant proprietorship. Fawcett was a
good deal amused by the difficulty of explaining to this
most exemplary official, responsible to some extent for the

---

[1] Fawcett became a member of the Political Economy Club (almost
the only place, I think, at which Mill was then to be met with in society)
on March 7, 1861. He introduced questions for discussion in 1862, 1863,
and 1866. As Professor of Political Economy at Cambridge he resigned the
ordinary membership and became honorary member in February 1867.

vast public works of India, the system of irrigation of the water-meadows round Salisbury. Yet Thornton's patient brooding over problems for which he had little apparent qualifications led him to some useful results, and he had the credit of converting Mill in regard to the wage-fund doctrine. In two letters of November 1862 I find Thornton supplying Fawcett with some statistical information about Indian products and railways, to be used in the 'Manual.' In the previous month he writes to Fawcett a letter, which I venture to quote, as it gives an interesting description of their common teacher, whilst it illustrates their feeling about him.

'St. Vevan, Avignon, October 1862.

'My dear Fawcett,—You will, I feel sure, be interested by a letter from this place, where I have been staying for a week domiciled with our friend Mill. It seems to be the custom in the South of France for all inhabitants of towns who can afford it to have a little country box, called in different places *bastide*, *campagne*, or *pavillon*, and consisting of one, two, three, or four rooms, to which they walk or drive on Sundays and holidays to pass a few hours, locking it up and leaving it empty on their return home in the evening. One of these *campagnes* Mill has bought and enlarged. It stands about a mile from Avignon, or, at least, from that part of it in which the hotel and shops are situated. You walk to it by the side of the beautiful Rhône, and then of an irrigation canal, through green meadows where the third crop of hay is now being cut, and through vineyards and plantations of mulberries. In front of the house is an oblong garden,

with an avenue of sycamores and mulberry-trees down
the middle, and at the end a trellis-work supporting a
vine, which serves as a verandah to the dwelling itself.
This is a small square building, whitewashed, with a tiled
roof and green venetian blinds without, and within three
small sitting-rooms on the ground floor and two on the
floor above, all fitted up very simply, but with English
comfort and neatness, and a mixture of French and
English taste.   Two of the lower rooms are the drawing
and dining-rooms; the third is my bedroom, at the
window of which, looking into the garden, I am now
writing.   Above are the bedrooms of Mill and Miss Taylor,
opening upon a terrace from which is a view of green
fields backed by ranges of mountains of most graceful
forms and constantly changing colours.   At eight o'clock
we breakfast; then, if there is no special plan for the day,
Mill reads or writes till twelve or one, when we set out
for a walk which lasts till dinner time.   In the evening
Mill commonly reads some light book aloud for part of
the time.   This, I fancy, is the ordinary mode of life
while here; but he is now laying himself out to entertain me, and almost every other day we make a carriage
excursion, starting directly after breakfast, and driving
twenty or thirty miles on end, and not returning till
sunset or later.   We have already visited in this way
Petrarch's Valley of Vaucluse, the Roman monuments
at St. Rémy, and the curious feudal remains of Les Baux;
and to-morrow we are to go to the famous Pont du Gard.
Mill tells me that they seldom let a week pass without
making some such excursion, but that this year they have
postponed all until my arrival.   I am enjoying myself,

and no small part of my pleasure consists in seeing how
cheerfully and contentedly, if I may not say how happily,
Mill is living. I feel convinced that he will never be
persuaded permanently to abandon this retreat; for here,
besides the seclusion in which he takes an almost morbid
delight, and a neighbourhood both very interesting and,
in its own peculiar way, very beautiful, he has also close
at hand the resting-place of his wife, which he visits daily;
while in his step-daughter he has a companion in all
respects worthy of him. I hope you will not find all these
details tedious. At any rate, having filled my paper with
them I must bid you good-bye, begging you to remember
me to Mr. Stephen and to Clarke, and to believe me

' Ever faithfully yours,

'W. T. Thornton.'

Thornton remained a warm friend during life.
Another friend who had a very strong influence upon
Fawcett was the late Professor Cairnes. Fawcett writes
to him on September 27, 1862, asking him to be his
guest at the meeting of the British Association which
was about to be held at Cambridge, and expressing warm
admiration for Cairnes's book on the 'Slave Power.' I
think that Cairnes was present. At this time he was still
in good health. Some time afterwards an accident brought
on the insidious disease which slowly crippled and finally
killed him. There was hardly anyone for whom Fawcett
entertained a more cordial affection. For years Cairnes
was a helpless invalid, and suffered cruelly. Fawcett, in
the midst of all engagements, was constantly running
down to his friend's house at Blackheath, cheering him

by his conversation, doing all he could to spread Cairnes's
reputation, encouraging him to collect and republish his
essays, bringing down anyone whom he thought likely to
be an amusing companion, and taking counsel with him
on the political measures in which they were both interested. The kindness was only part of Fawcett's invariable system, of which I have already given instances ; and
in this case Cairnes's vigorous intellect, which was never
weakened by his illness, made the congenial alliance profitable to both parties. During Fawcett's parliamentary career, Cairnes, so long as he lived, was one of his
most intimate advisers, whilst Mr. Leonard Courtney
made a third in this friendly union.

It was during this period that Fawcett gave a very
remarkable proof of his business powers, which may
come in here as a characteristic episode. His father
had been interested in Cornish mining, and had shown
the energy, inherited by his son, in the case of one ad-
venture. 'After many years of fruitless and dishearten-
ing toil and anxiety' (as Sir John Lambert tells me) 'he
brought to success a large mining undertaking in Cornwall, in consideration of which he was entertained at a
banquet by the shareholders and presented by them with
a costly service of plate.' Fawcett had himself made excursions in Cornwall with his father, and had been specially interested in the mining captains—an intelligent and
independent class whom he greatly respected. He wrote
several letters to the papers upon the condition of Cornish
miners and the mischief done by dishonest speculation.
He was also interested in some geological theories bearing
upon mines. A great rise in the value of some shares

in which his father was interested excited him and his
friends about this time, and I remember a good many
conversations at Cambridge upon the subject. Fawcett
for a time took part in speculations upon the mining
exchange. It is, I imagine, very rare for an outsider to
venture into such regions and come back without loss.
Fawcett clearly showed that he could hold his own, and
something more. He soon found, however, that such
an occupation would be incompatible with the political
career now opening before him. He withdrew at once
and entirely; and the only permanent result of his
operations was (as usual) an addition to the list of his
friendships. Mr. Hawke, of Liskeard, in particular, was
a lifelong friend. Fawcett stayed with him in 1868,
when he especially enjoyed some long swims in the sea,
which he visited from Mr. Hawke's house; and he went
there again in February 1883, after his dangerous illness
two months previously. Mr. Hawke tells me that it was
always thought that Fawcett could have made his fortune if he had devoted himself to mining speculations.
Fawcett himself refers apparently to something of this
kind in a speech made at Brighton before the election
of 1865. His friends had told him that he could never
get into Parliament, and that he had 'better go on to
the Stock Exchange and make a fortune.' 'I replied,' he
says, ' " No; I am convinced that the duties of a member
of the House of Commons are so multifarious, the questions brought before him so complicated and difficult,
that, if he fully discharges his duty, he requires almost a
lifetime of study." I said, " If I take up this profession,
I will not trifle with the interests of my country; I will

not trifle with the interests of my constituents by going into the House of Commons inadequately prepared because I gave up to the acquisition of wealth the time which I ought to have spent in the acquisition of political knowledge."' The sacrifice, as will be seen, was genuine.

Towards the end of 1862 it became known that there was to be a vacancy in the representation of Cambridge. Some of the leaders of the Liberal party in the town had naturally become known to Fawcett and had spoken to him of a possible candidature. Except for this local association, Cambridge was not a very suitable borough. It was a comparatively small constituency, much under the influence of party managers, and a good deal distracted by rather bitter feelings between Churchmen and Dissenters. No promising opening, however, had turned up since the contest for Southwark, and that contest had left some doubts of his ability to carry out a campaign to its legitimate conclusion. It might, therefore, be worth while to show that he could fight in earnest. A meeting of Liberal electors had resolved to put forward Colonel Adair (now Lord Waveney) as their candidate. A certain party of Liberals, however, objected to Adair, their chief reason being apparently that he did not sufficiently satisfy the Dissenters. A requisition, signed by 263 electors, was presented to Colonel Adair when he came to hold a public meeting in January 1863, in consequence of which he immediately retired from the contest. One of the leaders of the discontented party had seen Fawcett's friend Dredge, and now, without consulting Fawcett, made use of Dredge in getting up this requisition. Dredge had

not the delicacy to perceive the probable meaning of such
a manœuvre. He was horrified when he heard Fawcett's
view of the matter. Fawcett was, of course, shocked at
such a proceeding, which had taken place during his
absence and entirely without his knowledge. Fawcett,
in fact, had done his best to keep entirely apart from the
little squabbles of the place. The movement was calculated, if not intended, to make him the tool of the dissatisfied section. It would have been an underhand
proceeding, entirely alien to his nature, to have got up a
movement of this kind against a rival candidate. But
if it had come out that a man so closely connected with
him as Dredge had been concerned in the matter, the
candour of political opponents would not have been
equal to accepting his disavowal. As it was, Fawcett
was accused by his political opponents of being turned
to account by the malcontents; and that section may, of
course, have been encouraged by the expectation that he
would come forward.

With this, however, Fawcett had no concern. His
friend Macmillan was entirely free from any connection
with such intrigues, and had taken no part in any local
politics. His warm appreciation of Fawcett's abilities
made him eager to seize any opportunity of opening a
career to his friend. As soon as Colonel Adair retired,
Macmillan went to Fawcett and begged him to issue an
address. If Fawcett would write an address, he said,
it should be all over the town by the next morning.
Fawcett consented. 'If I am anybody's candidate,' he
said at the time, 'I am Macmillan's candidate;' but he
endeavoured to be nobody's candidate. The address

appeared on January 28, 1863, and the contest at once began. Fawcett's University friends did what they could to support him. Abdy, then Regius Professor of Civil Law, acted as his official election agent. Macmillan took the chair at his meetings; his friends Latham and Hopkins, then tutors of Trinity Hall, Gunson, Hammond, Clarke, Pryme, the Professor of Political Economy, and others appeared on the platform; and Mr. Fawcett senior came from Salisbury to support his son. The local Conservative journal of course assailed him, and published letters from 'Caustic' in the approved style of the provincial Junius. The worst they could say of Fawcett was that he was an advanced Radical, and that, although he called himself a member of the Church of England, he was ready to abolish Church rates, and, horror of horrors! to admit Dissenters to Fellowships. A terrible picture was outlined of well-known Dissenting ministers at Cambridge seated in Masters' lodges. The imputation that he was put forward by a clique of malcontents was also worked and probably to more effect. The party which resented Colonel Adair's expulsion abstained from voting. At the poll (February 10, 1863) Mr. F. S. Powell received 708 votes and Fawcett 627. The Conservative majority of 81 had been 67 at the previous contest of 1859; but the election, according to the Liberal organ, would have gone the other way had not the adverse section held aloof.

The contest cost some 600l., and was not very satisfactory. My clearest recollection refers to a dinner which was held in the college lecture-room to celebrate the event. The party numbered twenty-one, and I was

the only person present who had not the honour of being
the subject of a toast. The college servants were a
little scandalised at having to wait upon the strange
collection of Radicals and Dissenters which gathered
on this occasion within the academic precincts. Fawcett
enjoyed the excitement and fun of the election ; but he
gained by it only the proof, whatever it might be worth,
that he would go to the poll as well as make speeches.
Had he come forward again he would, I believe, have
united the Liberal party ; but he had seen enough of
the then condition of Cambridge politics to have little
desire for closer intimacy.

In the same year, as I have said, Fawcett was elected
to the chair of political economy ; and the triumph was
all the greater after so recent a manifestation of Radical
zeal. Soon after this, Fawcett at last found a chance, of
which he made good use, and which finally gave him a
firm foothold in politics. A vacancy occurred at Brighton
by the retirement of Mr. Coningham. The Liberals
were understood to have a safe majority in the borough,
and several candidates appeared. Mr. Kuper Dumas, a
member of the Stock Exchange, was the first to begin a
canvass. Mr. (now Sir Arthur) Otway, who had already
represented Stafford ; Mr. (now Sir Julian) Goldsmid,
who had much local influence, and Fawcett came forward
as Liberals. The Conservatives put up Mr. Moor, a
highly respectable resident, who had previously contested
the borough. To meet the danger of a split in the party,
a meeting of Liberal electors was held on January 19.
It was resolved to appoint a committee. The function of
this committee, as the mover of the resolution expressly

stated, was not to take a final decision, but to report upon the merits of the candidates and to arrange for a meeting at which they should make their own statements. The final decision was then to be made by a show of hands. Mr. Dumas declined to come before this committee, considering, apparently, that he had acquired a right by being first in the field. The other candidates agreed to accept its decision; and Fawcett in particular, in a letter written next day, declared very unequivocally that he would be bound by its report. Until the report was presented he would take no further steps in his canvass. He and his rivals had interviews with the committee. The committee told Fawcett expressly that the final decision did not rest with them. They further gave (as he said, without contradiction) a ‘distinct and solemn pledge’ that he should have an opportunity of addressing the electors. They told him that he had removed from their own minds any impression that his blindness was a disqualification, but they doubted whether he could remove that impression from the minds of the constituency. This was a matter of vital importance for him. The committee were only to report upon his merits, and, if their opinion were otherwise favourable, would leave him to convince the electors that his blindness was not a fatal disability. The obstacle, as we have seen, had been sincerely regarded as insuperable by many, both at Southwark and at the Cambridge professorship contest. It was certainly irremovable, and now again became a most prominent consideration. The committee agreed upon a report and called a meeting for the 25th. It became known that the report virtually set Fawcett

aside.   Hereupon he wrote to the committee stating that
he should attend the meeting; that if their report were
adopted, he should retire at once; but, if it were rejected,
he should, if called upon, address the meeting.

The committee apparently thought that the letter implied unwillingness to carry out his agreement. At the
request of some of its members, Mr. Willett, a gentleman
well known in Brighton for his high character and
public spirit, called upon Fawcett, then an entire stranger
to him, in order to discuss the matter, and was satisfied
with his explanations.   At the meeting, the report was
duly read.   It stated that Mr. Otway was the most
eligible candidate.   It then mentioned Mr. Goldsmid in
favourable terms; and said, finally, that though Fawcett
had every virtue, the committee, 'with deep regret, fear
that the constituency would deem that' his blindness
'would be some drawback to his usefulness.'   The committee, it must be noticed, did not express their own
opinion, but rested their decision upon an anticipation of
the opinion of the constituency.   This was to anticipate
precisely the point which (as Fawcett understood) had
been expressly reserved for settlement with the voters.
What else could be the sense of the promise that he
should have an opportunity of addressing them?   The
reading of the report brought about a most dramatic
scene.   Mr. Willett moved in formal terms that it
should be accepted.   The meeting, however, was crowded
by the friends of Mr. Dumas, who had been entirely set
aside by these proceedings.   One of them immediately
moved an amendment in favour of his candidate.   The
meeting was uproarious.   After much turmoil, the amend-

ment was put; and the chairman, after an inconclusive show of hands, had at last to pronounce that it was carried. Hereupon the meeting became a mere chaos of inarticulate hubbub. The chairman, apparently at his wits' end, called upon the candidates to speak. Messrs. Dumas, Otway, and Goldsmid uttered spasmodic professions of political faith which were swallowed up in the tumult. Then Fawcett came forward, and won probably the greatest oratorical triumph of his life. He began amidst great interruption ; but after a few sentences, says the reporter in a hostile paper, the vast body of electors 'listened with breathless attention.' You could have heard a pin drop, as a hearer has told me. Fawcett began by pointing out that the committee was appointed not to decide, but to recommend, and that it was pledged to give the candidates an opportunity of speaking to the electors —a matter of the most critical importance in his case. And then he told them his story. 'You do not know me now,' he said, 'but you shall know me in the course of a few minutes.' He proceeded with the account of his accident, during which, says the reporter, 'a deep feeling of pity and sympathy seemed to pervade the meeting.' He told them how he had been blinded by two stray shots 'from a companion's gun;' how the lovely landscape had been instantly blotted out ; and how he knew that every lovely scene would be henceforth 'shrouded in impenetrable gloom.' 'It was a blow to a man,' he said simply; but in ten minutes he had made up his mind to face the difficulty bravely. He would never ask for sympathy, but he demanded to be treated as an equal. He went on with the story of his previous

P

attempts to enter Parliament, and ended with a profession of his political principles. I do not think that
Fawcett ever again referred to his accident in public,
except in speaking to fellow-sufferers. His blindness was
apparently being made an insuperable obstacle; his best
and most natural answer was to tell the plain story of
his struggle, and he told it with a straightforward manli-
ness which completely overpowered the audience.

The meeting separated, and everything was now in
confusion. Mr. Otway told Mr. Coningham that night
that in his opinion 'Fawcett was the man for Brighton.'
Next day he had an interview with Fawcett, and asked
him what he should do under the circumstances. Fawcett replied at once that he now felt bound to persevere
for a time. If in a week he found that a majority of the
Liberals did not support him, he should retire. Mr.
Otway hereupon at once retired, and advised the committee to support Fawcett. Mr. Otway, if any man, was
the aggrieved party. As in all cases where important
conditions are left to be understood by verbal communications, angry charges were made, and Fawcett was accused
of having broken his pledge. Mr. Willett spoke to Fawcett
upon the subject. Fawcett at once challenged his ac-
cusers to attend a meeting which he held on Thursday,
January 28. They declined to come. A resolution was
passed all but unanimously, on the motion of Mr. Willett,
acquitting Fawcett of all imputations. Whatever the
weight of such a resolution, I think that upon this,
the only occasion of his life upon which any charge was
seriously made against his thorough straightforwardness, no real blame can be fixed upon him. He had, it

must be observed, nothing whatever to do with the rejection of the report. He had taken no steps whilst the committee was sitting, and he only spoke, with the other candidates, when he was called upon by the chairman. The only question could be whether he was justified in declaring to Mr. Otway on the next day that he intended to proceed with his candidature. The best possible test of a man's action in a case of this kind is the opinion of those who know all the circumstances. Fawcett won not only the acquittal but the active support and permanent friendship of honourable men. Colonel Fawcett (no relation to his namesake), a hearty and effective political leader, who had seconded the motion for the committee of selection, became the chairman of his committee. There was a story, I remember, that Colonel Fawcett had been making a speech on some previous occasion, when one of the smooth round pebbles which have been so lavishly provided for the benefit (amongst other things) of Brighton roughs, cut open his cheek. He went on without moving a muscle, with the blood streaming from the wound, and was ever afterwards a popular hero upon Brighton platforms. The colonel was from this time a cordial friend. Mr. Willett, who had made Fawcett's acquaintance through the dispute, became his vice-chairman, and threw himself into the cause with such enthusiasm that when, soon afterwards, the money obstacle threatened to be fatal he undertook to pay the costs of the election, and thus incurred a very considerable expense. Another friend whom I must mention was Mr. Merrifield, a barrister resident at Brighton, who warmly defended Fawcett in the press and became his life-long friend. Mr. Coningham, the previous member, also joined the committee. It was, I think, the view of these gentlemen that the committee were inclined to regard Fawcett as an intruder, and had been anxious to get rid of him by interpreting their powers, no doubt in good faith, but in a sense not properly admissible.

The split in the party now became hopeless. Various attempts were made to secure some arbitration. It was impossible to arrange any acceptable terms, and before long Fawcett, Goldsmid, and Dumas were all pledged to go to the poll. A trifling additional element of confusion was the candidature of a Mr. Harper upon purely Protestant principles. Fawcett set to work with his usual energy. He spoke constantly and effectively. During the heat of the contest Fawcett had to deliver his inaugural lecture at Cambridge (on the 3rd of February). He left Brighton in the morning and returned in time to address a public meeting in the evening. Dredge and C. B. Clarke were active in the committee-room ; and Fawcett's father and sister came over from Salisbury. One part of the campaign gave us a great deal of amusement. The local papers had taken the side of one or other of the rival candidates. We could not obtain insertion in them for an article which I had written on behalf of Fawcett's claims. Hereupon it was suggested by (I think) Mr. Washington Wilks, who had supported him at Southwark, that Fawcett should start for the nonce a paper of his own. Mr. Wilks sent down a sufficiency of type from the 'Morning Star ;' and during a week before the election we published a small newspaper—now, I fancy, of extreme rarity—

entitled the 'Brighton Election Reporter.' It was sold
for the modest sum of a halfpenny; and, as the newsboys
were allowed to keep the proceeds, it attained a very
lively circulation. I had the honour of being installed
as editor; and I may boast that I was also the chief con-
tributor. I cannot say upon a fresh perusal of its pages
that its wit or logic were such as to entitle it to a permanent place in literature. So much, however, may be
said of more important organs of public opinion. In any
case, it gave us the means of putting forward Fawcett's
claims, and enabled us to answer the imputations rising
out of the decision of the committee. A contest between
four Liberals necessarily turned a good deal upon personal
topics. We told the story of Fawcett's life; insisted
upon his vigour and independence; and pointed out that
our antagonists relied upon local influence, and that their
statements were in some instances trimming and am-
biguous. We considered ourselves to be eminently witty,
forcible, and at the same time laudably free from unworthy personalities. It is enough, however, to illustrate
our sentiments by quoting a few phrases from a final
appeal. We pointed out the difficulty of deciding between candidates, all professing the same principles in
general terms; and suggested that it was better for constituents to attend meetings and cross-examine the candidates themselves instead of trying to interpret carefully
prepared addresses. 'Let them go to judge whether he
(Fawcett) is not perfectly straightforward and honest in
the enunciation of his political opinions, and whether he
will not give a plain answer to a plain question. They
will certainly have the advantage of hearing manly and

sterling eloquence; and, if they know a man when they
see one, they will not come home without the pleasant
conviction that they have seen a true specimen of the
English variety of the breed.   They will probably
share our conviction that we have a chance of electing a
representative who will be a name and a power in this
country before many years are over.'

After a noisy nomination, in which rotten eggs and
Brighton pebbles played their part, the election finally
took place on Monday, February 15.   Fawcett headed
the poll in the early hours, when the working-men voted,
but he was passed before eleven, and at four o'clock the
votes were—Moor, 1,663; Fawcett, 1,468; Goldsmid, 775;
Harper, 82.   Mr. Dumas polled 175 votes, and retired,
being in a hopeless minority, at ten o'clock.   There was
some natural but, I believe, quite unreasonable irritation,
that Mr. Goldsmid had not felt himself at liberty to do
the same, as the addition of any considerable part of his
voters would have secured the Liberal triumph.   Fawcett,
however, took his defeat with perfect cheerfulness and
good humour; and indeed, though his friends were less
philosophical, he had some reason for complacency.   He
had won such a position that it was now certain that he
must be the accepted Liberal candidate at the next election.   Unless there should be a sudden change in the
balance of parties, his speedy success was therefore
assured.   He was, in fact, elected at the General Election
of 1865.   In the interval, he addressed various meetings
at Brighton.   His most remarkable speech was an
address upon parliamentary reform on September 13,
1864. The question was now beginning to excite popular

attention. Fawcett spoke of the honourable attitude of the
working-classes during the American war, and upon the
reception of Garibaldi in London.   They proved, he said,
that the questions which really roused enthusiasm in
the English people were those which appealed to their
moral sentiments.   He argued that something must be
rotten if a man at 20s. a week had not as much interest
in the peace and prosperity of the country as his neighbour with 10,000l. a year.   The sufferings inflicted by a
war fall chiefly upon the poor; and any argument which
implied that they should be rightfully excluded from the
franchise as incompetent and indifferent, was an argument denoting a degraded and unwholesome state of
feeling.   He proceeded to argue against the theory that
the rich would be swamped by the poor voters on the
ground that working-men were as much divided in
opinion as other classes.   He urged, however, significantly that any measure of reform should be judged in
accordance with our answer to the question, ' Do we think
it will cause the various sections of opinion to be more
independently and honestly represented ? '   He argued,
in fact, on the lines of his pamphlet on reform, though
without committing himself to special details or distinctly mentioning schemes of minority representation.
He feared, as I learn from a letter addressed to him by
Mill, that his language about Mr. Hare's scheme would
not be considered as sufficiently outspoken by its most
eminent supporter.   Mill replies that, on the whole, he
had been more favourably impressed than otherwise.
The speech was greatly superior to election speeches in
general.   He objects, however, to the argument against

the probability of a union of opinion amongst working-
men. It tends to depreciate the danger against which
Hare's scheme is directed, and is really unsound.
Working-men may be divided on other points, but not
the less united upon matters touching their own class
interests. Fawcett, as appears from later speeches, was
not convinced by this criticism.

When the election approached, a joint committee
was formed for Fawcett and Mr. White, the sitting
Liberal member. A great meeting was held in the
riding-school of the Pavilion, at which the two Liberal
candidates appeared, and resolutions in their favour
were passed; Colonel Fawcett and Mr. Willett both
speaking in their support. Fawcett's father was also
present, and enthusiastically received. Fawcett's own
speech indicates some of the difficulties which he had
to encounter. A Tory, he said, had summed them up
by saying that he would have to contend with ' 1,500l.
from the Carlton and a cart-load of slander.' The
slander seems to have been mixed; but the serious
arguments were that Fawcett was a poor man and
that he was plotting the ruin of the tradesmen by his
advocacy of co-operation. He replied with manly
eloquence by adopting both charges. He certainly had
advocated co-operation, and considered it the best remedy
for poverty. He certainly was poor; he had won an
income enough for independence by his own exertions in
an open field, and had deliberately preferred the study
of politics to the acquisition of wealth. Cobden—then
just departed—was a poor man; but he had 'vanquished
a proud aristocracy;' he had destroyed a gigantic mono-

poly and given bread and prosperity to millions of his
countrymen. When Fawcett visited the House of
Commons, he had found, he said, that every word uttered by Cobden made its impression, whilst the words
of millionaires might pass unnoticed; and he inferred
that poverty would not destroy a man's influence in the
House if he were thoroughly qualified for his position,
nor prevent his return by an independent constituency in
spite of all ostentation of wealth by richer men. Fawcett's independence excited respect and enthusiasm
enough to secure his return. But his avowed incapacity
to spend money was felt as an objection by some part of
the constituency. I do not think that I do injustice to
Brighton by saying that it contained some voters with a
preference for gentlemen who could encourage trade and
give handsome subscriptions to the races. For the
present, however, Fawcett's appeal to their higher feelings was triumphant. The objection to his blindness
seems to have vanished. The difficulty of catching the
Speaker's eye, he says, has ' become an interesting relic
of the past.' The number of the constituency had increased by 1,000. On the day of election (July 12, 1865),
6,492 out of 8,661 electors polled, and the numbers
were—White, 3,065; Fawcett, 2,665; Moor, 2,134.
The total expense of Fawcett appears to have been a
little over 900l., towards which, I believe, there was some
subscription from his friends.

CHAPTER VI.

MEMBER FOR BRIGHTON.

FAWCETT had thus, at the age of 32, achieved the great object of his ambition. He was at last a member of Parliament. His friends used often to talk over the probabilities of his success. He had shown by undeniable proofs that he could command the attention of a popular audience. The question remained whether he would be equally successful in the more fastidious assembly where, it is generally supposed, success depends upon some mysterious and indefinable aptitude. Critics who knew nothing of him personally took him to be an impracticable Radical, fitter to maintain abstract theses in a debating society than to take part in serious legislation. The better-informed felt no shadow of doubt that his force of character and intellect would make themselves felt in any assembly in the long run. But they doubted whether he might not have a severe ordeal to go through. He might, they feared, be too dogmatic and audacious ; whilst his blindness would be some obstacle to his acquiring the true orator's instinctive perception of the temper of his audience. He might be tempted to fall too much into the tone of a lecturer addressing obsequious pupils. Fawcett himself was fully alive to the possible dangers of speaking too

much, or upon subjects where he had not some claims to
speak as one having authority.

In the first Parliament (1865-68) he therefore remained comparatively quiet. The Parliament was one
which prepared the way for changes of vast importance.
The political condition originated by the Reform Bill of
1832 was coming to an end. Two of the great figures
of the preceding period passed away in this year :
Cobden died on April 2, and Palmerston on October 18,
1865. Cobden had been a warm personal friend.
Fawcett said in a speech at the Cobden Club, two years
later, that he revered the great agitator more than any
man he had ever met. The phrase, which I take from a
condensed report, was probably qualified in some way,
for he would hardly, even on such an occasion, have
implied that anyone came before Mill in his scale of
veneration. He had a regard, too, for Palmerston,
Cobden's greatest antagonist ; and, in a speech shortly
after Palmerston's death, explained his reasons. The
true secret, he said, of Palmerston's success was that
through life he showed ' a genial and an honest and
warm heart,' and never deserted a friend. To this,
which was a characteristic indication of Fawcett's own
sympathies, it may be added that Fawcett was fully
prepared to appreciate Palmerston's patriotic sentiments.
Though a Radical, Fawcett was as thoroughly hearty an
Englishman as any Conservative. In spite of his conviction that the Cobdenites had deserved well of their
country, he thought that their view of foreign politics
was in certain cases too much biassed by commercial
considerations. It was plain, however, that a new era

was approaching. The most remarkable election in
1865 was that of Mill for Westminster. Mr. Gladstone,
rejected for Oxford, came in for South Lancashire.
The period was beginning during which he and Disraeli
were to be the representatives of the chief opposite
tendencies. For the present, Mr. Gladstone still served
under Lord Russell, and Mr. Disraeli under Lord Derby.
The main result of the labours of the Parliament was
the singular series of operations by which the Reform
Bill of 1867 was ultimately carried. In 1866 the
modest bill introduced by Lord Russell's Government
was ruined by the famous defection of the ' Cave.' Mr.
Lowe and Mr. Horsman expressed the hearty distrust
entertained by the genuine Whig of the new social
strata to be brought within the sphere of politics. The
bill broke down, and Lord Russell finally disappeared
from active political life. In 1867 Disraeli succeeded
in educating his party ; it turned out that household suffrage was really a Conservative measure, and the nation
proceeded, as Carlyle puts it, to 'shoot Niagara,' with
consequences which will some day have to be summed up
by the impartial historian of the future.

Fawcett, though necessarily a subordinate in this
campaign, took, as will appear, a decided part in the
operations. I give the letter in which he describes his
first experience to his father : —

' 123 Cambridge Street, Warwick Square, London :
'February 1, 1866.

' My dear Father,—I have just returned from my first
experience of the House of Commons. I went there
early in the morning, and soon found that I should have

no difficulty in finding my way about. I walked in with Tom Hughes about five minutes to two, and a most convenient seat close to the door was at once, as it were, conceded to me; and I have no doubt that it will always be considered my seat. Everyone was most kind, and I was quite overwhelmed with congratulations. I am glad that my first visit is over, as I shall now feel perfect confidence that I shall be able to get on without any particular difficulty. The seat I have is as convenient a one as any in the House, and a capital place to speak from. I walked away from the House of Commons with Mill. He sits on the bench just above me, close to Bright. I sit next but one to Danby Seymour; White [his colleague for Brighton] is three or four places from me.

'Mother has indeed made a most wise selection in my lodgings. They at present seem everything I could desire; the rooms are larger than I expected, and Mrs. Lark and the servant are most civil and obliging. This is everything in lodgings. I can walk to the House of Commons in exactly a quarter of an hour; this is not too far.

'Accept my best thanks for the hamper. Everything has arrived quite safely, and all the contents will prove most acceptable. We are going to have the fowl for dinner to-night at seven. I hope now that I am so comfortably settled, some of you will often come to London. When am I to expect Maria?

'Give my kindest love to mother and her, and in great haste, to save post,

'Believe me, dear Father,

'Ever yours affectionately,

'HENRY FAWCETT

I may just notice that Fawcett's voice was heard almost for the first time in the House of Commons on February 23, 1866, when he asked why the wages of certain letter-carriers had not been raised by the Post-Office. Soon afterwards, he made his first serious experiment in a set speech upon the Reform Bill, on March 13. From Mr. Courtney, who was present, and from various contemporary references, I learn that it was decidedly successful; although, not unnaturally perhaps, it provoked some expressions of impatience. It was in any case characteristic. The sneers of the 'Cave' at the classes about to be enfranchised, and the insincerity of the previous treatment of the question by politicians, had roused Fawcett's indignation. He began with a spirited assault upon the prophetic warnings of Messrs. Lowe, Horsman, and other dreaders of democracy, and passed to a eulogy upon the high political instinct shown by the workmen during the American contest. He pointed out that the great questions of the future were those affecting labour and capital; and urged the importance of admitting the classes most deeply interested to a direct share in their decision, whilst maintaining (in spite of the previously noticed criticism from Mill) that the working-classes would not vote *en masse* more than any other class. The measure which he particularly noticed as likely to be favoured by reform was an extension of the Factory Acts. Confidence in the working-classes, who had been unjustly maligned by the sneers of his opponents, and the conviction that their enfranchisement would lead to a serious opening of the great social questions, was in fact the keynote of the speech. Probably dissentients

did not as yet fully recognise the strength of his convictions or distinguish his utterances from those of the
mere dealers in academic commonplaces; and it was
some of these phrases about the good sense of the working-
classes which appear to have struck his audience as
superfluous. Fawcett regretted, when addressing his constituents soon afterwards, that the Liberal Government
did not dissolve upon the defeat of their bill; but he
spoke warmly of Mr. Gladstone's leadership. Gladstone,
he said, was attacked by the leading journals because
they knew that he would not 'joke away the great
question of reform.' The sincerity of Gladstone's zeal
was proved by the rancour of his assailants, and Fawcett
called upon his hearers to express their determination that
he should be the ' great leader of the people of England.'
In the following session, however, Fawcett found himself
in a peculiar position. His leaders, Mr. Gladstone and
Mr. Bright, were dissatisfied with the Reform Bill
introduced by Disraeli. Although in Opposition, they
were still in a majority, and could therefore hope to
compel the Government to modify its measure so as to
meet their wishes. In the political campaign which
followed, both parties had occasion for all their skill in
parliamentary tactics. The mysterious compound house-
holder made his appearance at the most critical stage of
the proceedings and introduced intricate discussions not
easy and here quite needless to unravel. Fawcett's one
aim was to get the largest measure of reform, whether
it should come from the hands of the Government or
the Opposition. On the most critical occasion he had to
make a difficult decision. After some strange manœuvring

the House was about to go into Committee on the bill.
A meeting of Liberal members was held at Mr. Gladstone's house on April 5, at which it was decided to
move certain 'instructions' to the Committee. The effect
of the motion, if carried, would have been to upset the
Government, and probably to postpone indefinitely the
settlement of the question. Moreover, the instructions
were drawn so as to imply that the Liberal party were
for a narrower measure than the Conservatives. Messrs.
Gladstone and Bright were in favour of some limitation of
the franchise which would exclude the so-called 'residuum;'
and it was proposed to draw a line somewhere above
household suffrage pure and simple. Hereupon forty-
eight Radicals (of whom Fawcett was one) held a meeting
in the tea-room of the House of Commons. They became
famous (for a brief period!) as the 'Tea-room party';
they were denounced by the faithful as renegades and
mutineers, and compared to the Adullamites of the previous session. They were reproached for trusting the
natural enemies of reform instead of showing confidence
in their old leaders.

Fawcett was one of a deputation of five who waited
upon Mr. Gladstone to lay before him the resolution
adopted at the tea-room. Some private letters written
at the time, as well as speeches to his constituents,
explain his motives. He speaks with warm admiration
of Mr. Gladstone. He is obviously and sincerely
distressed at being forced to take up the attitude,
afterwards more familiar to him, of opposing his party
leaders. Mill, as well as Bright and Gladstone, had to
be opposed. He feels, however, that the Radicals cannot

allow themselves to act as though they had changed places with the Conservatives, and were for restricting instead of enlarging the proposed extension of the franchise. Disraeli had manœuvred to place them in that position. Mr. Gladstone gave way to the remonstrance of the Tearoom party, and the objectionable part of the instruction was withdrawn. The effect of this concession was that the bill was allowed to go into Committee. An amendment, however, was proposed in Committee by Sir J. Coleridge, embodying the remaining proposals of the Opposition. It was now drawn in such terms that the Radicals could vote for it; and Fawcett considered that Disraeli had been 'checkmated.' To his disappointment, Disraeli triumphed. The dissatisfaction of a small section of Tories produced no serious desertion from the ranks, whilst forty Liberals voted for the Government. Some of them, says Fawcett, wanted to annoy Mr. Gladstone; others dreaded a dissolution; but the remainder held that to support Disraeli was the shortest road to a satisfactory bill, and that they would be able before long to get rid of the various checks still proposed. Fawcett agreed to a great extent with this opinion, though he did not feel justified in again voting against his party. He perceived that Disraeli was resolved to pass a measure, and inferred that he could be got to pass a satisfactory one. The prevision was fulfilled; and, though Fawcett expresses his regret at Mr. Gladstone's vexation, he felt that his own action had been fully justified. The Liberals had been prevented from taking up a false position, and their ends had been achieved more completely than they could have hoped, though by the hands of their antagonists.

Fawcett was thus giving proof of independence, and came in for some of the reproaches directed against the Liberal seceders. The question, however, soon passed out of sight. On other matters, he appeared as a supporter of Mill in the questions which they both had most at heart. He spoke on behalf of Mill's amendment for admitting women to the franchise, which was rejected by 196 to 73 on May 20, 1867; and, with Mill, he supported a motion for a partial application of the principle of cumulative voting brought forwards by Mr. Lowe (July 5), and rejected by 314 to 173. Mill's great reputation had excited much curiosity, and some of his speeches were heard with respect and admiration. I do not know whether he succeeded in quite persuading the House of Commons that a philosopher could also be a man of business. Fawcett, I remember, used to regret that Mill erred by an excess of conscientiousness in his parliamentary capacity. He spoke rather ruefully of the hours wasted by the great thinker, who felt it a duty to nail himself to his seat whilst country gentlemen dilated at merciless length upon the cattle plague. But he also felt very strongly that Mill did much to raise the moral tone of his audience, and they were in close intercourse upon all the great questions of the day. In one question connected with the Reform Bill Fawcett appeared as the leader and Mill as the supporter. An Act for the Suppression of Corrupt Practices was got through the House in 1868 as a natural corollary to the Reform Bill. Fawcett protested more than once against the insincerity or half-heartedness of Liberals in regard to it; and in July proposed one of the reforms to which he always attached great importance. He moved that the expenses of the returning officer should be thrown upon the rates. Reform had certainly not hitherto tended to make access to the House easier for poor men. The expensiveness of election contests was an obstacle which he had good reason for appreciating at its full weight. He declared[1] that the chief danger which threatened representative institutions was the great and increasing cost of elections. When he exhorted young men of ability to adopt a political career, their answer was almost invariably that their first election would ruin them. It was impossible, he urged, to exaggerate the mischief of thus shutting out the ablest men from political life. To meet one obvious objection to his scheme, he proposed that every candidate should deposit a certain sum in order that mere men of straw might not come forward for the sake of notoriety. The difficulty of satisfactorily arranging this proviso was the cause or the pretext of the rejection of his proposal. On July 18 his clause was carried against the Government (after another favourable division of 78 to 69) by a majority of 84 to 76. Mill spoke soon afterwards (July 23) of the 'profound satisfaction' with which this vote had been received throughout the country, and declared that if the Government were wise they would adopt the proposal themselves. They preferred, however, to meet it by tactics which are not now worth examination. When Fawcett complained, Disraeli replied that the 'proviso' difficulty had turned out to be really insurmountable instead of being a mere pretext for evading a direct raising of the main issue; and Fawcett's last

[1] Speech at Brighton, January 27, 1868.

attempt to get the bill recommitted in order to introduce his plan was defeated (July 24) by 102 to 91.

By this time Fawcett's position in the House had evidently become stronger. He was recognised as a man whose utterances carried weight. He had already shown his power of dealing with questions which were to occupy a large part of his later activity. He had spoken upon popular education; upon University endowments; upon various financial questions; and upon India. The long wrangle over reform had occupied the attention of the House, and the great questions had obviously to be left over for settlement by the new constituency.

The education question was one of the most pressing. ' We must educate our masters ' was the phrase which expressed one common sentiment. Since we are compelled to admit the unwelcome guest, we must try to make him presentable. The argument from Fawcett's point of view was precisely the most conclusive justification of reform. It admitted, as he had asserted, that reform must lead to a system of national education, of which he had been an advocate from his boyhood. The only difference was in the spirit with which the change was contemplated. To his opponents, education was the best palliative for a necessary evil. To him, it was the natural corollary from a great act of justice. It was right to confer upon classes most deeply concerned in the national welfare a share in determining the national action. He did not doubt that, as one immediate result, a system of education would be claimed by them as a privilege, not imposed by their superiors as a defensive measure. He put this at a later period, when supporting

Mr. Trevelyan's motion for household franchise in counties (April 26, 1872). Mr. Lowe, he said, had been converted by the Reform Bill of 1867 to the policy of 'educating our masters,' and he now hoped that a similar process would bring people to see the necessity of educating the agricultural labourer. When advocating reform in January 1867,[1] he had expressed his view forcibly. He explained that he had no sympathy with the people who thought it necessary to 'stem the tide of democracy.' He desired to make the Government truly national, in order to promote the prosperity of all classes. The most prominent fact of the day was enormous wealth associated with the direst poverty. Beasts were so well protected, because 'powerfully represented in Parliament,' that all legislation was stopped till remedies were devised for the cattle-plague. Railways, because they were strong in parliamentary influence, were allowed to destroy the homes of thousands of the working classes and drive them to die in crowded fever dens without hopes of redress. The Factory Acts had been opposed by the rich on the 'paltry or cold-hearted plea that they would interfere with industry; as if it were the mission of a great nation simply to produce bales of goods and to swell exports and imports, even at the cost of sacrificing the health and blighting the minds of the young.' Why were not these Acts extended to the agricultural districts, where in many villages there was not one young man who could read the newspaper? It was because landlords and tenants were represented, whilst the agricultural labourers had not a single representative. This and other social reforms

[1] Speech at Brighton, January 15, 1867.

were, in his mind, essentially connected with political enfranchisement, and he was doing his best to call attention to the subject both in and out of Parliament.

In the House he endeavoured to bring forward a measure which always had a special and personal interest for him—the extension of the Factory Acts system to the agricultural labourers. He moved a resolution to this effect (on February 26, 1867), in a forcible speech, withdrawing the resolution on Mr. Walpole's assurance that Government meant to deal with the question. The report of a Commission upon the employment of women and children in agriculture had called attention to the mischiefs of the 'gang' system. Fawcett, in seconding a resolution moved by Mr. Dent in favour of some application of the Factory Acts to agriculture, contrasted, as at Brighton, the interest taken in the cattle-plague by some members with the want of interest in the 'more terrible plague which was ruining thousands of the constituents' of the same gentlemen. He had received 'scores of letters' corroborating the sickening details set forth in the Commissioners' report. He spoke emphatically of the necessity of rescuing the children from their degradation, and referred significantly to a remark recently made by Mr. Gladstone. The leader of the Opposition had said, with 'mingled dread and amazement,' that some agricultural labourers would be enfranchised by the Government measure. What a sarcasm on the existing system that such terror should be roused by a proposal to give a few thousand labourers a voice in the only body which could remedy their grievances!

Fawcett himself introduced a measure, intended, of

course, only to enforce attention to the subject, and withdrawn at the second reading. It proposed that agricultural children should have to attend school on alternate days, and gave magistrates the power of ordering schools to be built at the expense of the rate-payers. The proposal, as critics could easily remark, was no doubt crude enough, but it helped on a question which was now rapidly coming to the front. In the session of 1868 a Government bill was introduced, and another was brought in by Mr. Bruce (now Lord Aberdare), but both were withdrawn. Fawcett took one more opportunity, in the debate upon Mr. Bruce's bill, to enforce the claims of agricultural labourers; but by this time Parliament was moribund, and only desirous of handing over all important questions to its more democratic successor.

There was another group of measures connected with education in which Fawcett had the advantage of speaking as an expert, and in which he accordingly took a leading part. The second speech which he delivered (April 26, 1866) in the House was on going into Committee upon a bill introduced by Mr. Bouverie for opening Fellowships to Dissenters. Fawcett's view of the whole question was perfectly clear and straightforward. Every religious test which excluded any sect from the Universities should be abolished. Oxford and Cambridge should be the culminating bodies in a great organisation of national education, as popular schools, yet to be founded, should be its base. The main difficulty was that colleges still considered themselves to be sacred institutions, bound only to embody the wishes of their founders, and claiming freedom from all external interference and vulgar tests of utility. Fawcett's pride in his University and his warm appreciation of its merits might lead him to sympathise in some degree with its claims to independence, but not to such independence as would interfere with its national character. Neither colleges nor Universities could occupy a position worthy of them till every test was swept away which excluded any part of the nation. The greatest glory of Cambridge was that its rewards were given with absolute impartiality to intellectual excellence, but with the proviso that it must not be intellectual excellence in a Dissenter. That irrelevant proviso should be summarily and thoroughly abolished.

Fawcett's view has prevailed; nor do I think that many people will doubt that it was the statesmanlike view. The Liberal party, however, or its leaders, were slow to accept this, and preferred to go on nibbling at the question for years in a half-hearted fashion, proposing compromises and safeguards, and dealing with one fragment after another, till at last they contrived to sidle and twist into the position which Fawcett would have had them occupy at first. People who prefer such roundabout processes naturally resent the action of the plain straightforward persons who prefer to make only one bite at the cherry. Whether, as a matter of policy, it is or is not desirable to introduce a half measure in order to conciliate the prejudices of opponents is a question of expediency upon which it is always difficult to pronounce a judgment, especially at some distance of time, when the arguments for a half-measure have ceased to be intelligible. Considering the rapidity with which conversion has taken place, we may be inclined to think that an open assertion of the plain principle would have been the safest as well as the most straightforward course. Fawcett was probably justified in thinking that the reluctance with which his leaders took up the only firm ground in the matter covered some real distrust of the principle itself.

The question, meanwhile, was oddly complicated. There were, in the first place, tests upon taking degrees. At Cambridge a compromise had been arranged by which Dissenters were allowed to take the degree of B.A. without reserve; and to take the titular degree of M.A. without acquiring the privilege of a vote in the senate, almost the only tangible privilege which it conferred. At Oxford no degree could be taken by a Dissenter. In the next place, the Act of Uniformity imposed a test upon all Fellows; though, whilst this test was actually imposed at Cambridge, it had, oddly enough, fallen out of use at Oxford, because, I presume, Dissenters were there sufficiently excluded by the University regulations, which compelled all students to sign the Thirty-nine Articles. A Fellow had to take a degree, and was therefore incidentally compelled to be a member of the Church of England. In practice, many Dissenters of all varieties were admitted as students at Cambridge, and had distinguished themselves in examinations. They could also hold Scholarships, although they were forbidden to gain the higher reward of a Fellowship, and consequently of a place in the governing bodies of the colleges. Besides these tests, many Fellowships in both

Universities could only be held on condition of taking orders in the Church of England. Fawcett had already taken an active part in agitating for the removal of these restrictions. He had done what he could in the discussion of the college statutes. He had got up a petition at the end of 1861 for throwing open the Fellowships, which was signed by seventy Fellows, including twenty-eight Fellows of Trinity, and was presented to Parliament in the next session. In the two sessions of 1864 and 1865 a bill for the abolition of tests at Oxford had been brought in ; it was thrown out upon the third reading in 1864 by 173 to 171, and withdrawn in 1865 after the second reading had been carried by 206 to 190.

In 1866 the same bill was brought in by Mr. (now Lord) Coleridge, and passed its second reading by a large majority (217 to 103), but, after getting through Committee, was withdrawn in July ; the change of Ministry having probably made its further progress hopeless. This bill applied only to degrees ; but in the same session Mr. Bouverie introduced a bill for repealing the clause in the Act of Uniformity which imposed a test upon Fellows of colleges. A debate took place on the motion for going into Committee, in which Fawcett made his second speech. He said that 'the lifespring of the University' was the principle of electing the most distinguished men to Fellowships. Mr. Coleridge had apparently thought that Dissenters would be satisfied by admission to degrees. He claimed for them what was far more important, that they should 'have the full right to enjoy the endowments of the Universities.' Ironical applause from the Opposition benches showed that this claim was still taken to represent a monstrous greediness on the part of the Dissenters. Fawcett had pointed out that the grievance was not one which existed only in theory. Trinity had not had a senior Wrangler since 1846. Mr. Stirling, senior Wrangler in 1860, and the first to break this run of ill-fortune, had been excluded from a Fellowship because he was a Scotch Presbyterian. The senior Wrangler of 1861, again from Trinity, Mr. Aldis, was excluded because he was an English Dissenter. Mr. Aldis's two younger brothers had greatly distinguished themselves in 1863 and 1866, and were equally excluded. In many other cases the same restriction had caused injury to the college and injustice to the candidates. It was, indeed, a curious comment upon the ostensible motives of the supporters of the old system that Scotch Presbyterians, Wesleyans, Baptists, and Catholics should be excluded in order to maintain the purity of the faith in institutions where every clever lad studied Mill's Logic or Comte's Philosophy, and which were in point of fact the very centres of free speculation in the country. But it was not the interest of either party to insist upon this illustration of the national attachment to forms, however futile. This bill got into Committee by 206 to 186, and passed a third reading, but was finally withdrawn.

In 1867 both bills reappeared, with the addition of a third bill brought in by Mr. Ewart, allowing the admission of non-collegiate students. This bill was referred, on Fawcett's motion, to a Select Committee by 253 to 166 (April 10, 1867). He moved and carried that the bill for abolishing University tests should be made to apply

to Cambridge as well as Oxford. The success of his
motion was unexpected, and, as he says, so discouraged
opposition that the bill was allowed to pass without
alteration. It reached the House of Lords, where, on
July 25, the second reading was defeated by 74 to 46.
Fawcett also moved the second reading of the bill for
throwing open Fellowships; and upon this occasion Mr.
Gladstone made a speech indicating rather obscurely his
own view of the subject. He was, it seemed, in favour
of doing something in regard to the endowments as well
as degrees, but he desired some securities for religious
education after the admission of Dissenters to college
authority. He decided, on the whole, to vote against
the bill, the second reading of which was carried by
200 to 156 (May 29, 1867). The third reading was not
moved till August 7, when the bill was lost by 41 to 34.
Before the session of 1868 Fawcett had a rather sharp
correspondence with some of his allies. The Oxford reformers had come to the conclusion that it would be best
to separate from Cambridge, and to bring in a bill which,
besides combining the two bills for throwing open degrees
and Fellowships, should carry out various changes in the
constitution of Oxford, not directly applicable to Cambridge. Fawcett protested vigorously in the name of
the Cambridge Liberals. He could not understand the
policy of mixing the question of religious tests with an
entirely different set of questions, making the bill, he
said, 'an extraordinary jumble of discordant elements,' and
that at a time when success upon the main issue seemed
to be within reach, and many men were actually await-
ing election as soon as tests should be removed. His

Oxford allies were apparently not convinced by this very sound sense; but though they remonstrated, they at last gave way upon Fawcett's ·declaring that he should persist in moving the inclusion of Cambridge. An 'Oxford and Cambridge Universities Bill' was accordingly introduced by Sir J. Coleridge, Mr. Bouverie, and Mr. Grant Duff; the second reading was carried by 198 to 140 on July 1, though three weeks later the bill was withdrawn. The proposal was now to abolish all tests upon degrees (except degrees in divinity) and Fellowships, so far as these tests were imposed by Parliament. This would still leave untouched the tests imposed by college statutes; which might be altered after a more or less cumbrous process by the colleges themselves, with the approval of their visitors.

The question had reached this stage in Fawcett's first Parliament. He had been the leading representative of the Cambridge reformers. Another Parliament, with a strong Liberal majority really meaning business, might be expected to make short work of the remaining obstacles.

I leave to a future chapter an account of Fawcett's action upon another matter of the highest importance. He had already taken a share in certain discussions upon India which were destined to determine the direction of a great part of his parliamentary activity in later years. It is enough to say now that he had made a decided impression. He had worked upon some important committees, especially upon that which considered Mr. Ewart's bill for University reform, and upon one which considered the extension of the Factory Acts. He

had established beyond all dispute that his blindness
was no disqualification for taking an important part
in business or for the discussion of various financial
questions in which he had shown his power of dealing
with figures as well as abstract principles. Nor had he
done anything so far to make his independent attitude
offensive to his own party in general. The ' tea-room '
seceders could say that their action had been justified by
the passage of a measure of enfranchisement sufficient to
mark a substantial transference of political power. If he
had been a little too thoroughgoing for his party leaders,
a Radical constituency would find no fault with him. The
elections of November 1868 gave a large Liberal majority
in the country generally, but Fawcett had a rather sharp
contest. He was opposed by Mr. Moor, his previous
antagonist; by Mr. Ashbury, a Conservative who kept a
yacht; and by his old Liberal predecessor, Mr. Coningham.
Some complaints had arisen in part of the constituency
who would have preferred a rich resident. The poll was as
follows:—White, 3,342; Fawcett, 3,081; Ashbury, 2,917;
Moor, 1,232; Coningham, 432.

Fawcett's position at the time will be best understood
from the following correspondence with Cairnes. Fawcett
writes to Cairnes, on August 23, 1868:—

' I begin to be very confident that Gladstone will
obtain a great majority. The Irish Church would have
been a good cry to have appealed to the old constituencies,
but working-men neither care about the Irish Church nor
any other Church. The election, though satisfactory in a
party sense, will, I fear, return a House scarcely superior
in character to the last. Few good new men are coming out,

and more over-rich manufacturers and ironmasters are standing than ever. Before the next general election after the coming one, the working-men will have felt their power and will have learnt, perhaps by bitter experience, that Liberals do not all belong to the same species; in fact, a consummate naturalist, like Darwin, would classify Mill and Harvey Lewis as belonging to different and well-defined genera. Something must be done immediately Parliament meets to check election expenses. When last I saw you in Dover Street, I little thought that late that evening the Government would give notice of reversing the clause I passed for throwing necessary election expenses upon the rates. The shabby tactics of Disraeli have done much to make the country favour the clause. If I am returned I shall embody the clause in a bill and introduce it the first night of the session. I have had no news about Westminster since leaving London, but I cling to the conviction that Mill is safe. I spent a day at Brighton about a fortnight since, and everything there looks as promising as possible. Did you read Hooker's Address to the British Association? Some portions of it were most masterly; the " Spectator " is, I think, just in its criticism of his sweeping hostility to all metaphysics. When the next essay is written on peasant proprietors, the 26,000,000l. which have been subscribed in cash, a great portion of it by French peasants, to the recent loan, will provide a strong argument in favour of cultivation by the owner. I am staying in the midst of what is considered to be one of the most prosperous agricultural districts of England. It would be almost impossible to find a labourer who had saved a sovereign, and not one

in a thousand of these labourers will save enough to keep
him from the poor-rates when old age compels him to
cease work.   Yet nine Englishmen out of ten think that
it is in agriculture that we show our great superiority to
the French.'

Cairnes writes from Nice, November 21, 1868 :—

'My dear Fawcett,—I cannot repress the impulse to
send you a line of heartiest congratulation on your
triumph at Brighton, of which I have just received
intelligence. . . . But alas! that our exultation should
be dashed by the deplorable disaster at Westminster! I
can hardly describe the mortification it has caused me :
even the great gain of the Liberal party on the whole is
for me no compensation for this one loss.   The majority
was already large enough, if it were only of the right sort;
and who shall estimate the injury not only to Parliament,
but to the country, of being deprived of that exemplar of
far-seeing statesmanship, commanding views, and lofty
moral purpose which Mill's presence in the House
secured ?   And then to think how the enemies of truth
and light will blaspheme!   How the Philistines will
triumph! Is there any chance that any other constituency
will have the virtue to elect him ?   Greenwich, I see,
has elected Gladstone. In the event of G.'s being returned
for S. Lancashire, would it be possible to substitute
Mill at Greenwich ?

'I observe also with great regret that all the working-
men's candidates have been rejected—a most unsatisfactory feature in the case.

'It will be a relief to you that the hustings struggle
is over; and now will come on the struggle in Parliament.

But with such a majority as Gladstone will have all will
for a time be plain sailing; it is when the Irish land
question and the education question, English and Irish,
come forward that the quality of our Liberalism will be
tested, and it is then that Mill will be missed.'

Fawcett replies from Cambridge, December 11,
1868 :—

'You and I feel alike about the rejection of Mill.
Those who have watched him in the House of Commons
can perhaps fully realise the injury which his rejection
has inflicted on English politics. He diffused a certain
moral atmosphere over an assembly whose average tone
is certainly not high. A letter which I received from
Mill yesterday confirms me in the belief I have long
entertained that Parliament involved to him a most
severe personal sacrifice. He speaks almost with enthusiastic joy of being restored to freedom, and he is
evidently supremely happy in the prospect of being able
to work uninterruptedly. Still I am sure his sense of
public duty is so high that he would at once accept a
seat if one were offered to him. The working-men know
what a friend he is of theirs, and I believe they are determined to return him the first time a good opportunity
offers.

'The Liberal majority at the general election is of
course eminently satisfactory, but there is much in the
constitution of the present House which is very dis-
appointing. Intellectually it is inferior to the last,
and wealthy, uneducated manufacturers and merchants
are more predominant than ever. Mill always predicted
that this would be the case, thinking that the new voters

R

would require two or three years to understand the power
which has been given to them. I had a hard fight at
Brighton. Not only was there disunion in my own party,
got up by a small section who thought I did not spend
enough money in the town, but the Tory who opposed
me was very rich, and all that wealth could do against
me was done. My success was peculiarly satisfactory,
because it was obtained without a paid agent or a paid
canvasser; and we never held even a meeting at a public-
house. I quite agree with you that the present Government will have to be most narrowly watched with regard
to what they do upon education and the land question in
Ireland. Lowe, upon the subject, is as much in the dark
as any Tory.'

Mill's letter here noticed says that though the elections have gone against the most advanced party, they
have produced a House sufficient for the immediate purpose of making Gladstone Minister, and disestablishing
the Irish Church. Before the next general election the
working-classes will have had time to organise and insist upon due consideration of their claims. Meanwhile
Fawcett will be in the House to assert great principles,
and is as unlikely as any man to be discouraged. The
misgivings which find utterance in the above letters as to
the action of Mr. Gladstone's Government were prophetic.
In the Parliament, which lasted until January 1874,
Fawcett came to occupy a position in the House, and
before the country, which was remarkable, and may in
some respects be called unique. A Radical member under
a Liberal Administration is naturally part of a forlorn
hope. It is his proper function to condemn the caution of

leaders who lag behind a full acceptance of his principles. Fawcett had plenty of allies ready to find fault with Mr. Gladstone for not going fast or far enough. But his disapproval had a special colouring of its own. He was an almost isolated dissentient upon several important matters. He insisted upon exercising his right of private judgment. He held firmly to certain principles which involved a disagreement with some of his closest allies; and he especially devoted himself to the defence of causes which, as he thought, were neglected both by his official leaders and by the smaller band of thoroughgoing Radicals.

Such a position has its obvious dangers. I may assume, what no one, I think, ever doubted, that Fawcett acted upon principle; and, if it were necessary to prove the point, it would be sufficient to say that his action was not only unpalatable to the Government, but, in many ways, to his own constituents. Yet, whilst giving him the fullest credit for sincerity and uprightness, some critics might still maintain that he was crotchety or captious; that the love of independence degenerated into a desire of finding fault for the sake of fault-finding; and that he was not free from the weakness of courting the applause which is easily won by any man who speaks against his party. The answer to such a judgment, will, I hope, appear as we proceed. I shall, I think, be able to prove that his antagonism to the Government was not only upright and in full consistency with his strongest convictions, but also implied soundness (though certainly not infallibility) of judgment and generosity of feeling. This, however, must be shown by giving in detail the main objects of

his political activity. For the present I will venture to
point out one cause of difficulty which had an effect
upon his position throughout. Mr. Gladstone's personal
popularity became from this time one of the marked
factors in the political situation. It was due, as I think
I may say, to the fact that the great bulk of the constituents were convinced that he was thoroughly in
earnest; that he meant really to carry out great measures
of reform instead of making them mere stepping-stones
to power; and that he appealed to high moral principles
instead of questionable prejudices of temporary expediency. Fawcett shared this sentiment to a great
extent. He had spoken warmly of Mr. Gladstone's
sincerity upon the Reform question, and held him to
deserve the thoroughgoing loyalty of the Liberal party.
His private letters fully confirm his public utterances.
But there was a curious contrast between the two men.
Mr. Gladstone, if I may say so, was as typical a representative of the Oxford which obeyed the impulse of
Newman, as Fawcett of the comparatively plain, practical,
and downright Cambridge. Mr. Gladstone's astonishing
versatility of mind, the power of interesting himself in
ancient Greece or in modern theology which relieves his
political energy, was a source of wondering amusement
to Fawcett's strong, but comparatively limited, intellect.
He was rather scandalised than amused by the singular
subtlety and ingenuity in presenting unexpected inter-
pretations of apparently plain doctrines which makes the
history of Mr. Gladstone's opinions so curious a subject
for the psychologist. And these peculiarities led to one
important source of misunderstanding. No one admired

Mr. Gladstone as a financier more heartily than Fawcett. He often told anecdotes to illustrate Mr. Gladstone's power of grasping the most complicated figures, and of assimilating spontaneously the details of business questions, to the amazement of professional experts. But when Mr. Gladstone entered a different region Fawcett could no longer follow him so easily. As soon as the theologian showed through the financier he was annoyed by what enemies describe as the Jesuitical quality of the Premier's mind. He summed up his own opinion in a phrase which occurs in one of his speeches, and which I find written down on a separate scrap of paper. 'Gladstone,' said Fawcett, 'will go as far as he can in the direction of commercial liberty, and as far as he is forced in the direction of religious liberty.' Questions in which religious liberty was concerned played an important part in this Parliament, and Fawcett's distrust of Mr. Gladstone's sentiments affected his political attitude. The first matter of this kind was the old struggle over University tests, which, though not of the first order in politics, may be at once dealt with. Fawcett was especially interested in it, and the action of the Government made a considerable impression on his mind.

The bill of 1868 was again introduced by Sir John Coleridge (now Solicitor-General) in 1869, and supported by members of Government, though not as a Government measure. The second reading was carried (March 15) by 251 to 75. The effect of the bill was to remove all tests so far as imposed by Acts of Parliament; but Dissenters would still be excluded from a share of endowments until the colleges had altered their own statutes.

Fawcett urged that the matter should be settled for, not by, the colleges. He desired that in any case the process of removing tests from their statutes should be facilitated. He therefore proposed an amendment by which the colleges would have been enabled to remove the tests by a simple vote of the governing body instead of being forced to apply to their visitors or to the Queen in Council. This change was resisted by the Government. Fawcett's amendment was lost by 234 to 147. The bill passed the Commons, but was defeated in the Lords by 91 to 54. Fawcett thought that if Government had supported the bill, as they should have done, it might have been passed in this session.

In the next session (1870) Sir J. Coleridge once more introduced the bill, and now as a Government measure. The Government had by this time moved up to the position previously occupied by Fawcett. Sir J. Coleridge admitted explicitly that Fawcett had been right and that he had himself been wrong. The college tests were to be abolished without reference to the consent of the colleges. Fawcett, so far justified in his previous action, was still far from satisfied. He pointed out that many Fellowships (at least 130 at Oxford and 30 at Cambridge) were still tenable only by clergymen. He moved that these clerical restrictions should be abolished and that no one should hold a Fellowship or a Headship the longer in virtue of being in Orders. This amendment was rejected by 157 to 79, and the bill went up to the House of Lords.

Its reception there was remarkable. Lord Salisbury no longer met it with unqualified opposition. He virtually accepted the principle, which had seemed so scandalous a short time before, that Dissenters must be admitted not only to degrees but to Fellowships. He endorsed the view which had been taken by Mr. Gladstone in the previous Parliament. He pointed out—what was indeed sufficiently obvious—that the tests, if intended to fulfil their ostensible purpose of protecting the religious faith of students, excluded the wrong persons. They would keep out Mr. Stirling (the Presbyterian senior Wrangler of 1860), or Mr. Hartog (the Jewish senior Wrangler of 1869), but they let in essayists and reviewers, and by no means eradicated the leaven of Agnosticism. There, as he said with undeniable force, was the real danger; and he moved that the bill should be referred to a Select Committee, which might suggest such safeguards for a religious education as would be necessary after the admission of diverse sects. The motion was carried by the small majority of 97 to 83.

The Committee sat accordingly, was reappointed in the next session (1871), and produced a report. Meanwhile, the old bill had been again introduced in the Commons, and passed its second reading without a division. Fawcett renewed his attack upon clerical Fellowships in Committee. He was beaten by 182 to 160, and hereupon had a sharp passage of arms with Mr. Gladstone. He hoped, he said, that the Government would carefully consider their position; for though Mr. Gladstone had won a narrow triumph, a Liberal Government had never before found fewer Liberal supporters on a vital point of Liberal principles. Mr. Gladstone retorted that Ministers had pondered their position, and that their decision was irrevocable. They acted, as he had before explained, in deference to the House of Lords, which had shown itself ready to consider the question favourably, and which should therefore not have additional demands made upon it. At a later period of the session Fawcett had occasion to remind Mr. Gladstone of this (as he held) excessive politeness towards the Upper House.

The Lords now amended the bill in the light of their Committee's reports. They proposed to erect a barrier against the dangerous intrusions of Freethought by imposing a declaration upon tutors that they would teach nothing contrary to the authority of Holy Scripture; by making chapel services obligatory, exempting Heads of Houses from the bill, and one or two minor changes. The amendments were carried by small majorities (71 to 66 on the main point); but it is needless to inquire whether they would have done anything to keep at bay an enemy who was already within the walls. The House of Commons rejected them with a trifling concession about providing religious services for members of the Church of England. The House of Lords did not insist, and so at last the struggle ended, and the tests finally vanished. A restriction very injurious to Dissenters was removed, though it can hardly be affirmed that the influence of such feeble trammels upon freedom of thought was of any particular importance in other respects.

The impression upon Fawcett's mind was strong. Government had shown little energy at first in pushing the measure; they had slowly come to admit that the position which he had taken from the first was the right one; and they had still withheld one most important

part of the measure (the abolition of clerical Fellowships),
alleging a scruple founded upon tenderness to the House
of Lords, which certainly had little weight in other important matters. A straightforward and thoroughgoing
policy from the first would, Fawcett thought, have saved
much trouble and have proved that their hearts were in
the matter. It may be briefly mentioned, as some illustration of the rate at which opinion changes in such
matters, that under the Commission appointed in 1877
by the Conservative Government the abolition of clerical
Fellowships, for which Fawcett struggled so hard under
the Liberal Government, was quietly carried out (I believe
with scarcely an exception), and so far as I know excited
no protest.

Before this, other questions had arisen of greater
importance. Fawcett had expressed himself decidedly
in the first session (1869) of the new Parliament upon
various questions, in some of which he adopted the
ordinary Radical principles, though in most of them his
own personal convictions gave a special character to his
criticisms. He had again brought forward his proposal
for throwing election expenses upon the rates. He had
moved (April 9) that appointments in the civil and diplomatic services should be given by open competition.
This resolution was opposed by Government as too sweeping, although they contemplated a measure for introducing the same principle, and the resolution was rejected
by 281 to 30. He had attacked with some warmth some
provisions of a measure for regulating the pensions
granted to the holders of the great political offices. The
question seems to have stirred him considerably, as did

every question in which the purity and fairness of Government patronage came under suspicion. He alleged facts to prove that such pensions were often bestowed upon men who did not need them, or had merited them by no real services; and he complained that, whilst dockyard labourers were turned off at the first demand for economy, care was taken that the economic impulses of Government should not injure men in influential positions. Both in Parliament and in addressing his constituents he refers to this with some indignation. He interfered more emphatically in another more exciting piece of legislation, where there was also some question of imperfect purity. The great Liberal measure of 1869 was the Disestablishment of the Irish Church. Upon the main question Fawcett was, of course, in complete harmony with his leaders. The Church Establishment was doomed as soon as it was seriously attacked. But it was always intolerable to Fawcett that a measure, just in itself, should be advanced by anything savouring of jobbery. The stronger the case in point of principle, the more it should be independent of any appeal to lower motives. Mr. Gladstone had proposed an ingenious arrangement which was, perhaps, a little puzzling to the ordinary mind. The Irish landholders were to pay the tithe rent-charges for fifty-two years; and at the end of that time they would have redeemed the whole sum and be in possession of their estates without any charge whatever. Mr. Gladstone explained how this would be carried out by certain advances of funds, in such a way that all parties concerned would make a good bargain. Fawcett mentioned that this was, in fact, to make a present to the landlords, the value of which (that is, as I understand, of the ultimate capitalised value of the tithe rent-charges) he estimated at 7,000,000*l.*; and he declared it to be part of a process properly, though vulgarly, described as 'greasing the wheels' of the measure. His protest was unavailing. The clause was passed by 181 to 33. When the Lords' amendments were under consideration, Fawcett made a final protest, and complained that he had been the only Liberal member to object to the scheme. That his conduct was regarded as proof of an impracticable disposition is probable enough; and he had not even the complete sympathy of his most valued ally. Fawcett had, as usual, consulted Mill upon the point. Mill thought that as a matter of tactics the Government might be justified in making a present to the Irish landlords which cost it nothing and, in fact, only amounted to giving them the benefit of its better credit. He pointed out difficulties in the way of any other appropriation of the funds; and, though admitting that criticism in Fawcett's sense might be desirable, inclined against any directly hostile movement. Fawcett, however, acted upon his own view, the soundness of which I need not discuss. If on such points he was too much of a puritan, it was, at least, an honourable error.

In the following session (1870) questions arose of far more importance, upon which the division of sentiment between the Government and its supporters became more decidedly accentuated. Two great measures were passed— the Irish Land Bill and the Bill for Elementary Education—the last of which was probably the most permanently important of all the legislation of the time, and that in which Fawcett was most profoundly interested. The Irish Land Bill apparently received his complete approval. He took no part in the debates; but his view may be sufficiently gathered from an address to his constituents delivered (October 18, 1869) in anticipation of the Government measure, the nature of which was, of course, still unknown. Fawcett then stated that he had been much impressed by a pamphlet recently published by Mr. (now Sir) George Campbell. He proposed, on the strength of the Indian precedents adduced by Mr. Campbell, to have a periodical Government valuation of farms at intervals of twenty or thirty years. The tenant would have fixity of tenure in the interval, and at the end of each period would also have a right to the benefit of his own improvements. Fawcett was careful to point out that by this scheme no injustice would be inflicted upon the landlord. It has often been pointed out that fixity of tenure is incompatible with freedom of sale. If the tenant can part with his rights, the result of such a scheme may be only the creation of a new set of tenants in a worse position than the first. Fawcett therefore added that there should be in all cases a strict covenant against under-letting. He proposed, further, that if the tenant had injured instead of improving the land, the landlord should have the same claim to compensation as the tenant in the opposite case. Fawcett apparently justified the interference of the State on the ground that the existing sentiment in Ireland did in fact deny the existence of the landlord's absolute right in the soil; and that it was idle to overlook the facts or assume an 'ideal' state of society. His anticipation that such a measure would satisfy the demands of the Irish population was clearly erroneous. He thought, however, that the scheme involved no interference with the rights of property in the taking away from anyone of a single farthing which properly belonged to him. And it may be worth while to note what was his view before the question had passed into a different stage.

The Education question, however, was that which really aroused his closest interest. As I have already shown, the foundation of an efficient system of national education was the measure which, of all others, he had advocated from his earliest years ; which he believed, on theoretical grounds, to represent the most legitimate method by which legislation could contribute to the elevation of the people; and which he had already done his best to bring before the attention of Parliament. He had seen with satisfaction that public interest in the question had been rapidly developing, and that an adhesion to proposals for compulsory education was now popular, where four or five years before it had been regarded as a dangerous avowal. In the session of 1869 he had (March 12) opposed a motion by Mr. Melly for a further inquiry, on the ground that the time was already come for immediate action. On June 25 he had proposed a resolution calling for legislation upon that branch of the question which was of all others most interesting to him— the education of agricultural labourers. Government, he said, could not do much by direct legislation to improve the lodging or raise the wages of this neglected class ; but the extension of education was in their power and was of vital importance. He complained that the Factory

Acts had been extended to every class except this which most needed it.

The growth of public interest in the question was indicated and stimulated by the formation, in 1869, of the Birmingham League. Fawcett joined the League and spoke vigorously on its behalf at a congress held at Birmingham in October. His adhesion afterwards gave him some regret. Upon the main principle, as he understood it, there was indeed no difficulty. The aim of the League was the establishment of a universal system of compulsory education. Where necessary, the schools were to be supported by rates. Fawcett, as I have said, looked forward to a period in which there should be a complete system of graduated education from the elementary schools to the Universities, so that every meritorious person, of whatever class or creed, might have the chance of developing his faculties to the fullest possible extent. This was throughout the ideal which he contemplated and endeavoured to advance by every means in his power.

Questions, however, immediately arose, some of which were answered by the Birmingham League in what seemed to him a questionable manner. There was, in the first place, the difficulty of the relation between the new schools and the voluntary institutions which already existed, and which were almost universally associated with the Church of England or with some religious sect. The tests which still shackled the Universities were in process of removal; but it was a far more difficult problem how to reconcile universal compulsion with perfect religious equality. If secular and religious education could be absolutely separated, instruction in the purely secular matters might be secured by the State for every child, whilst the various sects might be allowed to provide religious teaching. The simple principle would therefore be that the State schools should be purely secular; and this was Fawcett's own view. Catholics, Protestants, and Secularists have the same letters, and accept the same rules of arithmetic, and might learn them at the same schools. Catechisms and creeds might be instilled elsewhere by priests and ministers. The Birmingham League, however, shrank from the name of irreligious and adopted the compromise of proposing that the Bible should be read 'without note or comment.' The schools, it was said, should be 'un-sectarian,' but not 'secular.' Fawcett characteristically confessed that he had found it rather hard to see the difference between the two words. He was willing, however, to accept the proposal for the present; though he afterwards expressed his regret for not having taken in this, as in other cases, the most plain and unequivocal position.

Beyond this, however, lay a more difficult point. Rate-supported schools might come into conflict with the voluntary schools. Fawcett, to whom it seemed infinitely more important that children should be taught somewhere than that their teaching should be confided to any particular sect, was willing to make use of all the existing machinery. He had no hostility to the existing schools. He hoped, he said, that their supporters might be stimulated to greater efforts in order to avoid the imposition of rates. The League, however, advocated a principle which, if fully accepted, would tend to the rapid

destruction of all voluntary schools. One part of their
programme was that education should be gratuitous as
well as compulsory. Fawcett does not seem fully to
have appreciated the bearing of their proposal in this
direction at the time. The scheme had not been reduced
to detail so as to reveal its tendencies; and all who desired a national and compulsory system of education,
and thought that the religious difficulty might be easily
set aside, could support the League in general terms.
Fawcett, however, objected to the gratuitous system upon
a different principle. It was, as is sufficiently clear,
entirely opposed to his general economical principles.
The fatal error was, as he urged, that it would diminish
the sentiment of parental responsibility. Government
might rightly interfere on behalf of defenceless children
and insist upon the parents teaching as well as feeding and clothing them. To bring a child into the world
was to incur a grave responsibility, and no action of the
State should tend to obscure that fact. But to relieve
a parent from the cost of his children's schooling would
most emphatically diminish his motives for forethought.
Yet Fawcett was so strongly impressed with. the importance of working for State education that, for the
present, he consented to overlook the point of difference.
He said that it was 'only a detail,' and that he was
'perfectly willing to sacrifice his own individual views.'

Mr. Forster introduced his measure on February 17,
1870. Fawcett immediately made the criticism which
determined his action during the session. The vital
question with him was that of universal compulsion.
The Government measure dealt with the difficulties of

introducing the new principle by what was called
'permissive compulsion.' The school boards were to
be empowered, but not compelled, to frame bye-laws for
enforcing attendance. This was, according to Fawcett,
the great blot upon the Government proposal. He wrote
a letter to the 'Times' (February 26), in which he
summed up very forcibly his objections to the principle.
He spoke upon an amendment to the second reading,
moved by Mr. Dixon, the representative of the Birmingham League, to the effect that no system would be satisfactory which left the question of religious instruction in
rate-supported schools to be decided by the local authorities. Fawcett took care to disavow unqualified sympathy
with the League, but upon this point he supported them.
The effect of the measure, he said, would be to set up a
religious difficulty in every school district. He maintained
that there should be an absolute separation between
religious and secular teaching, and he denounced permissive legislation as a fatal mistake. The amendment
was withdrawn. As the session proceeded Fawcett's
opposition became more pronounced. The provision for
'permissive school boards' was a timid, feeble compromise, implying a 'semi-paralysis' of Government. He
complained (July 8) that Government had not dared to
accept the principle of compulsion; he said that they had
no definite policy, and declared that their half-measure
was doomed to 'melancholy and disastrous failure.' 'Is
it well,' he had asked in his letter to the 'Times,' 'that our
statesmen should always wait to be influenced by platform
speeches, public meetings, and all the other forms of
popular agitation? If Mr. Gladstone and his colleagues

s

boldly declared that any policy were right and just, would they not thus do much to make the country accept it ? ' The criticism applied to many other questions besides this of education, and expresses one of his characteristic principles. A strong downright assertion of vital principles was the thing to command Fawcett's respect and excite his sympathy. He demanded it much more frequently than he got it.

Upon this point, however, it may be well doubted whether he did not miscalculate. Mr. Forster had stated distinctly that he was in favour of compulsion. But he thought it undesirable to be in advance of public opinion. An attempt to introduce compulsion without general support from those whom it would affect might undoubtedly have provoked a failure. It is impossible to say now whether he could safely have moved faster than he actually did in introducing a principle still so novel and so little accepted. The main question, after all, was whether the pressure would implant a system likely to be further developed or whether it would lead, as Fawcett predicted, to a disastrous failure. Fawcett quoted precedents of the frequent breakdown of measures framed upon the permissive principle. He argued that the Factory Acts would certainly have failed had they not been compulsory; he urged that exceptional legislation was always unpopular, and that a varying practice would make compulsion hateful in the districts which adopted it. He asked why the districts which had proved their zeal in the cause by a provision of adequate schools, and in which therefore the formation of school boards would not be required, should be deprived of the

benefits of compulsion. Perhaps there was some inconsistency in this reasoning. If the benefits of compulsion
were recognised, the introduction in some districts might
be expected to facilitate its introduction elsewhere.
That was Mr. Forster's view, who argued that in two
or three years we should be in a better position for demanding universal compulsion. Experience, I fancy,
has proved that Mr. Forster was right. Indeed, Fawcett
seems to me to have overlooked one principle which, in
the light of later experience, seems to be tolerably clear.
Permissive 'compulsion' may naturally fail when the
restrictions imposed are unpopular with the class affected,
or acceptable only on the condition of their being equally
applied elsewhere. But in this case the power of compelling attendance was to be part of the privileges of the
new school boards, and one to which they would naturally
cling. Now a body of this kind once established has a
wonderful vitality; it acquires a corporate spirit; it is
anxious to make itself felt; and it is much more likely
to grow and to develop itself at the cost of rival institutions than to die out for want of power. School boards
once set up had no difficulty in taking root. There was
in reality a greater danger that they would develop the
ordinary vice of official bodies, demand wider privileges,
and consider themselves to be infallible and immaculate
institutions.

It is not wonderful, however, that the early predictions as to the mode of working of a new system should
be as fallacious in this as in almost every case. Fawcett's
real complaint came to be that the system, as originally
devised, failed to affect the class for which his sympathies

were the liveliest.   The agricultural districts were comparatively untouched.   No compulsion was imposed upon
them.   The old national schools were left pretty much as
before, and no attention was paid to Fawcett's frequent
complaint that there was less need of more school accommodation in the country than of more security that existing schools should be filled.   He called attention to this
on May 27, 1870, in connection with the report of the
Commission upon agricultural labour.   He said that
in many districts schools had multiplied whilst education declined, because the tendency was now to set
children to work at an earlier age than formerly, and the
schools were often not half filled.   He maintained that
some system of universal compulsion was the only possible remedy.   Mr. Bruce stated that he preferred to
wait till compulsion had been tried elsewhere; and soon
afterwards the House was counted out.

The differences between Fawcett and the Birmingham
League did not hinder his co-operation at starting, but
they became gradually more pronounced.   They were,
in fact, vital.   The debates in 1870 turned to a great
extent upon the religious difficulty, the provision of an
adequate. conscience clause, and the conditions under
which payments were to be made to the denominational
schools.   The famous twenty-fifth clause, under which
the fees of children at such schools might be paid by the
school boards, passed without discussion at the time, but
afterwards gave rise to a prolonged controversy.   The
Dissenters, who were a main support of Mr. Gladstone's
Government, were alienated by the inadequate treatment
of their claims; and much eloquence was spent upon

various forms of the religious or ecclesiastical question. Tenderness for the consciences of parents and children was of course the ostensible motive. No one could propose that a child should be forced to a school teaching doctrines to which its parents objected. The question was how far the difficulty should be allowed to limit compulsion. The difficulty, it may safely be said, was one which looks more formidable on paper than in practice. Children and even children's parents were sufficiently guarded by a profound indifference to all dogmatic theology from any excess of scrupulosity as to the tenets taught in the schools. The English working-man unfortunately is quite incompetent to be a Davie Deans, with a keen sense for right-hand defections and left-hand backslidings. He would care little enough for any of the dogmatic controversies which divide the Protestant sects. But the objections raised covered also the differences which are rather ecclesiastical than religious. The Established Church derived a certain prestige from its position as the most effective organ of national education, even if its school teaching did little enough in the way of attracting converts. The jealousies between Churchmen and Dissenters found ample expression under the guise of an excessive desire to save the consciences of the most indifferent and ignorant classes.

Fawcett's great anxiety in this matter was that educational interests should not be sacrificed to such jealousies. Compulsory education could not be secured if the matter were not satisfactorily settled. Parents might be indifferent enough, and yet be ready to set up scruples as a pretext for avoiding responsibility. They might become

sensitive to the heresies of their teachers, if upon that
ground they might leave their children untaught.   The
League aimed at meeting the difficulty by the establishment throughout the country of a system of free 'un-
sectarian' schools, to which everyone might be compelled
to go.   The free school would be a terrible competitor
for the denominational school.   Few parents would
prefer school fees and orthodoxy to gratuitous teaching
and 'unsectarianism.'   To this, if it could be carried out
fairly, and with general consent, Fawcett did not object.
But he heartily distrusted any excess of Government interference.   He did not wish to attack the denominational schools, except by providing better schools and
allowing a fair competition.   The competition would not
be fair if one set of schools were to be gratuitous and the
other supported by fees; and, as we have seen, he objected
emphatically, on still more vital principles, to the gratuitous system.   His adherence to the League was therefore
always qualified.   He would let the denominational
schools die out if a better substitute could be found.
But he was also perfectly willing to use them if they
could be made useful.   The question as to a single system
of rate-supported schools or a system admitting of
voluntary schools was with him a secondary point, whilst
with the Birmingham League it was primary.   Secure
education for every child—that was the one main point ;
neither sacrifice the essential to the interests of religious
bodies nor to the enemies of religious bodies.

Two years later he expressed his views emphatically.
Mr. Dixon then moved a resolution to the effect that the
Education Act was unsatisfactory, because it did not

provide for school boards in all districts nor compel attendance, and because it allowed payments to be made to
denominational schools and promoted religious discord.
He was seconded by Mr. Richard, who gave expression
to the discontent of the Dissenting bodies. Fawcett voted
for the resolution (rejected by 355 to 94), but took occasion to make a kind of apology for his previous action.
He still considered the compulsory provisions as inadequate. He hoped that Government would introduce
some supplementary legislation; but he frankly admitted
that much good had been done. His main point, however, was his repudiation of the views of some of his
allies. One member (Mr. Leatham) had said that the
important point was religious equality, and that compulsory education, which he thought scarcely suited to
the country, was a very secondary matter. This was precisely the reverse of Fawcett's view. Fawcett regretted
the time wasted on a 'miserable religious squabble.' He
regretted the subterfuge about teaching the Bible ' without note or comment.' He held that the so-called
religious question was of infinitely less importance than
the question of compulsion. But he protested with still
more emphasis against the system, favoured by the
League, of free education. He had come to see more
distinctly the real tendency of the proposal, and to feel
the full force of the objections, to which he had never
been blind. Free education would diminish parental
responsibility; it would make the prudent pay for the
reckless; and would increase the general tendency to
make other people pay when we ought to pay ourselves
—a tendency which was the prominent characteristic of

modern Socialism. One of the papers in the 'Essays and Lectures' is a reprint of a letter to the 'Times' in the December of 1870, written by Mrs. Fawcett, but (as she informs me) expressing opinions which had his entire concurrence. Indeed, the principle involved is perhaps the most characteristic of his whole political theory. To ask whether he was in the right would be to raise a question in political philosophy which will not be settled until the distant period at which political philosophy becomes truly scientific. The issue meanwhile of the controversy will be decided by actual conflict rather than by argument. One form of Radicalism points towards Socialism. The remedy which it favours for this, as for other evils, is the transference to a great State department of the functions which had been inadequately discharged by Churches or individuals. Fawcett so far agreed with this movement as to accept fully the necessity of some State interference. He was as strongly impressed as anyone with the necessity of a national effort, and of getting rid of the obstacles raised by the jealousies of hostile sects. But in his mind this view was combined with a strong jealousy of excessive State interference. He wished to strengthen the sense of parental responsibility, not to take the burthen off the shoulders of parents. It is a question whether, in point of fact, the measures which he approved had not an inevitable tendency to hasten the adoption of those which he regarded as dangerous. If the State once insists upon compulsory education, it may become necessary that it should go further and provide education upon the easiest terms. In any case, I will venture to say that here, as elsewhere, the difficulties urged by Fawcett are the crucial difficulties, and that the problem for the advocates of the opposite system is precisely to devise some means of meeting them satisfactorily. So long as they are simply ignored or pooh-poohed, sensible observers will have to remark that a problem is not solved by a resolution not to look difficulties in the face.

This marks the point of divergence between Fawcett and a different school of so-called Radicalism which, according to Mr. Herbert Spencer, should be properly identified with old-fashioned Conservatism. For the present, however, this particular question ceased to hold a conspicuous position in politics. Fawcett was more occupied by the shortcomings of the measure in another direction. He was anxious to bring agricultural children within the range of compulsory education. For them comparatively little had been done; and in later years he continued on all occasions to advocate this corollary from the principles already applied in other cases. As the movement lay rather apart from the main lines of political activity I shall not again refer to it, and it will be enough to indicate briefly the chief results obtained. In 1872 Mr. Clare Read brought in a Bill for the Education of Children Employed in Agriculture, which was in substance a partial extension of the Factory Acts legislation. It was withdrawn after a second reading, but again introduced and passed in 1873. Mr. Mundella and Fawcett both protested strongly against the weakness of this measure, which still left a great difference between the agricultural and manufacturing districts, and led, I believe, to little practical result. In

the next Parliament Fawcett spoke strongly in favour of
a bill introduced by 'Mr. Dixon, in 1874, providing for
compulsory attendance and election of school boards. It
was opposed by Government and defeated. In 1875 he
brought forward a motion for giving to agricultural
children the advantages already enjoyed by manufacturing children, which produced an animated debate but no
specific result. In 1875 and 1876 he supported Mr.
Dixon, who again introduced his bill and was again
defeated in both years. In the last year, however, a bill
was introduced by Lord Sandon, and finally passed into
law, which marked a distinct step in advance. This Act
provided for the appointment of ' school-attendance
committees ' by the local authorities in districts where
there was no school board. It also extended the
principle of the Factory Acts, but the attendance committees were not compelled to make bye-laws, except on
the voluntary requisition of the ratepayers. Another
provision satisfied, for the time at least, the agitators
against the famous twenty-fifth clause. It allowed parents,
if unable to pay the fees, to apply to the guardians without being considered to be in receipt of outdoor relief.
Although the money thus payable to denominational
schools came equally from the pockets of the ratepayers,
whether it was paid out of the poor-rates or by the
school board, the remonstrances made against the preceding plan were dropped after the change. In the
following years (1877 and 1878) Fawcett took fresh
opportunities for urging the removal of all educational
differences between agricultural and manufacturing districts. Finally, in 1880, Mr. Mundella introduced a bill,

which was accepted unanimously, for making it imperative upon all school boards and school-attendance committees to frame bye-laws. Thus, for the first time, the
compulsory system was made to apply to the whole
population of the country. A few figures will illustrate
the development of the compulsory system. In 1872,
9,000,000 out of a population of 22,000,000 were under
school boards and 8,000,000 of these in districts subject
to bye-laws. In 1876, 11,500,000 were under bye-laws.
In 1879 bye-laws were in force under school boards in
districts with a population of 12,395,550, and under
school-attendance committees in districts with a population of 3,083,609. The whole population affected by
bye-laws was thus 15,479,159. In 1884, of the whole
population of England and Wales, amounting (according
to the census of 1881) to 25,497,439 persons, there were
16,081,618 in school-board districts, and 9,892,821
under school-attendance committees.

Fawcett thus lived to see the principle for which he
had uniformly contended carried out with a completeness
which would have seemed visionary at the beginning of
his political career. There was none to which he was
more attached. The arguments which he advanced
throughout were substantially the same, and were those
which have finally triumphed. It does not follow, of
course, that the statesmen were wrong who admitted
more compromise than he approved into the earlier
measures. Indeed, the rapid growth of the system
shows, as he frankly admitted, that they were right in ex-
pecting the system to develop itself when once planted,
and that some of his predictions of the failure of a

'permissive compulsion' were mistaken. Nor can it be said that the socialistic tendency of such legislation, which he saw with regret, has disappeared. The cry for free schools has certainly not lost its strength. So far, therefore, he was partly responsible for incidentally helping forward a movement which he thoroughly disapproved. He considered the system of compulsory education to be of such vital importance that he would introduce it even at the risk of misapplication. It may, in any case, be fairly said for him—and I should be most unwilling to say anything not strictly fair—that he advocated from the first, and in times when the advocacy was unpopular, the principles adopted a few years later even by his opponents; that he adhered to them unflinchingly, in spite of attacks from friends as well as foes; and that he did as much as any man not officially charged with the measures in question to force them upon the attention of Parliament and the country.

In the first sessions of his second Parliament Fawcett had gained a distinctive position. A contemporary journalist called him (in March 1871) 'the most thorough Radical now in the House,' and whilst it complained of his abstract dogmatism, admitted that he had acquired a lead amongst the extreme party. This view no doubt indicates the general estimate of his character. He had taken a prominent position in regard to several questions, upon which I shall have occasion to dwell hereafter, as well as upon the questions already noticed. In the session of 1871 he was a still more emphatic and powerful critic of the Government. The University Tests Bill had given occasion, at the beginning of the session, for a strong expression of dissatisfaction. As the session went on his attitude became more pronounced. In March he delivered a remarkable address to a crowded meeting at Brighton upon the 'future policy of the Liberal party.' He began by telling a story to which he often referred. Some old-fashioned Liberal had told him that after two hours' reflection he and his friends had been unable to answer the question, what there was left for the Liberal party to do. Fawcett said that he had enlightened his friend in the course of a short stroll, and he now proceeded to enlighten his constituents. He began by insisting upon the shortcomings of the previous sessions. The Irish Church had been disestablished, but at the cost of a bribe of 7,000,000l. The praise bestowed upon the Education Act was, as often happened, one more proof that it was 'a feeble and timorous compromise.' Time had been wasted in 'squabbling over a paltry religious difficulty,' which had been handed over to the local authorities instead of finally settled by Parliament. The University Tests had been only half settled. The Ballot Bill was a good measure, yet it left the most serious difficulty of election expenses inadequately treated. We had therefore still to make up leeway; but above all we had to introduce new ideas. He proceeded to speak more explicitly than he had hitherto done in public of the importance of minority representation. He said that the House of Lords required reform, and declared that there must be 'no more hereditary legislation.' He attacked the Church Establishment, insisted that the economy for which Liberals professed to pant should be made a reality, and that the rich sinecures should be cut down as well as the salaries of the poorer officials. The Army Reform Bill, he maintained, offended against this principle. And he insisted upon the many abuses connected with the poor laws, as bearing upon the greatest of all evils—the 'tremendous fact that one out of twenty of the population "was a pauper."' His book upon Pauperism had just been published, and expressed the opinions set forth on the platform. Undoubtedly the speech was a tolerably vigorous profession of a 'Radical creed,' and helped to emphasise his position. The points upon which he actually came into collision with his leaders were rather different. The Budget of this session provoked his indignant protest. It was the year in which Mr. Lowe proposed his famous match-tax with the little classical joke, 'Ex luce lucellum.' It would have been difficult to conceive anything more irritating to Fawcett. The tax itself, according to Fawcett, offended against every one of Adam Smith's canons. It was a paltry expedient, calculated to bear with great severity upon a miserable and defenceless class. The impression that the chance of letting off a classical pun had really contributed to recommend the proposal implied a degree of cynical flippancy which was intolerable. When the match-tax was blown to the limbo whither go 'all disastrous things' amidst general contempt, a new Budget was introduced, against which Fawcett, democrat as he was, felt all the more bound to protest. The additional expenditure was to be provided for by an increase of the income-tax; and Fawcett, in spite of various taunts, took more than one occasion of denouncing the unfairness of throwing the burden exclusively upon one class.

Another measure brought him more prominently forward. The bill which abolished the system of purchasing commissions in the army had passed the House with Fawcett's qualified approval. He of course sympathised with the main principle. But he complained that it left sinecure colonelcies untouched, whilst it made a saving by sweeping away 129 poor clerks at 100*l.* a year. He doubted, too, whether the abolition of purchase would not be secured at an extravagant price; and declared that a substitution of political patronage for purchase—which was not, he thought, sufficiently guarded against in the bill—would be a retrograde step. The bill got through the House of Commons in a rather mutilated condition, and the House of Lords were encouraged to decline considering the measure until the whole plan for army reorganisation was before them. Hereupon Mr. Gladstone found out that legislation was not required. A royal warrant was issued abolishing the system of purchase at a blow.

The faithful followers of Government were of course ready to accept a kind of small *coup d'état* which achieved their object. But this high-handed way of carrying out a principle was clearly inconsistent with Liberal principles and opposed to all Fawcett's notions of fair-play. He had pronounced in favour of reforming the House of Lords; but so long as it existed its action was not to be summarily put aside by an appeal to prerogative. The discovery that the measure needed no legislation came awkwardly after so much energy had been expended on the attempt to obtain legislation. The contemptuous treatment of the House of Lords was strange, as Fawcett rather bitterly observed, in a Minister who had so recently declined to carry out the Liberal principles in regard to the Universities from excessive politeness to the same body. Nor, as he showed by examples, was the objection to this use of prerogative a mere adhesion to an antiquated prejudice. Royal prerogative might not mean what it had meant in the days of the Stuarts, but a Minister might turn it to account for objectionable purposes. He might sell the rights of the Crown as in the case of Epping Forest, or give a charter to a sectarian University in spite of the opinions of Parliament. The force of this allusion will appear directly. Even in this case, though the immediate end was desirable, Fawcett quite sympathised with the demand of the House of Lords to know what was to be the substitute for the objectionable system. He would far rather wait, he said, to be sure of a sound measure than buy at such a price mere fragments of reform.

Fawcett took a leading part in the protest, though of course his action was for the moment unavailing. His conduct was intensely disagreeable to the Government. One official antagonist declared that, if Government had submitted, Fawcett would have been as ready to demand an application of the prerogative as he now was to denounce it. When Fawcett demanded some reason for this calm assumption, his assailant simply retorted that he made it because he was sure that Fawcett would in any case say whatever was most disagreeable. That was the natural official view. Nothing but a desire to be disagreeable could account for a member of the party opposing its leaders. Fawcett did, in fact, say the most disagreeable thing pretty often, because nothing can be so disagreeable as an opposition based upon principle, and upon the very principle of which the party claims a special monopoly. In this, and in many other cases, Fawcett was vexatious because his arguments were irrefragable from the point of view of the men whose principles he preferred to their practice. He might be called factious in opposing Liberal leaders, but he had the awkward retort that he was factious on behalf of the Liberal creed.

Fawcett's growing discontent showed itself in an article in the 'Fortnightly Review' for November 1871, 'On the Present Position of the Government,' which was one of his most vigorous performances. It was an indictment of the Ministry upon the whole course of their policy. Admitting that they had carried out, and deserved credit for carrying out, some of the chief measures for which they had been put in office, he called attention to their shortcomings. He said that they had alienated the friends of religious equality by their half-hearted treatment of University tests and elementary education; that they had mutilated the Ballot Bill by dropping all the clauses which really assailed the influence of money in elections; that the abolition of purchase had been so managed as to incur at least the danger of increasing political patronage rather than 'giving back the army to the nation' (the current phrase); that economy had touched the poor and left rich sinecurists unaffected;

T

that Mr. Lowe had first introduced a Budget alienating the
agricultural interest by a proposed tax on farm horses,
and injuring the poorest class by a tax on matches; and
that, when forced to withdraw, this prophet of the evils
to come from democratic tyranny had pandered to the
very evil principle which he had denounced by throwing
the whole additional taxation upon the payers of income-
tax; that, whilst doing something for the poor tenants
of Ireland, nothing had been done for the great social
questions of England; and that Government had actually done its utmost to promote the enclosure of English
commons, whilst denouncing the separation of the Irish
people from the land; and, finally, that the Cabinet had
not found time to spend a quarter of an hour upon the
momentous questions of Indian finance.

The importance attached by Fawcett to the last
points will appear more plainly hereafter. Meanwhile
he took pains to anticipate the objection that he was
blaming the Government for not coming up to the
demands of the extreme Radicals. He complained that
they lagged behind the main body of their supporters;
that they systematically waited till a policy was forced
upon them by external pressure; that a man who laid
down distinct principles and enforced them by strong
arguments was sneered down as a doctrinaire, and
virtually told that he must go elsewhere and excite the
people, till Government felt that hesitation was no longer
safe. Government took enormous credit to itself for
having, 'after much curious twisting and many a dubi-
ous halt, decided to accept a principle which years before
had been endorsed at a hundred provincial meetings.'

The justice, for example, of disestablishing the Irish Church, or of compensating Irish tenants for improvements, had been an accepted principle with every 'Radical shoemaker' thirty years before. Government, in his opinion, had injured itself, not by going too far, but by temporising, shuffling, and equivocating till it had disgusted the supporters whose enthusiasm might have been preserved by a vigorous adhesion to simple principles.

The utterance of these heterodox opinions was not calculated to improve Fawcett's position amongst the staunch adherents of the Government. During the later part of this Parliament he was regarded as so distinctly hostile that the Government 'whips' ceased to send him the usual notices. In the session of 1872 he came into further conflict with the Liberal leaders. The chief Government measure of that session was the Ballot Bill which had been sent up to the House of Lords in 1871 and rejected on the ground of insufficient time for consideration. Fawcett had been a constant supporter of the ballot. I do not think that he was an ardent advocate of secresy of voting—a principle to which Mill objected on grounds for which Fawcett must have felt some sympathy. Fawcett, I think, admitted that the measure was necessary as a protection against intimidation, whilst he could hardly approve of the view that the suffrage was a privilege to be exercised without any responsibility. He protested, for example (April 15), against a clause proposed in this session, the object of which was to make secresy compulsory by punishing anyone who should reveal his vote. He said explicitly that he attached much less importance to securing secresy of voting than to attacking the expensiveness of elections; and he complained bitterly of Government, in the session of 1871, for throwing over all the clauses except those which secured secresy. He had tried hard to engraft upon the measure his own plan for throwing the official expenses upon the rates. I have already mentioned the fate of his proposal in his first Parliament. After gaining a majority, he had been foiled by the tactics of the then Government. In 1869 he again introduced the measure, which was thrown out upon the second reading by a majority of 168 to 165 (March 3). In 1870 he postponed the introduction of his measure, as a Committee was sitting upon the whole subject. Afterwards (May 9) he complained that it had not been embodied in the Government measure introduced in that session. In 1871 it formed part of the Government bill, but Fawcett complained of the faintness of their support, and it was thrown out (July 31) by 256 to 160. Another clause, which declared that all payments not made through the official agent were to be held corrupt, was dropped, to his disgust. Though Mr. Forster promised that it should reappear next year, Fawcett insisted upon a division, and was beaten by 181 to 84 (August 1). He once more made an effort in support of his old measure in the discussions upon the Ballot Bill in this session (1872), and was defeated by 261 to 169 (April 25). The Ballot Bill thus passed without his favourite provision. He made a final effort in its support in the session of 1873. He complained pathetically that his bill had suffered from the patronage of the

Government, who had adopted it without catching his own parental affection. He hoped that it would regain vigour now that it had come back to the 'bracing atmosphere' of the benches below the gangway. The result, however, was unsatisfactory, for on a second reading (June 18) he was defeated by 205 to 91.[1]

The reception of his scheme was not calculated to raise his flagging belief in the sincerity of Government. Measures seriously calculated to diminish the expensiveness of elections did not find much real favour in a House composed so largely of rich men; and here, as elsewhere, Government waited for some external pressure. Another question was at last coming to the front in which he was greatly interested, and which he had done his best to urge upon his party. Already, in his first Parliament (1867), Fawcett had moved a resolution in favour of removing all tests from Trinity College, Dublin. In 1868 he was counted out; and complained afterwards that the whips of both parties had stood by the door to warn members from attending, and had thus quenched an inconvenient discussion.

In the next Parliament he did his utmost to gain a hearing. The question was one which profoundly

---

[1] In later years Fawcett made other attempts to promote this reform. In 1875 he proposed to engraft it upon a bill introduced by Sir Henry James to regulate election expenses; but his motion was defeated by 150 to 46. In 1882 he supported a bill introduced by Mr. Ashton Dilke, embodying his proposal; but the bill disappeared after the second reading had been carried by a small majority. A similar proposal made by Mr. Broadhurst in 1883 was rejected because it introduced controversial matter incompatible with the compact then arranged between parties. Fawcett had spoken warmly enough on the first two occasions to show that his interest in the question was undiminished.

interested his friend Cairnes. Cairnes, Fawcett, and
Mr. Courtney had constant discussions upon the subject,
Fawcett being the representative in the House of this
vigorous triumvirate. The question was superficially,
at least, the same as that of the English Universities;
but the religious difficulty, which beset educational questions in England, recurred in a far more formidable
form and associated with more intricate problems. The
exclusion of Protestant Dissenters from Oxford and Cambridge was clearly no real advantage to the interests of
the orthodox Anglican creed. The religious scruples
which hindered the establishment of elementary schools
in England had a very hollow ring, so far as the parents
and children were directly concerned. In each case
Fawcett might fairly maintain that the true interests
of national education were being sacrificed to miserable
sectarian squabbles. But it was not so easy to apply
the same principle to a country where the antipathies
between Catholic and Protestant are so profound and
deeply rooted as in Ireland. How are the principles of
toleration to be applied where there is so little of the
corresponding sentiment? Fawcett was perhaps predisposed by his own indifference to dogmatic discussions
to under-estimate the actual difficulty. The religious
views of his friends never gave him any trouble: he
could associate with Catholics, Protestants, and Free-
thinkers, and he did not see why they should not
heartily co-operate with each other.

Mr. Gladstone had declared that the Irish upas-tree
had three branches—the State Church, the land system,
and the education system ; he had dealt with the two first

after a fashion, and the third was now to be considered. The task was to be a difficult one. The method adopted in the case of the English Universities implied that, in point of fact, the various sects were ready to join in the same educational body, and that such a combination would work satisfactorily, because a teaching might be given which would offend no one, supposing a few easy precautions to be adopted. But if you have to deal with hostile Churches, ready to find cause of quarrel in every branch of study, and even considering a combined system of education to be in itself pernicious, the difficulty might become enormous or insuperable.

Fawcett, meanwhile, was directly concerned with the Dublin University alone. Dublin was so far more Liberal than Oxford or Cambridge that members of all creeds were already admitted as students, and could hold scholarships and take degrees. What was required was to remove the tests which excluded Catholics from membership of the governing body. If that were done, there would be a University as open to the whole nation as Oxford or Cambridge, though the question remained, how far it could take the same place as an adequate academical organisation for the Irish people.

Fawcett was content to work at the abolition of Dublin tests without for the present raising the wider question. In successive sessions he made one assault after another. In 1869 (August 3) he withdrew a resolution, after a speech from Mr. Chichester Fortescue (now Lord Carlingford), solely on the ground of the lateness of the session. Mr. Fortescue's speech, he said, pointed to a system of denominational colleges; and he warned the

Government that any such scheme would alienate their Liberal supporters. In 1870 (April 4) Fawcett again brought in a bill and was supported by Mr. Plunket, then just elected for the University of Dublin. Fawcett presented a memorial from the Provost and Fellows of Trinity College, showing that body to be itself in favour of enfranchisement. He complained of the obstacles which had been raised by both parties. Mr. Gladstone treated the motion as one of want of confidence, and the discussion was shelved by a majority of 232 to 92. In 1871 Fawcett again brought in the bill, which did not come up for the second reading until August 2. Mr. Gladstone expressed his approval of the principle ; but said that a more complete measure was required. The bill was talked out. In 1872, however, it came decidedly to the front. The bill was introduced early and came up for the second reading on March 20, Fawcett and Mr. Plunket being again mover and seconder. In order to meet Mr. Gladstone's objection to the incompleteness of the bill, clauses had now been introduced to alter the constitution of the college, chiefly to enable Catholics to obtain a position on the governing body more rapidly than would have resulted, in the ordinary course, from the simple removal of tests. Mr. Gladstone now criticised these clauses as crude, but offered to support the test clauses. Fawcett was moved to some indignation. He had added the constitution clauses precisely because Mr. Gladstone had said that the measure without them was incomplete, and Mr. Gladstone now himself proposed to reduce the bill to its incomplete state. After two adjournments, the second reading of the bill was carried (March 26) by 94 to 21.

The struggle broke out on the attempt to go into Committee. Mr. Gladstone again condemned the constitutive clauses as unsatisfactory, but offered to help the test clauses. Fawcett declined to allow his bill to be thus mutilated. After some sharp debate Mr. Gladstone stated that Government would resign if their proposed instruction for dividing the bill should be defeated. But he declined to treat the motion as one of want of confidence, and therefore to give a day for the discussion. The last discussion took place on April 25. Fawcett declared that he had only done what he had been told to do, and that now he was being hindered precisely for doing it. Government, he said, would not accept his challenge. 'For five years,' he said, 'I have been trying to obtain a decision. Twice my proposals have been talked out. Twice they have been counted out. Twice they have been got rid of by threats of a Ministerial resignation.'

Cairnes used laughingly to compare this to a more famous catalogue of direr calamities once endured in the cause of truth. It is enough to say that Fawcett was not likely to have his confidence in the Liberal Government strengthened. His distrust, it must be noticed, had been increased by the history of the 'supplementary charter' of the Queen's University.[1] A charter which would involve the introduction of a denominational system had been granted by Mr. Gladstone's Government at the very moment when they were resigning in 1866. It was granted, as its opponents maintained, so as to evade a

---

[1] A full account of this will be found in Professor Cairnes's *Political Essays*, pp. 323–326.

distinct pledge that it should first be considered by Parliament. The senate of the Queen's University, packed by the addition of six members, accepted it, but it was finally declared invalid by the Irish Master of the Rolls. Fawcett's intimate friend and adviser, Cairnes, had been especially indignant at this, as he considered, underhand attempt to introduce an obnoxious system. Fawcett was prepared to look doubtfully upon Mr. Gladstone's future action upon the same subject. But whatever the tactics employed against him, he would have been unreasonable not to admit that there was good ground for saying that the whole question should be treated in a comprehensive measure. His many attempts to bring it forward may have been unseasonable, but they no doubt made the introduction of a Government measure more imperative. At the beginning of the session of 1873 Fawcett once more brought in his bill, which was read a first time on February 7, stating at the same time that he did not wish to embarrass the Government, and should withdraw his bill if he were satisfied with the measure which they were now to introduce. That measure was introduced by Mr. Gladstone in a speech of which Fawcett said, that if a division could have taken place whilst the House was still under its influence the bill would have been almost unanimously carried. He was careful to suspend his own judgment until he had thoroughly analysed the bill and discussed it carefully with Cairnes. When opening the debate upon the second reading (March 3, 1873), he said that the time which had elapsed since Mr. Gladstone's speech had brought out an almost unanimous disapproval of the measure. It was one of the

compromises which are meant to please everybody and
which end by pleasing nobody.   Mr. Gladstone had proposed the amalgamation of the various existing bodies into
a single University.   Trinity College, the Catholic University, and the Queen's Colleges (with the exception of the
Galway College, which was to be abolished), were to form
parts of the new University, with a power of affiliating new
colleges which might hereafter be formed.   The difficulty
of bringing together the heterogeneous religious elements
was to be met partly by the so-called 'gagging clauses,'
excluding from the University course theology, moral
philosophy, and modern history.   The separate colleges
might make their own arrangements in regard to these
subjects, in which the University itself would neither
teach nor examine.   The scheme irritated the Irish Protestants, whilst it was rejected as insufficient by the
Catholics.   Fawcett attacked it energetically upon
various grounds.   He protested against the abolition of
the Galway College, and he declared that the proposed
excision of dangerous topics would make a satisfactory
treatment of all subjects, even political economy, for
example, hopeless.   His main contention was, in fact, a
protest on behalf of united as against denominational
education.   The bill, he urged, was an attempt to combine the two inconsistent systems.   A system of con-
current endowment was out of the question on account
of the prejudices of Irish and English Protestants, who
would not see education handed over to the Catholic
priesthood.   Fawcett held that, if possible, it would still be
wrong in principle.   To endow separate Universities, each
with a special sectarian colour, was, according to him, to

stereotype and intensify the bitter religious animosities which had been the bane of Ireland. The bill, which proposed to bring students of all religions together and yet to suppress all teaching upon the topics in which they differed, was to sanction the very principle of discord. Priests who forbade their disciples to associate with Protestants would now be entitled to say that the English Government admitted the danger of the association. He quoted a passage in which Cardinal Cullen had threatened with the censures of the Church parents who persisted in exposing their children to the dangers of united education. A Liberal Government had virtually aided and abetted this cruel and cowardly policy, when it had granted the abortive supplementary charter for the Queen's University. The effect of the present measure would be to help the priests to keep every Catholic out of Trinity College and the Queen's Colleges and thus to foster religious intolerance. Fawcett, in fact, regarded the religious difficulty in this case as he had regarded it in the case of English Universities and elementary education. It was really put forward by the classes which dreaded toleration, and the true remedy was a bold acceptance of the principle of united education. There is room here for some casuistical discussion as to the true bearing of the principle of toleration. It may, at any rate, be said that the question of fact has to be considered by a statesman. It is all very well to establish united education, but if the persons to be educated decline to unite your efforts will be thrown away. The question then occurs whether it is best to establish a system, rejected by those concerned, in the hope that it will gradually work its way into acceptance in spite of the intolerance of priests, or to endow the separate denominational bodies on the ground that even such education is better than none, or, finally, to do nothing. The question is one of statesman- ship enlightened by a knowledge of facts and of the sentiments of the population, and it is altogether beyond my power even to suggest the true answer. Fawcett, who thought comparatively little of the importance of the religious differences, accepted the first solution. The Catholics would have been content with nothing short of the second. Mr. Gladstone attempted a compromise which was equally unpalatable to both; and the result was the third possible conclusion—namely, that nothing was effected at all.

Catholics, Protestants, and the indifferent being all opposed to the measure, the power of Government was in- adequate to secure success. In spite of the great Liberal majority, the bill was thrown out by a majority of 287 to 284, and the Liberal Government received a fatal blow. Fawcett now brought in his previous measure. Govern- ment agreed to support it if limited to the clauses abolishing tests. Fawcett thought it best to accept the compromise, and the measure was finally passed after brief disputes on May 26.

Though Mr. Gladstone resigned, Mr. Disraeli refused to come in; and for the rest of this Parliament the Administration, which had come back to office, remained in a moribund condition until the dissolution of January 1874. Fawcett's action upon this occasion was amongst the main causes of the catastrophe, and he thus had the credit or discredit of finally putting that spoke into the wheels of the great Liberal Administration which finally threw the machinery out of gear.

Before summing up the results to himself of his action, I must speak of one other mode in which he had become conspicuous—not to the satisfaction of one part of his supporters. Fawcett, as will easily be believed, was one of the most clubbable of mankind. He had at an early period of his parliamentary career been the founder of the Radical Club—an institution consisting in equal numbers of members of the House and politicians, including ladies, who were not members. They met and discussed the questions of the day at weekly dinners. Mill was one of the original members. The club acquired considerable importance in later years and flourished until the elevation of several of its members to office in 1880, when by the constitution of the club they had to withdraw. It was perhaps as a kind of offshoot from this institution that a club calling itself by the more dreaded name of Republican was formed at Cambridge by Fawcett and some of his friends. Professor Clifford was secretary. The rules gave a formal definition of Republicanism, which meant ' hostility to the hereditary principle as exemplified in monarchical and aristocratic institutions, and to all social and political privileges dependent upon difference of sex.' The other rules were all devoted to securing a sufficiency of sociable dinners, with discussions of a conversational nature. Nothing could well be imagined more harmless than this club. It was purely private in its nature, and was scarcely more than a sociable meeting of a set of friends who amused themselves, after the fashion of young men at the University, by taking the title most significant of thoroughgoing opinions. It is superfluous to say that they were as little likely to proclaim a provisional Government as a meeting of the senior Fellows of Trinity to blow up the chapel with dynamite. A little audacious talk over a glass of wine would be the outside of the offending. Unluckily some erroneous account of this club got into the papers about the end of 1870 and gave a shock to some of Fawcett's supporters. To them, it appears, the name 'Republican' suggested Marat and Robespierre, or at least an expulsion of the Queen by force of arms like the recent expulsion of the Third Napoleon. One of Fawcett's best friends talked of moving an amendment to the usual vote of confidence at the general meeting of his supporters at Brighton in January 1871, partly on this ground, partly also on the ground of his attitude towards Mr. Gladstone. This attitude had not yet become so marked as in following sessions, and had been chiefly shown in a speech (August 1, 1870) in which he had said that we should have sooner avowed our resolution to stand by Belgium during the Franco-German war. Fawcett took the opportunity of giving a very plain exposition of his principles, though the threatened motion was judiciously abandoned. The principle to which he adhered was, he said, that of 'merit, not birth.' He disclaimed all disloyal feeling, and said (what was scarcely necessary to say) that no one would be more opposed than he and his friends to any revolutionary movement. He pointed out, however, some very practical applications of his principle, and spoke as usual of the honourable disregard of any consideration

but merit at Cambridge. A Fellow had been recently
asked before a Committee what was the ordinary social
position of Fellows of colleges. He replied (not quite
truly, I fancy) that he could not tell; for such a question was never asked at Cambridge. Fawcett hoped that
a similar feeling would come to prevail in politics, and
that a Prime Minister would never have to confess that
he had made a bad appointment because it was necessary
to provide for the son of a duke.

So far, indeed, Fawcett was a thorough Republican
in feeling. He would have admitted the force of the
plea for existing Monarchy that, under present circumstances, it provides a system under which the ablest
Minister has the best chance of coming to the head of
affairs. At any rate, he declared that he was not 'the
slave of an abstract principle,' and that nothing but
mischief could come from any attempt to upset the
Monarchy now. Yet Fawcett's Republican sentiment
perhaps went a little further. In the following session
he was in a minority of one against the dowry voted
to the Princess Louise, Mr. Peter Taylor and Sir Charles
Dilke acting as tellers upon his side. In the following year (on March 19, 1872) he was present at the
disorderly scene when Sir Charles Dilke moved his
inquiry into the Civil List, and was supposed to be
avowing some leaning to Republicanism. Fawcett spoke
amidst considerable interruption, and stated that, whatever his opinions might be, he objected to the question of Republicanism being 'raised upon a miserable
haggle over a few pounds.' His friends seem to have
thought that the utterance at that particular moment

showed some want of tact, and might tend to fasten upon Dilke's speeches a meaning disavowed by the speaker himself. But the sentiment was in itself thoroughly characteristic. Till the question could be raised in a worthier manner, Fawcett would have no desire to raise it.

The whole affair speedily passed out of mind. Fawcett was no revolutionist, if that word suggests the least disposition to violent changes. But perhaps he was more inclined towards Republicanism than most English politicians. He certainly had the heartiest possible contempt for that kind of vulgarity or ' flunkeyism ' which in these days sometimes passes itself off for loyalty. He spoke with a marked disgust of some Liberal politicians who warned him to be duly obsequious when there was a prospect of his having to examine a royal duke before a parliamentary committee. His utter indifference to any distinctions of rank made him more than usually contemptuous of such weaknesses and, I rather think, predisposed him to hold that the question between Republicanism and Monarchy might not be adjourned to so distant a period as is commonly taken for granted. For the present, however, he found no fault with the existing system, and discouraged any agitation in regard to it.

Fawcett had shown himself to be a very formidable critic; he had perhaps not entirely escaped the danger of wearying the House by his persistent endeavours to bring forward the awkward topics which, for various reasons, one or sometimes both parties would have been glad to keep out of sight, and by urging them perhaps at times with more self-confidence than tact. To the

U

regular official mind he had become thoroughly obnoxious. Various subordinate Ministers had endeavoured to snub him, to put him aside as factious and impracticable, and occasionally they had been even insulting in their language. A man in such a position runs no small danger of finding himself put down by common consent as a tiresome person who may be safely neglected.

Yet Fawcett had distinctly gained a position of real influence. He was regarded with feelings entirely different from those often excited by men of undeniable ability, who take up a similar position of independent opposition or make themselves the mouthpiece of a small party of impracticables. If his popularity was not so great or general as it afterwards became, he was not a man to be suppressed by sneers or by a tacit agreement to ignore him. The reasons for his success are probably not far to seek. In the first place, his action was in all cases clearly founded on principle. Nobody could affect to doubt that he really believed what he said, and that he spoke without any bias from considerations of what would please Ministers or constituents. It was clear, again, that he was not a stickler for mere crotchets. In every one of the cases in which he came forward a question of real moment was at issue, and he spoke after serious reflection and with the unmistakable impress of strong common sense upon all that he said. Nor could it be denied that he spoke, even when he opposed a Liberal Government, and when for that reason he went into the lobby with its Conservative opponents, as a genuine representative of Liberal principles. The motive of all the action already described was in one respect uniform. His complaint was that the Government lagged behind the bulk of the party ; that instead of laying down distinct principles, adhering to them boldly, and saying plainly how far it would go, it tried to compromise, to blink obvious facts, to pacify opponents by dexterous manœuvres, and so in the end came not only to lose credit by taking up its positions under pressure from the party which it ought to have led, but to cause more irritation than would otherwise have resulted. Supporters of the Government called him impracticable for his objection to compromise. Yet he might have retorted that the plainer or more manly course which he always desired would have been in the end the most practical. Mr. Gladstone's Government, according to its opponents, lost command of the country because it threatened so many interests. Fawcett said, in substance, that it failed because it excited the distrust both of supporters and opponents ; that it failed to take the plain course which would have roused the enthusiasm of Liberals ; whilst it equally failed to conciliate opponents, who never felt sure that it would not reach the Radical conclusions by devious and covert approaches. A masculine and outspoken opponent may excite more opposition for the moment, but he does not rouse the same antipathy as one who fails to speak out because he does not himself know how far he may be going. Whether the downright policy which would have satisfied Fawcett would have succeeded may be a question ; but, in any case, his thoroughly outspoken and masculine temper was already winning the recognition and respect both of friends and opponents. In after days it was said that Fawcett's popularity was

second only to Mr. Gladstone's. But the popularity was
not in his case balanced by a corresponding antipathy.
You cannot hate a man whom you cannot help trusting;
and Fawcett's most determined opponents could not but
admit that you might trust him implicitly in the sense of
knowing what he wanted. He, at least, had no reserve
of covert possibilities in the background. Moreover,
Fawcett's unmistakable geniality, the hearty good
temper and unfailing cheeriness of the man, his superiority to any petty malice or personal jealousy, made
themselves felt in politics as elsewhere. It was simply
impossible to dislike him.

Fawcett, again, was showing other qualities in political life than this of downright adherence to intelligible
principles. His complaints against the Government, so
far as we have gone, were based chiefly on its tendency
to subterfuge and compromise. But he had further to
complain that it suffered from that disease of officialism
which is so apt to beset the most virtuous reformers when
once in office. This indolent acquiescence manifested
itself in certain directions which involved indifference to
the grievances of the weak and helpless. Fawcett's
chivalrous hatred of oppression came out in his resolute
exertions towards calling attention to cases of this kind;
and, in the two cases of the enclosure of commons and
of the grievances of the people of India, he took so
prominent a position that I must speak of his action in
each case separately in the two following chapters.

CHAPTER VII.

COMMONS PRESERVATION.

I HAVE given some account of Fawcett's share in struggles which from time to time occupied the foreground of the political arena. Such struggles are not always so important as others which are fought out in comparative obscurity. This is perhaps true of the agitation for preserving open spaces, in which Fawcett took a leading part from the first session of his second Parliament. It attracted comparatively little notice at the time. Yet he more than once remarked to me that there was no part of his political career upon which he could look back with more unalloyed satisfaction. An open space, as he pointed out, once destroyed is destroyed for ever. To rescue it is often to confer a permanent benefit upon society, and a benefit without sensible drawback. There are few political achievements of which the same can be said. Though Fawcett did not initiate the movement, and was supported throughout by friends whose services he was always eager to acknowledge, he took a very prominent part in the conduct of the whole political campaign; and in no part of his career were his characteristic qualities more distinctly manifested.

The question interested him in more ways than one

His first published course of lectures (delivered in the October term, 1864) prove that his attention had already been called to the subject. After discussing the effects of a divorce of the great mass of the population from the soil, he referred to the mischiefs resulting from the enclosure of commons. He declared, from his own knowledge of the agricultural labourer, that cottagers could no longer keep a cow, a pig, or poultry; that the village greens had become extinct; and that the turnpike road was too often the only playground for the village children. He doubted whether the enclosure of commons involving the breaking up of pastures had, in point of fact, permanently increased the wealth of the country; but the wealth in any case was dearly purchased, if purchased by a diminution of the labourers' comforts. The compensation paid to the poor commoner had generally been spent by the first receiver; whilst his descendants were permanently deprived of many of the little advantages which might have helped to eke out their scanty resources.

The political economist of fiction is a hard-hearted being, who tramples upon such considerations in the name of an idol called Supply and Demand. Fawcett did not shrink from the strictest application of economic principles He gave full weight to the ordinary arguments, and only demanded that they should be fairly applied with a consideration of all the circumstances. Every increase of farming profit caused by more efficient systems of cultivation must undoubtedly tend to increase the demand for agricultural labour, and, so far, to raise the labourer's wages. But this, as he always insisted, represents only one part of the case. The remedial tendency may be slow to come into action. The labourer may be sluggish and ignorant, and therefore may fail to adapt himself to new conditions. The loss of his old advantages may induce him to lower his standard of living; his vitality may be weakened, his intelligence blunted, and thus even his industrial efficiency diminished. The improved organisation may be neutralised by the degradation of the human machinery of which it is composed. Such considerations lie outside the purely economical elements of the problem; but, as Fawcett was emphatic in asserting, they are not therefore irrelevant. On the contrary, they are precisely the points to which a statesman is bound to attend.

There was another aspect of the question to which he drew attention in the lectures already noticed. Government, he said, had allowed a considerable part of Epping Forest to be appropriated by private persons, and he observed that it was impossible to measure the social and moral injury inflicted by this change upon the dense masses of the metropolitan population. It was this aspect of the enclosure question which was soon to become most prominent. The process of enclosing common land has been going on rapidly since the early part of the eighteenth century. In many districts the injury done to the labourer, whatever it may have been, has been consummated. He has no longer any privileges to maintain. And, in any case, the preservation of the existing rights forms but a very small part of the great problem of a satisfactory system of land tenure. The other part of the question, on the contrary, steadily rises in importance. As the grimy masses of town building daily

engulph larger slices of green fields, the need of breathing
and recreation ground becomes continually more pressing.

Few Londoners are fully aware even now of the advantages which they owe to the survival of the ancient systems
of landed tenure. Within a radius of thirty miles from
the centre of London there is a great area of unenclosed
land, much of it of exquisite beauty and still apparently
steeped in the profoundest rural quiet. It is possible
even now to ramble for miles from one stretch of heather
and gorse to another, with pleasant interludes of field
paths or country lanes and occasional emergences upon
the fine springy turf of the broad chalk-ridges. With a
little judicious trespassing (and it is only right to express
gratitude for the liberality of many private proprietors),
one may wander from Windsor to Chatham through a
continuous range of lovely scenery still untainted by
London, and as beautiful in a quiet way as any part of
England. Happily for the lover of solitude, many such
spots still seem to be less known than most regions of the
Alps; though some which lie nearer to beaten paths
were already attracting public attention twenty years
ago. Hampstead Heath to the North, Wimbledon to the
South-west, and Epping to the East, were the most famous
haunts of the holiday-maker. They were all at this period
in serious danger. The growing value of building land
was of course the great cause of absorption in the
neighbourhood of London. The builder is always ready
to push out his incarnations of mean monotony till the
country is supplanted by something that is not town.
Further off, the more ostentatious masses of brick and
mortar generically known as 'institutions' delighted

to perch in their ghastly affectation of architectural pomp upon some open space where land is cheap and sufficient attention may be paid to the health of criminal lunatics and other interesting specimens of humanity. Railways naturally gashed commons with their disfiguring trenches and sliced off isolated corners—no longer worth preserving when dominated by the shrieks and steam-jets of the intrusive monster. A few years of neglect would have led to the disappearance of many of the best breathing-spaces round London, and allowed the huge web of suburban brick to be cast in continuous network over the whole area.

Public opinion was beginning to be aroused. In 1863 an Address to the Crown had been carried in the House of Commons against the further sale of forestal rights in Epping. A Committee had afterwards been appointed to consider the possibility of preserving open spaces in the Forest. Fawcett's reference to Epping, just cited, shows that his attention had been drawn to the subject. He did not, however, take a prominent part in the matter during his first Parliament. In 1865 a proposal to enclose some commons near Epsom was rejected by the House of Commons. Mr. Doulton, member for Lambeth, called attention to other encroachments: Wandsworth was being mangled by railways; Wimbledon was threatened with diminution by a third of its area and conversion into a park; Hampstead Heath was being carted away for gravel, and Epping enclosed. A Select Committee was appointed, of which Mr. Locke was chairman, and which included Mr. Charles Buxton, Mr. Shaw-Lefevre, and Mr. Cowper-Temple (then Mr.

Cowper, now Lord Mount-Temple). The report of the Committee laid down principles which soon received legislative sanction. The Commons Preservation Society was formed in July 1865 to advocate their adoption. Mr. Shaw-Lefevre became chairman, a position which he held, with a short interval, until he took office in 1880; and his services have been invaluable. Mr. P. H. Lawrence was honorary solicitor. Mr. Lawrence had taken a very prominent part in the defence of Wimbledon Common, and did, I believe, more than any man at this time to give shape and direction to the movement. Fawcett was an early member of the new Society, but took little part in its first operations. The Metropolitan Commons Act, passed in 1866, embodied some of the recommendations of the Committee of the previous session, and represented the policy of the Commons Preservation Society at that time. It provided, in the first place, that the regular machinery for enclosure should not be applicable to suburban commons.[1] The Enclosure Commissioners were also empowered to settle schemes for regulating commons on application from the persons concerned. The Commons Preservation Society hoped that these provisions would suffice to protect the most important recreation-grounds. By their suggestion, committees were formed in the neighbourhood of the threatened commons and suits were instituted in the names of the commoners. It was thought that the rights established by these suits would suffice to make enclosure impracticable ; and that all parties would then agree upon schemes

---

[1] That is, to commons within the Metropolitan Police District, or, roughly, within fifteen miles of Charing Cross.

for regulation. The facilities for the enclosure of
commons in the country no longer applied to the
commons round London. Parliament, it was still admitted, might fairly be asked to help in getting rid of
the old rural commons and the slovenly agricultural
system which they implied. But at least it was no
longer to do anything positively to encourage the substitution of brick and mortar for the open stretches of
turf or gorse in the neighbourhood of the metropolis.
And if Parliament would leave commoners and lords
of manors to fight it out, there were rights enough to
save the commons, which would then only require regulation by appropriate schemes.

Some incidents which soon followed helped to make
the agitation popular. There was the famous expedition
to Berkhampstead, where the fences erected to enclose
500 acres of a singularly beautiful common were thrown
down by an army of navvies. Mr. Augustus Smith, who
employed them at the suggestion of the society, then instituted a suit, which was decided in his favour in 1870.
Other suits, involving much antiquarian investigation,
took a considerable time, and it was not till 1869 that
the first scheme was certified under the Metropolitan
Commons Act. It was at this time that Fawcett first
took an active part in the matter. The procedure of
the Enclosure Commissioners had been defined by a
general Act passed in 1845. The Commissioners introduced an annual bill, which scheduled the commons to
be enclosed, and went through Parliament as a part of
the regular routine. It was almost always as much
taken for granted as the Mutiny Act. The Commis-

sioners were directed by the Act to inquire into the expediency of reserving part of the enclosures for recreation or allotments. In practice, however, they had been satisfied with an almost nominal compliance with this regulation. The bill introduced according to custom in 1869 scheduled 6,916 acres for enclosure, of which three were to be reserved for recreation and six for allotments. Amongst the doomed spaces was the pleasant common of Wisley, on the road from Kingston to Guildford, just beyond the pine-covered ridges of St. George's Hill.

Some metropolitan members protested against this particular enclosure. The bill had been hurried through its earlier stages after the debates upon the Irish Church. Mr. Knatchbull-Hugessen (now Lord Brabourne), Under-Secretary of State for the Home Department, who was in charge of it, stated (March 22), on the motion for going into Committee, that he would withdraw Wisley, in order that the case might be considered by a Select Committee. He remarked at the same time that it would be 'obviously unfair to stop unopposed enclosures,' and he therefore proposed to proceed with the bill, only reserving the case of Wisley. Fawcett made his first speech upon the subject, and protested that the House was in a position to decide for itself without further inquiry. A Select Committee was, however, appointed (April 5) to consider the Wisley case, and he was one of its members. It ultimately reported (April 26) in favour of a much larger reservation for allotments and recreation in the event of the enclosure of the common.

Meanwhile the attempt upon Wisley had apparently

called Fawcett's attention to the general character of the bill. Attention had been drawn to Wisley almost by accident. There was no security that other cases might not have been overlooked, and, at all events, the enclosure was tolerably sweeping. He immediately gave notice that upon the third reading he should move for a recommittal of the bill, in order that a better provision might be made for allotments. This motion brought about a struggle, in which Fawcett, with a very small band of supporters,[1] had to encounter the regular official phalanx, who, from their point of view, naturally enough resented his action. To the commonplace official, in fact, a proposal to convert a formality into a reality is an inversion of the rightful order of things. The Enclosure Commissioners and Parliament had been getting on quite comfortably so long as Parliament confined itself to simply endorsing the Commissioners' action. To propose that it should look into things for itself was to stop business and to inflict a hardship upon the various parties to the proposed enclosure. To Fawcett, on the other hand, nothing could be more offensive than a method of making things pleasant at the expense of the poor and ignorant, who had as little notion of interfering with Commissions and Parliament as with the thunder or the phases of the moon.

The Government whips decided upon circumventing Fawcett's vigilance, not as yet appreciating the difficulty of the proceeding. The third reading of the bill was set down for every Government night. It did not come on

---

[1] I believe that his chief supporters were Sir Charles Dilke, Mr. Locke, Mr. Thomas Hughes, Mr. P. A. Taylor, and Mr. Philip Wykeham Martin. Mr. Lefevre was now in office.

for discussion till the end of the evening's debates—that
is, often at 2 or 3 A.M.   The rule which now exists, forbidding the introduction of opposed business after half-past
12, was not then in force.   If Fawcett or his supporters
had failed to be in their places, the third reading might
have been achieved without opposition.   But night after
night he was ready, and the motion for the third reading postponed.   On one occasion Fawcett, as he used
often to relate, had caught a bad cold.   He sent a
message to the Government whip asking that the motion
might be once more postponed as it had been so often
before.   He received no answer; but, fancying that his
request would be granted as a matter of course, he was
retiring to bed.   A friend happening to call suggested
that it would be safer not to relax even for a night.
Fawcett struggled into his wraps, went to the House,
and found that business had been so arranged as to
secure the passage of the Enclosure Bill.   The whip
started 'like a guilty thing surprised' on the apparition
of Fawcett in the lobby, but good-humouredly admitted
the failure of his little bit of dexterity, and gave a formal
undertaking which enabled Fawcett to get once more
into bed with a safe conscience.

A Liberal Government, I imagine, is not less really
attached to official routine than its antagonists.   All
machinery, human or otherwise, has a certain *vis inertiæ*,
which resists all forces tending to displace it from its
regular grooves; but a Government which had just
come in with an enormous majority expressly to carry
out popular measures must have felt itself placed in a
false position when thus trying to suppress a protest of its

own supporters. The attempt to stifle the discussion was finally abandoned. Fawcett spoke with justifiable complacency of the success of his tactics. When in after days complaints were made of the half-past 12 rule, as facilitating obstruction, he would point to the hardship inflicted upon a small minority by the absence of the rule in this struggle. At last (April 9, 1869) the bill was allowed to come on at a reasonable hour, and Fawcett moved his resolution. He dwelt upon the absurdly small proportion of the acreage reserved for public allotments as a strong presumption of injustice to the labourer ; and he protested against the view avowed by Government speakers that the House had nothing to do but formally confirm the Commissioners' action ; or that the lords of manors and commoners had a right to the assistance of Parliament when they had once satisfied the requirements of the general Act. Fawcett was supported by Mr. Locke and Mr. Thomas Hughes ; and after an adjournment of the debate Government consented to the appointment of a Select Committee and the suspension during their deliberations of the Annual Enclosure Bill.

On April 20 a Committee was accordingly appointed upon Fawcett's motion to consider the working of the existing system, and the expediency of better provision for recreation and allotment grounds. The chairman of the Committee was Mr. Cowper-Temple. Fawcett, with Mr. (the present Sir William) Harcourt and some metropolitan members, opposed the existing system, which was defended by Colonel (afterwards Sir Walter) Barttelot and by Mr. Knatchbull-Hugessen, as representative of the official doctrine. Much evidence was taken, especially from the Enclosure Commissioners. These gentlemen frankly accepted the position which was assailed by Fawcett and his friends. The final cause of an Enclosure Commission is naturally to enclose. The preamble of the Enclosure Act of 1845 expressly declared that it was expedient to get rid of rights which obstructed cultivation and the productive employment of labour. It is a hardship to prevent the owners of any piece of property from distributing their various rights on terms upon which they all agree, and which presumably are most conducive to its profitable employment. The commons, it was held, were the private property of the lords of manors and the commoners. The public had no more to do with the common land than with the separate dwelling-houses of the owners. Enclosure meant simply the adjustment of the rights in the form most convenient for the only interested parties. If the public chose to keep commons open, it should pay for its requirements as it would pay for private land taken for public purposes.

Fawcett virtually contended in opposition to this that, before facilitating enclosure, Parliament was bound to consider the effect of its action upon the labouring class. He maintained that, in point of fact, the compensation given to the poor commoners had been mainly illusory. Country gentlemen and farmers had looked after themselves, but the cottager had been put off with some trifle, spent as soon as received. The evidence given by some of the witnesses confirmed this view. Mr. H. S. Tremenheere, the senior of the Commissioners appointed to inquire into the 'Employment of Women and

Children in Agriculture,' had calculated that of 320,855 acres enclosed, only 2,119 had been set aside for cultivation by the poor. The Enclosure Act had limited the allotments to a quarter of an acre to each of the existing population, without considering a prospective increase. The general effect of the enclosures had been to diminish the labourer's advantages, and to lessen his chance of rising to independence. Enclosure, in brief, was not simply a redistribution of private property, but was part of a social change injurious in many ways to the labourer.

The presumption afforded by such testimony which Fawcett, of course, took care to bring out was strengthened by evidence from local witnesses. Grievances would really be caused by the proposed enclosures. The commissioners had only given an acre for recreation at Withypool in Somersetshire because the rest of the land was 'too steep.' The villagers, represented by their parish clerk and the schoolmaster, complained that they were to be as badly off for open spaces as inhabitants of a town, and would only be able to play at the risk of trespassing. At Swaffham, the labourers had complained, but to no effect; and the allotments made had been quite unsuitable. Several of these simple protests made a strong impression upon Fawcett, who often referred to them afterwards, and quotes some of them in an article in 'Fraser's Magazine' for February 1870. He was particularly delighted with the evidence given by Mr. J. Reed, parish clerk of Withypool. When asked how far people would have to go for an open space, the witness replied: ' They could not find one for miles except they

x

did go on the common.'—Is there no open common
within reach of an ordinary walk? 'No; he would not
want any more recreation by the time he came to any
other common.—The people say 'they will be as badly
off as in a town.' Are there no fields where they can
walk? 'Yes, they can trespass, if they like that.'

The Committee reported after much animated discussion. Fawcett was solitary in persisting against a clause
inserted by the official members which provided that the
diminution of private rights should be taken into account
in determining the extent of public allotments. The
report, however, recommended certain alterations of the
previous system with the view of a more liberal treatment
of the claims of the labouring class; fuller notices of
meetings were to be given to all persons concerned; and
the reports of the Commissioners were to set forth more
clearly the grounds of their action and the statistics or previous enclosure. The report ended by adopting the main
principle advocated by Fawcett. The changed conditions of the country had made the benefits of enclosure
more questionable; and it was desirable that future
Enclosure Bills should be more carefully prepared and
the parliamentary scrutiny be made real and searching,
instead of passing as a mere matter of course.

The pending Enclosure Bill was allowed to proceed,
at the instance of the official and Conservative members
of the Committee, except Mr. (now Sir Henry) Peek, who
supported him throughout. Wisley and Withypool, however, were taken out of the bill, and it was recommended
that no further enclosures should be sanctioned by Parliament until the general law should have been amended.

Fawcett, supported by Mr. (now Sir W.) Harcourt, made one final effort to stop the bill till further evidence had been taken; and tried in the House to secure the omission of Pyecombe, where it had been proved that some of the inhabitants were opposed to the enclosure. He failed in this; the end of the session was approaching, and the Government had to push the measure through.

Fawcett's achievement, however, was a very remarkable one, and had gone far to establish his principles. Many had co-operated with him, and some had anticipated him, in calling attention to the absorption of the metropolitan commons. He was probably the first to direct the attention of Parliament to the case of rural commons. In any case, his dogged obstruction of the Enclosure Bill placed the question in a new position from this time forwards. It was due entirely to his independence and the support of a little body of friends that the system was radically changed. At the beginning of the session the passage of the Enclosure Bill was regarded as part of the regular administrative functions of Parliament, with which the public had no concern, and any interference with which was a wanton invasion of private rights. The report of the Committee had sanctioned the opposite theory, that Parliament ought to look sharply after all enclosures, and help them only when they were proved to be advantageous in the interest of all classes affected. The burden of proof was thrown upon the enclosers and security obtained against the neglect of the most helpless.

During 1869 Fawcett attended regularly the meetings of the Commons Preservation Society. Upon his motion

they agreed to extend the sphere of their operations to
the country at large, as well as the metropolitan district.
Meanwhile a question of special interest to Londoners
was beginning to press itself upon their attention. In
the days of Charles I. the royal forest of Waltham
stretched from the valley of the Lea across to the high
road between London and Romford. The little river
Roding may be said to bisect the angle thus defined, and
runs south-westwards between two broad low ridges, one
of which, between the Lee and the Roding, is still partly
covered by Epping Forest, whilst Hainault covered 4,000
acres on the other bank of the Roding. The forest
manors throughout the district had belonged chiefly to
religious houses. After the dissolution of the monasteries,
the Crown had re-granted the manors in Epping to private
persons, whilst it had retained in Hainault the large
possessions of the convent in Barking. Thus in Hainault
the soil of the waste belonged to the Crown; whilst in
Epping the Crown only enjoyed its forestal rights, the
soil belonging to the lords of about fourteen separate
manors. The effect of the difference of tenure was
curious. Up to 1851 there were about 7,000 acres in
Epping and 4,000 in Hainault. In 1851 Hainault was
disafforested by an Act of Parliament. After the various
claims of freeholders, lords of manors, and commoners
had been settled, the whole district was distributed
amongst the various private proprietors and the Crown.
It was then a wild forest tract, covered chiefly with
pollard oak and hornbeam, with occasional open spaces of
gorse and heather, where the forest trees grew 'unprimed
and of great size.' The Crown dealt with that part of

the district which fell to its share after the accepted
principles of the day. The timber was felled, fetching
nearly 21,000*l.*; the land was thoroughly drained and
fenced at a cost of 42,000*l.*; it was divided by rect-
angular roads and let off in farms which produced a
rental of 4,000*l.* The unimproved forest, we are told,
had only brought in 500*l.* annually, and the Crown thus
gained an additional income of 3,500*l.* for the loss of a
few scrubby patches of woodland, at which the Woods
and Forests felt the approval of a good conscience.

The Crown had attempted to enclose Epping at the
beginning of the century. The lords of manors and the
commoners had opposed the plan, which was dropped in
consequence. When Hainault was being improved out
of existence, the Crown bethought itself of making an
honest penny out of its rights in Epping. Between
1851 and 1863 it had sold these rights over 4,000 acres
to the lords of the manors, at an average price of about
5*l.* an acre. Epping began to go the way of Hainault.
The commoners, indeed, as was afterwards proved, still
retained rights not affected by the sale of the Crown
rights. The lords, however, considered the Crown to be
their only formidable competitors. They began to enclose the land, which was now becoming valuable for
building, and professed to have compensated or obtained
the consent of the commoners, if they did not simply
set them at defiance. They even declined in some cases
to buy the Crown rights, holding that rights which were
valued by the proprietors at so cheap a price would not
be defended at the cost of litigation. One gentleman
fenced in and ploughed up 300 acres without consulting

Crown or commoners. In another place where the Crown rights had been bought, the forms of statutory enclosure were gone through, without the sanction of Parliament or an application to the Enclosure Commissioners, and the lord of the manor and his neighbours appropriated 1,300 acres, condescending to set aside a plot of a few acres for a recreation-ground.

A labourer named Willingale had asserted his right to lop trees in a part of the enclosed land. Two of his sons, who had helped him, were arrested and sent to prison for three months with hard labour. Willingale and another small freeholder had then brought suits, which were taken up by the Commons Preservation Society, in order to test the validity of this enclosure. The suits virtually saved the forest for the time; they arrested building, though in 1869 they were languishing for want of funds.[1] The attitude of the Government in regard to these proceedings was remarkable. It is not without difficulty that one can realise the curious meanness of the official procedure. In 1863 the House of Commons had passed a vote against the sale of forestal rights. A Committee appointed in the same session had considered the question with a different result. They had reported that two courses were possible—either the Crown rights might be maintained without regard to expense, or the forest might be enclosed, the various proprietors compensated, and a portion set apart as a recreation-ground for Londoners. They held that it would be a 'course of doubtful justice'

[1] Willingale died before the final decisions of the questions. The rights of lopping were extinguished by payment of 7,000*l.*, obtained by the exertions of Mr. Lefevre, which was applied to build a public hall at Loughton.

to use the Crown rights as a means of preventing the enclosures to which the persons interested had the same right as all other persons similarly situated. They thought, moreover, that such action might fail, as previous experience showed, in securing the desired object. They therefore recommended the second course. The Open Spaces Committee of 1865 recommended, on the contrary, that the Crown rights should be enforced without regard to cost, so that the forest might be preserved in its wild state. They also advised immediate steps for abating the enclosures already made. In consequence of this recommendation, the custody of the forest had been transferred from the Office of Woods and Forests to the Office of Works ; the difference being that the Woods and Forests is supposed to administer property on simply commercial principles, whilst the Board of Works takes charge of ornamental property. The change, in fact, represented just the change of policy which was most required. The traditional view was to treat the Crown rights in a purely commercial spirit, and to leave entirely out of account every consideration but that of the Chancellor of the Exchequer. There is a story (mythical, I presume) of a monarch who asked his Minister what would be the cost of enclosing Hyde Park, and received for answer that it could be done for three crowns. No one in his senses could propose to let the London parks for farms or cut them up into building lots. But the forests of Epping and Hainault will be in the near future what Hyde Park was to our fathers ; and yet the only consideration had hitherto been how to make the most money out of them even at the price of their total dis-

appearance. Some persons who defended this policy
would have been the first to sneer at Fawcett as a
narrow-minded political economist, deficient in culture,
and therefore bound to ridicule all æsthetic or sentimental
considerations. In truth, it wants a very small smatter-
ing of political economy to perceive that the advantage
obtainable from bringing 4,000 acres of forest land
under the plough bears an infinitesimal relation to the
advantage of providing a huge mass of population with
a decent recreation-ground.

Meanwhile the enclosures remained unabated. In
May 1869 Fawcett was one of a deputation from the
Commons Preservation Society to Mr. Layard, then First
Commissioner of Works, which urged a vigorous assertion
of the Crown rights. Mr. Layard expressed his own
wishes for the preservation of the forest; but intimated
his dread of the Chancellor of the Exchequer (Mr. Lowe).
On August 2 another deputation bearded this formidable
official in his den. They came away with ears tingling,
if a round rebuke is enough for that effect. Mr. Lowe
declined to accept the principle recommended by the
Committee of 1865. He declared that he would not
advise the Crown to incur the expense of litigation,
which was certainly not likely to be recouped in money.
The deputation ventured to refer to a previous statement
of Mr. Gladstone's, who had expressed a hope that an
arrangement would be made which would satisfy the
lords and save part of the forest for the public, and had
practically shown his goodwill by the transference of the
forest to the Office of Works by a clause in the Crown
Lands Bill, 1865. Mr. Lowe sneered at the reply as very

'oracular.' A member of the deputation exclaimed that Mr. Gladstone was too honourable not to keep his promise. ' I don't understand,' replied Mr. Lowe, ' what it means ; it was evidently intended to please everyone, the lords of the manor included.'

Sarcasms of this kind are never perhaps very prudent, and it seems almost ungenerous to recall them now that they can only prove the short-sightedness of their brilliant forger. But the utterance must be mentioned, because it illustrates the spirit of the official taunts, which seemed to have been expressly calculated to irritate Fawcett or, indeed, any man of spirit. Fawcett immediately took the most straightforward and effective course. The Commons Preservation Society appointed a sub-committee to consider what was to be done. Fawcett proposed to move on the first opportunity for an Address to the Queen, praying that the ' Crown rights might be defended in order that the forest might be preserved for the recreation of the people.' Some of his friends appear to have thought that this was an act of excessive audacity on the part of a young Liberal who was bound to believe in the infallibility of his party leaders. But Fawcett never inclined to the extreme of superstition in that sense. He saw with his usual perspicacity that a simple enunciation of a broad popular principle would bring into relief the pettifogging and penny-sparing policy of the Chancellor of Exchequer, and compel the leader of the Liberal party to choose between accepting the Liberal view or appearing in the uncongenial character of a champion of private interests and the official *non possumus* against the clear interests of the people. It was only necessary to bring the two principles into clear contrast to make untenable the position hitherto occupied by the Government. Fawcett was for a time deprived of the help of Mr. Shaw-Lefevre, who was now in office; but he could look for support to many Conservatives. He was, however, as he used afterwards to say, alone at the time in deciding to bring on his motion and to force a decision. To say plainly what you want, when it may be inconvenient to the leaders of the party—even though it represents the essential party principles—requires, it would seem, something almost amounting to heroism in a member of Parliament. Praise of him for his courage would be too much like satire of his fellows; but it was at least one more example of his invariable independence of judgment.

Fawcett had his way, and brought forward his motion February 16, 1870. He spoke of the contemptible result of the economic measures. The Crown had sold their rights over 4,000 acres for 18,603*l*. 16*s*. 2*d*. They had imperilled a permanent source of healthful enjoyment to the people for a sum which, from the point of view of a Chancellor of the Exchequer, is scarcely visible to the naked eye. Ten times as much might have been saved in the time by abolishing a sinecure officer such as the Lord Privy Seal, and certainly, one may add, with less regret to lovers of the beautiful. The main argument which Fawcett had to encounter was significant. The forestal rights, according to Mr. Lowe, were relics of feudalism : they were useful to keep up deer for the royal hunting. Now that the Queen did not want to hunt, it would be unfair to keep them up for a different purpose.

A man may have no right to put up a fence to keep out
deer, but he may put it up to restrain a picnic party. The
Queen might not make over her rights to the public, but
must leave them to the lords of manors. The argument,
as Fawcett shrewdly pointed out, was an awkward one. If
a right ceases when the original purpose becomes obsolete,
what would become of the lords of the manors ? They
had ceased to discharge any duties : should they cease to
have any rights ? He ended by saying that the proposed
litigation was expected to cost 1,500l.; that it would almost
certainly succeed ; and that the Government which was
frightened by this amount thought nothing of spending
twice as much on bursting a big gun and smashing a
target.

Fawcett's motion was supported by Charles Buxton,
Mr. Beresford Hope, and Mr. Cowper-Temple. Sir John
Coleridge, the Solicitor-General, replied in the vein of
Mr. Lowe and ridiculed the idea of enforcing the shadowy
rights of the Crown. After a protest from Mr. Alderman
Lawrence against the tone of this speech, Mr. Gladstone
showed, as Fawcett had hoped, a wider appreciation of
the importance of the question. He admitted that
Fawcett had shown that it was the duty of Government
really to move in the matter and make themselves the
champions of the people of London by securing whatever
was practicable. He proposed a modification in the
terms of the motion, leaving the Crown more at liberty to
adopt such measures as might seem expedient. Fawcett,
of course, accepted the modification, and the motion
passed without opposition.

A great step had thus been made. Government had

accepted the leading principle, that the Crown was to aim at preserving the forest for the benefit of the people of London. The result was an encouragement to all who sympathised with the purposes of the Commons Preservation Society. They could no longer be treated as mere devotees of a sentimental crotchet when they were compelling Government to endorse their policy. Yet a Government convinced against its will is in the proverbial predicament. The Prime Minister could see clearly that Fawcett was in the right path; but it was another question whether he could impart the same conviction to his subordinates or induce them to co-operate heartily as well as approve formally. Mr. Lowe, who had sneered at his chief's former adhesion to the principle, was not likely to be converted by a renewed adhesion in a more deliberate form. Mr. Layard had been succeeded at the Board of Works by Mr. Ayrton; and Mr. Ayrton was supposed to be an ally of the Metropolitan Board of Works. That body was sceptical as to litigation; it did not believe in the possibility of establishing commoners' rights so as to prevent enclosure; and it therefore prepared to settle the problem by buying up the rights both of lords and commoners and selling part of the common for building. It was at this very time putting a stop to the Hampstead suit by buying the heath from the lord at the price of 230*l.* an acre. Mr. Ayrton, sympathising with this policy, was not likely to be keen in enforcing the Crown rights over Epping. The answer to the Address voted upon Fawcett's motion was suspicious. An awkward ' as far as possible ' intruded into the desire for the preservation of open spaces. No steps, in fact, were taken for some months. At last the representatives of the Commons Preservation Society were invited to meet a gentleman who was understood to speak with authority as to the views both of the Government and the lords of manors.

The proposal made on behalf of these powers appeared to the representatives of the society to be ludicrously inadequate. In spite of this, the Government were so far satisfied of the strength of their case, that in July a bill was introduced embodying the so-called compromise—one of those in which (in Mrs. Carlyle's favourite phrase) the 'reciprocity was all on one side.'[1] First of all, the lords of the manor and those who had bought of them were to keep what they had taken; that is to say, they were to keep more than half of the whole forest, or 4,000 out of 7,000 acres. Of the 3,000 remaining, the lords of manors were to take 2,000 more, to which they had not yet been able to help themselves. Of the 1,000 acres remaining, 400 were to go to the commoners and 600, possibly in various scattered plots of from one to 200 acres, to be reserved for recreation. This remnant was to be vested in the Metropolitan Board of Works, which was also to be enabled, if it saw fit, to acquire the 400 acres given to the commoners. Fawcett immediately gave notice of moving the rejection of this bill, but a decision that the Standing Orders had not been complied with caused it to fall through for the session; and even its partial exposure to daylight

[1] Mr. Ayrton, in a letter to the *Spectator* of July 25, 1885, says that this bill was introduced without his concurrence or knowledge, and in ' opposition to his known opinions.' It bears, however, his name with those of Mr. Gladstone and the Chancellor of the Exchequer (Mr. Lowe).

had been fatal to its feeble constitution. Government was not so ill-advised as to reproduce the monstrosity in the following session.

Fawcett at the next meeting of the society (August 8, 1870) moved that it should itself prepare a bill ' on the principle of forbidding further enclosures and acquiring the rights of the lords of manors on payment of a sum equal to the profits they derived from the unenclosed portions of the forest.' A bill upon the same principle had been introduced in regard of Wimbledon and Wandsworth Commons, in each of which Lord Spencer was lord of the manor, and had agreed to part with his interest to the public on consideration of an annuity equal to the proceeds from the commons in their open condition. Ten years later the same principle was applied to Epping, after the rights had been defined by litigation. At present it might have been premature. Notices of the bill as proposed by Fawcett were advertised in November. It was then intimated that Government would not re-introduce their measure; and the society thought it better to postpone their own bill, thinking that the passage of the Wandsworth and Wimbledon schemes would improve the situation, and also desiring, if possible, to obtain the initiative of Government.

Government, however, made no sign. There was talk of a compromise, when a measure was taken which precipitated affairs. The finest bit of forest—almost the only bit, I think, in which the trees are at present worthy of their position—is the grove known as High Beach. Elsewhere the trees are generally scrubby or pollarded, but in High Beach there is really a noble group of fine trees. The forest rights of the Crown had here been extinguished. The timber in the forest belongs to the lords of the manor, except where there are rights of lopping; and in this case no such right seemed to apply. It therefore seemed probable that the lords were within their right when notice was given that the trees at High Beech would be felled. At least it was a mode of gaining a compromise. What would be the good of the forest when all the trees were gone? Sir Henry Selwyn-Ibbetson, M.P. for South Essex, attended a meeting of the Commons Preservation Society to urge this view. Fawcett was present, and joined in the opinion that any compensation paid to the lords should be in money, not in land. Meanwhile, it became eminently desirable, in view of such possibilities as the permanent disfigurement of the forest, that Government should be stirred to action. It was agreed that a resolution should be proposed for the adoption of measures in conformity with the Address of the previous session. Fawcett, who suggested the motion, proposed also that it should be brought forward by Mr. Cowper-Temple, who would be able better to represent the less extreme party, and had already been First Commissioner of Works and a President of the Commons Preservation Society, and who, as chairman of the Enclosure Acts Committee, had been a staunch ally of Fawcett. No one was freer than Fawcett from the paltry jealousy which too often leads smaller men to prefer the glory of leading a movement to the success of the movement itself. Mr. Cowper-Temple threw out a suggestion—afterwards taken up—that the City of London might take action in the matter.

The debate (in which Fawcett thought it needless to
speak) had a most remarkable result. Government
opposed the resolution with its whole strength, and,
though nominally in possession of a large majority, was
defeated by a majority of 101 (197 to 96).

Government, warned by this significant vote, still
took time to deliberate; but at a later period of the
session a bill was introduced by Mr. Ayrton which
offered a fair solution. A Commission of three gentlemen was to be appointed to inquire into the various
rights of lords and commoners and to settle a scheme for
disafforestation and the preservation of the forest as an
open space. A struggle took place as to the composition of
the Commission, Fawcett declaring at one point that he
would rather the bill should be lost than the proposed
Commission appointed. Government yielded by placing
Mr. Locke, M.P. for Southwark, the Chairman of the
Committee of 1865, upon the Commission, and the bill
was finally passed August 18, 1871.

The long struggle over Epping was far from its
conclusion. At this stage, however, it passed out of the
parliamentary arena. It was happily discovered in the
course of the Willingale suit that the City of London had
certain rights in the forest; and the matter was taken up
with all the vigour of that powerful body. The Court of
Common Council passed a motion pledging the Corporation to use its resources in the cause. The City Solicitor,
Mr. (afterwards Sir Thomas) Nelson, took up the case
heartily; and Mr. Robert Hunter, honorary solicitor to the
Commons Preservation Society, was retained at Mr. Shaw-
Lefevre's suggestion for his assistance. A bill was filed
in Chancery on August 21, alleging a right in all owners

and occupiers of land within the bounds of the forest to turn out their cattle over all the wastes. Every lord of a manor was made a party to the suit and every enclosure made within twenty years was challenged. The result of this was the judgment of Sir George Jessel (Master of the Rolls) in 1874. All the enclosures were declared to be illegal ; and thus over 5,000 acres became permanently part of our national playgrounds.

It is impossible in such cases to assign to each man who has taken part in the struggle the precise amount of merit which is his due. Fawcett was scrupulously anxious never to arrogate to himself any credit which could be claimed for others, and I should regret to do it for him. But I think that it may be said without any possibility of injustice, that to Fawcett was due the chief credit for taking up a resolute attitude in the parliamentary struggle, and of laying down a simple principle which no Liberal could renounce in common consistency, and so by degrees forcing a Liberal Government to abandon the policy of pettifogging economy, and rousing public opinion to the degree necessary for overcoming the obstacles of vested interest and official stolidity.

A phrase or two from his article in the ‘ Fortnightly ’ of the following November will now be intelligible. He asked why the working-classes were losing their zeal for the Government. The reason was the indifference, or worse than indifference, of the Ministry to these questions. The few remaining commons are the only places ‘ where the people, except by sufferance, can leave the beaten pathway or the frequented high road. And yet this Government, so grand in its popular professions, so

Y

strong in its hustings denunciations of those who would
divorce the people from the soil, used the whole weight
of official influence to enclose the few commons that are
left !   So anxious were they to pursue this policy of
depriving the public and the poor of their commons,
that night after night the House was kept sitting to two
or three o'clock in the morning in order to pass an
Enclosure Bill; and the Ministry, apparently willing to
risk something more than reputation in the cause, were
disastrously defeated by those who were anxious to
preserve Epping Forest.'   Next to the Budget and the
Licensing Bill, he adds, the Government policy of
enclosure has been regarded by all the leading papers as
the main cause of a recent defeat of their party in East
Surrey.   Possibly Fawcett may have been rather hard
upon the Ministry in this passage.   But it is worth
noting on the other hand that they had come to stig-
matise him as 'impracticable,' precisely because he had
compelled them to admit the application of their own principles; and had so forced them into a line of policy of
which everyone now approves, and the adoption of which
at that time was of critical importance.   Impracticability,
one must confess, has its uses.

During this Parliament Fawcett had to interfere on
behalf of another district of surpassing interest.   He had
lived through his childhood on the edge of the New
Forest, and to the end of his life it was one of his
favourite resorts ; though I do not know whether he had
ever seen its beauties except through the eyes of others.
The Commissioners of Woods and Forests were doing
their duty according to their lights by destroying the

most characteristic glories of this unique region with a view to making it pecuniarily profitable. The Crown possessed the soil of 65,000 out of a total of 91,000 acres of forest as well as the right of preserving deer, and a large body of commoners had undisputed rights over 63,000 acres of the Crown land. In the last century the great value of the forest was supposed to consist in its supply of oak timber for the navy. By an Act passed in the time of William III., the Crown had what was called a 'rolling power of enclosure'—6,000 acres at a time were to be enclosed, till the young trees were past danger from browsing cattle, when the enclosure was to be thrown open and another area enclosed instead. In 1851, when some fatal spirit of money-making seems to have entered into the Government departments, an Act was passed by which the Crown undertook to remove the deer, and, in consideration of this, took a right to enclose 10,000 acres (in addition to the 6,000). The results of the new system were disastrous, as unfortunately may still be seen. Happily there are still many glades and groves in the forest, with noble oaks and beeches and tangled underwoods, such as might be the original of the most picturesque opening scene of all extant romances—where Gurth and Wamba are keeping swine in the Forest of Sherwood. But the 'old patrician trees' and the 'plebeian underwood' went down before the Commissioners like the leaders of the old *régime* before the Committee of Public Safety. The old woods, as one surveyor phrased it, should be cleared 'smack smooth!' Long lines of Scotch fir, drawn up in regimental order, supplanted the venerable intricacies of the old forest growth.

The alterations gave dissatisfaction to the commoners, who complained that the best lawns or pasture-grounds in the forest had been injured, and said that even the removal of the deer had done harm, because their mode of feeding improved the grazing for ponies and cattle. Inquiries were held and proposals made for settling the rather complex questions at issue. The official view was that the Crown represented the national interest as opposed to the private wishes of the landowners in the forest. In 1871 a bill for disafforestation was said to be in preparation. It was, however, abandoned in face of general unpopularity. Something must obviously be done to satisfy the conflicting interests and save the ancient woods. Fawcett was assured in answer to an inquiry that the woods should not be felled till the mode of treating the open spaces had been settled. Not content, however, with a bare assurance, he moved on June 20 that no ornamental timber should be felled, and no timber whatever should be cut, except for necessary purposes, whilst legislation was pending. The Woods and Forests issued a document (dated June 16, 1871), just before the debate on Fawcett's motion. This explained very clearly and opportunely their own view of their duties. The 'public,' it was pointed out, 'is a term frequently misunderstood. . . . Whilst the public really interested is the public of the United Kingdom, the public usually referred to is,' in brief, the tourist and the residential public. 'It can scarcely be said·that the suspension of the exercise of the Crown's rights in the New Forest would be advantageous to the taxpayers of Ireland or Scotland.' Their duty was to make an income for the nation, and to improve the property of the Heir-apparent in order that he might make a better bargain on the next settlement of the Civil List. It was added that a resolution of the House of Commons would not release the Commissioner in charge of the New Forest from the performance of his duties as trustee of a settled estate. He would have to disregard it, or violate duties imposed by Act of Parliament. Fawcett's resolution was evidently required when this was the official view. It was in fact supported on all sides, carried unanimously, and for the next six years it stood between the forest and the axe of the official tradesmen. The question, suspended for the time, came up again under the Conservative Administration. Fawcett's resolution, it was said, could not be considered binding for an indefinite time. In 1875 Lord Henry Scott obtained a Select Committee to inquire into the condition of the New Forest. An exhibition of pictures was opened by Mr. Briscoe Eyre and the late George Morrison to call attention to the beauties of the district.[1] Petitions against its devastation were signed at the same time and presented by Fawcett. He gave evidence before the Committee, taking the same ground as in the case of

[1] As long as the Deer Removal Act was in operation the policy was deliberately followed of trying to reduce the value of the common rights, with the view to make their ultimate purchase by the Crown less costly. See Mr. Briscoe Eyre's pamphlet, *The New Forest: its Commons Rights and Cottage Stock-keepers.* The Deputy Surveyor of the New Forest, Mr. Cumberbatch, wrote on December 31, 1853, to the Chief Commissioner of Woods: 'It appears to me to be important that the Crown should as soon as possible exercise its right of enclosing the 16,000 acres, because, exclusive of other advantages, *all the best pasture would be taken from the commoners, and the value of their rights of pasture would thus be materially diminished*, which would be of importance to the Crown in the event of any such right being commuted.'

Epping.   The forest, he said, should be preserved as a
national park.   Any money which could be made by its
enclosure was not worth considering in comparison with
the effects upon the health, happiness, and morality of
the people.   Even arguing the matter from a purely
economical point of view, he said that the influence of
the forest on the health and artistic faculties of the
people had a far greater money value than the money
value of the mere timber.   He got rid very summarily
of the main argument which fettered the hands of Commissioners.   They felt themselves bound, as honest
stewards, to make the utmost possible penny for the Heir-
apparent.   That defined their whole duty, and they could
think of nothing else.   Fawcett replied that the nation
would undoubtedly be delighted to pay a liberal compensation for the pecuniary loss due to keeping the
forest open.   To suppose that there was an unalterable
necessity of treating the forest as it would be treated by
a timber merchant, though neither the Crown nor the
nation desired it, was of course a mere superstition.
Fawcett judiciously pointed out that Mr. W. H. Smith,
Chairman of the Committee and Secretary to the
Treasury, had used the same arguments to good purpose
four years before on behalf of the Thames Embankment Gardens.   The Committee soon reported in accordance with this sound doctrine.   The ancient woods
were to be preserved, the destructive enclosures stopped,
and the Verderer's Court reconstituted so as to represent
the commoners more effectually.   An Act embodying
these principles was finally passed in 1877.

The general question of enclosures was still unsettled.

The Committee of 1869 had recommended the suspension of enclosures until a general measure should have been passed. An Enclosure Bill had, however, been introduced in 1870, but dropped upon Fawcett's remonstrances. A measure for amending the Enclosure Acts was introduced in 1871. Fawcett maintained that it did not carry out the recommendations of the Committee, and advocated its reference to a Select Committee. The bill was dropped. Other abortive bills were introduced in 1872 and 1873, but nothing was effected in this Parliament. The Enclosure Commissioners were thus forced to suspend operations. In 1872 they protested elaborately in their annual report against this inaction. They estimated that 8,000,000 acres, or more than one-fifth of England and Wales, consisted of common land, either waste or cultivated. Of this, 5,000,000 acres were mountainous, leaving 3,000,000 acres in the lowland districts of England. They thought that all the cultivated common land might be improved by being reduced to severalty, and that 1,000,000 acres of the waste might be profitably brought under the plough. A return made in consequence of this statement proved that the quantity of available land had been enormously exaggerated. The acreage was reduced from 8,000,000 to 2,632,000, and, of this, 1,500,000 acres were stated to be unfit for cultivation. The return of landowners in 1875, from the parish rate-books, reduced the quantity of common land to 1,524,647 acres, of which 326,972 were in Wales, whilst the greatest part of the remainder lay in the mountainous districts. The diminished estimate of the available area naturally strengthened the argument

against enclosure. In 1876, however, it was announced
in the Queen's Speech that a measure would be proposed
for setting the enclosure machinery once more at work.
The Home Secretary, Mr. (now Sir Richard) Cross,
introduced the bill accordingly. He called attention to
the changed conditions which made the preservation of
open spaces desirable, and stated that the bill aimed
rather at the preservation than the enclosure of commons.
The measure thus introduced represented a decided
advance in public opinion, but it failed to give satisfaction
to the opponents of enclosure. Mr. Shaw-Lefevre, now
chairman of the Commons Preservation Society, supported
by Fawcett, made a determined attempt to improve the
objectionable provisions. They held that it left too
much to the discretion of the Commissioners; that it
did not forbid parliamentary enclosure in the neighbourhood of large towns; and that it did nothing to put a
stop to the arbitrary appropriation of commons without
reference to Parliament, which had only been checked of
late years by means of expensive litigation. Mr. Shaw-
Lefevre moved a resolution to this effect on the second
reading. Fawcett supported him in a vigorous speech.
A previous speaker had approved the bill, as tending to
dispel the 'monstrous' notion that the inhabitants of
large towns had a right to wander over distant commons
as they pleased. Fawcett seized the opportunity of
endorsing this monstrous notion: the commons were
precisely a 'great and valuable possession' for the people
of the entire country, and he called upon Mr. Cross to
disavow the interpretation put upon his bill. He urged
that the bill would not effectually hinder the Commis-

sioners from acting upon their natural instinct of enclosing; that there were no sufficient safeguards for enabling the poorer commoners to put in their word; and no extension to the provinces of that system of regulating commons without interfering with existing rights which had been so effective in saving the London commons. The bill only amended the general Enclosure Act of 1845, of which the preamble still affirmed the desirability of facilitating enclosure. Nor did it prevent the arbitrary seizure of common land.

Mr. Cross vigorously denied in his reply that the bill would promote enclosures. Its aim, he said, was precisely to give facilities for keeping them open, and open for the benefit of the whole people, as well as those who had actual rights of common. Such an assurance from the responsible Minister was enough to justify Mr. Lefevre in withdrawing his motion. The bill was read a second time (February 18, 1876). Its further progress was delayed, however, till May 25. Though Mr. Cross had accepted the main principle advocated by the Commons Preservation Society, he had not admitted the inadequacy of his bill nor expressed any intention of amending it. The society had, therefore, reported against it, and Fawcett moved—on the motion for going into Committee —that the bill did not adequately protect the labourers, nor provide sufficient security against the enclosure of the commons required for recreation. Many petitions had been presented against the measure by agricultural labourers, and Fawcett remarked that it would be very differently received if the labourers had fifty representatives in the House. He protested against the tendency

of the bill to promote enclosure without reference to the
interests of this unprotected class. Under the Enclosure
Commission, he said, 5,500,000 acres had been added
to the estates of great proprietors, whilst villagers by the
hundred had lost their rights of pasture, and now found
it difficult to provide milk for their children. The
Commission, which had acted on this system, was still
to be trusted with full powers: they were still to be
under the guidance of the general proposition that enclosure was desirable; whilst in this very year they
showed their leaning by recommending the enclosure of
thirty-four commons, including the beautiful open spaces
at Wisley and the Lizard, and others near the crowded
populations of Sheffield and the Potteries. They had
proposed to enclose one common because it was used for
foot races, which, as he observed, was at least not worse
than pigeon-shooting at Hurlingham. And yet it was
proposed to except all these commons from the operation
of the bill. The 'worst and most mischievous of all
economies,' he declared, 'was that which aggrandised a
few and made a paltry addition to the sum total of
wealth by shutting out the poor from fresh air and
lovely scenery.' Fawcett as usual insisted upon a division, though he could not hope for a majority, and received 98 votes against 234 for the Government. As the
bill passed through the Committee, Mr. Shaw-Lefevre,
seconded by Fawcett and supported by some thirty or forty
members, fought the whole question doggedly. On the
main principles they were regularly defeated by the
Government, and generally by large majorities. They
failed to persuade the Legislature to substitute regulation

for enclosure, to except commons near large towns, or to give a definite proportion of future enclosures for recreation. They struggled long for another point. The more difficult the regular parliamentary procedure, the greater, said Fawcett, was the temptation to arbitrary enclosure. Various measures were therefore proposed for guarding against a process shown by experience to be too often successful. It was proposed to make unlawful enclosure a public nuisance, to allow others than commoners to take action against it, to impose a fine of 100*l.* upon anyone so enclosing, and to give the Enclosure Commissioners a *locus standi* to resist it. This last proposal was supported by Mr. Beresford Hope and other Conservatives, and only rejected by 189 to 155. The only concession was to a proposal made by Lord Henry Scott, making it necessary to advertise intended enclosures in a local newspaper.

Mr. Lefevre and Fawcett, however, met with much greater success in amending the procedure proposed in the bill. The Enclosure Commissioners were instructed not to proceed until they were satisfied that the enclosure would be for the benefit of the neighbourhood as well as of private interests. Securities were taken for an adequate testing of local opinion by means of public meetings; and amendments were directed against various clauses which had prevailed in regard to the system of allotments. The preamble of the bill was altered, and now expressly asserted the principle already embodied in the bill, that enclosure was not desirable unless it were clearly proved to be beneficial to the neighbourhood as well as to persons with definite rights in the commons.

Finally, the commons already scheduled in the report of
the Commissioners were taken out of the bill. Of the
thirty-eight commons thus affected, the Commissioners
reported two years later that eighteen were cases in
which they could not recommend enclosure, inasmuch as
‘ it was not proved to their satisfaction that it was for
the benefit of the neighbourhood’—a fact sufficiently
indicative of the importance of the principle of which
Fawcett’s persistent advocacy since 1869 had secured
the acceptance.

Mr. Cross’s bill was an improvement upon its predecessors, and he added to it the provision that every
enclosure scheme should be submitted to a Select Committee of the House of Commons before confirmation
in the general bill. The opponents of the bill had
done something to improve the procedure, and had
done still more by finally reversing the old presumption ; henceforth the burden of proof was thrown
distinctly by a legislative enactment upon the advocates
of enclosure. Any scheme now had to be supported by
clear proof that it was not injurious to the public interest;
whereas previously reference to the public interest was
treated as an impertinence. It was clear, too, that there
was a resolute and active party in Parliament determined
to make these concessions a reality. In this contest, it
must be added, Mr. Shaw-Lefevre and Fawcett were
not supported by the leaders of their own party. They
were backed by Sir Charles Dilke, Sir William Harcourt,
Mr. Cowper-Temple, and Lord E. Fitzmaurice. But no
ex-Cabinet Minister took any share in a work not unworthy of the exertions of the Liberal party.

The effect of the measure depended greatly upon the
spirit in which it would be worked by the Commissioners
and the Select Committee. Fawcett was a member of this
Committee when first nominated. In combination with
Sir W. Harcourt, he gave a direction to its proceedings
which showed that the new principle was really to govern
the operations of the Enclosure Commissioners. They
prepared four schemes, three of which related to contiguous
tracts, including altogether 4,600 acres in Rutlandshire,
and the fourth to a tract of 1,297 acres in Yorkshire. In
each case the principal part of the land was in cultivation, consisting of common fields. The case for
enclosure was therefore of the strongest kind, the change
involving very little appropriation of open spaces. It
was still questionable whether a distribution of the land
amongst private owners was preferable to its regulation
as common land, and whether, if this were satisfactorily proved, sufficient allotments for public use had
been set out. Fawcett and Sir W. Harcourt convinced
the Committee that the allotments proposed were insufficient, and the schemes were sent back to the Commissioners for amendment. After the rejection by large
majorities of the amendments proposed in the House, it
might still have been doubtful whether any great change
would come over the spirit in which the Commissioners
acted. The action of the Committee established that any
proposal for enclosure would be carefully scrutinised, and
that the Commissioners must take care of the interests of
the public, if the schemes which they proposed were to
have a good chance of passing into law. The precedent
had been successfully set. Up to the end of 1883 only

22,431 acres have been enclosed since the passing of the
Act of 1876. Nearly the whole consists either of common
fields or of mountain sides and moorland. An area of
260 acres has been set apart for recreation, and of 258
acres for field gardens. Where the purpose of enclosure
has been rather to avoid disputes between shepherds of
rival flocks than to promote cultivation, the public right
of recreation upon the space affected has been confirmed
so long as the ground remains unplanted. In the same
period, 22,529 acres of open land have been regulated,
and are therefore not liable to enclosure without the
deliberate action of Parliament. Comparing these figures
with the proposals resisted by Fawcett in 1869, when all
but three acres for recreation and six for field gardens
were to be enclosed out of 6,916 acres, it is obvious that
the tendency to enclosure has been greatly limited and
respect for the interests of the public has been enforced.
The title of the Enclosure Commission under the Settled
Land Act of 1882 was changed to Land Commission—
a sufficiently significant alteration. To Fawcett more
than anyone is due the reversal of what till his energetic
action in 1869 had been the settled policy of the Legislature in rural districts.

To complete the story of his defence of open spaces, it
is necessary to add a reference to a few less conspicuous
matters. Amongst the most powerful and insidious
enemies of open spaces are the great railway companies.
They can usually get the commons cheap; the lord of the
manor is glad to make something of his property, whilst
the commoners have no *locus standi* for individual opposition, and there have too often been opportunities for

acquiring cheaply a little additional space for sidings and ballast. Some attempts of the railways had been successfully opposed by the Commons Preservation Society in its early days, but no systematic check was placed upon railway aggression until 1877. In that year, the London and Brighton Railway proposed to mangle Mitcham Common, absorbing eight acres and cutting off many more; whilst the London and South-Western, which had already cut Barnes Common in two and erected a station upon it, proposed to take two more acres for sidings and coal-sheds. In such cases the public gets no compensation, the money going wholly to the private persons interested. The only real compensation would be the addition by the company of land equal in area to that absorbed. This, of course, is not easy to arrange, and the companies are strong in the House of Commons. Fawcett joined heartily in the successful opposition to the demands of the two companies in 1877; and in 1881, though he was in the Ministry, he voted in opposition to Mr. Chamberlain, then President of the Board of Trade, against the Surbiton and Guildford Railway Bill, which encroached upon Wimbledon and other commons. In 1883, again, he joined Mr. Bryce in a successful opposition to the proposal for a railway to High Beach, although the advocates of the bill, including the Corporation of London and some members of the Commons Preservation Society, supported it as making the forest more accessible to the public. Fawcett held that no such object could justify the sacrifice of part of the forest itself. In the same year he actively opposed the attempt of the London and

North-Western Railway to swallow up a burial-ground
near Euston Square; and in 1884 he spoke and voted
against a successful proposal of the Southampton Corporation to take a piece of common land for a cemetery.
He put aside with an amused smile of good-humoured
contempt the suggestion of some more timid members
of the society that its influence might be impaired by
defeat. It was not by shrinking from defeats that he
had succeeded in turning defeat into victory.

Fawcett frequently introduced this subject in his
speeches on various platforms and at public meetings
held for this special purpose. One of the few speeches
delivered after his illness at the close of 1882 was at the
meeting held at Reading to celebrate Mr. Shaw-Lefevre's
representation of the borough for a quarter of a century.
He reviewed the history of the movement in which he
and Mr. Lefevre had taken so important a part. On
other questions, which are still under discussion, he
showed his continued interest in the principle. Few men
had a livelier appreciation of the charms of the Thames.
Before his accident, I remember with pleasure a cruise
which I took with him and other friends from Henley to
London, when an experiment of his in steering nearly
ended in a catastrophe. One of our companions was Mr.
Fairrie, a famous University oarsman, who was one of
his lifelong friends; and in later years no recreation was
more to Fawcett's taste than a river excursion with
Fairrie or some other enthusiastic waterman. When,
therefore, the Thames needed protection, Fawcett alone
amongst the leading members of the Commons Preservation Society warmly took up a suggestion for establishing

a similar organisation on behalf of the river; and it was chiefly through his advice and encouragement (though his official position prevented him from acting personally) that Mr. Story-Maskelyne obtained the appointment of a Select Committee on the subject in 1884. And, finally, he strongly sympathised with Mr. Bryce's agitation against the system under which the harmless enjoyment of the beauties of the Scotch highlands is hampered by the selfishness of the proprietors of deer forests.

In these cases Fawcett could only look on sympathetically at the beginnings of movements in whose further development he was not to share. To the end of his life he was a warm supporter of the Commons Preservation Society, of which so much has been said. He attended its meetings regularly, and acquired in it a position of peculiar authority. It was not wonderful, indeed, that he should be there regarded with peculiar respect. His advice was always the expression of his characteristic strong sense. He formed his opinions carefully and independently, and expressed them resolutely. The justice of his main conclusions had been proved by the success of his conduct. He always went upon plain, simple principles; and one great secret of his success was his invariable practice of laying down definitely and explicitly the policy which he considered to be right, and then adhering to it inflexibly. Beyond this, no one could fail to recognise the simplicity and unselfishness of his purposes. He was fighting for a cause, in the justice of which he had the most unfeigned conviction. When it was out of favour, he was ready to put himself forward in spite of the unconcealed annoy-

z

ance of officials, of the leaders of his own party, and the majority of the House of Commons. When it was succeeding, he was equally ready to let other men take the prominent position if he thought that their support would be of more service to the cause than his own. The solid, sturdy strength, characteristic of his whole nature, may at times have given him the appearance of too much confidence in his own opinion. But, though independent and hard to shake from a fixed conviction, he was never overbearing. He had lost the occasional harshness of manner of his early youth. No man was readier to give a fair hearing to an opponent or more anxious to meet, instead of shirking, the real strength of the opposite case. In private life, Fawcett was one of the few men whose advice was really valuable from the care with which he would consider any point, his anxiety to avoid any bias even towards his friends, and the warm interest which at the same time he always took in their concerns. The same qualities made his lead especially valuable in this society, into whose cause he had thrown himself so warmly and unreservedly.

Fawcett had energetic supporters, some of whom took subordinate parts not likely to bring them the measure of credit which they deserved. Mr. Shaw-Lefevre, whom I have so frequently had to mention, was alternately his leader and his supporter. Mr. Shaw-Lefevre, with the advice of Mr. Lawrence, had been active in promoting the suits which saved the London commons in the years preceding Fawcett's activity. He was equally active and useful in later proceedings of a similar kind, especially in regard to Epping

Forest. Of other helpers I will only venture to mention Miss Octavia Hill, whose services on the Commons Preservation Society, where she was always a staunch supporter of the most energetic courses, form an additional claim to the many which she possesses upon the public gratitude. Fawcett always spoke of her with especial warmth. But without Fawcett the cause would have been far more doubtful; for its success was essentially dependent at the most critical part of the struggle upon his unflinching resolution, independence, and coolness of judgment. It is a reflection which has something of the pathetic for the future generations of Londoners who will enjoy the beauties of the Surrey commons and the forest scenery of Epping, that their opportunities of enjoyment are due in so great a degree to one who could only know them through the eyes of his fellows. When Fawcett lived at Lambeth he frequently took the railway to Putney and refreshed himself, after a night at the House, in the fresh breezes which still blow across the wide open space of Wimbledon Common. It is not long since I stood there one day by his side on the edge of 'Cæsar's Camp,' and noticed the interest with which he listened to a discussion as to the distant view. Was that the grand stand at Epsom ? Could we see the tower on Leith Hill through the gap of Mickleham Vale ? We prolonged the talk because Fawcett, instead of showing any sadness at his incapacity to follow us, seemed to derive pleasure from the livelier impression of the commanding position of our standing ground. It is surely a proof of unusual healthiness as well as kindliness of nature when a man

can thus delight in the vicarious sense of the beautiful instead of fretting over his own deprivation. It is pleasant
to think that so much of this enjoyment was still within
Fawcett's reach. It is not the less honourable to him
that, though no one could be more hopelessly shut out
from the direct appreciation of the remnants of un-
sophisticated nature, no one was more strenuous or
effective in efforts to preserve them in the interests of
his fellows and, above all, of the classes least able to enforce their own rights.[1]

[1] I have been giving an account of Fawcett's share in the movement
—not of the movement itself. For fuller information upon many
points which were not strictly relevant to my purpose, I am glad to refer
to Mr. Shaw-Lefevre's chapter upon ' Common Lands ' in his *English
and Irish Land Questions* (1881).

CHAPTER VIII.

INDIA.

I now approach what is in many respects the most remarkable part of Fawcett's political career. For many years he devoted the greatest part of his time and energy to Indian questions. He became popularly known as the 'Member for India.' He succeeded in impressing certain convictions upon English statesmen; he was the object of the enthusiastic admiration of large classes of our Indian fellow-subjects, and his strongest opponents ended by recognising the purity of his motives, the undeviating independence of his conduct, and even the value of many of the principles for which he endeavoured to obtain recognition. I shall do very little justice to Fawcett if I do not succeed in making clear the nature of his services to India. And yet the task is by no means easy. I cannot here, as in other cases, point to any definite legislative achievements. The effect of his action is to be found less in any specific changes than in the whole temper of English public opinion upon Indian questions. It is not possible to discriminate accurately his share in a result to the production of which many other causes contributed. It may be as well, too, that I should at once recognise frankly, what will be sufficiently evident, that I cannot affect to speak with any independent knowledge of Indian affairs. What I shall endeavour to do is to set forth as clearly as I can the main contentions to which he adhered from first to last, and to explain the chief grounds of his action. That can, I think, be done sufficiently to exhibit Fawcett's character, though I must of course leave to persons of far greater knowledge the task of deciding upon the value of his particular conclusions.

I am not able to trace the exact steps of Fawcett's interest in Indian affairs. His friend, Mr. Dale, Fellow of Trinity Hall, tells me that Fawcett once spoke to him in regard to some proposal for excluding undergraduates from the University library. Fawcett said that he had himself visited the library in his undergraduate days and had there taken up a book upon India which first specially drew his attention to the subject. India, as we have seen, is mentioned characteristically even in his school essays, and in the early letters to Mrs. Hodding. Various influences may have stimulated his interest. His intimate friends, Thornton and J. S. Mill, were both in the India Office, and qualified to speak with authority upon administrative details. Thornton gave him information about India for the 'Manual'; and in later days often discussed Indian questions with him. Mr. C. B. Clarke accepted an appointment in the Indian Educational Department at the end of 1865, and, when in India, wrote very full and interesting letters to Fawcett, giving the impressions of a keen political economist, not imbued with the ordinary official prejudices. Although Clarke's

views differed materially from Fawcett's, the letters incidentally illustrated many questions of Indian administration in a way calculated to suggest reflection. Fawcett's
first public utterance upon the subject was in July 1867.
It had been decided to give a ball at the India Office to
the Sultan on July 16. Fawcett asked whether the
expenses of this ball were to be charged to India. Sir
Stafford Northcote replied in the affirmative, and explained, in justification of the course adopted, that the
ball was a return for assistance given by the Sultan
towards telegraphic communication with India. Fawcett
was not satisfied. He consulted Mill. Mill, on the
whole, advised him to be content with having raised the
question. It was not the strongest case that could be
adduced. Sir Stafford Northcote's answer would be
regarded by many as satisfactory; and it was a more
important consideration that the real intention was
probably to induce the Sultan to give more effective
assistance than he had hitherto done. Fawcett was not
convinced by these arguments, which, in fact, hardly
seem to meet his point as to the fair distribution of the
charge. England, as well as India, was interested in the
telegraphic communication. On July 19 a motion was
made for a list of invitations to the ball. Some of the
usual parliamentary facetiousness was brought to bear
upon the supposed unfairness of the selection of guests.
Fawcett hereupon rose ' with great reluctance,' and said
that after ' anxious and careful consideration ' he felt it his
duty to express his feelings. The important question, he
said, was how the Secretary for India could ' reconcile
it to himself to tax the people of India for an entertain-

ment to the Sultan and Viceroy.' It might be proper for the officials themselves to give the entertainment. But ' why should the toiling peasant pay for it ? ' The Indian press was complaining of slowness in the measures for helping the sufferers from famine. It would have new occasion for sarcasms when a part of the Indian revenues was voted without the least compunction for an entertainment which would amuse good society and the people of London.

The protest, as Fawcett said soon afterwards, received no support and excited little immediate attention ; but it was the beginning of a long series of more important efforts. Fawcett had inherited the true Radical doctrines of economy and retrenchment. He was ready to condemn sinecures and needless pensions. But he had a specially hearty contempt for meanness, and this, as he afterwards said, was a ' masterpiece of meanness.' He always declined to base his criticisms of extravagant expenditure upon the simple question of pounds, shillings, and pence. It was lavish expenditure upon the rich, paid for by scrapings from the wages of the poor, which he specially scorned. The Sultan's ball was long a sore point with him.

At the end of 1867 he again came forward in the same sense. Parliament was summoned to provide for the Abyssinian war. Government proposed that the extraordinary expenditure should be paid for by England, whilst India should continue to pay the troops at the ordinary rate. Of course, the extraordinary expenditure was a very large proportion of the whole; but Fawcett held that a great nation should do things handsomely, and made a protest, though he was in a minority of 23 to 198 (November 28, 1867). His rising interest in Indian affairs was shown by two speeches made in the House of Commons during the next session.[1] On the last occasion he moved a resolution in favour of holding the Civil Service Examinations in Calcutta, Madras, and Bombay, as well as in London, in order to give natives of India an equal chance of obtaining appointments. Some of the obvious objections to this scheme were forcibly stated in the debate by Mr. G. O. Trevelyan. Taken by itself, as a serious proposal, this would, I think, tend more than anything to give plausibility to the charge of doctrinairism sometimes made against Fawcett. In fact, his love of fair play, and his belief in the system of open competition as accepted at Cambridge, possibly inclined him to a rather excessive estimate of the merits of such schemes in general. But it must also be said that the motion, which was withdrawn after a short debate, was intended chiefly to call attention to a most important principle. Through the whole of his career he took frequent opportunities of insisting upon the importance of giving fair play to the natives of India, and making use of their abilities in our service. The knowledge of his strong convictions upon this question had a considerable share in the gratitude with which native Indians came to regard him. The particular plan advocated in this resolution may have been impolitic. He does not appear to have attached special importance to it, and his perception of the difficulties in the way of any such scheme rather increased in later years. But he never lost an opportunity of urging

[1] March 27 and May 5, 1868.

the importance of the principle upon which it rested. If our Empire is not to be founded on simple terror and brute force, some plan must be found of giving a larger share in the administration to qualified natives, and enlisting their goodwill by providing them with a career. There were many other applications of this principle besides that embodied in the resolution; and Fawcett never lost sight of the importance of the question.

The sentiment which animated these speeches was that which lay at the bottom of all his interest in India. It was the chivalrous sympathy for the helpless and oppressed, in which he had never been wanting at any time, but which became a more pronounced feature of his character as he grew older and found more opportunities for its exercise. His love of fair play took a more tender and sympathetic development as he exerted himself to rouse others from an apathetic indifference to the wrongs of the weak.

In one of his speeches at Brighton (January 15, 1872), when he was becoming prominent as a critic of Indian administration, he expressed himself characteristically. He observed that the 'most trumpery question ever brought before Parliament,' a wrangle over the purchase of a picture or a road through a park, excited more interest 'than the welfare of 180,000,000 of our Indian fellow-subjects.' Constituencies, he added, were said to take no interest in the subject. He warned them that some day they would be forced to take an interest, if affairs were neglected in the future as they had been in the past. He quoted an official statement as to the neglect of Indian interests under the exigencies of English party

politics, and asked whether anyone who cared for the
honour of the country could remain quiet under such an
imputation.   'The people of India,' he said, 'have not
votes; they cannot bring so much pressure to bear upon
Parliament as can be brought by one of our great railway
companies; but with some confidence I believe that I shall
not be misinterpreting your wishes if, as your representative, I do whatever can be done by one humble
individual to render justice to the defenceless and power-
less.'   This conviction never left his mind.   As he said
in the House of Commons (August 6, 1870) upon another
occasion, he felt that 'all the responsibility resting upon
him as member of Parliament was as nothing compared
with the responsibility of governing 150,000,000 of distant
subjects.'[1]

At the time (January 1872) of the speech from
which I have quoted, most people thought, and the
newspapers warned him, that constituencies would
be indifferent to Indian questions.   When in 1874
Fawcett was defeated at Brighton and became member
for Hackney, he was able to say that his constituency
had never found fault with his attention to Indian politics,
and had always been warmly interested in his speeches
upon Indian affairs.   This is one of the cases in which
the highest principle turns out to be the most expedient.
Fawcett's Indian zeal became advantageous even from a
merely electioneering point of view.   His constituents
were proud of his achievements, and were interested—for
the time at least—by his expositions of Indian affairs.

[1] The population of British India in 1881 was estimated at nearly
200,000,000; besides 54,000,000 under native governments.

But it is equally true that no one who had an eye to popularity merely would have taken up the subject as Fawcett did. He relied, with his usual confidence in the good feeling of the people, upon their ultimate approval of his line of conduct. But it was because his motives were thoroughly pure from all taint of personal interest that he threw himself so heartily into the cause and believed that it would make its way.

In fact, he had to encounter not only the indifference of constituents, but the more active dislike of some members of the Liberal Government. It was only by slow degrees that they came to recognise his claims to serious treatment. In his earlier speeches he was met with the kind of contemptuous treatment with which the genuine official attempts to suppress the rash outsider who dares to question the wisdom and omniscience of his rulers. Fawcett gradually attained a position in which it was not only clear that he was an antagonist who could retort to some purpose, but that his words were entitled to serious weight. The cause of his success was not simply his obvious sincerity, but also the sound judgment with which he selected his position.

In fact, no one can deny that the prejudice against an outsider had some plausibility. It needs no demonstration that, upon many questions of vital importance to India, nothing but long experience can justify any man in speaking with confidence. The difficulty is rather to decide whether any Englishman, however long his experience, can obtain sufficient knowledge of the vast and complicated problems presented by the heterogeneous populations spread over so wide an area. Fawcett had never been out of Europe; he had enjoyed no special opportunities for gaining knowledge; he was not, in point of fact, more profoundly acquainted than many other Englishmen of his class with the religious and social organisation, the prejudices and customs, of the Indian races; and therefore he could have little to say upon many problems of internal policy. But this he clearly recognised. He limited himself to one question or class of questions upon which he could really speak to the purpose. It required no special knowledge of Indian peculiarities, though it did require faculties which he possessed in a high degree, to judge of the general position of Indian finances. He could say whether the balance-sheets presented by Indian statesmen were intelligible; whether they showed the revenue to be elastic or the reverse; whether they showed that the results promised for certain investments had or had not been achieved or been put in course of achievement; and whether there were indications that India was being made to bear expenses properly chargeable to England. He set to work to investigate these questions with an energy which is indicated by the results; and he limited himself very strictly to discussions where his competence to form an opinion was undeniable.

In truth, this strange phenomenon of the English Empire in India must present many problems to everyone who is not content to treat it simply as so much stimulus to national vanity. No thinking man can fail at times to ask the question whether the empire is or is not desirable for both races. Both the moralist and the politician may ask whether it can be possible for the ruling nation to discharge effectually duties so unprecedented, and for which we are clearly so unqualified in some ways, and whether the enormous burden of direct and indirect responsibilities with which we are laden is not a heavy price to pay for any conceivable advantages. If the utterance of such misgivings is generally hooted down, it is not because they are felt to be unreasonable, but because they are thought to be fruitless. Voluntary withdrawal from our position is out of the question, at least, till very radical changes have taken place in human society ; and we are doomed meanwhile to solve the problem by action instead of speculation. We shall doubtless hold on as long as holding on is possible; and if the empire should be dissolved, the dissolution must be the result of violence, not of prudential abnegation.

Fawcett accepted this necessity, and, I think, had little sympathy with the politicians who think our government of India essentially an evil. On the other hand, he sympathised still less with those who regard the maintenance and extension of empire as an ultimate aim to be upheld by all patriots, whatever may be the consequences to the subject race. He invariably preached that our rule was to be regarded as a sacred trust—good if so exercised as to be a blessing to the governed, and bad if exercised to their disadvantage. The question which he habitually put to old Indians was whether the condition of the masses under our rule was better than their condition under native rule.

His whole purpose was to aim by every means in his power at impressing upon his countrymen their enormous responsibility, and encouraging them to bear it in a worthy spirit. He felt strongly the difficulty of the position. The government of vast multitudes of an alien race by an assembly of some hundreds of English gentlemen, profoundly ignorant for the most part of the whole conditions of life of the subject population; elected by persons still more ignorant and indifferent, and for considerations which have the most indirect relation to their fitness for rule; profoundly interested, on the other hand, in questions of English politics, and ready to sacrifice the most important Indian interests to the most trifling questions of party warfare in England,—suggests enormous difficulties and may seem to justify despair. Swift illustrates the English view of Irish troubles in his day by the sentiment of Cowley's lover :—

> Forbid it, Heaven, my life should be
> Weighed with thy least conveniency.

The starvation of thousands of the native Irish was of less importance in the eyes of the English rulers, as Swift thought, than putting a few pounds in the pockets of the King's mistress. If the English rule in India were to be conducted on the same principles, the result must be the misery of our subjects and ultimately the collapse of our empire. But Fawcett thought that it was possible to rouse the nation to a worthier sentiment, and to this end he gave his best energy for many years. When an argument was urged against the interference of the House of Commons in matters of which it knew so little, he replied forcibly that, if the House did not interfere, India would suffer from all the evils of party government and have none of the advantages. We ought not, he said,[1] to be constantly meddling in details of Indian administration ; but we should do our best to protect the financial interests of India. Parliament was competent to see that India did not suffer by our shuffling off upon her charges which properly belonged to ourselves, though it might be quite incompetent to look after many questions in which local experience was essential to any wise judgment. This, in brief, was the principle upon which he always acted; and, in spite of indifference or more active contempt, he never failed to denounce every unfairness which came within his observation. He had for some years, he said in 1872, devoted all his spare time to the study of the subject; and the only result of his endeavours to bring it before the House had been to excite the Under-Secretary for India and to bring upon himself Ministerial rebukes. No amount of labour, no dread of an Under-Secretary, no Ministerial rebukes, should prevent him from doing what he could towards the creation of an adequate interest in this country in the affairs of our great dependency.

His first appearance, as I have said, was on occasion of the Sultan's ball. Whilst other members squabbled over the right distribution of tickets, he alone protested against the extreme meanness of charging the cost upon India. The case attracted much notice in India ; it was discussed in the native press; and he came to the next Parliament impressed with the conviction that the particular instance was a symptom of an evil existing on a much wider scale. His first active interference took place upon the introduction of the Indian Budget in

[1] Speeches of July 15 and August 9, 1875.

1870, when he complained—as he had frequent occasion to do afterwards—that the financial statement was not made until a period (August 5) at which the House of Commons was incapable of attending properly to anything. Its control of Indian finance could not be effective, if the question were not debated till the fag-end of the session. He had another piece of 'melancholy meanness' to mention, comparable to that of the Sultan's ball. The Duke of Edinburgh had been visiting India and distributing presents. The cost of these gifts (10,000*l.*) was to be taken from the Indian revenues. He quoted a statement recently made by Mr. Laing, formerly financial member of Council, to the effect that the finances of India were constantly sacrificed to the wishes of the Horse Guards and the exigencies of English statesmen. He dwelt upon various grievances, to be hereafter mentioned, showing that he had studied the question with close attention ; and he ended a remarkable speech by moving that it was desirable to appoint a Special Committee to inquire into Indian finance.

Mr. Grant-Duff (the Under-Secretary for India and the natural exponent of official views, and therefore, for some time to come, Fawcett's most prominent opponent upon these questions) spoke contemptuously of Fawcett's allegations. Mr. Gladstone, however, admitted the disadvantage of bringing on the Budget at so late a period, and spoke in favour of appointing a Committee in the next session. Fawcett withdrew his motion for the present, and in the next session it was taken out of his hands by Government, who moved the appointment of a Committee to inquire into the financial administration

A A

(March 9, 1871). The Committee sat during the three sessions of 1871, 1872, 1873, and its labours were continued by a Committee which sat during the first session of the following Parliament (1874). Fawcett was one of the most active and regular members of these Committees. Neither of them presented any definitive report; but a great mass of evidence was printed, including examinations of many of the most distinguished Indian administrators—Lord Lawrence, Sir Charles Trevelyan, General Strachey, and many of the chief officials from the India Office. The evidence is of the highest interest for any student of the great questions involved, and though no definite conclusion was reached, the facts elicited made a considerable impression upon public opinion.

In the course of the first session Fawcett presented a petition to the House from natives of India and European residents, demanding greater economy, and complaining of the expenditure upon public works. He moved that it would be desirable to send a Commission to India to obtain evidence on the spot. He withdrew his motion at the request of Sir Stafford Northcote, another member of the Committee, but had a sharp encounter with Mr. Grant-Duff, partly provoked by a misunderstanding, for which Mr. Grant-Duff afterwards courteously apologised. Mr. Grant-Duff, however, took occasion to observe that he did not wonder that Fawcett was dissatisfied with the Committee, seeing 'the writh-ings of the theories of the hon. member as witness after witness touches them with the light of fact, just as Ithuriel touched that other honourable gentleman with

his spear.' He spoke of Fawcett as employed in his
' congenial occupation of finding mare's nests,' and made
some fun of his indulgence ' in that branch of ornitho-
logical research.' Other members protested against
Mr. Grant-Duff's unusual asperity. Fawcett was content to reply by uttering a very characteristic maxim.
Five years' experience in the House, he said, had taught
him that a member was always right in bringing forward a question when the fact of his bringing it forward
caused the Minister concerned to lose his temper. I
would not refer to passing ebullitions of this kind, which
were, I would fain hope, forgotten or forgiven on both
sides, were it not that it seems necessary to show what
was the first sentiment aroused in Ministerial bosoms
by Fawcett's rough grasp of their optimistic convictions.
Mr. Grant-Duff was most sincerely convinced that the
Indian administration, though not, of course, faultless,
was rendering immense services to India; and held that
Fawcett was the unconscious instrument of discontented
and irresponsible persons magnifying the small imper-
fections inevitable in all human affairs into monstrous
injustice. Fawcett's function was in fact to insist that
the rulers of India should give a full account of their
stewardship. He neither asserted nor denied that on
the whole their rule was beneficial. But he did assert
that abuses existed and that his duty was to probe
them to the bottom. Some of the supposed cases
might be capable of full justification. Others might
turn out to be such venial blemishes as must occur
in all administration; and I cannot find that Fawcett
was ever slow to acknowledge the groundlessness of the

suspicions when a fair explanation was forthcoming.
But the habitual attitude of jealous examination of
official apologies and of refusal to take official statements
for granted is not likely to conciliate officials. . When, in
another encounter in this session, Fawcett criticised the
new Engineering College at Cooper's Hill as a deviation
from the principle of open competition, Mr. Grant-
Duff said in reply that competition was becoming a
fetish with the British people; to which Fawcett replied,
warning him against another fetish—the fetish of officialism. Widely different opinions might doubtless be
formed from a study of the whole evidence before the
Committees. I think, however, that it is impossible for
any reader to doubt that Fawcett's accusations were
justified in many particular cases. The question, of
course, remains whether those cases were to be regarded
as normal or exceptional. Fawcett did not himself draw
any further conclusion than this—that their occurrence
showed the necessity of strict supervision, improved
administration, and a better system of accounts. His
examinations of witnesses are admirable. Some witnesses were entirely upon his side; but upon other
occasions he had sharp encounters with officials who
strongly resented the c nclusions to which he tried to
force them. His especial merit was the clearness with
which he stuck to his points and the remarkable command of complicated accounts which he invariably
displayed. The longest and most generally interesting
of his examinations was that of General Strachey,
whose great experience and complete command of the
whole subject made him a formidable antagonist. They

had some tough passages of arms; and Fawcett's reputation in India was considerably heightened by the fact
that he could at all hold his own with a leading official
who was not only thoroughly well informed as to the
policy under discussion, but had taken a very important
part in securing its adoption. I imagine that the interrogator and his answerer parted with mutual respect;
especially as there is no indication of a want of frankness on either side, but simply some vigorous dialectical
fencing, such as used to delight Fawcett in old days
at Cambridge and might have pleased a Moderator in
the schools.

The power of effectually cross-examining a skilled
financier upon his own ground was specially remarkable
in a blind man, and the same power was shown still more
remarkably in two speeches upon the Indian Budget
which he delivered in 1872 and 1873.[1] A political opponent, Mr. (now Sir R.) Fowler, has said that he considered these speeches to be the most remarkable intellectual efforts he had ever heard. Without any of the notes
which help the ordinary speaker, Fawcett gave an admirably clear exposition of the complex questions which
might have raised the envy of the most accomplished
Chancellor of an Exchequer. His method, as is clear to
any reader of his speeches, was thoroughly to fix in his
head the cardinal facts and figures. He would get a
friend to help him,[2] and go over the ground again and

---

[1] They are reprinted in *Political Speeches*.

[2] Mr. Moulton, I believe, helped him in preparing the first of these
speeches. He received much help also from Mr. Dacosta, a retired Indian
merchant, and from Mr. James Hutton, formerly a journalist in India.
Mr. Dacosta was in communication with him for many years.

again until he was satisfied that the whole statement was perfectly arranged in the most lucid order. A friend with whom he prepared a speech upon the Endowed Schools Bill (in 1874) tells me that he thinks that Fawcett had prepared himself a little too carefully for purposes of debate, not leaving sufficient power of modifying his argument to meet other speakers. But he thoroughly secured the main result of working his thoughts into the clearest and pithiest form possible. He would quote a remark of Cobden's, that a speaker should not use more figures than he could carry in his head. Lucid arrangement was necessitated, to secure ease of recollection. In this respect the speeches are irreproachable. They do not affect rhetoric; and so long as he can make himself thoroughly clear he is not anxious to be epigrammatic or elegant or careful about repeating himself. The same illustrations and statements are apt to recur pretty often. When he said a thing in the best way he could, he was content to say it over again in the same way. He wished to hammer certain leading principles into people's heads, and for such a purpose it is often the best plan to repeat yourself, regardless of literary criticism. Fawcett certainly managed to make his views about India clear beyond all possible doubt, and to command more and more attention as time went on.

I will now endeavour as well as I can to sum up his main contentions. The groundwork of all his reasoning was the fact that India is a poor country. The vague impressions of its enormous wealth, derived from the days of the nabobs, had no doubt been to a great extent dissipated before his time ; but the English people still failed to appreciate the extreme narrowness of the margin which divides the great mass of the population from the starvation limit. Fawcett's first object was to make it obvious that India is a country in which one more turn of the financial screw, or a single failure of crops, will at once bring millions of our fellow-subjects into the direst necessity. The struggle for existence is always a terrible reality for the vast majority. Proof of this is to be found in the permanent condition of the revenues. The position of the national income was partly obscured, as Fawcett maintained, by the ordinary form of statement. The gross revenue of India,[1] for example, in 1879-80 amounted to over 68,000,000l.; of which over 22,000,000l. was derived from the Land Revenue ; over 26,000,000l. from various sources other than taxation (including over 10,000,000l. from opium, and 8,500,000l. from public works) ; and nearly 20,000,000l. from taxation proper. But a great part of this corresponds to a revenue which implies counterbalancing charges. It includes, for example, receipts for services, such as the post-office and telegraph, which are more than balanced by expenditure upon the same accounts. It includes also the gross receipts for opium and salt without deduction of the expense of production. When therefore, it is said that the revenue has greatly increased, we must remember that much of the increase implies a corresponding increase of expenditure, and therefore no real increase of resources. The great dif-

[1] See *Finances and Public Works of India* from 1869 to 1881, by Sir John Strachey, G.C.S.I., and Lieut.-Gen. Sir Richard Strachey, R.E., F.R.S. London, 1882.

ference between the gross and the net revenue makes it
necessary to avoid illusion, by fixing our attention upon
the net revenue, which represents the really disposable
resources of the country. Accepting this, the total net
revenue must be fixed at a very much smaller sum. On
Fawcett's mode of statement, it did not amount in 1876–
77 to quite 37,500,000*l.*; the gross revenue being at the
same period just under 56,000,000*l.* The main peculiarity of this revenue, as he constantly urged, was its
inelasticity. In England, a financier who requires to
raise a larger sum has numerous resources at his disposal. Without increasing the debt, he can add millions
to the national income by direct or indirect taxation.
The Indian financier, under similar circumstances, is at
his wits' end. The pressure is already as great as the
country will stand. He cannot raise an additional income of a few hundreds of thousands without provoking
a serious amount of discontent, in order to gain sums
disproportionately small. This, as Fawcett was never
tired of explaining, was the really vital problem of Indian
government. The finances are, as one witness said, the
key of the situation. To direct attention to these difficulties, and thus to obtain security for better administration and clearer statements in future, was his one great
object. His speeches in 1872 and 1873 are all directed
to this point. The financial question is of course inti-
mately connected with many social and political questions; but it was from the side of the finances, with
which of course he was most competent to deal, that
Fawcett attacked the difficulty, and did his best to drive
home his conclusions.

To make his points clear, I must follow him into some-what greater detail. And, first, we may observe that almost the whole revenue is derived from six sources— land, opium, salt, excise, customs, and stamps. From the land is derived nearly half of the net revenue. One-fifth of this, being derived from the districts under permanent settlements, is incapable of increase. In many other districts the payments are fixed for thirty years, and can only be raised as these settlements fall in. This revenue, I may observe, differs essentially, according to Fawcett and all orthodox political economists, from a tax proper. It is in reality a rent, enjoyed by the State instead of private proprietors, and, so long as it does not exceed a rack-rent, is not a burden upon any class of the community. He therefore was always opposed to the principle of the permanent settlement, which, as he held, prevented the State deriving any advantage in the most unobjectionable shape from the increased resources of the country. But, in point of fact, no large increase could be expected from the land revenue, whilst the depreciation of silver steadily lowered its real value. Opium is the next in importance of the sources of revenue (producing a net revenue of near 8,000,000*l*. on an average from 1877–81), and showed a considerable increase during the years of Fawcett's activity. It was, however, obvious that there was an element of un-certainty in an income dependent upon the demand from a foreign State, and which, in the opinion of some authorities, might be exposed to competition or prohibited altogether.

The salt-tax, which contributed about 6,000,000*l*. to

the revenue, is a very heavy tax upon a necessary of
life, pressing upon the poorest part of the population,
and already so high that an increase in the duty would
do much to check consumption. A man, according to
the evidence of Sir Cecil Beadon (Lieutenant-Governor
of Bengal), might live and support a family upon $4\frac{1}{2}d$.
a day, and would have to pay $1\frac{1}{3}d$. a week for salt. Salt,
duty free, would cost one-eighth of a rupee, and, with the
duty, sold for two rupees. No other indirect tax was
possible, with the very doubtful exception of tobacco.
The Lieutenant-Governor of Bengal said that he would
rather have his right hand cut off than be a party to
increase the salt-tax. The remaining sources of revenue—
the customs, excise, and stamps—brought in only about
5,000,000l. a year ; and the Government was constantly
under strong pressure to diminish them. In 1876 Lord
Salisbury pledged himself to repeal the cotton duties as
soon as the Indian finances would bear it. The duties
were accordingly reduced by Lord Lytton in 1879, in
opposition to the views of a majority of his Council.
The repeal was approved by the House of Commons in
April 1879, in spite of a protest from Fawcett, who,
staunch free-trader as he was, held that the sacrifice
of revenue was in this instance an unjustifiable concession to demands from Manchester, at a time when there
was unusual pressure upon Indian finances.

This brief survey, which is the substance of much
that was urged again and again by Fawcett in various
forms, will sufficiently indicate the grounds of his belief
that the revenues of India were singularly inelastic.
The authors of the 'Finances and Public Works of

India' take a much more favourable view. Although it is not for me to decide upon such disputes, I may notice that, even upon their showing, the net revenue remained almost stationary from 1869 to 1877; and that a considerable part of the increase in the next four years was due to opium and to increased taxation, though partly due also to increase of trade and in consumption of articles paying duty. The inelasticity is confirmed by the difficulty of discovering any new forms of taxation. The difficulties of direct taxation are sufficiently indicated by the objections to the income-tax. As Fawcett observed, an income-tax of $2\frac{1}{2}d.$ in the pound would raise 5,000,000*l.* in England, whilst in India it raised little over 500,000*l.* The discontent which it excited and the abuses connected with it were so great that it had to be abandoned, and, as Fawcett frequently observed, it was unequivocally condemned by three successive Ministers of Finance—Sir C. Trevelyan, Mr. Laing, and Mr. Massey. Lord Lawrence, in 1873, told the Committee upon Indian Finance that, after careful investigations, his Government had come to the conclusion that no new sources of income could be devised. When it was thought desirable to raise an additional fund to provide for famine expenditure in 1877, a license-tax was imposed upon all traders with incomes of over 100 rupees a year. It raised at its maximum about 820,000*l.* The limit of liability had to be raised when returns showed that more than a million people were taxed to raise only 340,000*l.*[1] Whatever may be the arguments in favour of such taxation, the extreme

[1] *Finances and Public Works,* p. 203.

practical difficulty of increasing the revenue is sufficiently obvious to justify Fawcett's general position. The ingenuity of the ablest financiers has been exerted to discover the means of a small increase to the revenue; and, in whatever direction they turn, they are immediately met by the danger of worrying an inert population, which will bear passively the burdens sanctioned by custom, but is frightened and harassed by novelty and uncertainty. Meanwhile, the burden of debt has been increasing by war, famine, and expenditure upon public works. The civil charges have risen enormously from the rise of prices and the natural growth of an expensive administrative system. To produce and maintain a perfect equilibrium, the rulers of India must have recourse, as Fawcett urged, to a strict and unrelaxing economy. A sound position must be attained rather by restricting expenditure than by increasing income. If Fawcett exaggerated the inelasticity of the revenue, even his critics would admit that he sufficiently demonstrated the necessity of economy. A fresh burden, such as might be cast upon India at any time by political necessities, would imply a strain for which the country should be prepared by setting it in order beforehand.

This brings us to one of Fawcett's main positions. Since the great mutiny, the abolition of the old Company and the development of means of communication have brought India into closer dependence upon her rulers. In more ways than it is necessary or possible to recount, changes in English politics have a direct reaction upon India, and the whole organisation of Indian government can be controlled and directed at every point by the home officials.

India, as he frequently said, is now in close partnership with England; a poor partner, therefore, is closely joined with a rich partner, and, moreover, with a rich partner who is able and inclined to assume the whole management of the concern. When measures were proposed which involved a heavy burden upon Indian finance, the opinion of the Indian Government was often not asked, and when it was opposed to the views of the Home Government, was summarily overridden. The old East India Company was a powerful and independent body, possessing strong influence in Parliament and in the country, and able to obtain a hearing for its protests. By the Act of 1858 a control over the Indian finances was given to the Indian Council, or rather to the Secretary of State in Council. This body had the right to veto charges of which they did not approve. But in practice they could not make good their opposition. The Secretary of State belongs to a Cabinet in which he is the only member specially interested in Indian affairs. If, with the support of his Council, he should oppose a demand from the Treasury, the result would be, as Lord Salisbury said before the Committee of 1874, to 'stop the machine.' 'You must either,' said Fawcett, 'stop the machine, or resign, or go on tacitly submitting to injustice.' 'I should accept the statement,' replied Lord Salisbury, 'barring the word "tacitly"—I should go on submitting "with loud remonstrances." Remonstrances, however loud, might be unavailing unless backed by the force of external opinion. And here there was the constant difficulty indicated by another of Lord Salisbury's replies. Under the pressure applied by the House of

Commons, every department desires to reduce its estimates. It is therefore tempted, without any desire to
be unjust, to get money in the direction of 'least resistance.' So long as the House of Commons is indifferent
to Indian finance, there will therefore be a steady temptation to shift burdens upon India. The jealous watch-
fulness of the House of Commons, said Lord Salisbury
in a phrase which Fawcett frequently quoted afterwards,
and in the spirit of which he had long acted, would be
the best protection of the people of India against such
injustice; and he spoke of the desirability of exciting the
public opinion of England 'up to the point of integrity.'

Instances of actual injustice came to light as the
Committee pursued its investigations. In his first
active protests Fawcett had been stirred by the cases of
the Sultan's ball and the Duke of Edinburgh's presents.
He dwelt upon the contributions made by India to
various consular establishments and objected to the payment from the Indian revenues of the two members of
the Judicial Committee of the Privy Council. He asked
why the colonies, which were equally interested, were not
called upon to pay equally; and suggested, as the too
probable reason, the simple consideration that the
colonies would not stand such a charge. A significant
and more important illustration of the tendency was a
story fully detailed before the Committee of 1871 by his
friend Thornton. The English Government were unlucky
enough to have a telegraph-cable on their hands, which
had proved unsuitable for the original purpose of con-
necting Falmouth with Gibraltar. Sir Charles Wood
(afterwards Lord Halifax), then Secretary of State for

India, agreed in April 1860 to join with the English
Government in laying it down between Malta and Alexandria, India paying two-fifths of the cost. He stipulated,
however, that the cost of a line in the Persian Gulf should
be also divided. The Treasury replied that this part of
the bargain should be left for after-consideration. The
Treasury, however, a month or two later sent in their bill
for the cable and demanded payment. Sir Charles Wood
protested that his assent had been conditional; but in the
end he was forced to submit. India was left to construct
the Persian cable at her sole expense, which (with some ex-
tensions) came to a million. After some years, the Malta
cable had to be sold for a trifle, of which India received
two-fifths. The total loss upon the transaction to India was
115,946*l*. As a corollary bearing upon another topic
often noticed by Fawcett, it may be noticed that the sum
finally received was considered as ordinary revenue.
You borrow money to buy a thing, said Fawcett to a
witness, sell it at an enormous loss, and then put down
the result to income. And he summed up the transaction
between the two countries by saying that similar conduct practised by an individual A. to another B. would be
regarded as ' uncommonly sharp practice.' ' Yes,' was the
reply, ' it is impossible to suppose that any individual B.
would submit to such treatment.'

Such transactions, however indicative of an objectionable tendency, did not by themselves imply a loss of
much significance to the national revenue. The existence of a similar spirit in regulating the main branches
of national expenditure would be a far more serious
matter. The most expensive part of the State organisa-

tion is, of course, the army. The military expenditure of India is great in itself; its amount becomes more remarkable when compared with the revenue which supplies it, and especially, as Fawcett pointed out, when it is measured against the net, instead of the gross, revenue. The amount for 1876–77 was estimated by Sir John Strachey at 17,000,000l. This is a large enough fraction of the gross revenue of 56,000,000l., and when set against the net revenue of only 37,500,000l., it amounts to 45 per cent. of the whole—a proportion so large as to make this the cardinal fact in regard to all Indian finance. Moreover, in many directions the expenditure was apparently as elastic as the revenue was the reverse. Causes beyond the control of the Government contributed to swell it. The rise of wages and prices in the world at large enforced a rise of the soldier's pay and of the cost of stores. It was stated, for example, by officials examined in 1873, that whilst the European forces in India had been reduced, during the nine years preceding 1872, from over 69,000 to under 59,000, and the Native army from 134,000 to 116,000, the total cost had risen slightly contemporaneously with the decrease of numbers.

Various causes were alleged for this; but it was clear, in any case, that the matter was of primary importance. As Fawcett pointed out, the clearest proof that the increase was due not to extravagance, but to the irresistible force of circumstances, would not diminish the necessity for careful inquiry. The more inevitable the growth of expenditure, the more necessary every possible measure for securing economy. The Committees devoted a great deal of time to taking a mass of evidence upon these heads from the most competent authorities. They reported, in 1872 and 1874, that the 'most serious consideration' was necessary, and that further inquiry was desirable. The whole problem is of course one of great complexity. Fawcett followed the whole discussion carefully, and examined many of the witnesses. His main efforts were directed to the inquiry how far Indian interests and opinions had been consulted, and how far the total expenditure was directed towards maintaining a really efficient army. Many matters were of course discussed, upon which experts contradicted each other, both upon questions of policy and questions of arithmetic, with great freedom and confidence. Much of the controversy lay beyond the province of finance. There were discussions as to the principles of military organisation, and occasionally excursions into curious and insoluble points of casuistry as to the equity of the arrangements for distributing the burden between England and India. Without entering into all these discussions, Fawcett brought out, I think, ample grounds for his demand for a close supervision of the whole matter, and for the careful protection of Indian interests against the thoughtlessness and selfishness of English politicians.

The Mutiny of 1857 had necessitated a complete reconstruction of the military system. The Native army had in great part vanished, and the political relations between the two countries were radically changed. If the English rule was to be maintained, it was obvious that a considerable European army must be provided, at whatever cost. That was, in any case, the starting-point

B B

of the inquiry. The question remained whether due attention was secured for Indian interests, and the enormous pressure upon Indian revenues kept within the narrowest possible limits. And upon this question there was ample ground for keen and persistent controversy.

The first step had been the amalgamation of the English and Indian armies. According to some very high authorities—opposed, it is true, by others perhaps equally high—this amalgamation was a gigantic blunder. One thing, at any rate, was clear. It had been adopted, as Lord Salisbury stated in 1874, against the opinion of 'almost every available Indian authority.' Lord Lawrence said, in 1873, that the Indian Council had objected to it unanimously. Out of fifteen members of the Council fourteen had recorded their protests against it. These protests were before the House of Commons, but the House took no notice of them whatever. The Governor-General had also sent home his objections, rather late it appears, but in any case without producing the slightest effect. Right or wrong, the change thus adopted, in spite of the unanimous objection of the party most concerned, had involved a great increase of expenditure. A large number of officers of the old army had become superfluous in consequence of the disappearance of their soldiers; and it was desirable in some way to give them satisfaction. The amalgamation was carried out under a commission of Indian officers of experience, which, as Sir Charles Trevelyan expressed it, was 'setting the wolves to guard the sheep.' Concessions were made after a time, the effect of which was to give a certainty of comfortable retiring pensions to a large number of the old officers. Under the old system, a man had to wait for promotion until some post involving actual service was vacant. Under the new (after a concession granted in 1866) he was to rise in rank, whether there was a vacancy or not, simply in virtue of the length of his service. An officer who had served for thirty-eight years thus acquired a right to a permanent allowance of 1,100*l.* a year. The staff corps, the new body which was to discharge duties formerly assigned to the officers of the native army, numbered, before 1866, 1,485 officers; and on the concession being made, it was at once 'swamped,' as a witness expressed it, by the immediate accession of nearly a thousand additional officers. The charge to be ultimately imposed by these allowances was variously estimated at from 577,000*l.* to 1,000,000*l.* a year, which represents the cost of making things pleasant for the old army. An immense boon had been conferred upon them at the cost of the Indian revenues; and a very large sum has to be paid for non-effectives, though, in course of time, when the system is fully established, this will no longer be the case.

Another effect of the amalgamation was, that every change in the English army involves a corresponding change in the conditions of Indian service. The introduction, for example, of the short-service system involved changes in India, the precise effect of which was the subject of much entangled controversy. An increase in the pay of the English army, made with a view to purely English requirements, involved, according to one witness, an increased expense of 400,000*l.* a year to India.

A specially entangled dispute raged over the question of
recruiting.   On the old system, the Company had a
single recruiting depôt at Warley.   On the new system,
the rule comes to this—that a fifth part of the officers
and non-commissioned officers of every regiment serving
in India are maintained at home in the various depôts
at the cost of the Indian revenues.   Fawcett urged
strongly, with the support of various official witnesses,
that these troops really constituted part of the effective
force in England ; and said that the correct statement
would be that a certain portion of the English army was
maintained at the cost of India.   In any case, it was admitted that the cost of recruiting was greatly increased.
England, as Fawcett expressed it, had a monopoly of
the raw material, and could therefore compel India to
buy it at such prices as she chose to fix.   The differences
of the system made any direct comparison difficult.
According to one estimate, the difference was that
whereas India had formerly obtained a recruit for the
infantry at a price of 42l., she now had to pay 82l.   In
an official letter (May 15, 1873) from the Indian Government to the Duke of Argyll, it was stated that the charges
for recruits were now fixed at about 58l. for an artillery-
man, 63l. for an infantry and 136l. for a cavalry soldier;
whereas the average charge for all arms from 1849 to
1859 had been under 20l.   It was replied, amongst other
things, that the recruits were now drilled before instead
of after their voyage to India ; and I, at least, should
not venture even to have an opinion upon the subject.
Debates between the highest authorities as to the distribution of such charges between India and England

brought out the fact that, in the opinion of the Indian Government, charges which they were driven to describe as ' scandalously unjust' had been imposed upon them, in spite of their repeated protests.

This brief indication of some of the points at issue may serve to show the complexity of the controversy. Fawcett abstained from entering into that part of it which may be called purely military. But if he did not prove, he had the assent of many of the highest authorities in arguing, that the partnership of England and India had involved an extravagant expenditure on the part of the poorer partner—the necessity of paying more for a given article than was needed for her own purposes, and the necessity of compensating vested interests at an excessive rate, and of paying enormously for the non-effective part of the services; whilst all her protests were liable to be summarily overridden whenever they came into awkward collision with the needs of the more powerful partner.

Another large expense connected with the army leads to a different part of the subject. The change had involved the necessity of building barracks for the English troops. The total expenditure from 1862–63 to 1872-73 appears to have been about 5,500,000*l.*, whilst an outlay of at least two or three millions more was contemplated. General Strachey said that we should have spent nine millions upon barracks by the end of 1873. It was disputed whether the whole scale of these barracks was not extravagant; whether they were not mere 'suntraps,' and so forth. It was, at any rate, acknowledged on all hands that the estimates had been greatly exceeded.

and that the work had in some cases been shamefully
scamped. The walls of one building had quietly tum-
bled down. At Sangor 165,000*l.* had been spent upon
barracks which turned out to be unfit for human habi-
tation. One of a committee of examination had poked
his walking-stick into the walls, and the mortar ran out
' like corn out of a sieve.' Another case, not connected
with military expenditure, which was a good deal discussed before the Committee may be put beside this.
The Governor of Bombay sold his official residence at
Poonah for 35,000*l.* He obtained leave from the
Governor-General (Lord Lawrence) to spend this sum
upon building a new one. A year afterwards it turned
out that he had already spent 90,000*l.* upon this purpose,
and before the house was finished it had cost nearly
160,000*l.* The question of the responsibility for this
expenditure was the subject of much argument. Such
incidents, in any case, seemed to prove that Indian
expenditure upon public works was not always conducted upon business-like methods. The expenditure
upon public works in general is a matter not less
important than the military expenditure, and to questions of this kind Fawcett devoted a large and increasing share of his energies.

He complained, as I have said, that Indian expenses
increased along with a great increase of debt. The fact
of such an increase is of course admitted; but the reply
is that the debt was incurred by borrowing money for
public works. If the money so borrowed has been
judiciously spent, if it has developed the resources of the
country, and that development has more than counter-

balanced the additional burden, the policy is obviously justified. Fawcett, indeed, would have been the last man to deny that it was a duty to act energetically in that direction. The English rulers of India have to do much which in England would properly be left to the energy of private persons. He said emphatically that public works were most desirable ; but he also urged that, where so great an expenditure was taking place, a scrupulous economy and a careful investigation of the probable results of our operations were essentially necessary. The East India Company had spent certain sums upon public works, charging them simply against revenue. Two years before its abolition, Mr. Bright declared that during the preceding fourteen years the Corporation of Manchester had spent more upon public works for the good of its own population than the Company had spent during the same period upon the whole of its vast territories. This, if true at the time, was soon to be changed. When the Company disappeared a great system of public works was speedily developed. On the plan first adopted, guarantees were given to various companies. They were to receive 5 per cent. upon their capital, whatever the results of the undertaking. The system produced dissatisfaction ; companies safe of making a respectable percentage on all the money expended had no sufficient inducement for spending it to the best advantage ; and the pressure brought to bear upon the authorities in favour of very doubtful schemes was often successful in overcoming their prudential motives. Towards the end of Lord Lawrence's Viceroyalty (1867–68) a great change was made. The system of giving guaran-

tees was abandoned. Public works were to be divided
into two classes—ordinary and extraordinary. The ordinary works were to be made from revenue, being works of
such a nature as not to return a profit. Extraordinary
works were to be those which were to be constructed
from borrowed money, and were to be only undertaken
in cases where a net return was anticipated equal at
least to the interest of the money borrowed. Under both
systems an immense sum has been spent upon railways
and irrigation works. Thus, in 1880-81 the capital of all
the public works amounted to 142,223,000*l.*—composed
of 97,728,000*l.* for guaranteed railways, 26,689,000*l.* for
State railways, and 17,806,000*l.* for irrigation works.
It had been already proposed before 1872 to adopt plans
which would involve an expenditure of 30,000,000*l.* upon
railways and 40,000,000*l.* upon canals. The question
therefore remained, how far these millions had been, or
were likely to be, judiciously invested for the benefit of
the country. The history of the operations already
carried out was not calculated, as Fawcett urged, to en-
gender much confidence either in the judgment which
preceded the undertakings or in the economy with which
they would be executed.

The investigation was one of considerable difficulty.
The distinction between ordinary and extraordinary
works led to great obscurity in the accounts. The term
'extraordinary' ceased, as the authors of the 'Finances
and Public Works'[1] tell us, to bear its original meaning.
They were intended to be works for which money was
borrowed upon the ground that the returns from them

[1] P. 49.

might be relied upon to exceed the interest of the loans. For this reason they were excluded from the 'ordinary' expenditure of the year. But they came to be any works the expense of which could not be met from the revenue, 'whatever might be the conditions or circumstances under which they were undertaken. The question of the probable early, or even ultimately, remunerative character of the works was in some important cases altogether set aside, the justification for the outlay having been found in considerations of a political or administrative character.' The Indian Government had set out with the intention of openly and deliberately borrowing money, on the ground that the loan should be invested in speculations certain to pay. But the convenience of a fund which did not appear in the ordinary Budget produced a temptation to which financiers yielded, and they borrowed money which was applied without regard to future profit. The evasion of the original condition complicated the statement of accounts, and in spite of repeated orders from successive Secretaries of State against undertaking any but remunerative works, the system was not finally put down.

There were great difficulties in many cases in determining what had been the actual results of works already taken. Fawcett examined General Strachey at great length upon this head. He urged that it was impossible to make out how far the loans for reproductive works had been used for the avowed purpose, and how far deficits had been made up from the ordinary revenue. General Strachey fully agreed that the accounts had not been definitively made up in such a way as to bring out precisely the mode in which the funds had been applied. He said that he had strongly urged the advantage of making such a statement upon Lord Mayo, who was himself anxious for it; but that the difficulties had not hitherto been overcome. Fawcett maintained that under these circumstances the accounts were 'absolutely untrustworthy,' and though General Strachey thought that with some trouble the desired information might be elicited, he agreed that the accounts were not what they ought to be. Fawcett endeavoured to prove that, if proper charges had been made, the rate of interest with which some works were credited would be reduced from a little over 5 to 3·8 per cent.; and this led to some pretty logical fencing which reached no definite conclusion. Fawcett, in my judgment, had the best of the logic, and at some points succeeded in placing his opponent in a difficulty.

In certain cases, however, there was no need for any minute questions of account-keeping. It was plain, beyond all dispute, that the Indian Government had been led into some disastrous bargains. There was, for example, the Mutlah Railway. The Secretary of State (Lord Stanley) had given a guarantee for this line, which was to connect Calcutta with Port Canning. At least twice the necessary sum (according to General Strachey) was spent upon the construction. It never paid its working expenses, and Government was at last forced, by the terms of the contract, to buy it for 500,000*l.* or 600,000*l.* The port was ultimately abandoned. The Carnatic Railway had received a guarantee, in regard to which the Indian Government was not consulted, and the result had been that Government had paid 43,500*l.* to the proprietors, whilst the aggregate net profit from the working of the railway was only 2,600*l.* Some three-quarters of a million had been spent upon the Godavery navigation works, from which there was no return, whilst the anticipated result of opening up a new line of traffic had not been attained. It was thought better to abandon the three-quarters of a million than to spend another quarter in the faint hope of obtaining some better result from a completion of the works. Government had guaranteed interest on 1,000,000*l.* to the Madras Irrigation Company. It had afterwards been forced to lend the company 600,000*l.* to save it from a collapse. Though part of this had been repaid, the final result was that 1,372,000*l.* was swallowed up without return. The Orissa Company had a similar history, which Fawcett summed up in a statement accepted by General Strachey : 'The Secretary of State entered into a complicated arrangement which he could not carry out, then remitted it to the Government of India, who entered into another complicated arrangement, and, in the end, to get out of the difficulty, the Government bought the company' (paying 1,050,000*l.*), 'at considerably above the market price of the shares.' A somewhat similar case was that of the Elphinstone Company at Bombay, where it was alleged that Government had paid 2,000,000*l.* upon shares really worth a much smaller sum. The accuracy of this statement was disputed by one of the managers of the company, and Fawcett's examination of him upon that occasion is a conclusive proof by itself that he would have been a most effective

performer at the bar. He drew admissions from a reluctant witness to prove that Government had made
a bad bargain, and that the effect of their purchase
had been to prevent the proper development of the
property.

Such cases as these proved, according to General
Strachey, that human beings were liable to blunder, and
that Indian officials were neither perfect nor omniscient.
They proved, according to Fawcett, that the system
which admitted of such blunders, and which made it
very difficult to track them through its complex system of
accounts, was radically unsatisfactory, and not calculated
to attract confidence in the great undertakings announced
for the future. His researches had certainly resulted in
something more than a discovery of 'mares' nests.'
And upon certain points his conclusions were borne out
by General Strachey, as well as by witnesses less inclined
to an optimist view. General Strachey, in fact, fully
agreed that the accounts hitherto given were unsatisfactory, and would not show whether a fair profit had been
obtained; that disastrous bargains had been forced upon
the Government by the pressure of interested persons;
that the worst extravagance had occurred where the
opinions of Indian officials had been overridden by
the Home Government; that a better distribution of
responsibility in the administration of public works,
both in the buying of stores in England and the carrying out of the works in India, was urgently needed; and
that Parliament would only do its duty by insisting upon
a careful limitation of such expenditure and of the debt
incurred for the purpose. He held that the railways

and irrigation works had produced excellent results in
the development of Indian resources; and in common
with most authorities he maintained that these results
could only have been attained at the time through the
guarantee system. He agreed, however, that the great
expenditure which it involved made a new plan necessary; and that without such a change of policy the
construction of new railways in India would become
' absolutely impossible.'

Fawcett's labours in the Committee during the
sessions of 1871, 1872, 1873, were untiring, and it is plain
from many parts of his examination that he had taken
great pains to prepare himself by independent examination
of the facts and by communication with well-informed
persons outside. His able speeches upon the Indian
Budget showed that he was already a very competent and
vigorous critic of financial affairs; and his name became known to all persons interested in such questions.
He came to have an extensive correspondence with
English residents in India, with many members of the
Civil Service who sympathised with his views, though
disqualified by their position from openly avowing their
opinions, and, as time went on, with members of the
Indian Council and other official personages in England.
He soon attracted the attention of such natives as
were able to follow English parliamentary discussions.
Addresses were voted to him by a great number of
Native associations of India. A meeting at Calcutta, for
example, in October, 1872, voted an address to Fawcett,
and another to the Mayor of Brighton thanking the
constituency for returning such a worthy representative

and disinterested friend of India. He was frequently entrusted with petitions setting forth the complaints and
grievances of the Native or non-official community, and
was strongly impressed with the importance of obtaining
a fuller hearing for the Native view of our policy. In
June 1871 he moved that it was desirable to send a
Commission to India in order to take evidence from the
natives themselves. The Committee of 1873 so far
adopted his view as to request that natives might be sent
home at the expense of Government to give evidence;
and two were accordingly examined. Upon one matter
connected with this Fawcett took a characteristic line.
Applications were made to him, when his advocacy of
Indian interests became conspicuous, to represent the
grievances of various Indian magnates before Parliament. He invariably declined such requests, on the
ground that he was too poor a man to have anything to
do with princes. He was strongly impressed throughout
his career with the importance of keeping himself absolutely free from the remotest suspicion of any pecuniary
bias. I remember his speaking to me in early days
of the respect rightfully entertained for a conspicuous
member of the Conservative party who had resigned
office rather than compromise with his conscience, when
a few days' longer tenure would have entitled him to a
pension. It would be impertinent to praise Fawcett for
being free from the least taint of pecuniary motive. He
was not only free from such taint, but scrupulously
delicate in all such matters. When, on his first entrance
into Parliament, it was proposed to him to become
director of a company, he declined at once, feeling that

such appointments, however compatible they may be with strict integrity, must tend to lower a man's political position, especially if he be a poor man, and may throw some doubt upon the absolute purity of his motives. Whilst upon these grounds Fawcett carefully avoided any dealing with princes, he spared no trouble in trying to be of service to poor men who had, or thought they had, some grievance to complain of. He was both kind and serviceable to natives who came to be educated in England with introductions from his friend Clarke and others; and I have letters expressing the warmest gratitude from one of these gentlemen to whom he had been able to render assistance.

During Mr. Gladstone's first Administration, Fawcett had thus made himself known as a prominent critic of Indian policy. The general feeling about him may be traced in some contemporary comments. In March 1871 an able, and on the whole a friendly, journalist had reflected what was probably the average opinion, by complaining of his 'rigidly theoretic Radicalism,' which prevented him from regarding the 'political world' as a merely practical world. A couple of years later (February 1873) an article in the 'Economist,' probably by his friend Bagehot, took a shrewder view. It said that his influence was due not only to his courage, but to the 'hard common sense and adherence to scientific principles by which his Radicalism was modified.' He was free from the 'pulpiness' and 'sentimentality' of most Radicals of the present day. Instead of making 'wild speeches against Indian administration,' he accepts the duty, and labours with all his might to have it done in the way he approves. His vigorous adherence to plain facts enabled him to bring 'extreme Liberals into full connection with the quiet mass of hard-headed opinion existing in the country.' He talks a Radicalism which Whigs can understand, and which therefore induces them to examine it more closely and dread it less. This was the quality, in fact, for which Fawcett was gradually obtaining credit. He was not a mere abstract theorist, but a man with a keen eye for realities, and a 'theorist' only in the sense that he held unflinchingly to what he took to be the true account of the facts.

The election for the next Parliament took place at Brighton on February 5, 1874. The result was a complete defeat of the Liberals. The numbers polled were—Ashbury, 4,393 ; Shute, 3,995 ; White, 3,351 ; Fawcett, 3,130. The successful candidates, according to the papers of the day, were a 'wealthy and successful yachtsman' and 'a distinguished cavalry officer.' Both of them, it is added, were 'personally most respectable men;' but it was neither expected, nor did it in fact happen, that they would take any conspicuous part in politics. Mr. White, it may be seen, received nine more votes, and Fawcett forty-nine more, than on the previous occasion, whilst the Conservative vote was greatly increased. It does not appear from the figures that Fawcett's differences with his party had really lost him any support. The change in the vote was no doubt due to the general causes which led to the great Conservative reaction of the time.

The feeling expressed in the country generally upon Fawcett's defeat was significant of the position which he had already attained. Fawcett had incurred whatever odium falls to the man who becomes a keen critic of his own leaders. The remarkable thing about Fawcett was, as I have said, that, whilst taking this dangerous attitude, he had succeeded in gaining respect and influence. He might, and he did, urge that he differed from Mr. Gladstone's Government in a more thoroughgoing adherence to their own principles. And yet he was equally pronounced in his attachment to doctrines repudiated by the popular theories of his own party. He never wavered, for example, in proclaiming his adhesion to the doctrine of minority representation, and repudiated all the favourite schemes of Radicals which were, in his opinion, incompatible with fair play to antagonists or to the widest principles of individual liberty. He would have nothing to do with such measures as the Permissive Bill; he had already separated himself from Mr. Mundella upon the question, then exciting much interest, of the extension of the Factory Acts to new fields of women's labour; and he never condescended to conceal his hostility to some of the favourite nostrums of the party to which he belonged.

Holding this position of unbending independence, it was the more creditable to him that his temporary exclusion from the House was regretted on all sides. The Indian papers spoke strongly of his unique position, and a fund of 400*l.* was raised and transmitted to England to pay the expenses of another contest. It arrived too late, but went towards the expenses of the contest at Hackney in 1880. Another sum of 350*l.* was then raised in India, which was placed in the hands of trustees with a view

c c

to a future election, and will now be devoted in due time
to some purpose connected with India. Soon after the
Brighton election, there was a prospect of a vacancy at
Hackney. Fawcett was immediately selected as a candidate, and he addressed the electors for the first time on
March 18, 1874. His speeches were remarkable for
their outspoken avowal of principles supposed to be
unpopular. He was greatly impressed at this time by
what he regarded as a discreditable competition between
the two great antagonists. Mr. Gladstone had said that
if he should be returned he would repeal the income-tax.
Mr. Disraeli immediately followed suit by announcing
that he would do the same. Fawcett denounced these
promises as incapable of fulfilment, sure to lead to
disappointment, and intended only to catch votes. He
expressed his resolution to continue his attention to
Indian affairs, then complicated by the threatened famine
in Bengal. Even the 'Saturday Review,' not generally
favourable to his party, hoped for the return of Fawcett
as the one man out of official circles who cared for India.
He claimed credit from a Metropolitan constituency for
his defence of Epping Forest ; but he stated unequivocally that he would not vote for the Permissive Bill, that
he was opposed to the Nine Hours Bill, and that he should
resist all attempts to throw more charges upon the
Consolidated Fund. In spite of a complete refusal to
adopt any vote-catching professions of faith—or, let us
hope, partly by reason of it—Fawcett was enthusiastically
welcomed. He and his fellow-candidate, Mr. Holms,
were opposed in the Conservative interest by Lieutenant

Gill,[1] and the poll, on April 24, 1874, was—Holms, 10,905 ; Fawcett, 10,476 ; Gill, 8,994.

From this time Fawcett occupied a safe seat, and the general satisfaction at his return to the House proved that Hackney was only reflecting the general state of public opinion.[2]

He was at once added (April 30, 1874) to the Committee on Indian Finance, which had been appointed (April 20) a few days before his election. I have already spoken sufficiently of the nature of his labours upon this Committee, which was substantially a continuation of those appointed in the preceding Parliament. During the Parliament of 1874-1880, Indian questions occupied a larger proportion than before of his whole energy. I shall not go into the details of much that engaged his attention during this period ; for he was mainly employed in insisting upon principles already asserted and applying

[1] Lieutenant Gill was a young officer of Engineers, who was murdered with Professor Palmer in 1882 in attempting to open communications with Arab tribes.

[2] A passage may be quoted from a contemporary journalist. The *Times* of April 27, 1874, says : ' Mr. Fawcett is of all men the most independent. He offended the publicans by refusing to use their houses as committee-rooms ; he offended the advocates of the Permissive Bill by declaring his resolution to vote against it ; he offended shopkeepers by his zeal in favour of the co-operative movement; he offended working-men by his opposition to the latest movement for limiting the hours of labour of adult women ; he offended old-fashioned Liberals, and Liberals who are getting old-fashioned, by his persistent advocacy of reforms that had not come within the range of their education when they were young ; and Liberals of a later growth remembered how often he had found himself unable to acquiesce in Mr. Gladstone's policy and plans. Yet he must have secured the support of men of all these sections, who concurred in sending him to Parliament because they believed that his presence there would be advantageous, in spite of errors of opinion which each section in turn lamented.'

them to various questions which arose from time to time. I may observe in general that his position was in one respect materially improved. Officials no longer treated him as a nuisance to be suppressed contemptuously from the heights of superior knowledge. His criticisms, if not always welcome, were at least received with respect, and frequently fell in with the doctrines admitted in general terms, if not always applied in practice, by the responsible authorities. The change may have been due in part to the change of persons in office. Fawcett himself had softened and was less severe in his language as he became more familiar with the intricacies of the subject. Moreover, he acted in the spirit of a proposition which he frequently laid down, that it was altogether unworthy to treat Indian questions as belonging to party politics. The principles which he had most at heart— the principles of generosity to the subject race and of scrupulous care in managing the finances and sharing the burdens of the empire—were happily not the property of either political party. As a matter of fact, Lord Salisbury seems to have come nearer to him in point of principle than the other Secretaries of State during the period. Towards the end of this Parliament, indeed, Lord Beaconsfield's policy involved momentous results to India, and was criticised accordingly by Fawcett. During the first years he was chiefly occupied in trying to secure the acceptance of the principles which had, in his judgment, been established by the Committees on Finance. Lord Salisbury had laid down strict rules against borrowing money for unremunerative purposes. Lord Northbrook (Governor-General from 1872 to 1876) was energetic in the reduction of expenditure. Fawcett expressed his confidence in the good intentions of the authorities. He thought that a steady pressure of parliamentary opinion would strengthen their hands, and more than once appealed to Lord Salisbury's approval of that view. The evidence published by the Committees had no doubt had a marked effect in strengthening the demand for economy. Fawcett's speeches had served to rouse the attention of the House of Commons, and to prove that even popular constituencies might be induced to take some interest in the matter. He was now doing his best to make use of the advantage he had gained. Whenever a measure was brought forward affecting the finances of India, he insisted that it should not pass without careful scrutiny. He complained in 1875 that the Government had declined to reappoint the Committee upon Indian Finances, and pledged himself to make 'astonishing disclosures' if the opportunity were granted. He complained that, whilst this Committee was allowed to drop, another Committee was appointed to consider a question of compensation to English officers, and said that the House of Commons was always brought in to compel additional expenditure and never to insist upon saving (August 9, 1875). In February 1877 he moved for a Committee, when Lord George Hamilton (now Under-Secretary for India) explained that the previous Committee had finished all practical matters and that it would be idle to go into ' wide speculative questions.' Fawcett's motion was lost by 173 to 123. He took various opportunities to criticise measures in which he thought that Indian interests were neglected. In 1875, for example, he moved that the whole expenses of the Prince of Wales's visit to India should be paid by England. Mr. Gladstone united with Mr. Disraeli in opposing him, and by a majority of 379 to 67 (June 15) it was voted that India should contribute 30,000l. towards the expenses. In the next year he opposed a measure for giving pensions to members of the Indian Council; and in 1877 protested against the abolition of the cotton duties, a motion for which was brought forward in the interests of Manchester and in the name of free trade. On these and other points Fawcett was of course defeated, and occasionally convinced that a good ground might be assigned for some of the measures which he challenged. Even in such cases he was fully justified by his principles in insisting that the explanation should be given. He was attempting to carry out his self-imposed duty of enforcing responsibility to the House of Commons.

Fawcett had to complain in 1876 that Lord Salisbury's directions restricting the accumulation of debt for non-remunerative works had been insufficiently observed. He attacked the distinction between ordinary and extraordinary expenditure, which, as he urged, made a fair estimate of the results impossible. Before long, events took place which gave additional weight to these considerations. After the famine of 1874, Lord Northbrook had stated that famines could no longer be regarded as abnormal calamities. Three serious famines had occurred within the previous ten years. He argued with the approval of Lord Salisbury that, to meet such difficulties in future, we should secure a regular surplus of revenue above expenditure in prosperous seasons, by which debt might be discharged or protective works carried out. These principles were accepted by Lord Lytton's Government. On January 1, 1877, the great Durbar was held at Delhi, at which was announced the assumption of the Imperial title by the Queen. 'It will long be remembered in India,' says one who was then a resident, 'that before the echo of the guns in honour of that event had died away, and long before the high officials had returned to their posts, the increased death-rates in several Madras districts were announcing with emphasis that a terrible famine had begun. Before it ended, in spite of strenuous efforts and a vast expenditure, it swept away more than two millions of people.' The actual expenditure on famine relief, in the five years from 1873 to 1878, including remissions of land revenue, was nearly 16,500,000*l*.[1] To meet such emergencies, it was decided that the revenue should be increased by 1,500,000*l*. a year, and new taxes were imposed for the purpose. The finances of India were meanwhile exposed to danger from two other causes. The first of these was the depreciation of silver. The revenues of India are payable in silver, whilst the interest on the debt contracted in England, and most of the other home charges, are payable in gold. The consequence is that India has to pay a considerable sum which appears in the accounts as 'loss by exchange.' This first became serious in 1876; in 1877 it appeared as more than 2,000,000*l*., and has ever since represented a serious additional burden. To this subject Fawcett had long paid attention. He

[1] *Finances and Public Works of India*, p. 159.

frequently endeavoured to attract notice, and to expound
sound economical theories; but I shall not give details
upon a question which requires so much that is only intelligible to experts. To these difficulties, arising from
causes altogether beyond their control, the Conservative
Government added a third, in the shape of a heavy war
expenditure. The whole cost of this is set down at
18,748,300*l.*, to which England ultimately contributed
5,000,000*l.* It is needless to observe that the estimates
for this war were, at starting, exceedingly modest by
comparison.

The pressure, however, upon the Indian revenues led
to the appointment of a Committee upon Public Works,
which took evidence in 1878 and finally reported in 1879.
Fawcett again took an active part in its deliberations. The
conclusions at which it arrived are noteworthy, and go far
to justify the opinions upon which he had all along insisted.
The report goes over the history of the previous policy and
considers the results obtained up to the latest date. The
expenditure upon guaranteed railways had now amounted
to over 95,000,000*l.*, and that upon State railways to over
18,500,000*l.* The Committee comes to the conclusion
that this expenditure has not been 'financially remunerative.' The returns had not been equal to the guaranteed
payments, except in 1877–78, when an exceptional profit
was derived from the carriage of food during the famine.
Up till 1873-74, the net loss upon railways had increased.
Since that year, however, there had been an improvement; and this improvement, it may be added, has been
maintained, so that the railways are worked at a profit to
the State. The railways constructed by the State since

the abandonment of the guarantee system are still imperfect, and were partly constructed with a view to political or military considerations, as well as with a view to profit. They showed a similar result. The irrigation works, however, had been far more unsatisfactory. Taking, indeed, the total of the capital and the total returns, some profit had been realised. This, however, includes quite different categories. Of 17,000,000*l.* actually spent, 5,500,000*l.* spent upon one set of works had returned a very handsome profit. The profits, for example, on the Cauvery works are given at 81·30 per cent. on the capital. But some of the profitable works have been constructed upon the deltas of the Madras rivers under the most favourable circumstances, whilst others, such as the Cauvery, are based upon old Native works, and no credit is given upon the original outlay. Moreover, the Cauvery works had only increased the irrigated area by one-half, whereas they were credited with the land revenue over the whole irrigated area. The remaining works, costing 11,500,000*l.*, have barely paid their working expenses, and therefore pay little or nothing towards the heavy interest upon the sums borrowed for their construction. The Committee point out very clearly the causes which limit the value of irrigation to certain especially favourable districts. They give the history of Lord Salisbury's attempts to restrict the amount of borrowing, and the difficulties which had hitherto prevented compliance with his regulations. They show the difficulty of ascertaining beforehand whether any given undertaking will or will not turn out to be remunerative, and say that the effect of the distinction between ordinary and extraordinary expenditure is that works which have turned out failures may be transferred to the category of ' ordinary ' simply upon that ground, when their maintenance will be charged against revenue and their original cost will be lost sight of.

They propose various regulations for the future in order to enforce a stricter economy. The total sum borrowed in any one year is not to exceed 2,500,000*l.*, whereas it had averaged about 4,000,000*l.* The debt for productive works is to be separated from the permanent debt; all expenditure upon such works is to be treated as borrowed money, and a full statement of their position is to be comprised in the Annual Financial Statement. These recommendations have been adopted by the Government; changes have been introduced into the system of accounts, and the restrictions upon borrowing money have been maintained.[1] The effect is a substantial recognition of the principles for which Fawcett had perseveringly struggled during twelve years. It is for more competent persons to say how far their recognition was wise and what have been the results in practice. I will only venture to say that although his share, or that of any individual, in such results is necessarily absorbed in the working of much wider causes, Fawcett might congratulate himself on having partly fulfilled his programme of forcing upon the English Parliament some real consideration of the requirements of the subject race.[2]

[1] *Finances and Public Works*, p. 95.

[2] I may here add that in 1879 Fawcett sat upon a Select Committee, which considered the terms of purchase of the East Indian Railway. He moved a resolution, in accordance with the decision of the Committee,

In February, May, and October 1879 Fawcett published three essays upon Indian finances in the 'Nineteenth Century,' which give the latest and clearest exposition of his views. In the last of them, called 'The New Departure in Indian Finance,' he is able to say that the Indian Budget was discussed on May 22, instead of in August, and that it excited so much interest as to last for three nights. This, he says, is a striking contrast to former years, when it was generally hurried over in the closing hours of the session. The vital importance of limiting taxation and reducing expenditure had been acknowledged by the highest authorities, and an obstacle had thus been surmounted which had hitherto stood in the way of all serious reforms. He proceeded to point out the dangers and difficulties which still lay in the way. He had objected to reckless borrowing for the construction of works; but he insisted on the importance of developing the resources of the country, and for that reason reducing the expenditure until there should be a fair surplus to spend upon works of real value. Such retrenchment might be aided by reducing the charges for civil administration, which had been rapidly growing ever since the transference of India to the Crown; and he insisted upon one point, to which he always attached especial importance: a great economy might be effected, and a great political advantage gained at the same time, by opening a wider field of employment for natives. He thanked Lord Lytton, with whose policy he was far

and accepted by the Government, to the effect that the bargain had been unduly favourable to the Company, and that, although it could not be set aside, it should not be taken as a precedent.

•

enough from sympathising in most respects, for his efforts in this direction, and gave some telling illustrations of the importance and practicability of such a policy. After calling attention to the heavy military expenditure, he ends with the expression of a hope that a new financial era is really being inaugurated.

These essays produced a remarkable impression. They were received with a unanimity of approval which surprised Fawcett himself. He observed that it illustrated the uncertainty of any forecast of the effect of an appeal to the public. After years of labour, apparently productive of little result, he had suddenly become an exponent of accepted principles. In fact, it was the difference generally observable between the reception accorded to the utterance of opinions of a comparatively unknown man and the utterance of the same opinions by a man who has slowly won his way to a prominent position.

The military difficulty noticed in these essays was soon to become prominent. The English Embassy entered Afghanistan in September 1878. It became an invasion, and the treaty of Gandamak was signed in May 1879. Then followed the massacre of English officers and the Afghan war, involving, amongst other things, a bill of 18,000,000*l*. Fawcett, of course, shared the objections of his party to the so-called 'forward policy:' He took part in the agitation against it. He joined in forming the Afghan Committee which in the end of 1878 tried to rouse public opinion in England. He was in close correspondence with Lord Lawrence, who gave him much advice and information. He addressed public

meetings at Bethnal Green and Hackney, denouncing
the underhand conduct of the˙ Indian Government
towards the Ameer ; demanding that Parliament should
be summoned, and arguing from the opinions of high
authorities—especially Lord Sandhurst—that an occupation of Cabul would involve an intolerable burthen of
three or four millions upon Indian finances. At the
close of the session of 1878 he had protested vigorously
against the famous move of bringing Indian troops to
Malta. The proceeding proved, as he urged, that we
had before kept up too large an army in India, or that
the garrison was now too small. If an Indian army
could thus be used for Imperial purposes, the temptation
to raise its numbers beyond the needs of India would be
overpowering, whilst the constitutional control of Parliament would be evaded. When, in December, Parliament
met to approve the expenditure incurred in Afghanistan,
Fawcett proposed a motion, seconded by Mr. Gladstone,
condemning the Government plan which threw the main
share of the expense upon India. Once more he made
an emphatic protest on behalf of the Indian revenues.
He complained that when it was a question of declaring
war, the Government had boasted that they were carrying out a great Imperial policy ; when it was a question
of paying for the war, they represented it as a mere
border squabble. He said, characteristically, that the
course adopted by Government was unpopular because
it was a course marked by meanness and ' entire absence of generosity.' He declared that his constituents
at Hackney would prefer to pay their fair share of the
expenses. His motion was rejected by 235 to 125.

In the session of 1879 he returned to the charge.
The expenses of the war were now estimated at 2,600,000*l*.
—a sum which turned out to be ludicrously inadequate.
It was proposed that the English contribution should be
a loan of 2,000,000*l*. free of interest, to be repaid in
seven years. The result, according to Fawcett, would be
that, allowing for the interest, India would pay seven times
as much as England. Mr. Gladstone again supported
Fawcett, and he was defeated by the narrow majority
of 137 to 125 (July 25). He remarked afterwards
that twenty-nine members of Government voted in this
majority, which was a sufficient indication of the tendency
of independent opinion. The only tangible good effect
of the discussion was that it had really roused attention
to the necessity of economy; and on the debate upon
the Budget (May 22, 1879) Fawcett was able to withdraw a motion for the reduction of expenditure on the
ground that Government had virtually accepted his
position.

He brought forward one other matter in this session,
in which he had long been interested, and to which he had
occasionally referred in Parliament. He asked (February 28) for a Select Committee to inquire into the
Government of India Act. That Act had constituted
the Council of India to discharge the same functions of
controlling financial measures which had, under the old
system, belonged to the Company. In theory it had an
absolute vote upon all measures involving expenditure.
An Act passed in 1869 had diminished its independence
by making the office tenable for ten years instead of for
life. Radical differences of opinion came out in the

debates as to the actual powers enjoyed by the Council. Lord Salisbury and Lord Cairns had taken a much higher view of its authority than Lord Hatherley and the Duke of Argyll. Lord Cairns had even said that, in case of an invasion of Afghanistan by Russia, the consent of the Council must be obtained before declaring war. Yet Lord Cairns was a member of the Government when Afghanistan was invaded without even a previous consultation of the Council. Fawcett maintained that, in point of fact, the opinions of the Council had received no attention in most important matters. One member of the Council who was in constant communication with him maintained that the result of the system was that the fifteen men of greatest Indian experience were disqualified for expressing their opinions on Indian policy in public, and not allowed to exercise any effectual control over it in their official capacity. Fawcett pointed out other difficulties in regard to the legal interpretation of the Acts of Parliament. He urged that in any case the position of the Council should be accurately ascertained and defined. Government, however, refused to grant an inquiry. They held that the Council exercised an effectual financial control, and that matters of high policy must necessarily be decided by the Cabinet. Fawcett's motion, supported by the Liberal leaders, for a Committee was rejected by 139 to 100. In the following years he was unable to obtain any action in the matter from Mr. Gladstone's Government, which for various reasons held that the discussion would be inopportune.

After Fawcett's acceptance of office in 1880 he spoke

rarely upon Indian affairs. He had indeed accepted office with the full intention of continuing his interest in India, and with the understanding that he would be allowed to take part in Indian debates. His attention to the affairs of his department necessarily absorbed the chief part of his energy, and, for whatever reason, he had few opportunities of expressing his views at any length except upon occasion of the Indian Budget of 1880. The recent discovery of the singular error of nine millions in the accounts of the Afghan war then gave additional weight to a principle upon which he had frequently insisted—namely, the necessity of securing some more effective responsibility in the management of Indian accounts. When a blunder even of this magnitude was committed, the one thing clearly established was that it was nobody's fault.

Some complaints were made that he had not fully acted up to his previous principle in the matter of the war expenses. Fawcett's reply to such a criticism from a constituent was that, although he could not approve fully, he thought that the compromise ultimately adopted in the cases of Egypt and the Afghan war was the best obtainable. Although therefore he declined, in spite of some pressure, to vote for the motions confirming it, he did not consider himself bound to give further expression to his convictions. The policy of the Indian Government during the remainder of his life was generally in the direction which he approved; and he had the satisfaction of seeing that the principles for which he had so long striven were obtaining official recognition. I have thus attempted to bring out the main outlines of

Fawcett's share in directing Indian policy. To my mind his action was scarcely less remarkable for its independence and thorough disinterestedness than for the remarkable soundness of judgment with which he confined himself to discussing questions upon which he could speak with authority and to enforcing principles within the line of practical politics. Even those whom he criticised most severely, felt, as Sir Henry Maine has observed, that they had to deal with a scrupulously honourable antagonist, who was utterly incapable of underhand attacks or of any conscious unfairness towards opponents. No man was more anxious to give full credit to friend or foe, wherever he saw that it was due. And therefore his long and persistent struggle against what he took to be abuses left no bitterness even in those assailed, whilst it secured for him the hearty admiration of all who sympathised with his main purposes.

CHAPTER IX.

THE POST-OFFICE.

THE story of Fawcett's life under the Beaconsfield Administration must fill a comparatively small space in these
pages. But I must beg my readers to bear in mind
that this is not due to any decline in his energy or
his influence. He laboured as vigorously as ever, and
more tasks offered themselves as his experience and
reputation increased. Part of the story, however, has
been told by anticipation in order to give a continuous
narrative of his action in regard to particular spheres of
labour. His interest in education, in the preservation
of commons, and in India had not diminished; and his
activity in regard to India in particular was unintermitting
and effective. I have, however, said what seemed desirable to be said upon these points. For another reason
this part of his career must be more briefly treated. My
aim is to set forth the man and his principles, not to give
the history of all events in which he had a share. During the Parliament of 1874-1880 he was less frequently
fighting for his own hand. He had fallen into the ranks
of his party, instead of being an independent leader of
irregular forces. Opposition naturally brings men together. Differences of opinion which may prevent com-

mon support of a substantive policy may be quite compatible with a joint assault upon a common enemy. Fawcett had disapproved, and had felt himself bound to utter his disapproval, of many parts of Mr. Gladstone's official policy; but he thoroughly sympathised with the Liberal opposition to the policy represented by Lord Beaconsfield. On the questions which came to be most prominent there was thus no difference between his party and himself. Other questions upon which the main differences had arisen had partly passed out of sight, and in some his party had virtually accepted his own position. In one direction, indeed, there was a great and growing difference between Fawcett and one wing of the Liberal party. His objections to all policy looking towards Socialism or paternal government were at least as strong as ever, and were perhaps more outspoken. In his divergence upon such matters from some Radicals there might be the germ of future discord. He recorded his protest against certain measures favoured on both sides of the House, and his protest was received with respect, but it led to no party struggles. For the present the party issues did not turn upon points of this kind.

The removal of old causes of irritation and the spontaneous development of his character improved his general position. He was making friends in all parties. His thorough strong sense and straightforwardness had now gained general recognition, and the respect for his motives was blended with cordial liking for his cheery good-nature. His popularity both in and out of Parliament was steadily increasing.

A short reference to one or two points will therefore be sufficient. In the session of 1874 Fawcett took a leading part in a discussion which revived some of the old feelings about denominational education. The Endowed Schools Act of 1869, passed in the flush of the Liberal victory, had given some offence to Conservatives by declaring that no schools should be confined to the Church of England, either as to the character of the teaching or the qualification of governing bodies, unless in accordance with the express terms of the original instrument of foundation. Lord Sandon (now Lord Harrowby) introduced a bill in 1874 which allowed the Church of England to establish a claim under easier conditions. A provision ordering the scholars to attend church services would now be sufficient. A usage of a hundred years was to establish the connection of a school with any denomination. The act relieving dissenting schoolmasters from the subscriptions required by the Toleration Act had not been passed till 1779. Therefore in 1874 hardly any school could claim to have possessed for a hundred years the right to teach any other than the Anglican doctrines. Lord Sandon used an unguarded phrase, which was taken to proclaim an intention of retaking the guns which had been lost under the previous Adminstration. He disavowed this meaning, which, however, was thought by his opponents to represent the tendency, if not the intention, of the measure. It was significant of Fawcett's improved position with his party that he was now selected as their natural spokesman upon this matter. He moved in a very spirited and carefully prepared speech that no schools should be controlled by any religious body which had been thrown open by the last Parliament. Though his motion was rejected, the opposition to anything savouring of a reaction was so determined that Disraeli found it expedient to modify the measure. The bill passed after some sharp debating, but merely as a measure for transferring the functions of the Endowed Schools Commission to the Charity Commission. In spite of the Conservative reaction, the results obtained in the previous Parliament in favour of religious equality were definitive.

In the same session, Fawcett took the very active part which I have already noticed [1] in opposition to the extension of the limitations upon women's labour. He was opposed on all sides, denounced as a coldblooded political economist, and had only the satisfaction of having laboured hard in what he held to be the cause of justice to women. In 1875, besides much activity in regard to India, he spoke with great power upon various social and financial questions; upon the Agricultural Holdings Bill; upon artisans' dwellings; upon savings' banks; and upon the poor law and local taxation. I shall not dwell upon these questions, which came up again in later years, because his general principles have been sufficiently indicated, and his action did not affect his political career. It is enough to say that they had his constant attention, and that he defended consistently and weightily views which were often opposed to the general current of opinion, and unpopular with many of his constituents. Frequent remonstrances, for example, from supporters who were anxious to induce him to make

[1] See p. 174.

some compromise as to the Permissive Bill met with a
courteous, but unequivocal, refusal to comply.

In 1876 the Eastern Question began to overshadow
all other political interests.   It led Fawcett to take a
part too characteristic to be passed over.   He shared the
indignation aroused in England by the Bulgarian atroci-
ties; he presided at a great meeting held at Exeter Hall
on September 19, 1876, and called upon his hearers to
pronounce themselves emphatically in support of Mr.
Gladstone, who now came from his partial retirement to
head the popular movement.   He criticised severely the
levity shown by Disraeli on the first news of the events,
and complained that the indifference and mysterious
silence of the Government was giving the impression
that England would support the Turks.   He spoke again,
in obedience to a call from the audience, at the National
Conference at St. James's Hall in the following December.   Mr. Gladstone was then the principal orator at a
meeting intended to prove that the resolution of Englishmen to withdraw all support from Turkish abuses was
confined to no political party, nor to those who generally
concerned themselves with politics.   In the following
months the indignation cooled, and jealousy of Russia
began to show itself.   Public opinion was veering to
the side of the Government; and in the next session
the leaders of Opposition seemed to be flinching from the
policy implied in their previous declarations.   Fawcett
was grievously disappointed.   He urged in vain upon
the leaders that the agitation of the previous months required corresponding action.   At last, supported by the
more Radical section of his party, he moved a resolution

(March 23, 1877), on his own responsibility, demanding that the Powers should insist upon guarantees for an improved administration of the Christian provinces. He declared in his speech that he was resolved to say in the House what he had said on the platform. He charged the Government with shrinking from the logical consequences of the despatches in which they had themselves condemned Turkish misrule. He taunted them for their want of resolution. They had bragged about a ' spirited foreign policy.' They had now adopted a mere ' do-nothing policy ; ' and he disavowed for his own part a wish for ' peace at any price ' or absolute non-intervention. An exciting debate followed. Fawcett was accused by Conservative speakers of approving a ' bloody war.' Lord Hartington, the leader of his party, repudiated any responsibility for the motion, which he regarded as ' inopportune,' and, with Mr. Gladstone, suggested that it should be withdrawn. Fawcett felt himself bound to consent ; the want of unity in his party would lead to a discouraging division ; but the majority objected to permit of the evasion. After a two hours' struggle, and the rejection by large majorities of several motions for adjournment, Government at last permitted the adjournment to take place without a direct vote on the resolution.

War was presently declared by Russia (April 24, 1877). Directly afterwards Mr. Gladstone proposed four resolutions which substantially agreed with Fawcett's motion. They condemned the Porte's reception of Lord Derby's despatch, affirmed that it had no right to material or moral support, claimed a system of self-government for the Christian provinces, and said that such a system should be introduced by the concert of the European Powers. This, however late in the day, was to lay down the line of policy which Fawcett approved and held to be only the logical consequence of the principles avowed in the autumn agitation. He was again disappointed. Mr. Gladstone decided at the last moment, in obedience to the doubts of moderate Liberals, not to move the third and fourth resolutions defining the policy to be adopted, and to confine himself to the bare condemnation of the Turks embodied in the two first. Fawcett complained in his speech of this irresolute policy. Mr. Gladstone's arguments, if good for anything, were good for his conclusion as well as for his premisses. The Conservatives, strengthened by the irresolution of the Opposition, were triumphant, and Mr. Gladstone's first resolution was rejected by 354 to 253. Fawcett, it will be seen, did not share the sentiments of the extreme peace party. During the Franco-German war he had complained of Mr. Gladstone for not coming forward more resolutely to avow the English responsibility for Belgium; and on this occasion he was again in favour of a decided line of action. Lord Beaconsfield, for the present, was at the height of his power, and the Opposition could only remonstrate. In the following years the development of the forward policy brought Fawcett into the field as a defender of the Indian finances. I have already spoken of his protests against the despatch of Indian troops to Malta, and his share in the agitation against the Afghan war. He had thus taken an important part in the assault which was finally ruinous to the Beaconsfield Administration, and he naturally had his reward. I may as well add here that although Fawcett had voted for Mr. Forster (and against Lord Hartington) as leader of the Liberal party upon Mr. Gladstone's retirement, he came before long to entertain the highest respect for Lord Hartington, whose loyalty and solidity he fully appreciated, and to whom he gave a cordial support.[1]

In the elections of 1880 the Liberal party again triumphed, and Fawcett's own victory was decisive to a degree which astonished him. His colleague, Mr. Holms, stood with him, and they were opposed by Mr. G. C. T. Bartley. The poll, taken on March 31, 1880, resulted as follows: Fawcett, 18,366; Holms, 16,614; Bartley, 8,708. Just 1,500 votes were divided between Fawcett and Bartley, showing that Fawcett's majority over his colleague was mainly due to the favour of some of the Conservatives. The cost of this election, in proportion to the number of voters, was less than in almost any election of the time. It was afterwards regarded as setting a standard of the minimum of necessary expenditure.

Fawcett's position in the Liberal party was now sufficiently prominent to ensure his holding a place in the new Ministry. He received and accepted from Mr. Gladstone the offer of the Postmaster-Generalship. Several of his friends, whilst congratulating him on his

---

[1] I am permitted to state that in October 1880 Lord Hartington offered to Fawcett a seat in the Indian Council. Whilst speaking very kindly of Fawcett's claims to a higher political position, he pointed out the opportunities of usefulness to India in the Council. Fawcett declined with cordial thanks, saying that he thought that he could be more useful as an independent member, if he should at any time resign office. His view of the unsatisfactory position of the Council had also, I believe, some weight with him in this decision.

new position, expressed their regret that he had not received a place in the Cabinet. It is not for me to form
any opinion upon the general question. It was, however,
understood that Fawcett's blindness was now for the last
time an obstacle to his promotion. He had felt some fears
that it might be regarded as an obstacle to his holding office
at all. A member of the Cabinet has to see many confidential papers, and there would be a difficulty in admitting one who would have to use other eyes for reading
them. The only reference made to this by Fawcett himself, so far as I know, was in the letter (April 28, 1880)
in which he announced his appointment to his parents.

'My dear Father and Mother,—You will, I know, all
be delighted to hear that last night I received a most
kind letter from Gladstone offering me the Postmaster-
Generalship. It is the office which Lord Hartington held
when Gladstone was last in power. I shall be a Privy
Councillor, but shall not have a seat in the Cabinet. I
believe there was some difficulty raised about my having
to confide Cabinet secrets ; this objection, I think, time
will remove. I did not telegraph to you the appointment
at first because Gladstone did not wish it to be known
until it was formally confirmed by the Queen ; but he
told me in my interview with him this morning that he
was quite sure that the Queen took a kindly interest in
my appointment.' He adds that Mr. Gladstone said
'that he has given me the appointment in order that I
might have time to speak in Indian and other debates.'
He goes on to make some arrangements for fishing at
Salisbury. On May 4 he tells his sister of his first visit
to the office, and of how kindly he has been introduced

by Lord John Manners [1] (his predecessor) and welcomed by the permanent officials.

Fawcett was thus installed in office ; and the remainder of his history is chiefly the account of his administration. He spoke rarely henceforward except in one or two Indian debates, and upon the business of his department. I have shown that Fawcett fully sympathised with the avowed principles of the Ministry of which he was now a member. At the same time, I cannot doubt that, had he still been an independent member, he would have found much to criticise in their action. His position as a Minister without a seat in the Cabinet imposed reserve, whilst it did not enable him to exert any direct influence upon the policy of Government. On some points I can only conjecture his probable views. Mr. Gladstone's Government was especially notable for its Irish and Egyptian policy. In both cases I imagine that Fawcett's sympathy must have been imperfect. The relegation, for example, of political economy to Saturn cannot have been quite to his taste. I have given his view of the proper mode of dealing with the Irish land question in a previous chapter.[2] He held, I think, that exceptional legislation of some kind was absolutely required. Political economy, on his view, does not lay down rigid principles irrespective of the condition of the people affected, but must give different results in different cases. He thought that it was necessary to take into account, as a first element of the

---

[1] I cannot mention Lord John Manners without saying how generously and warmly he has done justice on more than one occasion to the merits of his successor and political opponent.

[2] See p. 252.

problem, the wishes and convictions of the Irish people themselves. No one, indeed, could be more opposed to Home Rule, which, as he said, meant the disruption of the empire. He would rather, as he said on one occasion (May 24, 1877), that the Liberal party should remain out of office ' till its youngest member had grown grey with age ' than be intimidated into voting for Home Rule. Still he held that some such legislation as that embodied in Mr. Gladstone's Land Bill was necessary; though I do not think that he had very strong anticipations of good results from this particular measure. One of the reminiscences published on his death describes him as sitting amidst a party of friends who were discussing Irish irreconcilability, and repeating as if to himself, ' We must press on and do what is right.' In a letter to his father of January 27, 1883, I find a phrase which confirms the anecdote. ' There is nothing for it,' he says, in view of some new proof of disaffection, ' but to persevere in doing justice in spite of all provocation.' I do not doubt that, on the whole, he considered Mr. Gladstone's measure to be in the direction of justice, but I have no means of knowing his precise opinions.

In regard to Egypt, I can only say that he shared the uncomfortable feeling of other members of the party and the Government. He felt it to be the weak point of the Administration. He, like others in his position, only heard of the various false steps after the mischief was done, and when remonstrance would be too late. He was, I have reason to believe, one of the first to take alarm at the joint Note from England and France to the Khedive which led to the bombardment of Alexandria

and the subsequent complications. He looked with suspicion at the employment of Indian troops, and refrained
on one or two occasions from voting. But, whatever his
views, I can only say that he did not feel himself so far
divided from his party as to be disqualified for taking a
share in administration. Divided as he must still have
been on some points from Mr. Gladstone, I find in his
private correspondence frequent expressions of admiration for some of the Premier's qualities. He speaks of
the pleasure of doing business with such a master of the
art, and refers with satisfaction to favourable reports of
Mr. Gladstone's health. Past disputes had certainly left
no ill-will, though I cannot say that his judgment of his
leader had materially altered.

I shall now proceed to give such an account as is
possible of his administrative career. Fawcett came
into office at the age of forty-six with no previous experience of official work. He had a strong conviction of the
evil of 'officialism,' the 'fetish' which he had often
denounced. Officialism may be described as the evil
spirit engendered by the tacit assumption that the nation
exists to maintain the office, instead of the office to serve
the nation. The 'red tape' so often denounced is
doubtless necessary in a great organisation, which can
only be worked by adhering strictly to fixed rules, and
where the mainspring of action for the great mass of
the employed must be discipline rather than private
interest, or even irregular zeal. It is the essence of
machinery to operate regularly. But when the machinery
is taken as an end in itself, and the rules taken for sacred
and unalterable laws instead of means for securing the

proper discharge of the function, the official spirit of
order may occasionally degenerate into superstition, and
the head official becomes a high priest, enveloping himself in mystery, and resentful of any external interference. From all that I have heard, I imagine that the
department of which Fawcett was now to be the head
was honourably free from this superstition. To him,
at any rate, it was entirely uncongenial. His merits
may best be defined as the antithesis to the most beset-
ting sins of officialism. He held himself to be a public
servant; he was ready at any time to give an account of
his work, to welcome all fair inquiry from his employers,
and to make it his sole aim to give them every reasonable
satisfaction. He threw himself into his duties as vigorously as if he had been an enterprising capitalist trying to establish a successful business by dint of good
management.

The Post-Office has in fact to carry on a vast business, and should act upon business principles. To a
Chancellor of the Exchequer it naturally commends
itself by its contributions to the right side of the Budget.
Fawcett always held this view to be inadequate. He
regarded the Post-Office as an engine for diffusing
knowledge, expanding trade, increasing prosperity, encouraging family correspondence, and facilitating thrift.
He thought, therefore, that it should not be crippled by
the desire to raise from it the maximum sum in aid of
taxation. In spite of objections, of the real force of which
he was fully aware, he thought that it might be safely
extended under proper precautions, not simply by applying part of the annual income, but by the investment of

capital. The last experiment of this kind, the purchase of the telegraphs, had not been very encouraging ; but he was still convinced that an energetic development of the business would do much to increase the public welfare. He spared no pains in doing what he could in this direction, though his means were necessarily limited by the degree of sympathy of his colleagues. He distinguished himself not so much by devising new schemes as by his readiness to adopt suggestions on all hands, and his determination to push business through instead of allowing it to remain permanently in the stage of preparation and circumlocution. He succeeded during his tenure of office in winning fresh popularity for the department by convincing the public that he at least was earnest in his desire to serve them.

The Post-Office is naturally the department which comes most into collision with private organisations. In every extension of its activity Fawcett had more or less to encounter the jealousy of companies or private persons already discharging some of the functions to be undertaken. Nothing could be more opposed to his principles than any action really tending to suppress or diminish private energy. But he was convinced that the vast machinery under his command was able to discharge a number of functions for which private enterprise was altogether inadequate ; whilst in other cases its action might be so regulated as to stimulate instead of discouraging the activity of its competitors. The mode in which the Post-Office could in fact be turned to account so as to invigorate the national life may be best understood from a brief account of his main achievements.

Writing to his father on April 7, 1883, he says that he expects that nothing will be more popular in Mr. Childers's Budget than the proposal to reduce the price of telegrams. 'Curiously enough,' he adds, 'before I had been a fortnight at the Post-Office I felt that there were five things to be done—(1) The parcel post; (2) the issue of postal orders; (3) the receipt of small savings in stamps and the allowing small sums to be invested in the funds; (4) increasing the facilities for life insurance and annuities; (5) reducing the price of telegrams. The first four I have succeeded in getting done, and now the fifth is to be accomplished.' These five reforms, to which may be added the measures in regard to telephones, were in fact Fawcett's chief performances, and I shall briefly indicate their nature.

When the Post-Office was in its infancy certain complaints were made against Docwra, the inventor of the 'Penny Post' for London, from which it appears that the post then (1698) carried such articles as bandboxes, tradesmen's parcels, and apothecaries' mixtures. Patients complained, wisely or otherwise, that they did not get their physic in time. The high rates of postage afterwards suppressed the carriage of everything except letters. Various schemes for a parcel post had been discussed in later times. Sir Rowland Hill contemplated such a scheme; the Society of Arts proposed one in 1858; the Royal Commission on Railways advocated a plan in 1867; and, as all Englishmen know who have had occasion to forward their knapsacks in Switzerland, the plan was already working on the Continent. It had spread to most countries, and in 1880 a Convention, to which

England sent two delegates, met to arrange for an international parcel post throughout Europe, with the almost solitary exception of Great Britain. Two years before, Lord John Manners had opened negotiations with the railway companies in regard to a parcel post, and Fawcett on taking office immediately asked for and obtained authority to proceed in the matter. After long discussions, the negotiations dropped in 1881, as the terms of the companies were unacceptable. In 1882, however, Fawcett made a new effort; an agreement was at length reached, and the Parcel Post Act was passed in that session.

The negotiation required firmness and a clear head for business. Fawcett could not take matters with a high hand. The public, though grateful for the boon, were not so eager beforehand as to exert the pressure of a popular agitation. His colleagues had business enough on their hands to make them unwilling to sacrifice much time to such objects in Parliament. The Treasury is never too eager to advance schemes which must be expensive and are not certain to be remunerative. The railway companies were not willing to admit a powerful competitor, unless they could exact terms clearly favourable to themselves. In the negotiations already started, it had been decided to treat with the companies as a single body, instead of making terms with each company separately. Fawcett sometimes expressed the opinion that better terms might have been made if the subject had been approached differently, through an alteration in the scale of the letter post, so as to admit of the carriage of heavier packets. When, however, a different plan had once been adopted, a change of front would have implied a hostile attitude, and the general opposition of the railway interest would have been fatal under the circumstances to the speedy adoption of any scheme. The railways must therefore be conciliated; and he resolved to adopt a plan from which the public might derive a profit, even though the railways were enabled to exact more than their fair share.

He offered, therefore, that the railways should receive 50 per cent. of the total postage on the parcels carried by them; and he finally conceded 55 per cent. The sum is divided amongst the different companies in proportion to the amounts of their own parcel business. The Post-Office undertakes the collection, sorting, packing, unpacking, and distribution of the parcels; whilst the railway companies undertake the carriage and transference of the parcel baskets between the mail van and the train. The work thus done by the Post-Office represents, as experts consider, more nearly two-thirds than one-half of the total expense. The companies have also the advantage that the payment to them increases in proportion to the increase of traffic; whereas, in the case of the letter post, the increase of traffic increases the weight of the bags, without an immediate increase of the payment. Each railway makes its own bargain for letter-carrying from time to time for a fixed sum, not for a share of the postage. There is thus a means of readjustment which does not exist in the case of the parcel post. Fawcett, however, deliberately resolved to carry out a measure which he regarded as beneficial to the public, even though a somewhat disproportionate benefit should accrue to the co-operating companies.

The Act was finally passed on August 18, 1882. Nearly a year elapsed before it could be brought into operation. During Fawcett's illness in the winter of 1882–83, Mr. Shaw Lefevre undertook the discharge of his duties, and was most energetic and helpful in forwarding the preparation of the scheme. A careful examination of every detail was required before so vast a business could be added to the previous operations of the department. Fawcett took a lively interest in discussing every detail submitted to him by the subordinates, who had, of course, in the first instance to work out the new arrangements. He went with zest into such minutiæ as the formalities to be observed in posting and the weights to be assigned to rural letter-carriers. His main anxiety was to prevent any dislocation of the letter-service. After careful preparations, the new service was at last started on August 1, 1883. Fawcett, with his wife and daughter, went down to the 'circulation office' on the first evening, and writes the same night to his parents, describing the scene, the extraordinary variety of objects posted, and the 'smartly painted red vans.' He begs them to come and have a look at it. Three days later he reports that things are working smoothly, and speaks warmly of the zeal of all concerned, from the head officials down to the humblest letter-carrier. He says that he shall soon issue a general notice of thanks to the persons co-operating in the result. The only difficulty has arisen from the public inexperience in the art of packing.

The parcel post was not at first a financial success. The number of parcels was, in the first month, at the rate of only 15,000,000 annually, whereas it had been estimated at 27,000,000. The average weight also, and consequently the payment for postage, was rather below the estimate. The estimate, it must be observed, had to be made very much at random, from the absence of any previous experience ; and Fawcett was of opinion that the demand of the Treasury for an apparently precise statement was a rather futile formality. He energetically laboured to reduce the cost by better organisation, and especially by amalgamating the parcel post with the letter post, so far as this was possible. His report, when the system had lasted for a year, sums up the results so far. The new post had been introduced without the least interference with the older services. The number of parcels conveyed had increased and was now at the rate of from 21 to 22 millions a year. Simplifications, and consequent economies, had been introduced, and further improvements were under consideration. He is especially glad to record one result which might have aroused jealousy in some official minds. The railway companies had set about a competition with the service from which they had wrung such excellent terms. They had at once advertised an improved service of their own ; and Fawcett is able to declare in his report that the fears of a suppression of private enterprise have not been realised. He is glad to have stimulated instead of suppressing a competition for the better service of the public.

He ends by pointing out that it always takes some time—as was the case, for example, on the first introduction of the penny post—to gain general appreciation of the new advantages offered. In fact, the numbers of parcels began to rise in the following autumn. In September there was a marked improvement. In October the results were still better, though the improvement probably came too late to be known to him. At the present time, the original estimate has been nearly reached.

Various subsidiary questions arose, the chief one concerning the registration of parcels. Mr. Lefevre, whilst discharging Fawcett's duties, decided that in the case of the parcels post insurance for value would be better than simple registration, as in the case of letters. Fawcett, on returning to his post, had gone very fully into the question, but had not reached a final decision. He was also desirous of introducing a more minutely graduated scale of payments. He was at work to the last, but I need not give further details upon the achievement with which his name will probably be most frequently associated. In those, and in other cases, I have only to say that the results which are palpable to the public give a very inadequate idea, unless to those who will take the trouble to reflect, of the amount of labour behind the scenes which is required to produce the visible change. The introduction of the parcels post required a considerable expenditure of energy; but it was only one of several important reforms.

One matter in which he was greatly interested was the lowering of the charge for telegrams. His interest was especially excited by the consideration that under the existing system the benefit of telegraphic communication is chiefly confined to the richer classes. Persons engaged in speculation, whether on the Stock Exchange or in the betting-ring, are the most active patrons of the telegraph. Fawcett regretted that in this capacity the

Post-Office was of comparatively little use to classes in which he took a livelier interest, the workmen and small traders. It was on their behalf in particular that he wished to improve the public machinery for the diffusion of rapid communication. In the summer of 1880 he received a deputation from the Society of Arts asking for cheap telegrams. He at once took the matter up, obtained estimates, and made a very carefully considered speech to the deputation (July 17, 1880), which sufficiently showed his own leaning. Upon the plan which then seemed to him most advisable, and which has been adopted since his death, the first cost was estimated at 167,000*l.* a year. The question remained whether the Chancellor of the Exchequer would think it worth while to make a temporary sacrifice of this amount. If that official saw his way to it, no difficulty would be raised by the Post-Office. The telegraph business, which had been prosperous in the first year of Fawcett's administration, increased from various causes at a much slower rate in the years following. In his report for the year ending March 31, 1882, he mentions the fact that though the proportion of telegrams to the population is greater in England than in any other country except Switzerland, the proportion of telegrams to letters is less than in many other countries. Here the proportion was one telegram to forty-four letters; whilst in France the ratio was one to twenty-nine; in Belgium one to twenty-four; in Holland one to twenty-two, and in Switzerland one to twenty-three. The decision, however, rested with the Treasury. The purchase of the telegraphs for a large sum (over

10,000,000*l*., for a property valued at 7,000,000*l*.) has caused the financial results to be so far unsatisfactory. It was only in the year 1881, as Fawcett stated in his report, that the net returns were sufficient to meet the interest. The Treasury was therefore inclined to doubt the policy of a scheme involving increased expenditure even for a time, though Fawcett urged that it should properly be regarded as expenditure on capital instead of deduction from income. If the telegraphs had been bought for a reasonable sum the returns, even with a sixpenny rate, would have covered the interest. When a proposal for cheap telegrams was brought forward by Dr. Cameron in the House of Commons in 1880, Fawcett sufficiently showed (as he had done in speaking to the Society of Arts) his own preference for a word-rate of a halfpenny, with a minimum charge of sixpence. His known inclinations encouraged fresh agitation in the House; and in 1883 Government was outvoted and the adoption of sixpenny telegrams became certain. Much, however, had to be done in the way of preparation. New plant had to be provided, and the trained staff increased. There arose, also, the question of the abolition of the free addresses, which would involve a heavy burden on the Post-Office. Fawcett had proposed that in reckoning the halfpenny charge words used in addresses should be counted as well as those in the messages. It was urged that this would press hardly upon the poor whose addresses are generally long in proportion to the obscurity of their abodes. The objection had especial weight with Fawcett, who spared no pains to require information and advice. His death came before a conclusion had been reached. Although he did not live to see his views adopted, there can be no doubt that his known opinions helped to secure the ultimate result.

It will be as well to deal here with another matter which was amongst the most difficult and delicate of all that engiged his attention. The telephone was a recent invention when Fawcett took office, and two companies had been started to bring it into operation. The law officers of the Crown advised him that the companies were infringing the monopoly secured to the Post-Office by the Telegraph Act. It became his duty to apply to the courts, who decided (December 3, 1880) that a telephonic message was a kind of telegram, and that, consequently, the monopoly was infringed by the companies. The judges added an expression of an opinion, the justice of which was obvious, that companies which had introduced so beautiful an invention into public use, without intentional breach of the law, deserved consideration from the Postmaster-General. They had obviously a moral claim either to compensation or to a license. Fawcett decided upon the latter course, and the companies received a license on terms of paying a royalty of ten per cent. on their gross receipts and restricting themselves to a given area. At the same time the Post-Office acquired a supply of telephones from other sources and established telephonic exchanges in many large towns.

The development of the system and the growth of new companies soon produced many complications. Telephonic areas previously distinct could now be brought into connection. 'Trunk wires' to join distant centres were required, and licenses were granted upon special terms. New companies asked for licenses in districts already supplied; and districts supplied by the Post-Office asked to be supplied by companies. To refuse these applications would be to create monopolies. The United Telephone Company—formed from the two original companies —had already occupied the most important centres. The licenses had been originally given on the principle of ' one telephone exchange for one town.' Upon this principle the Post-Office would be itself prevented from competing with the company, whilst it would forbid competition with itself elsewhere. Though there are obvious advantages in the unity of an agency, which is useful in proportion to the number of those who communicate through it, Fawcett felt that such monopoly was undesirable, as tending to crush enterprise directed to the development of the new invention. The public would have no security that the best invention should be adopted. Fawcett therefore announced in his report of 1882 that he had resolved to give licenses to responsible persons, and to establish post-office telephone exchanges where needed, irrespective of previous occupation of a district. Licenses accordingly were issued, which contained a new stipulation. In return for permission to infringe the monopoly of the Post-Office, the new companies were to allow the Post-Office a supply of their patented instruments. New companies accepted these terms; but the company already in possession of the most advantageous field rejected the new terms. They preferred to keep to their old limits rather than extend their area of operation on condition of allowing the Post-Office to use their patent.

They were strong enough to buy off or defy competitors. Persons living outside the area served by them began to complain of inadequate accommodation. The Post-Office once more appeared to be suppressing enterprise and raising difficulties; and the action could only be defended on the ground of their own interest in the national monopoly of the telegraph. Fawcett felt the position to be intolerable, and in the spring of 1884 invited the companies to a fresh discussion of the question.

Some companies asked for a monopoly of their own districts. The main proposal was that the royalty of ten per cent. should be abandoned, on condition that the companies should make good to the Post-Office any loss caused by the use of telephones in place of telegraphs. This proposal also implied a monopoly, for a company could not afford a guarantee unless it were protected against competition. Fawcett finally came to the conclusion that there were only two courses: Government must acquire the telephones, as it had acquired the telegraphs; or it must leave the field open to competition, simply taking care that companies should confine themselves to telephonic communication. He announced his terms on August 7, in Committee of Supply. He proposed in brief to give the widest possible liberty to responsible persons to establish telephone exchanges in districts, occupied or unoccupied, to abolish all restrictions as to the area to be served, and to abandon the demand for patented instruments.

The royalty of ten per cent., and an undertaking to deliver no written messages, were the only conditions imposed upon the companies. The companies were at once satisfied, and almost his last official act was the approval of a license embodying these terms. It was signed without alteration by his successor, Mr. Shaw Lefevre. His last interview at the office was with a gentleman who begged for protection for a small company in which he was much interested, and which would probably be driven out of the field. Fawcett listened patiently and kindly; but was compelled to refuse decidedly.

In this case, as in the case of the parcel post, Fawcett could feel that his action extended the utility of the Post-Office, and called out increased energy in private enterprise. If the Government should come to monopolise the services, it would be only because experience had proved that it could discharge them most efficiently.

In another direction, the Post-Office had to deal with a powerful interest. The Post-Office, in fact, is a great banking concern, though it is confined chiefly to operations too minute to be profitable for private banks. In transmitting small sums and encouraging minute savings, it has an advantage from the vast scale upon which it can work; and therefore rather supplements than supplants private enterprise. Any extension, however, of its functions is naturally scrutinised with a certain jealousy by bankers. On coming into office, Fawcett at once took up a measure which had been prepared by a committee some years before. The established system of Post-Office orders was in one respect defective. Each order cost the department 3d., and it would be unjust to lower the charge beneath the cost, and so to confer a benefit upon the transmitters of money at the cost of the community. The charge, however, was in certain cases

excessive. If, as he put it, a boy wanted to send to his
mother the first shilling he had saved, he would have to
pay 2*d*. for the order and 1*d*. for postage. On the great
number of small orders (94,500 orders for a shilling had
been issued in a year) the cost of transmission thus
amounted to 25 per cent. He proposed, therefore, to
introduce the new system of postal orders which had
been already devised under his predecessor. They were
to differ from the Post Office order in these respects :
that the sender was not to give his own name or that of
the payee ; that they might be cashed at any money order
office ; and that the commission charged was to be fixed
at a lower rate. The main difficulties raised were the
increased facilities for theft, and the danger of creating a
small paper currency. Bankers in the House dwelt upon
these objections, and a good deal of private negotiation
was required. Fawcett expressed his readiness to con-
cede any change thought necessary in order to avoid the
creation of the currency. After some discussion, however, the measure was carried almost in the shape
originally proposed. A proposal to reduce the period of
currency from three months to one was rejected after a
division, as it would have greatly diminished the convenience offered, especially to persons who wished to lay in
a stock of orders. On the other hand, Fawcett consented
to an amendment, making it necessary to insert the name
of the payee. This satisfied his critics, though it seems
to make little real difference. The measure was passed
and was the most rapidly successful of any proposed by
Fawcett. He observed in 1884 that the number of
orders issued had at first scarcely realised the estimate

of 50,000 a week; but that four years later it amounted
to 350,000 a week. In the year ending March 31, 1882,
the whole number issued was about 4,500,000; in the
next financial year, nearly 8,000,000; and in the next,
over 12,000,000. A slight alteration was made in the
rates, and permission was given to make up broken
amounts by adding stamps, by an Act which came into
operation on June 2, 1884; and in the following year, over
20,000,000 orders were issued. The amount transmitted
rose from near 4,500,000*l.* in the year ending March 31,
1882, to near 8,500 000*l.* in the year ending June 2, 1885.
He could also announce in 1882 that as the average
period of circulation was only six days, the fears of a
small currency had proved to be without foundation.

Fawcett was more profoundly interested in the various
institutions by which the Post-Office endeavours to stimulate thrift. In his first year of office, he took up the
question of the Post-Office savings-banks. They had been
in action since 1861, when Mr. Gladstone had introduced
a measure embodying a scheme suggested by Mr. (now
Sir W. C.) Sikes, and Mr. Chetwynd of the Post-Office.[1]
The measure was signally successful. The Post-Office
savings-banks throve and became more popular than
their old-fashioned rivals, the trustee savings-banks. A
considerable deficiency meanwhile had arisen in the old
banks, owing to the fact that too high a rate of interest
had been allowed upon deposits. In 1880, Mr. Gladstone, as Chancellor of the Exchequer, introduced a bill
to make up the deficiency and to reduce the rate of

---

[1] See *History of Savings-Banks,* by William Lewins (1866), for full
details.

interest in future. At Fawcett's suggestion he added a
provision raising the limit of permissible deposits in the
Post-Office banks from 200*l.* to 300*l.*, and the amount
which might be deposited in one year, from 30*l.* to 100*l.*
Mr. Gladstone also spontaneously added provisions for
enabling investments to be made in Government
securities through savings-banks of both kinds. The
bankers objected to the proposed extension of limits.
They argued that this change would involve an interference with private enterprise; and divert large sums
now applied to trade and agriculture by the bankers
towards investment in Consols. The result of their
opposition was that this part of the measure was
ultimately withdrawn. Fawcett regretted the necessity,
and a bill including similar provisions was introduced by
him and Mr. Courtney in 1884. There was again
sufficient opposition to compel its withdrawal. In his
report of 1884, Fawcett gives some information which
he had collected to show the needlessness of the jealousy
which had been aroused. He pointed out that in
Cambridgeshire a population of 190,000 had only 10
places provided with a bank, whereas there were 47 towns
provided with a Post-Office savings-bank. He inferred
that the Post-Office banks might attract savings, where
private enterprise would not offer the necessary facilities.

Meanwhile Mr. Gladstone's measure was passed when
lightened by the withdrawal of the obnoxious clauses.
A good deal of discussion was directed to lowering the
proposed limit of investment in public stocks, which
according to the bill was fixed at 10*l.* Fawcett pointed
out some difficulties in this change whilst fully approving

its aim, but he promised to keep his attention upon the question and to propose a reduction of the limit if there should appear to be any desire for the investment of smaller sums. To another plan suggested for establishing a savings-bank at every post-office, Fawcett replied by describing a plan which he had started experimentally. It consisted in sending a clerk to village post-offices to receive deposits and money orders once a week. The plan had been tried for a month with apparent success, but it ultimately failed to attract business enough to justify perseverance. Another scheme adopted at the same time was far more prosperous. Mr. E. W. Harcourt suggested in the debate that the limit of deposit in the Post-Office savings-banks should be lowered beneath the old limit of a shilling. Fawcett replied that the small accounts were the costly ones ; and that a free use of the investment clauses would diminish the number of the larger and more profitable. He described, however, a scheme which had been suggested to him by the late Mr. Chetwynd, Receiver and Accountant-General of the Post-Office. It had been fully worked out, and Fawcett resolved to try it as one mode of meeting the various difficulties which had arisen. This is the now familiar scheme of 'stamp slip deposits,' which would have rejoiced the heart of Benjamin Franklin. Blank slips issued at every Post-Office may be filled up with twelve stamps and will then be received at the savings-bank as a shilling deposit. The plan was first tried in certain selected districts in September 1880, and succeeded so rapidly that, on November 15, Fawcett decided to extend it to the whole country. By the end of March

1881, 576,560 slips had been received and 223,000 new accounts were estimated to have been opened in consequence. In his report of 1882, Fawcett states that the daily average of receipts was 248*l*. In 1884 he observes upon the great increase in the number of children who are depositors. In four years the total number of depositors had increased by a million, of whom not less than a quarter were young persons. By thus encouraging the habit of saving in early life, the Post-Office, he remarks, is probably doing more to assist than to retard private enterprise. The clauses for investment contributed to the popularity of the savings-banks. The total amount invested in Government stocks at the end of the financial year March 31, 1884, was 1,519,983, held by 20,767 persons. The high price of stock and the commercial depression have, no doubt, considerably affected the results.

In the winter of 1880 Fawcett took very great pains (with the assistance of Mr. James Cardin, of the Post-Office, a gentleman for whose abilities he had a high respect) to prepare a small pamphlet called ' Aids to Thrift,' of which about 1,250,000 copies were gratuitously circulated. His aim was to translate into perfectly simple language the technical phrases given in the Post-Office Guide, whilst it was of course essential to avoid giving any false impressions. There could not be a better bit of literary practice; but in any case Fawcett would not grudge the trouble involved. About the same time he was deeply moved by an incident which may be noticed by way of preface to another part of the subject. A poor neighbour employed in a mill near Salisbury, had fallen ill. He had insured himself in a certain society which was to pay him an allowance in case of illness. The allowance was stopped upon certain pretences strongly suggestive of fraud. Fawcett, to whom he appealed, immediately called at the offices, where the secretary, not recognising his visitor, treated him with considerable insolence. Fawcett brought the man to his senses, extracted certain sums from the society, and took steps to investigate the nature of its business. He had the satisfaction of obtaining something for the poor man, who died not long afterwards. Fawcett did what he could for the family. The facts which came under his notice gave him a vivid impression of the difficulties which beset a poor man who desires to provide for the future. The poor are induced to confide in societies which devote a very large proportion of their receipts to 'expenses of management,' and make such conditions that a good many of the insurances lapse after the payment of premiums. Upon a trial for fraud it came out that in one of these societies only 5 per cent. of the policies came to maturity. The powers of the Post-Office could hardly be turned to better account than in providing a good substitute for agencies of this variety and giving the best security for the savings of the poor. A system of life insurance and annuities had been adopted by the Post-Office in 1865. Much pains had been taken by the officials concerned, to work out the new scheme and secure a good start. For whatever reason, however, the progress had been languid. Insurances had fallen off and few annuities were bought. Fawcett took up

F F

the question, and in February 1882 moved for a Select
Committee to inquire into the system. A scheme was
proposed by Mr. Cardin for simplifying and improving
the arrangements, which was approved by Fawcett and
by the Committee and embodied in a bill introduced
in the same session.

The main purpose of the scheme was to take all
possible trouble off the hands of customers. Saving
was to be made as simple and easy as possible. All
needless formalities were to be abolished. The business
of annuities and insurance was to be more closely
associated with those of the savings-banks. The main
changes came to this : that, henceforward, a person
who desired to insure his life or to buy an annuity
might apply at any office where there was a savings-
bank—that is, at any one of 7,000 offices, instead of
being limited to 2,000. When the terms were accepted
he might pay his premiums wherever he pleased, instead
of having always to pay at the same place. Finally, he
could pay in any sums and at any time, instead of
having to pay an exact sum at a particular time. The
Post-Office would take charge of all sums, and apply
them in accordance with a direction given once for all.
The depositor had only to take care that there should be
a sufficient sum to his credit when the premium became
due. Fawcett further induced the Committee to recommend the enlargement of both the upper and the lower
limits of allowable insurances and annuities. It was
also recommended that in cases of small amounts
medical examination might be omitted, provision being
made against loss to the Post-Office if the insurer died

within two years. It was thought that the necessity of going before a doctor often involved the loss of a day's work and would discourage insurance, whilst the security given by medical examination becomes very small for a period exceeding two years. The proposal for an extension of the limits was resisted by the insurance companies and bankers, as in the analogous case of the savings-banks deposit; and the proposed extension was diminished in order to meet their objections. The bill was then passed without further modification in August 1882.

The necessity of providing new tables and settling various details, in the discussion of which Fawcett took a keen interest, prevented the scheme from coming into operation until June 3, 1884. Shortly before this (May 28, 1884) he had an opportunity of pointing out its main provisions. Some letter-carriers and sorters asked him to establish a system of compulsory deduction from their wages with a view to providing pensions. Fawcett, in reply, pointed out the difficulties of this proposal, and observed in particular that it would not encourage self-help. He then showed, by example, the advantages of the system about to be started. By taking the slight trouble of placing a penny stamp every week on a blank form, and depositing it when filled at a savings-bank, a lad of 15 would entitle himself to an annuity of 2*l*. 10*s*. a year at the age of 60. The penny a week would result in a shilling a week. A person who has 20*l*. in a savings-bank at the age of 20 may give a simple order, in consequence of which he will at the age of 60 receive an annuity of 5*l*. or a policy of 25*l*. Or by saving 2*s*. a week from 20 to 50, an annuity will be secured of 18*l*. a year, to commence at the age of 50. Annuities may be purchased on the terms of a return of the purchase-money if the annuitant changes his mind; and a person may nominate his wife or child to receive the insurance money on his death without making his will or going through further formality. Fawcett disclaimed any intention of urging the adoption of any particular plan; and spoke with his usual earnestness of the importance of all such means of saving as building societies and co-operative institutions, and the advantage of bringing the whole energy of the department to bear upon the encouragement of thrift. A short paper, called ' Plain Rules for the guidance of persons wishing to make provision for the future by the aid of the Government,' was widely circulated. So far it seems that the scheme has not achieved the success which may be hoped when its provisions are more generally understood. There are, however, permanent difficulties arising, especially from the impracticability of providing, in schemes of State management, for allowance in time of sickness, or of employing agents for collecting premiums, as is done by private societies.

Fawcett was always on the watch to spread the savings-bank system. The number of new banks annually opened under his administration rapidly increased. It rose in 1881 to 280 from 185 in the previous year, and in 1882 to 486; whilst in the five years to the end of 1884, 1,693 new offices were opened. The number of depositors increased with remarkable rapidity. In 1879 there were 96,000 new depositors; in 1880 196,000, and in the three following years nearly a million. He would often remark that almost the only satisfactory symptom in Irish matters was the increased use of the savings-bank, even in the more distressed districts. He was constantly examining such statistics to trace the effect of past legislation and find suggestions for the future.

I have now spoken of the principal results of his administration. When a fair estimate is made of the labour and thought implied, it will, I think, be clear that Fawcett turned his four years and a half to good account. In truth he was not merely interested in his work, but took to it as though the administration of the Post-Office had been less a duty than the passion of a lifetime. He delighted in talking over the business of his office and canvassing new suggestions, as a man delights in amusing himself with some favourite hobby. Besides the more imposing reforms, he introduced a number of small improvements. Miss Smith, of Oxford (sister of his friend, Professor Henry Smith), happened to tell him of the indicators used abroad to show when the last collection had been made at pillar-boxes. He at once made inquiries, and finding that a similar plan had been in successful operation at Liverpool for two years, he decided that, in spite of some objections to the expense, the Liverpool system should be extended to the whole country. A similar suggestion led him to introduce the reply post-card. He would watch the effect of any new facilities, and was interested in hearing of the results in convenience and increased correspondence due to the erection of a pillar-box near his old home in Salisbury.

He multiplied pillar-boxes in railway stations, and had letter-boxes fixed to the travelling post-offices in trains. He was always eager to improve the mail service to remote towns; and would observe that one good result of State management was the consideration of out-of-the-way places. A private management, he said, might probably have introduced a halfpenny post in London, and have left the country worse served than at present. Amongst other little improvements he either adopted, or was preparing to adopt, the German plan of allowing the sale of stamps by tradesmen who were willing to dispense with a commission in consideration of the customers attracted to their shops, and by the abolition of the distinctive telegraph stamp he was enabled to allow telegrams to be deposited in pillar-boxes at night in order to be forwarded on the first clearance. He provided for the issue of postal orders on board ship; and earned the gratitude of many pensioners by arranging (at the suggestion of the War Office) for the transmission of the sums due to them by money orders, thus relieving them of the necessity for a journey. He positively enjoyed the discussion of the minutiæ which are tiresome to any man whose heart is not in his work. Some proof of this may be found in his annual reports. Such documents are generally quoted in the newspapers for anecdotes of the remarkable persons who send 'live kittens and dead rats' by post; but they also afford evidence of the care with which Fawcett watched every available indication, at home and abroad, of the success of the various schemes for increasing the utility of the Post-Office.

It will be easily understood that the consideration of
the multitudinous details involved in these plans required
steady and determined labour. Fawcett was scrupulous in
going into matters for himself to a degree which, if anything, erred by excess. His minutes upon papers laid
before him always showed that he had given his mind to
the question. Instead of simply approving the draft of a
proposed letter to be signed by a secretary, he would direct
a letter to be prepared for his own signature, in order that
the receiver might know that the matter had received his
personal attention, and that, if desirable, its terms might
be softened. His secretary had to read papers which came
before him daily, except on bank-holidays, and to get
them up thoroughly, for Fawcett, instead of passing them
as a matter of form, was certain to ask minute questions
about them. He frequently had personal interviews
with subordinate officials in order thoroughly to understand their views in cases even where such interviews
were beyond the ordinary practice of the department.
He was thus able to get at first hand the opinions of
the persons immediately concerned, to be sure that his
own views were understood by them, and to count with
confidence upon their cordial support. Such interviews
did much to strengthen good feeling on all sides. When
differences of opinion arose, he would discuss the question at 'almost wearisome length,' from his dislike to
overriding a subordinate's judgment, and his eagerness
if possible to carry conviction. His evident wish to conciliate took away the sting of adverse decisions when
they became necessary. He was always anxious in the
same way to attend personally to applications backed by

no official influence. If, for example, a cottager asked that letters might be delivered to him personally, instead of being left at the house of his employer, Fawcett would investigate the petition as carefully as if it had been a request from a colleague. This system, adopted from conscientious motives at the cost of severe labour, might be pushed to excess. Some people thought that he went too much into details, and wasted energy on matters which should have been left to subordinates. Mr. Blackwood, who has kindly given me his impressions of Fawcett as an administrator, thinks that this excess, if it were an excess, of zeal arose partly from his inexperience in administration, partly from his desire to base his decisions on the fullest information, and partly from unwillingness to let drop any of the strings which he had once taken up. Mr. Blackwood adds that it had, in any case, the good effect of enabling him to master the complex details of the service. It enabled him to obtain a thorough command of all the business for the conduct of which he was responsible, to infuse energy into his subordinates and attract public confidence. If the strain upon his own energies was severe, he never neglected important matters in his attention to comparative trifles. His dread of falling into the vice of 'officialism,' of substituting routine for active judgment of particular cases, confirmed him in a practice to which he adhered with deliberate conviction. In connection with this, I may refer to his answers to the parliamentary 'question'—a phrase which, as in another use of the word, seems to be nearly equivalent to torture. Some officials may be justified in thinking that a question is presumably an impertinence, and should be answered in kind by an evasion or a retort. Fawcett's answers are really attempts to give information. He tried to say as much, not as little, as possible. And at the same time they are remarkable proofs of his minute knowledge of details and his really astonishing power of producing full statistical statements. Their obvious candour did much to improve his general position.

It was of course inevitable that Fawcett should gain the esteem of the permanent officials of the Post-Office, as of every other class of men with whom he had much intercourse. His courtesy, kindliness, and sincerity were as obvious in this as in other relations of life. I may add that he returned their esteem. He frequently remarked to me upon the high standard of honour in the public service, observing that officials in receipt of moderate salaries had often to decide upon questions, such as mail contracts, involving large sums of money, and that there was never the slightest suspicion of their turning their opportunities to private profit. Besides his general attention to their wishes and opinions, he was always scrupulously careful to give them all possible credit. He was keenly alive to the danger of unfairly appropriating the labours of subordinates whose position enforces silence as to their own claims. He never introduced a scheme without assigning the original suggestion and elaboration to the right author. He took great pains to obtain those honorary distinctions for his subordinates which are often the only mode of rewarding their zeal or making known to the outside world the fact that they have been useful servants. I will add that his

position gave him particular pleasure when it enabled
him to reward merit.   Few things, as I judge from his
private letters, pleased him more than an opportunity of
appointing Mr. Hunter to the solicitorship of the Post-
Office.   Mr. Hunter's fitness had been recognised by
independent persons, and Fawcett considered the appointment as also a recognition of Mr. Hunter's great
services in the preservation of commons.   He was equally
gratified by later experience of Mr. Hunter's fitness for
his post.

As Postmaster-General, Fawcett was the commander
of a civilian army numbering (if we include those who
give a part only of their time to the Post-Office) over
90,000 persons.   To maintain the public spirit of this
body was a very important part of his duties.   Several
important questions at once arose.   Many of the telegraphists were dissatisfied with their rate of wages, which
stopped, after previous advances, at 28s. a week, until they
could be promoted to a higher class.   There were threats
of a strike ; and the case was taken up by members of the
House.   After a careful examination of the case, involving
much comparison with rates of wages in other employments, Fawcett induced the Government—not without
difficulty—to re-classify the telegraphists, so as to admit
of a steady rise to a salary of 80l. a year.   The scheme
applied also to the postal staff, who had not taken part
in the agitation, and the concession satisfied the persons
concerned.   The charge to the country would amount
ultimately to 150,000l. a year.   He afterwards raised the
rate of payment to sub-postmasters, at the cost of 34,000l.
He made other arrangements to improve the position of

postmen in towns, and extended to the whole country a system of good-conduct stripes, carrying with them an increased pay of 1s. a week. Three such stripes may be earned, and the cost was estimated at 63,000l. a year. He also gave an annual week's holiday to country postmen. The proposed additions were not carried out without remarks in some quarters upon the principles of political economy. Should not wages be fixed by supply and demand? Fawcett of course accepted the general principle, and gave due weight to it by investigating the actual rates in the open market. He never lost sight of the principle that one class should not be unduly benefited at the expense of the community. But he did not admit that the rate should be the lowest which would attract any class of physically capable persons. The end should be to have such a rate of wages as would secure really efficient service by obviating discontent. He quoted a statement of the Postmaster at Glasgow, that the system of stripes gave him the pick of the labourers instead of the refuse, as a strong illustration of the efficacy of his measures.

Another change enlisted his strongest sympathies. He was especially anxious to extend the system, already in operation, of employing women. The clerical work connected with the new postal orders was entirely entrusted to female clerks. In his report of 1882 he observes that the number of women employed in various capacities has increased in the year by 299, and says that the system has been so satisfactory that he hopes to extend it. The next year the number was increased to 2,561, and is now 2,919. He introduced in 1883 a new class of female sorters in the savings-banks to arrange the various documents; and he had the satisfaction in 1882 of appointing a lady to a medical post—an appointment fully justified by the large number of women employed. He also appointed female medical officers at Liverpool and Manchester. He was thoroughly satisfied by subsequent experience of the results of this increased employment of female labour in all directions. When he took office women were appointed by limited competition to clerkships in the savings-banks, three being nominated for each vacancy. Fawcett felt very keenly the responsibility of nominating candidates. He tried to avoid personal influence, and one of the first persons he nominated was the daughter of a policeman who had no influence to back the application. He would go through the lists carefully and repeatedly, but could not satisfy himself that he had chosen those most in need of employment. He therefore determined to introduce open competition. He took, however, the most scrupulous care not to interfere with the interests of women already nominated by his predecessor. The telegraphists were treated in the same way. The result has been that last year 2,500 women competed for 145 clerkships, whilst there have been 30 applicants for every vacancy in the telegraph department. The severity of the examination and the limits of age for admission have had to be raised.

One other point may be noticed. When Fawcett took office it was the practice to transfer the appointment of a postmistress who married to her husband. She would therefore lose her appointment if the husband misbehaved. Fawcett tried to find some way of obviating the hardships which occasionally resulted. No plan could be suggested till the passage of the Married Women's Property Act in 1882. He then decided that a woman should in every case have the option of retaining the appointment in her own name. The arrangement was confirmed by Mr. Lefevre.

Fawcett was especially anxious in all cases when the dismissal of a subordinate was proposed. He felt it painful to confirm such an order, and asked carefully what the man had said in his defence, and whether he could not have another trial. A friend tells an anecdote of his delight upon one occasion when he had directed a suspension of judgment, in spite of strong circumstantial evidence. The real criminal had been acute enough to suspend his depredations during an experimental removal of the suspected person. At last, in consequence of further investigations directed by Fawcett, the character of the man accused was fully cleared. I am bound to add that in this direction Mr. Blackwood thinks that Fawcett occasionally pushed clemency to weakness. Fawcett's leniency, he thinks, made him unwilling to enforce punishments really called for in the interests of the necessary discipline, whether it arose from his dislike to inflicting pain or from a conception of personal rights connected with his political principles. I rather think that Fawcett's politics were as much the consequence as the cause of his extreme good-nature. His dread of officialism, too, counted for something in this as in all his official activity. He could not bear to make a human being the victim of a rigid formula. A certain inclination to this side seems to me characteristic of Fawcett. I remember his leaning to the good-natured view in the little world of college, where questions of discipline would also occasionally arise. Any deviation from strict justice would certainly be in the direction of mildness; and the tendency fell in not only with his natural kindliness, but with the cheery optimism which predisposed him to the pleasantest view of things, and made him unwilling to believe in the existence of evils or in the necessity of inflicting pain. But a different view may be taken of the facts. Fawcett's good nature was blended with a strong sense of justice. He was righteously unwilling to dismiss a man, often with a stigma for life, unless he was thoroughly convinced that the charge was fully proved; and he might be right in refusing to accept the decision of a man's superior, even though the superior might be annoyed. I know that some qualified observers attribute the best effects to Fawcett's scrupulous attention to such considerations. His gentleness was in any case appreciated by those whom it concerned. They felt that their superior was really sensitive to their welfare. I will venture in this connection to quote part of a letter from a post-office clerk sent with a wreath to be laid upon Fawcett's coffin. After speaking with genuine feeling of Fawcett's fairness, sincerity, determination to do the right, and ' gentleness in dealing with delicate and difficult cases,' the writer adds, ' The humblest servant within the dominion of his authority was not left uncared for. During his history as Postmaster-General, a greatly improved state of feeling has been introduced among the officers in their general tone towards each other and towards those beneath them,

and the whole service in all respects has been greatly
and wonderfully improved.'

I have sufficient testimony that Fawcett's influence
in maintaining and raising the tone of the official departments more immediately under his influence was
marked and elevating. I have given the only two adverse criticisms which Mr. Blackwood thinks may be made
upon his administrative powers. But these blemishes
—which are at worst exaggerations of good qualities—
are noticed by Mr. Blackwood as the sole drawbacks
from remarkable excellence. 'Nothing struck me more
forcibly in Fawcett's character,' he writes, 'than his
extreme thoughtfulness for the wishes, feelings, and convenience of everyone with whom he had to do. As a
Minister of State he could, of course, command the
services of all his subordinates, and his blindness might
have been regarded as justifying him in requiring their
aid to an exceptional degree. But I invariably observed
that he would sooner expose himself to inconvenience,
and even deprive himself of what appeared to be official
assistance of an almost indispensable character, than
subject those from whom he might have demanded it to
inconvenience. Numerous instances have occurred to
me when he preferred to wait for information rather than
cause an officer to forego his leave of absence, and even
miss a train or his usual luncheon-hour. There were
few things about which he was more determined to put
matters right than the health of the staff in the various
offices, and the sanitary conditions under which work was
performed. He was keen at once to observe the failure of
health, however slight, in any of the officers with whom

he came in contact, and at once to suggest that they should recruit themselves by leave of absence. He never forgot the particular circumstances connected with each case in which he had been interested. He took the greatest interest in the official career of his subordinates, and often suggested some beneficial change of employment. Whilst very cautious in deciding to administer blame, he never shrank from the unpleasant task of doing it personally in any delicate case, or when he thought that it would have a better effect as coming directly from himself.

' 'His quickness in discernment of character struck me as most remarkable. A few moments' conversation with an officer, or the manner in which another treated a case, though only on paper, was sufficient to enable him to form a very accurate idea of a man's capabilities and calibre.'

'For nearly five years,' says Mr. Blackwood in conclusion, 'I was almost daily in Mr. Fawcett's company, and I can truly say that I never served, or could wish to serve, under a more able, upright, and conscientious chief, and that the friendship I was permitted to enjoy with him inspired a most sincere affection and the strongest regard for his memory. The Post-Office could never, I believe, have a more capable Postmaster-General, nor its officers a truer friend.'

Upon Fawcett's death, the officials who had been most associated with him subscribed to make a present to his widow, as a token of their 'affectionate remembrance' of a beloved chief.

Here I close my account of Fawcett's official life.

No one will require me to enforce the obvious conclusions by any additional comments. I shall only say that to the friends who had long watched his career with sympathy the success of his administration gave peculiar pleasure, whilst it even surpassed their anticipations. He had victoriously established the one point upon which doubt might still be possible. It had long been certain that he possessed some of the most essential qualities of a statesman—independence, soundness of judgment, and a power of commanding the sympathies without flattering the meaner instincts of the people. He had now established beyond all dispute that he was not merely not disqualified for office by his blindness, but that he had unusual qualifications both for discharging the most onerous duties of a responsible post, and for conciliating public confidence in his department. Few men have ever made such a mark by a brief exercise of administrative functions. It could hardly be doubtful that he would achieve the one remaining victory—that, on some future occasion, he would be member of a Liberal Cabinet, and be able to render invaluable services at a time when it is daily becoming more important that the accepted leaders of the people should be men who fear to speak an insincere word, and fear nothing else.

CHAPTER X.

CONCLUSION.

FAWCETT's administration of the Post-Office had greatly
extended his popularity. His occasional utterances in
public were received with marked respect. They were
reassertions of his old principles in a perceptibly gentler
tone. One only need be mentioned. On October 13,
1884, he delivered his last address to his constituents at
Hackney. Its calmness and fairness were brought into
relief by the angry discussions then raging between the
rival parties. Fawcett never forgot that his antagonists
were human beings—a fact which is too frequently
overlooked by politicians. In nothing, indeed, is his
example more commendable than in the rebuke which it
tacitly administers to a spirit of mutual intolerance. He
was now unconsciously saying his last word upon
matters in which he was most deeply interested. He
expressed his conviction that the enfranchisement of
women, already dictated by justice, would soon become a
necessity, and he spoke emphatically in favour of proportional representation. In the following session the
decision of the Government to adopt a measure incompatible with this principle led to the resignation of

Fawcett's old friend, Mr. Courtney. I am able to say that Fawcett had made up his mind to adopt the same course. Some critics have thought that this decision implied an excessive attachment to a mere crotchet. I need not say a word as to the value of the doctrine itself. Upon that question I have never been able to follow Fawcett's teaching, which I mention only to give more emphasis to the further statement that I cannot admit the force of the adverse criticism upon Fawcett's action. Not only was Mr. Hare's scheme the very first political question upon which he had uttered himself in public, not only had he adhered to it till the last through good and evil report, but he held that it was the means of giving effect to that respect for the rights of a minority which was a first principle in his code of political morality, and which in his opinion was an essential condition of combining justice with progress. He was therefore fully justified in the view that he could not continue without gross inconsistency to hold office in a Government which acted in opposition to his most cherished convictions.

During this period Fawcett received several of those honours which are to any man welcome proofs that popular approval of his character is ratified by more critical judges. The University of Oxford gave him the honorary degree of Doctor of Civil Law. The University of Würzburg, in August 1882, on occasion of its tercentenary celebration, conferred upon him the title of Doctor of Political Economy: the only other person upon whom that degree had been conferred being M. de

Laveleye. The Institute of France elected him, in May 1884, a corresponding member of the section of Political Economy. The Royal Society paid him the high honour of electing him to a Fellowship. In 1883 the University of Glasgow gave him the LL.D. degree, and in the same year he was elected to the Lord Rectorship of the same University, his opponents being Lord Bute and Mr. Ruskin. The delivery of the customary address was prevented by his death. No notes of his intended remarks had been preserved. Mrs. Fawcett therefore printed and presented to every student of the University a copy of his last speech at Hackney. As a political speech, it is, as she says in a few prefatory words, of course quite different from what he would have said in an address; but she adds, ' It appears to me so characteristic of him on whom the choice of the students fell, so free from party passion and prejudice, so fearless in saying what he knew would not be popular, so instinct with devotion to principle and love of justice, that I cannot believe it will be useless or unacceptable to young men just beginning the battle of life.' Nothing could be better said, and there are few speeches indeed delivered by a strong partisan in the heat of a bitter political contest which would have the same qualifications for being turned to such account.

And now, before I come to the end, I must briefly revert from Fawcett's political career to his domestic life. The stream of domestic happiness had indeed been running freshly and fully beneath all the agitated surface of political contest. To Fawcett I have often thought was specially applicable a passage in a poem which I now always associate with his memory. The 'happy warrior,' says Wordsworth, is one

> Who, though thus endued as with a sense
> And faculty for storm and turbulence,
> Is yet a soul whose master-bias leans
> To homefelt pleasures and to gentle scenes;
> Sweet images! which, wheresoe'er he be,
> Are at his heart; and such fidelity
> It is his darling passion to approve;
> More brave for this, that he hath much to love.

Over some elements of his happiness I must pass very lightly. I need only say that in his last years, as previously, Mrs. Fawcett was his adviser in the most serious matters; and that when she was temporarily absent he would put off a decision of great moment in his career until he had been able to obtain her opinion. On all occasions he was acutely sensible of the value of her advice and encouragement. Their one child, Philippa, born 1868, was now growing up to an age at which she could be frequently her father's companion, and the development of her talent was a source of constant and growing interest to him. He enjoyed also the intimacy of Mrs. Fawcett's family, members of which have taken a most important part in proving the capacity of women for wider spheres of activity. A visit, always greatly enjoyed, to his wife's parents at Aldeburgh was part of his regular programme for the annual holiday. His delight in society was unfailing; but he delighted more and more in small parties or in the family circle, where conversation could be intimate and informal. A walk across Clapham or Wimbledon Common, a row with his old friend Fairrie, or with the 'Ancient Mariners,'

a ride with two or three friends along the Cambridgeshire
roads, or a chat over a cigar with some old college crony,
gave him unfailing satisfaction. He was not one of those
who become tongue-tied at home. He would pour himself
out upon all the topics in which he was most deeply interested, over his own table, when there were no guests,
as freely as when he had other listeners. His passion
for talk and his invariable affability sometimes subjected
him to trials of patience.   He was mean enough at times,
I fear, to shift such burthens upon his wife. He would
laugh over an anecdote of a diplomatic struggle, when he
and a neighbour had tried to transfer to each other the
company of an excessively talkative friend, who had intruded upon them during the morning hours reserved for
hard work.   Fawcett got the worst of it on this occasion,
but few men could submit so patiently to such inflictions
or were less susceptible to the grievance of being bored.
Talk was a necessary of life to him.   The seat which he
occupied in the House of Commons became notorious as
a centre of gossip.   Wherever he went he dispelled
reserve. His utter indifference to distinctions of rank
enabled him to cultivate human relations with all classes.
His own servants loved him, and the servants of his
friends had always a pleasant word with him. He was
scrupulously considerate in all matters affecting the convenience of those dependent upon him.   I will venture
to add that one inmate of his house, well known to all his
friends, was a little dog called Oddo, after a character in
' Feats on the Fiord.' Oddo came from the refuge of lost
dogs to act as watch-dog in the garden at the Lawn.
His good qualities made him a pet, treated with rather

excessive tenderness in matters of diet by his master, who, however, took a lively interest in his education, and always considered him as a humble friend. Oddo returned his affection, and survives to be loved for his master's sake.

Of Fawcett it might be said in adaptation of Johnson's remark upon Burke, that if you had taken refuge with him under a haystack from a shower of rain you would have discovered his genius for friendship. Wherever he recognised valuable qualities, friendships germinated with astonishing rapidity and enjoyed a vitality hardly to be expected from the rapidity of their growth. The certainty with which he remembered a voice once heard in a friendly talk often amazed his acquaintance. The number of persons upon whom he sincerely bestowed the title of intimate friends was surprising. And all the overgrowth of new friendships seemed rather to strengthen than to stifle the earlier ties. When he went to Salisbury he made a point of visiting his father's old labourers and renewing the old associations by talking over the matters which interested them. How successful he was in throwing himself into their feelings may be inferred from an anecdote of his father's old farm-servant Rumbold. Rumbold was one day giving to Fawcett's mother the last news from his sties; 'and,' he added, 'mind you tell Master Harry when you write to him, for if there's one thing he cares about 'tis pigs.' It was one thing, though hardly the one thing. His home affections steadily gathered force. He had been in the habit of writing a weekly letter to his parents. He happened one day to ask his sister what gave them most pleasure? She

replied, 'Your letters.' From that time, though overwhelmed with parliamentary and official work, he wrote
twice instead of once. Many of these letters lie before
me. They are homely and affectionate; giving any
interesting bit of news; occasionally enclosing such letters
as could be shown without breach of confidence; com-
menting briefly upon the state of politics; and full of little
requests or suggestions prompted by his affection. He
tells of any successes or compliments which are likely to
gratify his parents; he reports with pride the remarks
which he has heard upon his father's remarkable
immunity from the infirmities of old age; he praises his
father's power of packing, as shown in the preparation of
certain hampers which frequently passed between them;
he sends birthday presents, and is always thinking of
some trifle, a pair of ' Norwegian slippers ' or the like,
which may contribute to the paternal comfort. The letters
everywhere imply that constant desire to give pleasure
which is more significant than the strongest professions
of affection.[1] I need not say with what affectionate
pride these letters must have been received, nor what
comfort must have followed the reflection that the blow
innocently inflicted by his father's hand had furthered
rather than impeded the son's career.

[1] I venture here to insert an anecdote which reached me too late
to occupy its proper place. The Rev. Sir James E. Philipps, Bart., now
Vicar of Warminster, was curate of Wilton at the time of Fawcett's
accident. Mr. Sidney Herbert (as he then was) rode over immediately
to see Mr. Fawcett, senior. Sir J. Phillips happened to be at Wilton
House on his return. Mr. Sidney Herbert, on being asked about the
family, replied that Mr. Fawcett had said to him, ' I could bear it if my
son would only complain.' That was almost the only consolation which
he never received.

The increase of Fawcett's income upon taking office made no difference in his modes of life. He was profoundly sensible of the importance of preserving absolute independence in money matters. Except that he spent a little more upon riding, he lived precisely as he had done before. He was able also to allow himself the luxury of a few more presents to his family; and nothing gave him more pleasure than to entertain his parents and sister at his house; to provide seats for them at concerts and so forth; or to take his father with him to the House of Commons and bring some of his political friends for a chat under the gallery.

A trial was now to befall all who loved Fawcett. During the summer of 1882 he had worked with little intermission. He came to town in November for the autumn session, and on returning from the Lord Mayor's banquet on the 9th, Mrs. Fawcett heard that the illness of a cousin, Miss Rhoda Garrett, to whom she was strongly attached, had taken a serious turn. She immediately went to the house to take a share in nursing. Miss Garrett died on the 22nd. Besides discharging his parliamentary and official duties, Fawcett had to attend to his lectures at Cambridge, and was persuaded to go to Salisbury to speak at an election meeting. His speech (on November 17) was spirited, and his father was present to witness and share the enthusiastic welcome of the son. After the meeting, Fawcett seemed fagged. He returned to town on Monday, the 20th, lectured at Cambridge on the 22nd, returned to town, and on the 23rd went to the House and did business.

He complained of feeling ill, but apparently suffered
from nothing worse than a cold. He grew worse, and
Mrs. Fawcett, who had been at Miss Garrett's funeral at
Rustington on the 25th, returned to town on the 27th,
and was alarmed at his condition. On Wednesday, the
29th, Sir Andrew Clark pronounced the case to be one of
diphtheria. Miss Agnes Garrett, Mrs. Fawcett's sister,
had fortunately happened to be calling at the beginning
of the illness, and stayed to the end. Mrs. Fawcett
devoted her whole energies to the most assiduous care of
her husband. Dr. Ford Anderson, Mrs. Garrett Anderson's brother-in-law, took up his lodging in the house to
be always at hand. Complications soon appeared. The
presence of typhoid was suspected, and Sir W. Jenner,
who was called in, confirmed the opinion. A bulletin
stating the new danger was issued on December 2,
and caused general anxiety. The fever was expected to
reach its crisis on December 9; and upon that day it
was hoped that the worst was over, when a violent
hæmorrhage took place in the evening, which threatened
to produce choking. Happily Dr. Ford Anderson was
immediately on the spot. The danger was surmounted,
and no serious return occurred. After this there was no
further relapse, and at the end of the week the patient
was considered to be out of danger.

Fawcett was frequently delirious during the first fortnight and remembered little of what had happened. He
said that he had made up his mind that he should not
recover, and remarked upon the little importance of an
expectation of death during serious illness. He insisted
upon hearing the bulletins, which were read to him

with certain omissions. He remembered the date of an important election at Liverpool and inquired for the result. He spoke, when at his worst, of a custom which he had for many years observed, of making presents of beef and mutton to his father's old labourers or their widows at Christmas. As soon as he became distinctly conscious, he told his secretary to be sure to make the necessary arrangements. He would also ask whether the inmates of his family or the doctors who came to see him were getting proper attention to their meals.[1]

Rarely has any case of illness been watched so anxiously by the outside world. Letters and messages poured in, not only from colleagues, subordinates, and personal friends, but from persons in all ranks—from the Royal Family down to many whose communications were not the less welcome because betraying that the pen was an implement only used under strong pressure of feeling. The Queen often telegraphed twice a day for the latest news. Everywhere, in meetings of working-men and third-class carriages, the last news of Fawcett was discussed and the progress of his illness followed with eager attention. When once convalescent, Fawcett gained strength rapidly. Daily relays of lady friends came to read to him ; they got through the whole of ' Vanity Fair.' Fawcett was deeply

---

[1] During this terrible struggle for life, Fawcett received the most unstinted devotion of his family and physicians. Besides his regular attendant, Mr. E. Wright of Clapham, Sir Andrew Clark, Mrs. Anderson, and Dr. Ford Anderson, were in daily attendance, and did all that could be done by skill and affection. Miss Agnes Garrett and Mr. Dryhurst were equally devoted. Miss L. M. Wilkinson and Miss Cowie also came daily to the house to help as occasion served. They have all, I have reason to know, earned enduring gratitude for their labour of love.

touched by the kindness. When it became possible to bring
back two maids who had been left at Cambridge for fear of
infection, they brought with them Oddo and a cat named
Ben ; and a little family festival took place, in which both
dog and cat did what their nature permitted to join in the
general congratulations. After three weeks' silence, he was
able to dictate a letter to his parents. On January 8 he was
taken to the house of his father-in-law at Aldeburgh, where
his friend Mr. Sedley Taylor came to help in amusing him.
There he received a congratulatory address, signed by some
350 inhabitants of the little town, claiming a special interest in him, and rejoicing that their bracing air had contributed to his convalescence. He afterwards paid visits
to Sir B. Samuelson at Torquay, to Mr. Hawke at Liskeard (where he played cards for the first time), and to
Lord Portsmouth at Eggesford, and he reached Salisbury
on February 26. Though still suffering from rheumatism
and sleeplessness, he was rapidly gaining strength. With
Mrs. Fawcett's help he prepared a new edition of the
'Manual '; and in March he resumed his duties at the
Post-Office, which in the interval had been undertaken
by his old friend and colleague, Mr. Lefevre. His reception on again entering the House of Commons was such
as could only be given to a universal favourite just
escaped from imminent danger.

Fawcett appeared to himself, and to others, to have
made a complete recovery. His strong constitution
seemed to have triumphed completely. He had always
been careful in matters of health, scrupulous in diet,
taking regular and moderate exercise, and anxious to a
degree which was a cause of friendly ridicule to guard

against chills by warm clothing. One or two slight attacks of cold showed the necessity for caution, and his friends sometimes remarked that his stride was less vigorous than of old, especially in going up hill. But this was easily explained by his increase in weight. All anxiety had disappeared, and to inquiries after his health he would answer that he was never better in his life. His cheerfulness and vigour of mind seemed fully to confirm the statement; though there can now be no doubt that the shock had left permanent weakness.

In the summer of 1884 he was again prevented from taking a proper holiday. The telephone question gave him much worry and anxiety. In September he visited Wales, made a vigorous little speech at Bala, and after visits to Mr. H. Robertson and Mr. Osborne Morgan, returned to Cambridge at the end of September. He was to give his lectures that term, but he was frequently in London upon business, and made his speech at Hackney on October 13. Parliament met in the same month. On Thursday, October 30, he lectured, and his voice was weak from a cold caught a day or two before. After a visit to London, he returned to Cambridge on Saturday, November 1, where Mrs. Fawcett's younger sister, Mrs. Salmon, had come with her husband for a visit. He enjoyed a ride with them in the afternoon, which was damp and raw, and appeared none the worse on his return, but still complained of cold. Two or three friends dined with him in the evening, and one of them laughingly maintained the superiority of a cold of his own to Fawcett's. The claim was generally admitted. Next day Fawcett stayed in bed, having passed a bad night, and did some Post-Office work with his secretary. Dr. Latham was called in in the evening and said that a congestion of the lungs was threatened. On Monday Fawcett put off his lecture and made arrangements for postponing some official work. In the evening the case became graver. On Tuesday he suffered much pain from the development of pleurisy. Mrs. Fawcett wrote to Mrs. Anderson, who came from town on Wednesday after-noon. She took a grave view of the illness, but was forced to return to town, promising to come back with Sir Andrew Clark if an improvement did not take place. After she had gone there was an improvement. At his request, Mrs. Fawcett read some passages of Dickens to him and he laughed over them heartily. In the evening he sent a request to Mr. Lefevre to act again as his deputy. In the night he became very restless, but would not allow Mrs. Fawcett to be disturbed, after her pre-vious want of rest. On Thursday morning (November 6) he was evidently worse. Dr. Latham and Dr. Paget, who had also been called in, found that the action of the heart was weakened. Fawcett was able to speak to his secretary about sending notice of his illness to the papers. A telegram was sent to Mrs. Anderson, who reached Cambridge about four in the afternoon with Sir Andrew Clark. With Dr. Latham and Dr. Paget they went to his room and found him dying. He was still able to speak in a voice strong enough to be heard outside his room. He inquired whether dinner had been provided for Sir Andrew Clark. Presently his hands and feet began to grow cold. Fancying that the weather had changed, he said to Mrs. Fawcett and Mrs. Anderson, who were applying hot socks to them, ' The best things to warm my hands would be my fur gloves ; they are (which was true) in the pocket of my coat in the dressing-room.' He never spoke again. Mrs. Anderson had left the room to speak to the doctors, when he fell into a doze for a few minutes, and suddenly died about half-past five, in presence of his wife and daughter.

It was decided to bury him in the churchyard of Trumpington. Something was said of his native town, but it was thought unadvisable to incur the risk of additional excitement for the aged parents, still living in the Close of Salisbury. On Monday, November 10, he was therefore laid by the quiet little church, whose square tower is so familiar to all Cambridge men. Leslie Ellis, the poet and mathematician, and John Grote, most kindly and modest of metaphysicians, familiar names to the older generation of Cambridge, had already been laid there. It was associated with many pleasant rides and walks. The churchyard and the neighbouring roads were thronged by a great crowd of all classes. Besides his nearest and dearest, there were official colleagues, the chief authorities of the University, representatives of his college, of the University of Glasgow, of Brighton and Hackney, his two constituencies, and of various bodies specially connected with him ; and there were many friends, to some of whom the scene brought crowded memories of old happy days. As they stood in silence by the coffin, they saw some who had been already seniors in his undergraduate days, many fresh young faces and a few who had grown up side by side with him. They thought, perhaps,

more of the gaps. Whilst Fawcett lived, the dream of
the past had not been quite a dream. The old memories
had been so fresh and bright whilst he was there to dwell
upon them with unabated youthfulness that they seemed
still to preserve a partial reality. Now a gulf was
suddenly opened, and the memories sank back into the
phantasmal abyss of the past. About every old college
building and street in the old town there still hung
echoes of the boyish laughter and exulting talk of the
time when everything seemed possible except failure. But
for the future such memories would carry with them a
bitter regret. And yet they felt even then that the
last farewell to a brave man should not be dictated by
simple sorrow, and still less by despondency. Even
then they might feel with a certain glow of mournful
pride that the old blood must still be running warm and
strong in the race which had put out so noble an offshoot; and that in the University which he loved so
well, and the youth from which it is supplied, there must
be many ready to follow in his steps and be invigorated
by the example of so gallant and generous a leader.

A few words remain to be said. Many hearts were
chilled by the sad news which spread through the country
on that dreary evening. A noble career had been
snapped, and a beloved friend was taken from many.
Letters of condolence poured in from all sides, and if
the writers could not but feel the difficulty of giving any
fresh expression to a universal sentiment, they might at
least feel that no genuine word of sympathy is quite unavailing. It falls soothingly upon wounds beyond all

power of healing. I will not, however, venture to dwell upon them. They came, as the previous congratulations had come, from all classes and parties; from the officials of this and most other countries; from many political and social bodies whose causes he had served; from the circle of friends, more extensive than almost anyone has ever possessed; from many who had scarcely seen him, but had received some passing kindness from him; from servants whom he had treated with kindly confidence; from anonymous writers who wished to make acknowledgment of benefits derived from his actions; from many bodies of Post-Office officials, and from associations of working-men. The Queen wrote to the widow one of those letters which reveal her touching and spontaneous sympathy with those who have suffered under the heaviest of human sorrows. Mr. Gladstone wrote a sympathetic letter to Fawcett's father, saying that there had been no public man of our day whose remarkable qualities had been more fully recognised by his fellow-countrymen and more deeply embedded in their memories. But I will only quote two letters, which may illustrate the feeling of the class in whose interests he had most energetically laboured. One, which is an example of several, ran thus:—

'Pangbourne, November 8, 1884.

'Dear Madam,—I hope you will forgive us, but having followed the political life of the late Professor Fawcett we felt when we saw his death in the papers on the 7th that we had lost a personal friend, and that a great man had gone from us.

H H

'The loss to you must be beyond measure; but we as part of the nation do give you who as been his helper our heartfelt sympathy in your great trouble, and we do hope you may find a little consolation in knowing that his work that he has done for the working classes has not been in vain.

'We, as working-men, do offer you and your child our deepest sympathy, and beg to be

'Yours respectfully,

'HARRY Cox, Carpenter.
'CHARLES EDDY, Carpenter.
'RICHARD BOWLES, Carpenter.
'G. LEWENDON, Bricklayer.
'GEORGE BROWN, Bricklayer.
'WILLIAM Cox, Carpenter.
'CHARLES Cox, Blacksmith.
'M. CLIFFORD, Postmaster.
'F. CLIFFORD, Clerk.'

Another letter deserves to be given :—

'11 Elder Place, Brighton, November 11, 1884.

'Dear Mrs. Fawcett,—Excuse me in not writing you sooner, on the sad death of your dear lamented husband. Several of his old friends at the Brighton Railway works has wished me to ask you privately how you are situated in a pecuniary sense. We always thought that the Professor was a *poor man* and only had what he earned by his talents; his three years of office could not have brought in much money for you and the family to live in ease and comfort for the rest of your days. It is our opinion that you are richly entitled to a public pension. Failing this, would you accept a public subscription, say a penny one, from the working classes of this country, for the many good and noble deeds your noble partner done for the working classes of this country. His advice was always sound, good, and practical, and full of sympathy, a good private friend to all men.

'I see you had a plentiful supply of flowers, but those flowers soon fade and are no support to the poor and fatherless ones. I am confident, if you could make up your mind to accept a penny testimonial, the working classes would give cheerfully, not in the shape of charity, but for public and striking services rendered by one of the best men since Edmund Burke. We only wish he had lived twenty years longer.

'Pray excuse my plain way of writing to you, as an honest workman, one of his supporters from first to last. His last letter to me a month back was full of sound and good advice concerning our Provident Society.

'Believe me your sincere friend and well-wisher,

'JOHN SHORT, Senior.'

Mrs. Fawcett, whilst deeply touched by the good feeling which prompted this letter, was able to say that her husband's forethought and prudence had left her in a position to make it improper for her to accept either a pension or a subscription. 'Our men at the railway works,' as Mr. Short replied, 'say that you are entitled to all honour for refusing a pension or a public subscription from the working men; also that your dear husband and our best friend has practised what he always preached to us, private thrift!'

Various proposals were immediately made to honour Fawcett's memory. A statue is to be erected in the market-place of Salisbury, near a statue previously erected to Sidney Herbert, on the spot where he took his first childish steps, and to which he always returned with fresh affection. In Cambridge there is to be a portrait by Mr. Herkomer of the figure so familiar for a generation. Measures are still in progress for some appropriate memorial in India to the man who showed so unique a power of sympathy with a strange race. A national memorial is in preparation, which is to consist of a scholarship for the blind at Cambridge, some additional endowment for the Royal Normal College for the Blind at Norwood, and a tablet to be erected in Westminster Abbey. A memorial is also to be erected in recognition of his services to women; and the inhabitants of Trumpington are placing a window to his memory in their church. Such monuments are but the outward symbols of the living influence still exercised upon the hearts of his countrymen by a character equally remarkable for masculine independence and generous sympathy. My sole aim has been to do something towards enabling my readers to bring that influence to bear upon themselves.

APPENDIX.

THE following list of Fawcett's published works is exclusive of occasional letters to newspapers and a few reprints of reported speeches. His independent publications, all of which, except the first, were issued by Messrs. Macmillan, are as follows :—

1. 'Mr. Hare's Reform Bill,' simplified and explained by Henry Fawcett, M.A. Fellow of Trinity Hall, Cambridge. (James Ridgeway, 1860.)

2. 'The Leading Clauses of a New Reform Bill,' June 1860.

3. 'Manual of Political Economy,' March 1863. Six editions have appeared, the last in August 1883. Each edition was carefully revised, but the bulk is not much altered. Up to June 1884, 21,750 copies had been printed. In the fifteen months to June 1864, 1,031 copies were sold ; and 1,673 copies in the year to June 1884.

4. 'The Economic Position of the British Labourer,' September 1865. Substance of a course of lectures delivered in autumn of 1864.

5. 'Pauperism : Its Causes and Remedies,' April 1871. Substance of a course of lectures delivered in the autumn of 1870. Substance embodied in later editions of the 'Manual.'

6. 'Essays and Lectures on Social and Political Subjects,' March 1872. Containing eight essays by Mrs. Fawcett, and the following by H. Fawcett—(1) Three lectures

forming part of a series delivered in the Lent Term of 1872 upon 'The Programme of the International Society economically considered,' and dealing respectively with 'Modern Socialism,' 'The General Aspects of State Intervention,' and 'The Regulation of the Hours of Labour by the State'; (2) an article reprinted from *Macmillan's Magazine* for October 1868, entitled 'What can be done for the Agricultural Labourer,' with a postscript dated January 1872 upon 'The Education Act and the Agricultural Commission'; (3) an article upon 'Pauperism, Charity, and the Poor Law,' reprinted from the *British Quarterly* for April 1869; (4) an article upon the 'House of Lords,' reprinted from the *Fortnightly Review* for October 1871.

7. 'Speeches on some Current Political Questions,' October 1873.

8. 'Free Trade and Protection,' May 1878. Substance of a course of lectures delivered in the autumn of 1877. The sixth edition, edited by Mrs. Fawcett, appeared in February 1885. Nearly 6,000 copies had been printed by June 1884.

9. 'Indian Finance,' January 1880. Three essays reprinted, with introduction and appendix, from the *Nineteenth Century*.

10. 'State Socialism and the Nationalisation of the Land,' July 1883. Separate publication of a chapter in the sixth edition of the 'Manual,' which also appeared in *Macmillan's Magazine* for July 1883. It was sold for 2d., and 9,000 copies were printed up to June 1884.

11. 'Labour and Wages,' April 1884. A reprint of five chapters from the sixth edition of the 'Manual,' on 'Remedies for Low Wages,' 'Trades-unions,' 'Strikes and Copartnership,' 'Co-operation,' and 'State Socialism, and the Nationalisation of the Land.' This has been translated into French by M. Raffalovich.

The following articles appeared in reviews :—

Macmillan's Magazine : (1) ' On the Social and Economical Influence of the New Gold ' (July 1860) ; (2) ' Co-operative Societies : their Social and Economical Aspects' (October 1860) ; (3) ' A Popular Exposition of Mr. Darwin's " Origin of Species "' (December 1860) ; (4) ' On the Exclusion of those who are not Members of the Established Church from Fellowships, and other Privileges of the English Universities' (March 1861) ; (5) ' Mr. Mill on Representative Government ' (June 1861) ; (6) ' On the Present Prospects of Co-operative Societies' (February 1862) ; (7) ' Inaugural Lecture on Political Economy,' delivered before the University of Cambridge on February 3, 1864 (April 1864) ; (8) ' State Socialism and the Nationalisation of the Land ' (*see* above).

Westminster Review : ' Strikes : their Tendencies and Remedies ' (July 1860).

Fraser's Magazine : ' Inclosure of Commons ' (February 1870) ; ' The Indian Deficit ' (January 1871).

British Quarterly : ' Pauperism, Charity, and the Poor Law ' (April 1869 ; *see* ' Essays and Lectures ').

Fortnightly Review : (1) ' To what Extent is England Prosperous ? ' (January 1871) ; (2) ' Boarding out of Pauper Children ' (February 1871) ; (3) ' House of Lords ' (October 1871 ; *see* ' Essays and Lectures ') ; (4) ' The Present Position of the Government ' (November 1871 ; and separately reprinted (1872) with ' Postscript in Reference to recent Ministerial Statements ') ; (5) ' The Nationalisation of the Land ' (November 1872 ; part of a course of lectures delivered in the Lent Term of 1872 in continuation of those published in ' Essays and Lectures ') ; (6) ' The Incidence of Local Taxation ' (May 1873) ; (7) ' Wealth and Increase of Wages ' (May 1873) ; (8) ' The Position and Prospects of Co-operation ' ; (February 1874) ; (9) ' Professor Cairnes ' (August 1875).

Nineteenth Century : (1) ' The Financial Condition of India ' (February 1879) ; (2) ' The Indian Budget of 1879 ' (May 1879) ; (3) ' The New Departure in Indian Finance '

(October 1879 ; *see* ' Indian Finance ' above) ; (4) ' The next Reform Bill ' (March 1880).

Cassell's Magazine :—

(1) June 1872.—' The Condition of the Agricultural Population of England ' (three articles).

(2) October 1872.—' The Poor Law and the Poor ' (two articles).

(3) February 1873.—' Increasing Prosperity and Advancing Prices ' (two articles).

(4) April 1873.—' Local Taxation ' (two articles).

(5) August 1873.—' Our Present National Expenditure ' (two articles).

(6) November 1873.—' The Income Tax and Small Incomes ' (one article).

INDEX.

ABD

ABDY, Prof., 205
Aberdare, Lord, 231, 260
Aberdeen, 144, 183
Abyssinian war expenses, 344
Adair, Col., 203, 204
Addison, Joseph, 5, 14
Afghan war expenses, 392, 396–398, 400, 408
Agricultural labourers, education of, 229–231, 252–254, 260, 265, 267
'Aids to Thrift,' 432
Aldeburgh, 127, 452, 460
Alderbury, 7, 58
Aldis, Mr., 235
American Civil War, 89, 215, 222
Anderson, Dr. Ford, 457, 458
— Mrs. Garrett, 458, 459, 462, 463
Archer, Mr., 190
Argyll, Duke of, 372, 399
Army Purchase, abolition of, 29, 270–273
Ashbury, Mr. J., 238, 384
Assington, 164
Austen, Jane, 95
Austin, Charles, 23, 27
Australia, 41
Avignon, 198
Ayrton, Right Hon. A. S., 316, 317, 320

BACON, 95
Bagehot, Mr., 383, 384

BRI

Bala, 461
Ballot Act, 269, 275, 276
Barnes Common, 335
Bartley, Mr. G. C. T., 409
Barttelot, Sir W., 303
Bass, Mr. M. T., 64
Bateman, Bishop, 77, 133
Beaconsfield, Lord. See Disraeli, Right Hon. B.
Beadon, Sir Cecil, 362
Belgium, 287
Beresford-Hope, Right Hon. A. J., M.P., 315, 331
Berkhampstead, 299
Besant, Dr., 32
Bessborough Gardens, 128
Bethnal Green, 397
Billiards, 17, 20, 21
Birmingham Education League, 254–257, 260, 262
Blackheath, 200
Blackwood, Mr. S. A., 440, 445, 446, 447
Blindness, 44–72, 182, 183, 193, 207–210, 217, 218
Blore, Rev. E. W., 84
Boarding-out system, 153, 154
Bolton, 196
Botting, Mr. W., 59
Bouverie, Right Hon. E. P., 231, 234, 237
Bowen, Mr. E. E., 28, 29
Brabourne, Lord, 300, 303
Bradford, 98, 158, 184
Bridges, Dr., 174
Briggs, Mr. (of Methley), 164

BRI

Bright, Right Hon. John, M.P., 4, 40, 188, 223, 224, 375
Brighton, 60, 128, 239, 381
— elections, 206–214, 216, 217, 238, 240, 242, 347, 384
'— Election Reporter,' 212, 213
—, speeches at, 128, 214, 215, 227, 229, 252, 269, 346, 347
British Association meetings, 99, 116, 119, 144, 183, 184, 185, 200
Broadhurst, Mr. H., M.P., 277
Brontës, The, 95
Brookside, Cambridge, 129
Brougham, Lord, 184, 185, 189, 190
Brown, Mr. Edward, 63, 73, 74, 83, 119, 183
Bruce, Right Hon. H. A., 231, 260
Bryce, Mr. J., M.P., 335, 337
Buckle, Henry, 98
Burke, Edmund, 95
Bute, Marquis of, 452
Butler, Rev. H. M. (Dean of Gloucester), 28, 29
Buxton, Charles, 297, 315

Cæsar's Camp, 339
Cairnes, Prof., 82, 142, 144, 157, 200, 201, 238–242
— and Irish University Reform, 278, 281, 282
Cairns, Earl, 399
Calcutta, 378, 381
Cambridge, 23, 26, 73–94, 96, 457, 461, 468
— election, 203–206
Cameron, Dr., 425
Campbell, Dr. C. J., 70, 71
— Sir George, 252
— Mr. R., 108
Canterbury, 196
Cardin, Mr., 432, 434
Cards, 55
Carlyle, Mrs., 317
— Thomas, 13, 24, 98, 116, 136, 139, 220

COO

Carlingford, Lord, 279
Carnatic railway, 378
Cauvery works, 393
Chamberlain, Right Hon. J., M.P., 335
Chesterfield, Lord, 78
Chetwynd, Mr., 429, 431
China, 42
Cima di Jazzi, 60
Clarendon Woods, 60
Clark, Sir Andrew, 458, 459, 462
—, Mr. W. G., 83
Clarke, Mr. C. B., vii., 15–17, 21, 22, 32, 35, 63, 74, 89, 121, 122, 153, 185, 188, 197, 200, 205, 212, 342, 383
— and King's College, 15–17
— — Brighton election, 212
— — Cambridge, 21, 22, 32, 74, 89
— — India, 342, 383
— — professorship election, 121, 122
Clayhithe, 61
Clifford, Prof., 86, 286
Cobbett, William, 5, 141
Cobden, Richard, 4, 83, 84, 89, 216, 217, 219, 358
'Cobdenites,' 29, 219
Cockburn, Chief Justice, 113, 132
Coleridge, Lord, 225, 234, 237, 245, 246, 315
Common land, amount of, 327, 334
Commons Bill of 1869, 299–307, 322
— — — 1876, 328–332
— Preservation Society, 298, 307, 310, 312, 313, 316, 317, 328, 329, 335, 337
Comte, 235
Coningham, Mr., 206, 210, 212, 238
Cooke, Mr. C., 36
Cooper, Mary, afterwards Mrs. W. Fawcett. See Mrs. W. Fawcett
Cooper's Hill College, 356
Co-operation, 164–166, 216, 387

COR

Cornish mining, 201
Courtney, Mr. L., M.P., 117, 120–122, 201, 222, 278, 430, 450
Cowie, Miss, 459
Cowper-Temple, Mr., 64, 297, 303, 315, 319, 332
Cricket, 57
Crimean War, 29
Critchett, Mr. George, viii., 35, 45
— Mr. G. Anderson, 35
Cross, Rt. Hon. Sir R., M.P., 169, 174, 328–332
Cullen, Cardinal, 284
Cumberbatch, Mr., 325
Cumulative vote, 226
Cunningham, Mr. J. W., 16

Dacosta, Mr. J., 357
Dale, Mr. A. W. W., 342
Darwin, Charles, 98–102, 239
Delhi, 391
Democracy, 170–173, 186, 187
Dent, Mr., 230
De Quincey, 95
Derby, 220
— Lord, 42, 188, 378, 407
Dilke, Mr. Ashton, 277
— Rt. Hon. Sir C. W., M.P., 288, 289, 301, 332
Disraeli, Rt. Hon. B., 186, 220, 223, 225, 227, 239, 285, 386, 388, 390, 403, 405
Dixon, Mr. George, 257, 262, 266
Docwra, 416
Donaldson, Dr., 57
Doulton, Mr., 297
Dredge, Mr., 191, 192, 195, 196, 203, 204, 212
Driving, 59
Dryhurst, Mr. F. J., 55, 62, 70, 74, 458
Dumas, Mr. Kuper, 206–209, 212, 214

Eastern Question, 406–408
'Economic position of British Labourer,' 136

FAW

'Economist' newspaper, 383 384
Edinburgh, Duke of, 353, 366
Edmonson, Mr., 9, 10
Education of agricultural labourers, 167, 168, 229–231, 253, 254, 260, 265–267
— compulsory, 28, 29, 167, 168, 170, 175, 228 231, 253–269
Edwards, Mr. J., 17
Egerton, Rev. J. C., 36, 98
Egypt, 400, 412
Election expenses, 226–228, 239, 249, 276, 277, 385, 386
Eliot, George, 95, 164
Ellis, Leslie, 463
Elphinstone Land Co., 379
Ely, 58, 61
Enclosure Commissioners, 298–301, 304-306, 310, 327, 330, 331, 333, 334
Endowed Schools Act, 358, 404, 405
Epping Forest, 295–297, 308–322, 339, 386
Epsom, 297, 339
'Essays and Lectures,' 160, 177, 264
Euclid, 16, 142
Euston Square burial ground, 336
Ewart, Mr., 235, 237
Exeter, Lord, 188
Eyre, Mr. Briscoe, 325

Factory Acts, 174–176, 222, 229–231, 237, 253, 254, 258, 265, 266, 385, 386
Fairrie, Mr. E. H., 336, 453
Fawcett, Henry, birth, 1 ; at a dame school, 6 ; Mr. Sopp's, 7, 8 ; early diary, 8 ; at Queenwood College, 8–15 ; boyish writings, 11–14 ; at King's College, 15 ; goes to Peterhouse, Cambridge, 18 ; personal appearance, 18, 19 ;

FAW

undergraduate life, 19-33; Trinity Hall, 30; Cambridge studies, 24-27; the Union, 27-30; Mathematical Tripos, 32; Fellowship, 32, 33; parliamentary ambition, 38-40; the bar, 33, 34; Putney Heath, 34; Westminster Debating Society, 34; affection of the eyes, 35-37, 41, 42; Paris, 36; French oculists, 36; letters to Mrs. Hodding, 38-42; visits House of Commons, 42; accident, 43-52; decides on his career, 47, 51, 52; letter from Mr. Hopkins, 48-51; life at Cambridge, 73-90; lectures at Bradford, 98; British Association meetings, 99, 116, 119, 144, 183; defence of Darwinism, 99; correspondence with J. S. Mill, 102-104, 187, 188; University reform, 104, 116, 133; writings on political economy, 182-188; contests Southwark, 189-195; sounds other constituencies, 196; contests Cambridge, 203-206; Professor of Political Economy, 117-123; lectures, 123-125, 146, 294; his work in political economy, 134-169, 293-296; first contest at Brighton, 206-214; second contest and election, 214, 216-218; enters House of Commons, 218-222; re-election to Fellowship, 126; marriage, 125-129; returned for Brighton in 1868, 238; attitude towards the Government, 242, 245, 268-277, 289-292; article in 'Fortnightly Review,' 273, 274, 321, 322; defeated at Brighton in 1874, 384; elected for Hackney, 380, 387; candidature for Mastership of Trinity Hall, 130-133; parliamentary reform, 214, 222-227; election expenses, 226, 228, 239, 249,

FAW

276, 277; education of agricultural labourers, 229-231, 253, 265-267; University reform (in Parliament), 231-237, 245-249; open competition, 249; political pensions, 249, 250; Irish Church question, 238, 250, 251; Irish land question, 252, 253; Irish University question, 277-286; compulsory education, 253-268; the budget of 1871, 270, 271, 274; army purchase, 271-273; commons preservation, 293 340; India, 341-401; endowed schools, 404; Eastern Question, 406-409; second election for Hackney, 409; Postmaster-General, 409, 410; views of Irish question and Egypt, 411-413; principles of Post-Office administration, 413-416; parcel post, 416-421; cheap telegrams, 421-424; telephones, 424-427; postal orders, 427-429; savings banks annuities and insurance, 429-437; takes up a case of hardship, 433; minor improvements, 437, 438; internal administration, 439-443; employment of women, 443, 444; influence and ability in his administrative capacity, 444-449; last address at Hackney, 450; honorary distinctions, 451, 452; illness in 1882-83, 457-460; last illness and death, 460-464; public feeling on his death, 464 468; parliamentary position, 289-292, 388, 402, 403; character, 37, 38, 52, 53, 67, 72, 85-87, 129, 130, 177-181, 195, 196, 218, 219, 243, 291, 292, 337-340; family affection, 46, 455, 456; kindness to sick friends, 84, 85; friendships with younger men, 85, 86;

FAW

habits and amusements, 53–72; love of scenery, 59, 60, 71; regard for Cambridge training, 90–94; business capacity, 201–203; views on Republicanism, 286–289; domestic life, 452–457

Fawcett, Mrs. (wife of Henry Fawcett), 53, 58, 62, 125, 127–129, 264, 452, 453, 460, 462, 467

Fawcett, Miss Philippa Garrett (daughter of Henry Fawcett), 54, 62, 453

Fawcett, Mr. William (father of Henry Fawcett), biographical details, 1-4, 11, 17, 18; share in his son's accident, 43, 45, 46, 63, 65, 201, 205, 212, 216, 220, 221, 456

Fawcett, Mrs. (mother of Henry Fawcett), 2, 3, 65, 121, 122, 221

Fawcett, Miss Maria (sister of Henry Fawcett), 2, 11, 36, 41, 42, 44, 122, 212, 221

Fawcett, Mr. William, junior (brother of Henry Fawcett), 2, 4, 57

Fawcett, Mr. Thomas Cooper (brother of Henry Fawcett), 2

Fawcett, Col., 211, 216

Fearon, Mr., 15, 17

Fellenberg, 9

Fellowship system, 75, 76

Fellowships, tenure of, 30, 104–116

Finsbury, 196

Fishing, 8, 63-67

Fitzmaurice, Lord E., 332

Fitzroy, Mr. F., 108

Forster, Right Hon. W. E., M.P., 256, 258, 259

Fortescue, Right Hon. Chichester (Lord Carlingford), 279

'Fortnightly Review,' 273, 274, 321, 322

Foster, the Messrs. (of Cambridge), 122

Fowler, Sir R. N., M.P., 357

Franco-German War, 287

GOL

Frankland, Dr., 10

Free education, 256, 262-265

'Free Trade and Protection,' book on, 136, 146-149

Froude, Mr. J. A., 137

Fuller, Prof., 24

GANDAMAK, 396

Gardiner, Mr. W. D., 22

Gardner bequest to the blind, 70

Garibaldi, 215

Garrett, Miss Agnes, 458

Garrett, Miss Millicent. See Mrs. (Henry) Fawcett

Garrett, Mr. Newson, 127

Garrett, Miss Rhoda, 457

Geldart, Dr., 78, 130

George, Mr. Henry, 141

Gibraltar and Falmouth cable, 366

Gill, Lieut., 387

Gladstone, Right Hon. W. E., 40, 42, 86, 89, 220, 223-225, 230, 236, 238-240, 242-245, 247, 248, 250, 257, 260, 278-287, 291, 292, 312, 313, 315, 317, 353, 383, 385-387, 390, 397-399, 403, 406, 409-413, 429, 430, 465

—— on Afghan War expenses, 397-399

—— Commons, 312, 313, 315

—— Eastern Question, resolutions on, 407, 408

—— English University reform, 236, 247, 248

—— Income-tax, 386

—— Irish University reform, 278-287

—— oratory, 40, 42

—— Parliamentary Reform, 223-225, 230, 244

Glasgow, 184, 194; rectorship, 452, 463

Godavery works, 379

Godwin W., 150, 151

'Gogmagog Hills,' 58

Gold discoveries, 13, 144, 183

Goldsmid, Sir Julian, 206, 208, 209, 212, 214

GOO

Goodeve, Prof., 17
Gorst, Sir J. E., 28, 29
Granchester, 58
Grant-Duff, Right Hon. M. E., 237, 353-356
Greenwich, 240
Grote, John, 463
Guildford, 300
Gully, Mr. W. C., 20, 28
Gunson, Rev. W. M., 84, 205
Gurdon, Mr., 164

Hackney, 176, 397, 461
— elections, 347, 385-387, 409
— speeches at, 386, 397, 450
Hadley, Mr., 31, 32
Hainault, Forest, 308, 309, 311
Halifax, Lord, 366, 367
Hall, Prof., 17
— Mr. W. H., 62, 63
Halpin, Mr., 191
Hamilton, Dr. (Dean of Salisbury), 17
— Lord G., M.P. 389
Hammond, Mr. J. L., 83, 85, 205
Hampstead Heath, 296, 297, 316
Hann, Mr. James, 16
Harcourt, Right Hon. Sir W., M.P., 27, 303, 307, 332, 333
Hare, Mr. Thomas, 82, 87, 89, 103, 170, 184, 188, 197, 215, 216, 450
Harlowe, Clarissa, 84
Harnham Hill, 43
Harper, Mr., 212, 214
Harris, Mrs. (schoolmistress), 6, 17
Hartington, Marquis of, 407, 409, 410
Hartog, Mr. N., 247
Hatherley, Lord, 399
Hawke, Mr. R., 202, 460
Haynes, Mr. A., 74
Hayward, Mr. T. H., 3
Henley, 336
Hennessy, Sir J. Pope, 34
Herbert, Sidney, 456
Herschel, Sir John, 49

IND

Hertz, Mr. and Mrs., 184
High Beach, 318, 319, 335
Hill, Miss Octavia, 339
— Sir Rowland, 416
Hoare, Mr., 66
Hobbes, 142
Hodding, Mrs., viii., 34, 38, 60, 342
Hofwyl, 9
Holmes, Mr. (factory commissioner), 174
Holms, Mr. J., M.P., 386, 387, 409
Home Rule, 412
Honorary distinctions, 450, 451
Hooker, Sir John, 239
Hopkins, Rev. F. L. (of Trinity Hall), 205
— Mr. W. (mathematical tutor), 24, 26, 27, 48-51, 99
Horsman, Right Hon. E., 220, 222
Hotham, Dr., 84
Houghton, Lord, 27
House of Commons, 17, 38, 40, 52, 202, 203, 217, 220, 221
— — Lords, 246, 248, 269, 271, 272
Hughes, Mr. T., 221, 301, 303
Hume, David, 98
Hunter, Mr. R., 320, 442
Hutton, Mr. James, 357
— Mr. R. H., 118
Huxley, Prof., 83, 99, 167

Ibbesley, 64, 65
Iddesleigh, Earl of. See 'Sir S. Northcote'
Immigration, protection of labour from, 184
India, 13, 41, 181, 228, 237
— financial injustice to, 365-373, 380
— government of, by England, 348-352, 364-366
— irrigation works in, 393
— income-tax, 363
— English neglect of, 346, 347, 366

IND

India, private grievances in, 382, 383
— public works, 374–378, 380, 381, 390, 392–394
— railways, 392
— revenue inelastic, 360, 362–364
— — net amount of, 359, 360
— — sources of, 359, 361, 362
— subscriptions from, 385, 386
Indian Army expenditure, 368–373
— barracks, 373, 374
— Budgets, 353, 357, 360, 380, 398, 400
— Civil Service examinations, 345
— cotton duties, 362, 390
— Council, 365, 370, 381, 398, 399, 409
— Essays, 395, 396
— famines, 391
— finance accounts, 376, 377, 380, 400
— — Committees, 353, 354, 356, 366, 369, 381, 387, 389
Irish Church, 238, 250, 251
— land question, 252, 253, 411, 412
— University question, 277–286

James, Sir Henry, 297
James, Mr. Henry, jun., 80
Jenner, Sir W., 458
Jessel, Sir George, 321
Jevons, Prof., 144
Johnson, Dr. Samuel, 81, 86, 455
Jones, Mr. Daniel, 22
— Richard, 119

Kay-Shuttleworth, Sir J., 158, 184, 194
Kelso, 65
King's College and School, 15–17
Kingsley, Charles, 116
Kingston, 300
Kirby-Lonsdale, 1

MAC

Knatchbull-Hugessen, Right Hon. E., 300, 303

Laing, Mr. S., M.P., 353, 363
Laissez-faire, 149, 159–163, 166-176
Lamb, Charles, 95
Lambert, Sir John, 2, 17, 201
Lambeth, 339
Laplace, 86
'Lardner's Encyclopædia,' 49
Lark, Mrs., 221
Latham, Dr., 462
— Rev. H., 31, 131, 132, 205
Lawn, The, 51, 128, 129
Lawrence, Alderman, 315
— Lord, 354, 363, 370, 374, 375, 396
— Mr. P. H., 298, 338
Layard, Sir A. H., 192, 194, 312, 316
Leatham, Mr. E. A., M.P., 263
Leeds, 164
Lefevre, Right Hon. G. Shaw, M.P., 298, 301, 310, 315, 320, 328–332, 338, 340, 419, 421, 427, 459, 461
Leicester, 196
Les Baux, 199
Leslie, Prof. Cliffe, 118
Lewins, W., 429
Lewis, Mr. Harvey, 239
Lincoln's Inn, 33, 52
Liskeard, 202
Lizard, The, 330
Locke, Mr. John, 189, 297, 301, 303, 320
Longford, 4, 44, 51, 59
Loughton, 310
Louise, The Princess, 288
Love, Mr. (of Southwark), 190
Lowe, Right Hon. R., 118, 220, 222, 226, 229, 242, 270, 312–317
Lushington, Mr. Vernon, Q.C., 28
Lytton, Sir E. B., 34
— Lord, 132, 362, 391, 395

Macaulay, Lord, 27, 98
MacLaren, Mr. Duncan, 194

MAC

Macleod, Mr. H. D., 117, 122
Macmillan, Mr. A., 116, 204, 205
' Macmillan's Magazine,' 197
Madras, 391, 393
Madras irrigation works, 379
Mahomet, 13
Maine, Sir Henry, 34, 132, 401
Major, Dr., 15
Malta, 397
— and Alexandria cable, 367
Malthus, 5, 97, 137, 142, 150–156
Manchester, 158, 375, 390
Mandeville, 148
Manners, Lord John, 411, 417
Mansergh, Mr. J., 9
' Manual of Political Economy,' 116, 117, 134–136, 141, 145, 157, 163, 169, 197, 198, 342, 419, 460
Markby, Rev. Thomas, 15
Marriage, 127–129
Marriott, Mr. W. T., 29
Marten, Mr. A. G., Q.C., 28
Martin, Mr. P. Wykeham, 301
Massey, Right Hon. G., 363
Match-tax, 270
Mathematics, 14, 16, 17, 26, 32
Mathematical Tripos, 31, 32
Maurice, Rev. F. D., 24, 116
Maxwell, Prof. J. Clerk, 25
Mayo, Mr. A. T., 184
— Lord, 378
Mayor, Mr. J. B., 117–120, 122
Melly, Mr. J., 253
Memorials, 468
Merivale, Mr. Herman, 118
Merrifield, Mr. F., 211
Methley, 164
Metropolitan Commons Act, 298
Mickleham Vale, 339
Mill, J. S., 23, 24, 64, 82, 96, 97, 100, 102–104, 118, 125, 134 –136, 139–142, 145, 157, 159, 160, 165, 170, 182, 185–188, 190, 197, 200, 215, 219–222, 224, 226, 227, 235, 239–242, 251, 286, 342, 343

NEW

Mill, J. S., at Avignon, 197–200
— correspondence with, 82, 102, 188, 190
— and Darwin, 100
— defeat at Westminster, 239–241
— election expenses, 227
— enfranchisement of women, 226
— India, 342, 343
— Irish tithe rent-charges, 251
— liberty, 103
— Parliamentary reform, 224
— political economy, 24, 64, 96, 97, 134, 139–142, 157
— position in the House of Commons, 226, 240, 241
— proportional representation, 170, 185–188, 215, 226
— Radical Club, 286
— working-men's representation, 242
Miller, Mr. (butler, Trinity Hall), 79
Mills, Prof. R. H., 118
Milston, 5
Milton, John, 95
Mitcham Common, 335
Molesworth, Sir Wm., 190
Monckton-Milnes, Mr., 27
Moore, Mr. (free trader), 4
— Mr., 206, 214, 217, 238
Morgan, Mr. Osborne, 461
' Morning Star, The,' 189, 190, 194, 212
Morrison, Mr. George, 325
Moulton, Mr. J. F., 86, 357
Mount-Temple, Lord. See ' Mr. Cowper-Temple '
Mundella, Right Hon. A. J., 174, 176, 265, 266, 385
Munro, Rev. H. A. J., 84, 129
Music, 23, 55
Mutlah Railway, 378

Napier, Sir Charles, 189
Napoleon III., 287
Nelson, Lord, 64
— Sir T., 320
New Forest, 65, 322, 326

NEW

Newmarch, Mr. W., 118
Newmarket Heath, 19, 63
Non-collegiate students, 235, 237
Normal College for the Blind, 70, 71, 468
Norman, Mr. G. W., 118
Normanton, Lord, 64
Northbrook, Lord, 388, 390
Northcote, Sir S., 118, 343, 354

Oddo (a dog), 454, 460
Oldham, 196
Old Sarum, 2, 6, 141
Orissa irrigation works, 379
Otway, Right Hon. Sir A., M.P., 206, 208-211
Oude, annexation of, 29
Ovid, 7
Owen, Robert, 9
Oxford, 231, 233, 234, 236, 244

Paget, Dr., 462
Palmerston, Lord, 40, 42, 89, 182, 219
Pangbourne, 465
Parliamentary reform, 30, 214, 222-227
Pattison, Mark, 98
'Pauperism,' book on, 136, 152-154
Peasant proprietorship, 165, 239, 240
Peek, Sir H., 306
Pellatt, Mr. Apsley-, 191
Pembroke, Lord, 64
Pensions, 249, 250
Permissive Bill, 386, 387, 405
Peterhouse, 18, 20, 22, 24, 44, 56
Philipps, Rev. Sir J. E., 456
Pinckney, Mr. (of Salisbury), 1
Pitman's shorthand, 9, 11
Plunket, Hon. D., M.P., 280
Poland, 29
Political economy, 96, 97, 124, 125, 137-145
— — Club, 197
Pont du Gard, 199
Poonah, 374

ROB

Pope, Essay on, 30
Porter, Rev. J. (Master of Peterhouse), 24
Porter, Mr. W. A., 24, 45
Portsmouth, Earl of, 459
Post-Office, 414-448; annuities, 433-436; improvements, minor, 437, 438; letter-carriers, 222, 435; parcel post, 416-421; postal orders, 427-429; salaries, 442; savings banks, 429, 430, 436, 437; savings, investment of, 431; stamp slips, 431, 432; telegraphs, 421-424; telephones, 424-427; women in, 443, 444
Powell, Mr. F. S., 205
Prince of Wales's visit to India, 390
Prize Fellowships, 113-116
Proportional representation, 184-188, 215, 216, 226, 451
Pryme, Prof., 117, 205
Putney Heath, 34, 239
Pyecombe, 307

Queen, The, 459, 465
Queenwood College, 8-15
'— Chronicle and Reporter,' 9, 10
Quoits, 20

Radical Club, 286
Radnor, Earl of, 4
Railways and Post-Office, 417, 418
— State management of, 185
Rathbone, Mr. Harold, viii.
Read, Mr. Clare, 265
Reed, Mr. J., of Withypool, 305, 306
Republicanism, 286-289
Ricardo, 96, 97, 155, 156
Richard, Mr. A., M.P., 263
Riding, 54, 62, 63, 461
Rigby, Mr. J., Q.C., 22, 23, 32
Ringwood, 64, 66
Roberts, Dr., vii.

ROB

Robertson, Mr. H., 461
Rochdale, 164
Rogers, Mr. Thorold, M.P., 118
Romford, 308
Romsey, 7
Rottingdean, 60
Routh, Dr., 22, 24, 25
Rowing, 56, 57, 58, 336
Roxburgh, Duke of, 54
Rumbold, Henry, 455
Ruskin, Mr., 136, 137, 452
Russell, Lord John, 29, 185, 220

St. George's Hill, 300
Salisbury, 1, 3, 60, 198, 212, 432, 463, 468
— Lord, 246, 365, 370, 388-390, 393, 399
Salmon, Mr. and Mrs., 461
Samuelson, Sir B., 460
Sandhurst, Lord, 397
Sandon, Lord, 266, 404
'Saturday Review,' 386
Saugor, 374
Savings banks, 168
Scott, Lord Henry, 325, 331
Scovell, Mr. (of Southwark), 191-194
Selwyn-Ibbetson, Sir H., 319
Senior Nassau, 119
Seymour, Mr. Danby, 221
Sheffield, 158, 185, 330
Sherbrooke, Lord. See '— Lowe, Right Hon. R.'
Short, Mr., 466, 467
Shorthand, 9, 11
Shute, Gen., 484
Sichel (oculist), 36
Sikes, Sir W. C., 429
Silver, depreciation of, 391
Six-Mile Bottom, 62
Skating, 53, 60-62
Smith, Adam, 97
— Mr. Augustus, 299
— Miss E., 437
— Prof. Henry, 80
— Mr. Lumley, Q.C., 108
— Miss McLeod, 62

THA

Smith, Right Hon. W. H., 326
Smoking, 55
Social Science Association, 158, 184, 185
Socialism, 156, 157, 160 163
Somerset House, 15
Sopp, Mr. (schoolmaster), 7, 8, 9
Southampton Cemetery Bill, 336
Southwark, 120, 207-212
— election, 189-195
Spencer, Earl, 318
— Mr. Herbert, 160, 265
Squarey, Mr. A. T., vii., 4, 33
Stafford, 206
Stanley, Lord, 188, 378
State interference, 149, 159-163, 166-176
Steele, Mr. (mathematical tutor), 22, 24, 25
Stephen, Mr. Justice, 27
— Mr. Leslie, 18, 20, 25, 31, 46, 57, 59, 74, 100, 108, 122, 126, 200, 206, 212, 213, 336
Stirling, Mr., 235, 247
Stonehenge, 9
Story-Maskelyne, Mr., M.P., 337
Strachey, Sir John, 359, 368, 376, 391, 394
— Gen. R., 354, 356, 359, 373, 376-381, 391, 394
Strikes, 164, 184
Sultan's ball, 343, 344, 352, 353, 366
Surbiton and Kingston Railway, 335
Swaffham, 305
Switzerland, 60

Tait, Prof., 22, 25
Talfourd, Judge, 79
Taylor, Miss Helen, 199, 200
— Mr. P. A., 288, 301
— Mr. Sedley, 164, 460
Tea-Room Party, 224, 225, 238
Tennyson, 23
Tests, religious, 231-237, 245, 249
Thackeray, W. M., 82, 95, 458

THA

Thames protection, 336, 337
Thomson, Sir William, 24
Thornton, Mr. W. T., 82, 118, 157, 165, 197, 200, 342, 366
'Times, The,' 165, 193, 257, 387
Tizard, Mr. Samuel, 65
Tooke's 'History of Prices,' 97
Tremenheere, Mr. H. S., 304
Trevelyan, Sir C., 354, 363, 370
– Right Hon. G. O., 345
Trinity College, Dublin, 277–286
— Hall, 30, 31, 56, 73, 77–80, 83, 126, 130–133
— — at Christmas, 77–79, 82, 83
— — Master of, 76
— — statutes, reform of, 106–112
Trollope (schoolfellow of H. Fawcett), 8
Trumpington, 58, 463, 468
Tyndall, Prof., 10, 13

UNEARNED increment, 165
Union Society, Cambridge, 27–30
University Reform, 28, 30, 96, 104–116, 231–237, 245–249

VANSITTART, Mr. Augustus, 57
Vice-Chancellor of Cambridge, 123

WAGE-FUND theory, 155–159
Waley, Prof., 118
Walking, 57, 58
Walpole, Right Hon. S., 231
Waltham, 308
Walton, Izaak, 12
Wandsworth Common, 318
Warley, 372
Warminster, 144
Waveney, Lord, 203, 204

WRI

Webb, Mr. Jonas, 82
Westminster, 239-241
— Abbey, 468
— Debating Society, 34
' — Review,' 164
Wheaton, Mr. S. W., 65, 66
Whewell, Dr., 49, 90, 119, 120, 122
Whist, 21
White, Mr. James, 216, 217, 221, 238, 384
Wilberforce, Bishop, 99
Wilkinson, Miss L. M., 459
— Rev. M. M. U., 22, 74
Wilkes, Mr. Washington, 194, 212
Willett, Mr. Henry, 208, 210, 211
Willingale, 310, 320
Wilson, Mr. E., 22, 24
— Right Hon. E., 40
Wilton, 5
Wiltshire labourer, story of a, 140, 164
Wimbledon, 296–298, 318, 335, 339
Windsor, 296
Wisley Common, 300, 301, 306, 330
Withypool, 305, 306
Wolstenholme, Dr., 32
Women, education of, 173, 174
— enfranchisement of, 127, 176, 177
— employment of, 385, 443, 444
— position of, 173–177
Woods and Forests Department, 309, 311
Wordsworth, W., 95
Working-men, representation of, 240, 242
Wright, Mr. Aldis, 95
— Mr. E. (of Clapham), 459
— Mr. Elias, vii., 64, 65, 164, 165
— Mr. (of Manchester), 40

Spottiswoode & Co., Printers, New-street Square, London.